THE BETTER
ANGELS

Also by Charles McCarry

THE MIERNIK DOSSIER
THE TEARS OF AUTUMN
THE SECRET LOVERS
CITIZEN NADER

THE BETTER ANGELS

Charles McCarry

E. P. Dutton △ New York

To Joseph Judge

All characters and events in this book are entirely fictitious.
Its time is invented also, and chronological anomalies are
intentional.

For information contact: E.P. Dutton, 2 Park Avenue,
New York, N.Y. 10016

Library of Congress Cataloging in Publication Data
McCarry, Charles.
The better angels.
I. Title.
PZ4.M12265Be   [PS3564.A2577]   813'.5'4   78-26968

ISBN: 0-525-06631-4

Published simultaneously in Canada by Clarke, Irwin & Company
Limited, Toronto and Vancouver

10 9 8 7 6 5 4 3 2 1

First Edition

The mystic chords of memory, stretching from every battlefield, and patriot grave, to every living heart and hearthstone, all over this broad land, will yet swell the chorus of the Union, when again touched, as surely they will be, by the better angels of our nature.

ABRAHAM LINCOLN
First Inaugural Address

MIDSUMMER

PATRICK GRAHAM, as he chose his necktie, called out a piece of gossip to his wife. One of their friends had detected her husband in adultery and was suing him for divorce. "Damn!" said Charlotte Graham. "That means we'll be two short for dinner Wednesday week. Stella might at least have rung me up."

Charlotte sat on a bench at her dressing table, vigorously brushing her long hair. "I shall be so glad when Americans can admit that they, too, live in a country where someone else is likely to be the past or present or future lover of the person they happen to be married to," she said. "That's the first sign of a civilized society, and it makes entertaining *so* much easier."

Charlotte, an Englishwoman who was the daughter of a peer, had been waiting for this sign all through the fifteen years of her exile in Washington as Patrick Graham's wife. She and her husband were talking to each other through the open door between their bedrooms as they dressed for the evening. "*Why* are your women so solemn about their snowy American bottoms?" Charlotte demanded. "If they weren't, we wouldn't have to give this awful party every June."

A hundred people, many of them strangers to Charlotte, would invade the Grahams' fine Federal house in Georgetown in the next half hour. These were men and women to whom Patrick owed a favor, social or more often professional—people who were not quite those he wanted at one of the twenty dinner parties for six that he and Charlotte gave each year for his important sources. Patrick was

1

the most famous television journalist in America; Charlotte was the most exhilarating hostess in Washington. The last President, a man Patrick loathed, had told her that she would have made a perfect wife for Charles II. One of her ancestresses *had* made that monarch a perfect mistress, and the king had created her complaisant husband an earl.

Patrick came into the room and smiled at Charlotte's image in the mirror. Her wide green eyes, amused and knowing, met his in the glass. Charlotte never wore anything except stockings beneath a dress and she was naked to the hips. Her head was thrown back and her hair fell free. Filled with auburn lights, it crackled under the brush. She had always had a lovely throat, and her small breasts, with some help from the plastic surgeon, remained firm. Bones were beginning to show through the taut flesh of her back; Charlotte had been as supple as a cat when Patrick married her, but she had grown angular in the years since, and her skin had lost its freshness. She blamed the awful climate of Washington, but Patrick believed it was constant dieting and too much alcohol that had spoiled her figure and complexion; eating and drinking as she did, the results would have been the same even if she had remained in the English mists.

"You don't really mind this party," Patrick said. It was always held on the nearest Saturday to Midsummer Day, Patrick's birthday; he was approaching fifty, but looked younger than his wife.

"No. I rather adore it, actually—seeing the fresh crop of lambs each spring, they're so new to the world and so pretty. It makes one feel quite maternal."

Charlotte called this annual event "the Lambs' Party" because most of the guests were very young; it was no small part of her wit that she put a comical name to everything. Charlotte never meant to wound; she had no malice. But ordinary emotions—innocence, envy, ambition, anger, jealousy, political fervor—were so alien to her own nature that she was seized by mirth when she encountered them in others.

Like most people of their kind in the last decade of the twentieth century, the Grahams had no children. They had never wanted any. The instinct to breed was feeble in Charlotte's ancient family; her father had died, penniless and raving, without male issue, and his line was extinct. Patrick, in his heart, thought that his own nation deserved to be extinct; America, the whole West, was dying at last of its appetites, like a rich drunk who refuses to give up bad habits and challenges his doctor to keep him alive.

Charlotte stepped into her dress and Patrick helped her with the

2

zipper. She handed him her ruby necklace and lifted her hair so that he could clasp it around her neck; she wore a jewel on every finger, but no wedding band.

Charlotte knotted his tie for him. Patrick wore only one kind of necktie—silk, a small white polka dot on a sober blue or maroon background. It was a sort of trademark, something he'd begun years before, when his career was just starting to prosper. Like many of the marks of Patrick's outward appearance, the ties had been Charlotte's idea. She always thought of things that took a long time to be noticed, but which, once remarked, were never forgotten.

"Charlotte Swan Neck," said Patrick as Charlotte turned to admire her necklace, and their laughing eyes met again in the glass. They were friends; accomplices. Patrick kissed Charlotte's cheek, a fleeting pressure of dry lips on painted skin. He couldn't bear the taste of makeup, or its coarse perfume.

Downstairs, the doorbell rang and they heard voices in the hall.

"The Lambs are all arriving at one time," said Charlotte. "Come help me herd the poor things."

The Grahams' Midsummer party, in truth, had a way of running itself. Charlotte organized it perfectly, a bar in what she called the drawing room, another in the garden, young Englishmen in footmen's livery weaving among the guests with trays of drinks and canapés. The British upper class had become, in the Washington of the 1990s, a sort of posh servant class. Once or twice she had discovered that a waiter hired to serve at a party or to hand round the courses at dinner was a blood relation.

"Well, it's really only three steps down to the scullery from being a viscount, you know," she was saying now to the British chargé d'affaires, "so I was hardly amazed when the young chap Kadowaki the caterer sent over to serve cocktails turned out to be Billy Macdonald's second son Nicholas. It was the Japs who started the whole thing—they all suddenly wanted English servants, you know how faddish their millionaires are, and of course the British working class wouldn't wait on a lot of Wogs with low kneecaps, so who was left but the peerage?"

Charlotte, in her long green gown and her jewels, was strikingly beautiful from a distance of ten feet. She stood at one end of the long living room, drinking Scotch and milk, a mixture for which she was famous; no one else in Washington drank it, but Charlotte drank it from morning to night and never showed the slightest sign that she had swallowed anything more powerful than milk alone. "Liver like a rugby ball," she said of herself; "everything else works awfully

3

well." Between Charlotte and Patrick, stationed at the opposite end of the room, milled the great crowd of guests. It pleased Charlotte that they were all dressed so well, it showed that they regarded the Grahams' least important party as an event.

Mostly, the people who were drinking Patrick's excellent liquor and nibbling Kadowaki's sashimi and tempura were fresh and slim; many of the women had obviously got new clothes for the affair. They belonged to that peculiar American class, the showily educated, ostentatiously intelligent, terribly serious children of parents who had been just like them. The air was charged with their nervousness. They drifted from one group to another, wearing the same clothes, flashing the same expensive smiles, uttering the same opinions. Charlotte found them touching. They had all gone to the same schools and now they went to the same shops and had the same ambitions. Yet they didn't know one another, as people of their kind did in other countries; America produced a ruling class by lottery with each new generation. Names meant nothing; celebrities had cinders for fathers and ashes for sons. No wonder Americans were obsessed when they were young and mad when they were old. Charlotte was kind to all of them, especially to the women whether they had careers of their own or not; Patrick was going to be in business in Washington for a long time to come, and the Grahams knew the wisdom of planting a young tree for every old one that fell in the political forest.

At the other end of the room, Patrick was smiling down at a young woman. She was a small female with black hair and a face that glowed with intelligence; Patrick, for reasons Charlotte knew well, had a weakness for the type. He made a joke and the girl laughed. Patrick was a handsome man, made lustful by his fame. The girl's husband, standing forgotten beside her, smiled and said something. Patrick didn't answer him. He took the raven-haired girl by the arm and led her through the open french doors into the garden.

Her husband stood alone for a moment, then approached a little ring of people, and, smiling once again, introduced himself. He hadn't been introduced to Charlotte. Patrick must not regard him as a comer. Certain of tonight's guests were almost ready to be invited to a dinner party. Patrick introduced these to Charlotte with a special formula: "Charlotte, really you must meet so-and-so"; for the ordinary run of guests, if he bothered to bring them over to her at all, he merely said, "This is my wife," and told Charlotte their names. The Grahams had a whole system of verbal signals; Charlotte, who knew so much more about society than Patrick, had been surprised,

4

in their early days together, that she had to teach him about such things.

No one had devised a signal to warn of the approach of Clive Wilmot. The British chargé d'affaires, who had returned to Charlotte in order to say good-night as the party approached its end, caught sight of Clive as he entered the room. "Oh, dear," he said, in Clive's own public school accent. Charlotte lifted a questioning eyebrow. "I'm afraid Clive has arrived," said the chargé. "Oh, dear, indeed," said Charlotte, and went quickly across the room, smiling and touching those who were left in the thinned party, so as to lead Clive away if he needed leading. Patrick had vanished. Charlotte supposed he was in the garden; he loved to show it to people.

"A drink, a drink, a very large drink!" Clive Wilmot cried. A waiter appeared at his side with a tray of glasses. Clive took two of them.

"Clive," said Charlotte, "how nice. It's always a surprise to see you at one of our parties."

"I can't think why. I always turn up."

"Yes. But you're never invited."

Wilmot's dark woolen suit was speckled with dandruff and cigarette ash. In the breast pocket he carried a large number of pens and yellow pencils and a red and white tube of Colgate toothpaste. The suit, tailored in London, was too heavy for the climate. Wilmot wore a red-checked shirt under his pin-striped vest, and a Guards tie. Wilmot had made a life for himself as an outrageous character; he loved to crash parties, start rows in restaurants, pass himself off as a drunk. Charlotte looked closely at his eyes and saw that he was quite sober; he usually was.

Patrick came in from the garden. "Ah," he said, "the Regency buck. How are you, Clive?"

Elsewhere in the room, the remaining guests were putting down glasses and preparing to leave. "Just let us have a moment to say good-bye to our invited guests," Charlotte said.

"Don't want to drive them out," Wilmot said. "Probably all future senators, Supreme Court justices, inventors of bombs that only kill the vegetation and leave the mammals to eat each other up."

The Grahams were smiling at Wilmot. Charlotte had always liked him for his mockeries, and Patrick knew that he was the head of the Washington station of what remained of British intelligence. Patrick didn't quite trust him, but he was a useful man to know.

"Stay!" Wilmot called to a small group of departing young people. "We're going to have a wonderful discussion. Want to speak to you about the virtuous qualities of your President. Wonderful chap. New type of human, only took two and a half centuries of feverish cross-breeding to produce him. *Homo americanus*. Fucks no one but his wrinkled wife, great example to the rest of us. Sends messages óf love to the benighted—uplifts the miserable of the world."

Most of the Grahams' guests worked, in one way or another, for Bedford Forrest Lockwood, the President of the United States. His administration had drawn a great troop of young idealists to Washington. Patrick had called them the largest influx of intelligent reformers to come into the capital since the New Deal. They were listening to Clive Wilmot in silence, their faces hostile. He was touching a sensitive nerve. Lockwood, in his first term, had put policies into effect, idealistic programs that he had promised in his campaign for the presidency, which had placed his re-election in doubt. The President's altruism, his open displays of sympathy and understanding for the miserable, his insistence that the sacrifice of self-interest was the only true self-interest, had brought him close to becoming a figure of fun. Lockwood's followers had very little sense of humor about him, and even less about his program. They were the first generation in a very long time that had been given something to believe in. They would believe in Lockwood, and in his ideas, for the rest of their lives. Patrick Graham had said of them, in one of his television commentaries that had helped in a subtle way to elect Lockwood, that they were fighters of a new kind—fighters against disillusion.

Now Patrick's raven-haired girl stared at Clive Wilmot and her delicate face was a mask of disgust. Charlotte took her hand in both her own.

"You mustn't mind Clive," she said. "He's quite harmless."

"I'm sure he is. Good night, Lady Charlotte."

She left and the others followed her, quietly saying good-night to the Grahams. Clive Wilmot gave each departing couple a cheerful wave with one or the other of the two glasses of Scotch whisky that he held in his hands.

Usually Wilmot subsided when his audience left. Tonight he went on babbling, standing in the spot he had chosen when he entered, near the cold fireplace. He drained one glass and helped himself to another. Charlotte watched him consume four Scotches in less than fifteen minutes, while Patrick was in the hall, tipping the waiters. Charlotte wasn't concerned. Wilmot could hold a lot, and the drinks were very weak—she always had them watered after the first trays were passed. All the same, Wilmot seemed to be getting

6

drunk very rapidly. He must have a reason to behave as he was doing.

"Clive, you're a rude beast and a tiresome show-off," said Charlotte. But she was amused by him; she always was. Years before, when she was twenty and he was only a few years older, they had been lovers during a whole winter in London. He was just back from Ulster, where he had lost a leg to an IRA mine. He compensated for his mutilation by a maniacal cheerfulness and great sexual inventiveness. Clive had a friend who owned a theatrical costume shop and he would borrow clothes from him; Charlotte, dressed as a flapper, might be tumbled by Clive attired as a Czarist dragoon in full dress uniform; the historical periods were always mixed. So, because Clive was often female in his sexual desires, was their lovemaking. Wilmot's shouting, his artificial speech from the plays of Noël Coward, his drunken brawls, these were really his honesty. One night as Charlotte lay on his body, making rhythmic love, he had recited "The Owl and the Pussycat" in the same solemn cadences, like those of a tipsy evangelist, with which Dylan Thomas, on old phonograph records, had recited his jumbled poems. The experience, intense orgasm combined with uncontrollable laughter, had been one of the sweetest in all Charlotte's life. She did not often see Clive without remembering that moment.

Long afterwards, Wilmot had had bad luck. Posted to Baghdad —he had read Arabic at Oxford—he'd been exposed as a British intelligence officer and sent home in open shame, persona non grata ever afterwards in the Near East.

Banishment from the Arab world was a disaster. For a generation, Arabs had controlled the world's wealth; because they controlled the sources of the world's energy, they controlled the world. A sheikh's thumb lay on the windpipe of every Krupp, every Mitsubishi, every manufacturer on earth. There were no more Arabs than there ever had been, and their territory had not enlarged. Territory meant little, in modern terms: large countries in cold climates were poor countries because they had to burn fuel to keep their people alive, and there was very little fuel outside the deserts of the Arabs. The Arabs were, as the rich and the powerful always are, the objects of burning curiosity. They were the prime target of every intelligence service in the world. To know what one imam or sheikh or emir might do, and to know it before anyone else, could mean billions in gold, or even national survival.

Clive Wilmot, who had known Arabs and Arabic so well, had by some misstep been, as it were, blinded. He was no longer of much use to his intelligence service or his country. Everyone knew it. Most were glad enough to see him transformed into a beggar. At length

7

Wilmot had been sent to Washington, where there was virtually nothing for him to do except to have lunch once a week with a middle-grade officer from the American intelligence service. It was a social, not a professional post; when the Americans wanted to deal with the British secret service, they did so through their own chief of station in London. It was believed in Langley that Wilmot was unstable; like Patrick, the American intelligence people didn't quite trust him. To Patrick they spoke quietly of Wilmot as a man who had lost a brilliant future through a single mistake. That was what everyone said about him. If the men of the Foreign Intelligence Service of the United States, that cautious organization which had supplanted the CIA, knew what exactly Wilmot's mistake in Baghdad had been, they weren't willing to share the knowledge with Patrick Graham.

Patrick returned to the empty living room and took a place beside Charlotte on the sofa. Wilmot sat opposite, his body lax on a fragile antique chair and footstool.

Patrick said, "All that about Lockwood, Clive—those young people resented it. They don't understand the weary humor of the Old World, you know."

"Oh? I *am* sorry. I do understand. I see what Lockwood is—all elbows and honesty. Lincolnian. No wonder he inspires belief. You still love him, do you, Patrick—you, yourself? Think he's the man the world's been waiting for?"

"I wouldn't go that far. He's the best we've had for a long time."

"Better than his foul predecessor, eh? After all, everyone knows you put Lockwood where he is today. It was you who threw Herr Mallory out of the White House like a shitting cat."

"Come, Clive."

"True!"

And it was. Almost four years before, on the eve of a presidential election no one had thought Lockwood could win, Patrick had discovered Franklin Mallory to be involved in a secret plot. Mallory had conspired with politicians in the western provinces of Canada to secede from their own country and join their territory and people to the United States. Hundreds of millions in bribes had been paid by American corporations to buy votes in the plebiscites that would decide the issue of secession. There had been a worse rumor—never proved but widely believed because Mallory's enemies thought him capable even of murder—that Mallory had tried to assassinate the prime minister of Canada. Terrorists had fired a hundred rounds into the prime minister's bulletproof limousine and left an American-made machine gun on the pavement in Ottawa as they fled. The Canadian, though wounded, had escaped with his life. Patrick, tapping sources that he still held secret, had pieced the story together and broadcast it a week before the election. He had the largest audience of any commentator in America. His own outrage infected millions of his listeners. Opinion had been swayed. Lockwood had been elected by a plurality of two hundred thousand votes, a fraction of one percent of the total number of ballots cast.

Now Clive Wilmot asked, "Patrick, I've often wondered, did you really believe that Franklin Mallory had a hand in that shooting in Ottawa?"

Clive had stopped drinking. His whisky glasses stood on the table beside him and he himself sat quietly on the chair. Patrick had begun to take an interest in Clive and in what he said. He saw, as Charlotte had done earlier, that he was not affected by liquor. Clive was up to something.

"It was certainly possible," Patrick replied. "Everyone knows what Mallory is capable of."

"You're against assassination, then—no matter who is assassinated, no matter who orders the assassination?"

"Of course. That's a damn silly question."

"I suppose it is. I just wanted to be sure we were on the same philosophical ground."

Clive spoke very clearly now and he seemed less disheveled. There was a stillness in him. Charlotte began to pay closer attention to what was happening between the two men. Patrick's interest was engaged, he had caught something in Clive's tone; his senses were as acute as a snake's when a story blundered near, and he could strike as quickly. Patrick asked no questions; he waited for Clive to come closer to him.

"Assassinations are rather fascinating," Clive said. "I wonder, Patrick, if you were at all puzzled by the death of another of your heroes. . . ."

"Does Patrick have heroes?" asked Charlotte.

"I think so. Lockwood seems to be one, Patrick's always talking him up on television. So was the chap I was referring to, Ibn Awad. Patrick, it was you who called Awad 'the new Gandhi,' wasn't it?"

"Yes. That's what he was. It was obvious to the whole world that he was an authentic saint. Like Gandhi or Pope John. They don't come along often, but when they do, people see them for what they are. I saw it, too."

"Yes, you built him up wonderfully. I remember your broadcasts from Hagreb—old Ibn Awad in his white jibba, praying and passing barefoot over the burning sands."

As in so many things, Patrick Graham had been first in the discovery of Ibn Awad's sainthood. The emir of a desert tribe, Awad had resisted the drilling of oil wells in his backward country for twenty years. When finally he permitted it, he used the enormous income from his wells to build mosques and hospitals and a powerful radio transmitter over which he broadcast prayers for peace and brotherhood and the purification of Islam. Though he was one of the richest men on earth he had gone on living the life of a Bedouin, wandering in the desert. He made long pilgrimages, traveling on foot, to Mecca and other holy places. Patrick had done a series of extraordinary interviews with him, the two of them talking into a camera with the limitless empty sands all around them. Ibn Awad's simple faith, his goodness, had shone out of his weathered old face. He had been small like Gandhi, but he had had the head of a falcon, not the humble face of a martyr, under his windblown kaffiyeh.

Charlotte said, "But Ibn Awad wasn't assassinated, surely? Patrick was *there*."

"So was I. We all thought he had had himself killed. A last appeal to the world, an example of self-sacrifice. What did you call it, Patrick? Crucifixion of the self?"

Charlotte spoke because she saw that Patrick wanted her to do so. She often asked the obvious questions for him; it didn't matter how ignorant she seemed, but Patrick was supposed to know everything. "I must say he chose a bizarre death. Having his own son shoot him, and then the son being beheaded for the crime." She shuddered. "The television pictures were awful. Patrick, your voice trembled, coming over the air."

"I don't wonder," said Clive. "You must have been close enough to smell the blood when they took off the boy's head. Normally one smells nothing in the desert, there are no odors. A sudden gout of blood *can* knock one back a step or two."

Still Patrick said nothing. But Charlotte, seated by him, could feel the tension in his body. Sometimes, when Patrick was onto something big, a story that engaged his emotions, his whole being would tighten—mind, feelings, the very muscles of his body—and nothing could set him loose except the discovery of the truth.

"I'm afraid I have something rather disagreeable to tell you, Patrick," Clive said. "Ibn Awad was assassinated by President Lockwood."

Nothing had ever made Patrick feel sicker than Clive Wilmot's words—not even that gout of blood in the desert or the cloud of black flies that had come from nowhere to settle on the slippery red stump of Prince Talil's severed neck. A huge man had beheaded Ibn Awad's favorite son with a ceremonial sword. Patrick had

10

watched the polished steel blade flash in the sun, had seen the head leap from the body, had seen the red ejaculation of blood. For a long moment his mind could not connect the memory of that horror with Bedford Forrest Lockwood.

Then, striking time after time, he began to ask Clive questions.

Clive gave Patrick details. Patrick attacked the evidence. He demanded proofs.

Clive shrugged. "There are no documents when one head of state orders the death of another."

"Then you can't prove this?"

"I can show you how to prove it to yourself," replied Clive. "I wonder if you can bring yourself to believe it even after you have all the evidence in hand."

Patrick was on his feet. Clive's rigid artificial leg rested on the brocaded cushions of the footstool. He lifted what was left of the leg with a grimace.

"What reason could there possibly be?" Patrick demanded. "Why would Lockwood, of all people, want to kill Awad, of all people? It's crazy."

"Yes, isn't it? But then perhaps it takes one to kill one. They were both great ones for saying their prayers in public, weren't they?"

"There are such creatures as men of good will. Nothing you've said to me so far convinces me that Lockwood and Awad fall into any other category."

"Then you are going to have an unhappy month or two," said Clive. He removed a pencil from his bulging breast pocket and handed it, together with a single sheet of cheap notebook paper, to Patrick. "I'd rather you wrote this in your own hand," he said. He dictated a name and address; it was a common Arab name, obviously false, followed by the name of a cheap hotel in Baghdad.

"Go and talk to this chap," Clive said.

"Who is he?"

"You'll recognize him when you see him."

"Is he going to tell me again what you've told me tonight?"

"Perhaps a bit more."

Clive lifted his artificial leg, locked its hinge, and heaved himself to his feet. When he sat down or got up, one leg stiff and the other normal, his amputation was noticeable. When he was tired he dragged the bad foot. He walked out of the room without offering to shake hands with Patrick, or even making a last joke with Charlotte.

They heard the door close, and, a moment later, Clive's unmatched footsteps shuffling by the garden wall. The french doors

11

into the garden were still open and the faint scent of roses came into the room along with the muffled noises in the quiet street.

Patrick read the name and address again and put the slip of paper into his pocket.

"What're you going to do?" Charlotte asked.

"Go to Baghdad, for starters. Even if Clive's story is a lie it's interesting. Why would he tell me this?"

"I wondered why you didn't ask him that."

"He'd lie. It's his profession."

Patrick picked up a telephone. Charlotte listened to him tell somebody at the network to book him a seat on the SST to Beirut the next morning; he'd have to fly a local airline from there to Baghdad. He was taking no camera crew with him. He was taking no one at all.

When he hung up the phone, Charlotte said, "I'm surprised you don't just ring up Julian Hubbard and ask him to let you talk to the President. This business of meeting in Baghdad with mysterious Arabs doesn't sound good to me."

"Time enough to talk to Julian when I get back."

"I don't like Baghdad. Bullets, knives, bombs. That's where those lunatics killed poor Rosalind Wilmot."

"They won't kill me, any more than they killed Clive. Men are safe as long as someone has an idea they're useful."

Patrick rose and walked to the other end of the room and back. Charlotte watched him as he looked at his Daumier bronzes, his pictures, his new tapestry copied from an Ingres painting. There were no windows in the room except for the french doors into the garden; they had had to brick them all up in this age of terror and murder before the insurance company would issue a policy on Patrick's life. Looking at the tapestry, Patrick was forty feet away from Charlotte and his back was turned. But he had no trouble hearing her question.

"*Can* you?" she asked. He didn't reply, and although she knew he understood her meaning she finished the question. "Can you bring yourself to believe what Clive told you if you do find it's true?"

"Yes," said Patrick, running a finger over the weave of the tapestry. "That's *my* profession."

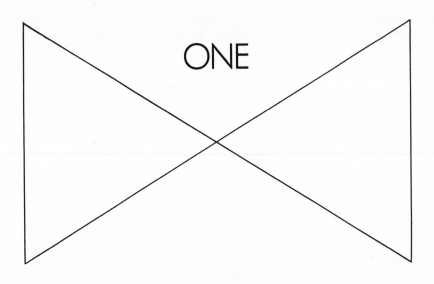

ONE

1

Julian Hubbard, President Lockwood's principal assistant, was six feet five inches tall, and as he shaved he had to stoop a little in order to see his face in the mirror. It was a Sunday, the morning after the Grahams' Midsummer Night party. Julian hadn't gone to the party, and though his life and Patrick's had mingled for twenty-five years and more, Graham was the last man he was likely to think about today. Julian had been reminded, moments after rising, that this was his dead father's ninetieth birthday, and as he lathered his long jaw his mind was crowded with memories of his parent—or, to be as precise as Julian liked to be, his thoughts were on himself in relation to his family: as son, father, brother, husband.

Julian had awakened at six o'clock, as he had trained himself to do, with his new wife lying beside him, slender and nude and deeply asleep. Smiling with pleasure, he spent several minutes examining her body—the fine ankles, the graceful legs, the hips that were so narrow when she was clothed and so full when she was not, the tumbled heavy hair streaked by the sun. She had already got a tan, and her skin, under its coat of bleached down, was golden in the lambent first light of day. They had been married only six months, and her beauty still surprised him.

The scent of Washington in the early morning, like that of a woods freshened by rain, came in the open window. Julian got up without touching his wife and closed the sash. Mist drifted from the lawn in the walled garden below as the rising sun, already strong, burned away the dew. Julian listened for a moment to the birds as they began to stir, and identified the call, loverlike and quavering, of a purple finch, one of a pair that nested in a young elm he had planted at the back of the garden; it pleased Julian that these two American species, the bird and the tree, once so common and now so rare, should come together in his yard. His wife uttered a faint groan, shuddered, and moved her tongue with a clicking sound in her dry mouth, but didn't wake. Julian covered her with the sheet that lay on the floor beside the bed in a tangle with her nightgown and his pajamas. She was twenty-eight years old, nearly twenty years younger than Julian. She had his mother's name, Emily.

Julian had wanted to have a birthday party for his father on this day, bringing his half-brother Horace back from abroad, finding such friends of his father's as might still be alive—college classmates, lawyers who had worked with him in the New Deal, officers who had served with him in the OSS, the politicians and bankers, musicians and editors, ballplayers and actresses who had been his New York friends. President Lockwood had been asked to come to the party, accepting with transparent pleasure, and had suggested using the presidential yacht. Lockwood had met Julian, and many others who had helped to make him President, at Elliott Hubbard's table.

But then, in February, Elliott had died, instantaneously, of a massive stroke, alone in his own house, as he would have wished. No good-byes. There never had been any between Julian and his father, perhaps because the son was always going to places—Exeter, Yale, the Navy, Washington—where the older man had gone before him. Elliott Hubbard almost never advised his son, never criticized him; Julian's father believed in leaving things unspoken, and so far as Julian could tell, unjudged. The strongest emotion Elliott Hubbard ever showed, at least in Julian's presence, was amusement. Perhaps the strongest one he actually felt was disgust. All his life, when he was separated from his father, Julian had missed him intensely; he missed him now.

On the day he left for school, Julian had drawn Elliott Hubbard into conversation about an antique Persian hunting carpet that hung on the wall of the study in their New York house. The scene in the carpet, swarthy horsemen in sparse black beards hunting stags through a forest, had always fascinated Julian; he had liked to bring his books into the study to do his homework and daydream over it. Into the silk, in Farsi characters, was worked a motto. Julian's older brother, a student of languages, had already told him what it meant,

14

but now he asked his father for a translation. "I'm told," Elliott Hubbard said, with his impish smile, "that those are the three rules of character that nobles in ancient Persia taught their sons: to ride, to shoot straight, to tell the truth. Very little else, in their view, was useful in a man's life."

On that same afternoon, a bright day in September, Julian's father had given him his first alcohol, a glass of manzanilla, and then sent him, alone with his baggage in a taxi, to Grand Central Station. "Play football if it appeals to you, there's a lot of enjoyment in it after it's over," Elliott Hubbard had said by way of farewell. "And don't let anyone lie to you. Bullshit is the curse of boarding school—of life, in fact."

Ever since, inflexibly, Julian had demanded the truth of others. It was a painful trait. Other key rules he had guessed correctly, from observing his father: drink only dry wines and good liquor, and drink everything sparingly; work very hard without letting others see the effort involved; think what you please, but never speak unkindly of another man; forget any woman who has stopped loving you.

Julian was the child of his father's second wife, a woman much younger than he who had left him, not for a lover, but for an illusion. She thought she was a painter. It was evident to Julian, even as a boy, that his mother had no talent; it was just as clear that putting color on canvas, rising every morning and spending the whole day doing this, brought her intense happiness. She deserted her husband and her child when Julian was eight and went to live in a cottage in Normandy. It was a very small stone house, heated by a fireplace, without electricity. The roof was thatched, with blue and yellow iris growing along the ridgepole, and these flowers were always in bloom when Julian arrived to spend the summer. At night he heard animals—mice and squirrels and nesting birds—rustling in the thatch above his bed.

He always came to France by ship, and his mother would meet him outside the customs in Le Havre. She never spoke to Julian of school or his father, or of anything that had to do with his life in America. She did not write to him in winter; he was alive to her, and real, only when he was with her. Julian spent ten summers with his mother. She never cooked except to fry eggs in a blackened skillet for their breakfast; she would arrange the eggs, yolks all broken and running into the porous grain of the bread, edge to edge on a split baguette, and then cut this long sandwich in two, giving the larger part to Julian. At other meals, taken whenever they were hungry, they ate cheese and cold meat and fruit with their fingers

15

and drank rough red wine, diluted with spring water, from the thick tumblers that were almost their only dishes.

Julian's mother wore jeans, never a dress, and wiped her brushes on them as she worked, so that her lean thighs were streaked with her paints. She knew everything in nature—the names of trees and wildflowers, even those of stones and soils, the birds and their songs. She taught them all to Julian, and thirty years afterwards he could identify the call of a warbler, the bark of an oak, the petals of loosestrife with as little conscious effort as he recognized a popular tune or read English. Yet for all her love of the natural world, Julian's mother never painted anything as it was. She reduced everything to an abstraction. Julian didn't know whether she lacked the technique to reproduce living things in their true form, or whether she had some flaw—perhaps it was a gift—that made her see things as color only. She would work the whole day, gazing fixedly at a landscape, holding up the handle of a brush to measure perspective, and at the end of her labors show Julian a canvas smeared with pigment, suggestive of nothing. Sometimes her work had a kind of luminosity: the light in a cloud or the rain falling through the industrial smoke of Le Havre across the river would find its way through her eye to her hand and onto the surface of the painting. She was invariably happy with what she had done; she would smile at the picture, and then put it away and forget it. The cottage was filled with her works, all unframed, stacked with faces against the walls.

Julian and his mother swam in the Seine and sailed a dinghy, exhilarated by the river's dangerous tides and currents. At night they read and went to bed early. They talked almost never; like his father, she never asked questions. Before they slept, his mother sometimes played the mandolin and sang old parlor songs about lost and ruined girls—"Sweet Genevieve," "Ben Bolt," "The Gypsy's Kiss." Her voice was melodious even when she shouted, and could be heard a long way across the water. She had beautiful white teeth. She died of cancer at forty, in winter like Julian's father, also alone. Julian never saw a pretty woman smile or heard his daughter, who had a sweet soprano voice, singing in some far room of the house, that he did not remember his mother.

Now Julian had married a young woman as a second wife, just as his father had done. She passionately wanted a baby. Julian's Emily spoke of this every day. She was in the grip of an overwhelming instinct to conceive and give birth. Each menses was a stain of failure; Emily told him in the night that she could never be a whole person, a completed female, until she had borne his child: "No one else's baby, Julian—yours, with your life and mine mixed in him."

16

Julian wondered if his mother had been the same, if his father had made her pregnant with him, Julian, as reluctantly as he was bringing himself to get his own bride with child. The children of his first marriage, a son named Elliott and a daughter named Jenny, were twelve and ten, old enough to accept an infant. Julian loved them now with his whole heart, but he had detested the illnesses, the noise, the stench, the mindless tyranny of babies. He could not tell Emily that; she could not understand what she hadn't yet lived through. Instead, he told her that there was so much in his life, since he had fallen in love with her, that he had no room for more.

Emily insisted on her own needs. Julian must honor her emotions. "I won't live by *words*! I know what I feel!" she cried.

Julian recoiled. He had heard this before, the words and their very tone, all during his first marriage. He yielded to Emily, as he had yielded so often to his earlier wife, because they had ardor as their weapon while he, like his father, had nothing more powerful in his emotional arsenal than good humor and good manners. In his job, he was a passionate and ruthless man who rewarded the President's friends and destroyed his enemies without compunction. In the White House, in politics, Julian was acting according to his beliefs; he was doing what was important. Emily was his pleasure. President Lockwood was his duty.

Julian hoped that, if a baby came, it would be as lucky as he had been in his older brother. Horace had been the best friend of Julian's childhood, as he was his best friend now—almost an extra parent because of the ten years' difference in their age. Horace was the only confessor Julian had ever had; he could tell his brother anything. Somehow, he never asked Horace anything about himself: Horace told him what he thought he needed to know.

Their father had been forty when Julian was born. After Julian's mother left, Elliott and his young son were alone a good deal. They had two residences, a tall stone house on Ninety-third Street that Elliott had bought when he became senior partner of his law firm, and a rambling wooden mansion in the Berkshires called the Harbor—really it was an eighteenth-century farmhouse with innumerable ells and wings—which was the seat of the Hubbard family. They wintered in New York and summered on a mountainside where the lawns and the rose gardens and the rare trees planted by a botanizing ancestor were a green island in a hemlock forest that was as blue as the Atlantic on a fair day, and as unbroken.

The Hubbards did not belong to New York society, and such society as there had been in the Berkshires withered when the mills that had been the source of its wealth and self-esteem had moved south to escape high labor costs and irksome safety laws. Elliott sold the Hubbard mills as soon as his father died, when they still had some value. He moved to New York sooner than that, right after finishing law school. He was the first member of his family who chose his own friends.

Elliott Hubbard cared greatly for male company, and both houses were full, most evenings, with supper guests. Julian ate with his father's friends from the time he was able to stay awake. They were, all of them, men who did things—wrote books, made movies, produced plays, ran banks and brokerage houses, dug up lost cities, pitched for the Yankees. These men accepted Julian, and Horace when he came home, as equals. They all laughed a good deal, and drank a lot of wine, but Julian never encountered a fool or a drunk until he went away to school.

As there was never any child's talk in Elliott's houses, there was never any child's food. Julian ate what his father ate, and the diet ran to raw foods: oysters, steak tartare, marinated fishes, large chewy salads. Steaks and roasts were bloody, vegetables were crisp and barely heated through by steam. Julian's father believed that most of the value of food was lost when it was cooked. When Julian went to Exeter he had a hard time adjusting to the soft, starchy diet that the school provided, and for the rest of his life he found it difficult to deal with food prepared in the ordinary way.

After dinner, when they were alone, father and son played cribbage or chess, one game, on alternate nights, and Julian's rare victories were earned. It was only when Julian went to bed that his father treated him as a child. He read him to sleep—fairy tales in the years before Julian's mother left them, then Kipling, *The Jungle Books* especially, and poetry: *A Shropshire Lad* and what Julian remembered as the complete works of Byron, bound in tan limp leather. The old man's face, reading glasses perched on his nose, was always happiest when he was reading Byron; Julian realized now that Elliott had loved the poet's reckless life as much as he loved the voice in the poems.

Julian, half-crouched over the sink in his bathroom in Washington, wiped lather from his cheeks. In the mirror, he looked like his father: the same great height, horse-faced, fierce-eyed, with the identical arched narrow nose and wide mouth, the shaggy eyebrows and the dark hair going gray at the temples. There were many similarities, and Julian was not the only one who noticed them; a good many men still alive in Washington had known Elliott Hubbard in his political phases—he'd been a government attorney in Roosevelt's last term, and much later, a lawyer who had saved old friends who had given way to idealism from McCarthy

18

and Nixon. Elliott had worked quietly, almost secretly, as brilliant lawyers do. He had had a reputation. Julian, working for the same causes a lifetime later, had fame. He didn't like it, but he accepted the saturation of publicity that went with his job and made his name almost as familiar as the President's.

Julian grinned at his image in the glass. The main difference between him and his father, he sometimes thought, was that the older man had spent his life in large beautiful houses while Julian had lived in small ugly ones. His father had had bathrooms built specially for a man of his height. Julian had spent the quarter century since he had left home doubled over low washbasins as he brushed his teeth and removed his whiskers. He shaved morning and evening, lathering twice each time: four backaches a day. Friends told Julian that the "restored" brick house in Georgetown for which he had had to pay a million dollars was a jewel, but it was dark and narrow and low, and within his own lifetime it had been part of a slum. He had civilized the house with the things his father had left him—a few pieces of good French furniture; a dozen carpets; a row of Post-Impressionist paintings on the sitting room wall; a Sargent portrait of his grandmother as a girl: the lovely intelligent white face under a summer hat in a field of shimmering black.

Julian had no interest in possessions for their own sake. Very early he had accepted a set of political beliefs that made the love of property impossible, and he lived by those beliefs as best he could. But these inherited objects were parts of the consciousness of his family—the Seurat and the Cézanne had been bought from the artists by his great-grandfather; the Empire tables and chairs had been found in Paris by his grandmother; the Tabrizi carpets had been owned in Shiraz by a great-uncle, an archaeologist who had lived in Persia most of his life, digging for Harvard, as his sisters had said, and had come home to die bringing nothing but the rugs with him. Julian's brother had been named for this relative, and, like him, had spent the greater part of his adult life abroad, mostly in the Near East.

Horace had come back from Beirut for the funeral, and he and Julian had buried their father in the Hubbard plot in West Stockbridge. It was a bitter day, fifteen below zero at noon, the sun a pale disk on the southern horizon, snow blowing against the plain stones that bore the same Christian names generation after generation: Elliotts, Horaces, Julians, Aarons, Jonathans. There were no flowers, just the plain pine coffin Elliott had ordered for himself; and no other relations. Elliott's sisters were dead, and he had been

19

the youngest child and the only male of his generation. Horace had never married, and Julian's son was the last Hubbard. The Order for the Burial of the Dead was read by a young curate whose wind-stung hands, gripping the Book of Common Prayer, turned red and trembled violently. His surplice whipped around his legs, revealing green hiking boots and thick woolen socks, and his black stole blew behind him like the tail of a school scarf. The grave seemed very deep because the workmen had gone down through four feet of snow before striking the frozen earth. As Horace and Julian drove away in the undertaker's car they saw their father's yellow coffin lying beside the open grave. Snow eddied around the var-nished box; in the jump seat the curate held his frostbitten hands in his armpits and sucked his breath through his teeth in pain.

Two days later there was a memorial service in New York at Saint Thomas Church, where Elliott had been baptized, confirmed, and married to his first wife—and, it turned out, where he, the un-believer, had gone to morning prayer every day for the last quarter century of his life. The President came, along with two hundred others who had been invited by the family. Even here Elliott's diffi-dence prevailed. There was no eulogy, just the plain Episcopal service: prayer, psalm, lesson, hymn, blessing.

After leaving Saint Thomas's, the President and his wife and a dozen others went back with the family to the house on Ninety-third Street. Horace and Julian gave them sherry while Wilfred and Maria, the couple who had kept house for Elliott for forty years, changed from their church clothes to their uniforms. Lock-wood draped his long body in a chair that crackled under his weight and drew Jenny onto his lap. Soon he said something to make her laugh, and she covered her mouth. Lockwood took Jenny's flying hand gently in his and kissed it through the white glove she had worn to church. "Go ahead," he said, "a good honest laugh is the thing your grandpa would like best to hear from you." But the house seemed cold and changed; Elliott had died in the room where they were, and Maria had sprayed something in the air that had killed the scent of him. Julian, watching his child's solemn face as Lockwood stroked her hair, wondered if any of them would ever come back here.

The family had supper alone, and Jenny and Elliott, tired by a long day filled with strangers, went up to bed after the dessert.

Horace looked across the broad table at Emily. They had met only once before, at her wedding. "You look very well in the pearls," he said. "The pearls are always worn on solemn occasions."

20

The long double rope of pearls around Emily's neck were among the jewels Horace had returned to the family when his mother died. Caroline, Julian's first wife, had left them behind, with the children and all the rest of the Hubbard jewelry, when she got her divorce.

"Patrick Graham mentioned the pearls—how fine they'd looked on Caroline," Emily said. "Was he such an intimate of hers?"

The brothers exchanged a look. Emily caught it and said, "What does *that* mean?"

"Patrick and Caroline have a long history," Julian said. Emily, aglow with curiosity, began to ask a question, but Horace interrupted.

"Why was Patrick there?" he asked. "Did he know Pa?"

"They may have met." Julian smiled. "Patrick likes to be in the right places, and he's known me for a long time."

"And loved you. He went through the crowd on the church steps like a monkey going through a card index, looking for Caroline."

Emily rapped on the table. "What *is* this?"

Julian didn't answer, but after a long gaze from Horace, raised his eyebrows, giving him leave to speak.

"Patrick was in love with Caroline," Horace said. "He lived with her while Julian was in Vietnam, and for a long time afterwards. Then Julian stole her away."

"It wasn't quite that simple," Julian said. "How do you know these things, Horace?"

"Brotherly concern. And then again, old Caro wasn't what you'd call discreet. For years she expected Patrick to kill you."

Julian made an impatient gesture. "All that happened at least twenty years ago. Besides, it was Caroline's choice. Even Patrick could see that she wasn't the sort of woman anyone could steal. She took what she wanted."

"Smart girl," said Emily. Her eyes, lit by mischief, darted from one brother to the other. She was too young and too pretty to feel jealousy of the past. "I want to know all about this."

Horace smiled and looked at his watch. "Pry it out of Julian. I have to take the morning plane to Beirut and Julian and I—and you, too, Emily—really ought to have a talk."

"Ah, the reading of the will," said Emily. "I'll go upstairs and leave you to it."

She kissed them both. Horace watched her walk out of the room; he gave Julian and himself more wine. When he heard the bedroom door close at the top of the stairs he said, "I must say,

21

Julian, you have a way of having smashing girls fall in love with you. This one isn't as disputatious as Caroline. That must be a relief."

"It is."

Horace was his father's executor; he was the elder son and the banker. "I've been through Pa's assets," he said to Julian. "Sebastian Laux has always been his banker, so it was simple enough. In brief, there is no ready money."

"None?" Julian's face broke into a fond smile and Horace returned it; both men liked this last act of nonchalance on their father's part.

"You may have noticed, Julian, that Pa lived in a kind of nineteenth-century rapture. He kept Wilfred and Maria in this house and Lipton at the Harbor year-round. He belonged to three clubs, kept boxes at the ball games and seats at the Metropolitan and the Philharmonic."

Elliott had had an income from his law practice, but he hadn't really worked for years. He'd educated his sons and paid for his women, and all his life he had been freehanded with himself.

"All that's left, really, is the two houses, both mortgaged," Horace said. "We'll have to sell them to pay taxes and debts and pension off Wilfred and Maria and Lipton—they're old now, so there ought to be enough. Everything in the houses, the paintings and furniture and so on, goes to the two of us to divide as we agree." There would be no trouble about that, and Elliott had known it. "I'd like the hunting carpet and the Pissarro," Horace said. "All the rest you can have, I've no room for it." Julian protested: the Post-Impressionists and the Sargent and the rest were worth a lot of money.

"No more than Pa had to give my mother in reparations for falling into bed with yours," Horace said. "That's where the capital went, and Mother went to Paris after the divorce and spent her life throwing it away so Pa would never get it back. She'd have risen from her deathbed and flung the jewels into the Seine if she'd imagined that any wife of yours might have worn them." This was the most Horace had ever said about his own mother.

"Did she really hate Pa and my mother that much after all those years?" said Julian. He was incredulous.

Horace, just for a moment, lost the expression of mild amusement that was habitual to him. When he stopped smiling he had his mother's cold face and her pale, unreadable eyes. But when he spoke, it was in their father's voice with its peculiar soft timbre; this was his only physical inheritance from Elliott Hubbard.

"That's twice tonight you've suggested there's some statute of limitations on hatred," Horace said. "Do you really think it dies like love or fades like sorrow?"

Julian, in that instant, realized that his father was truly dead. Looking into Horace's wintry eyes he saw once again the coffin in the snow at West Stockbridge, the mountains veiled by the storm, the stripped trees bent by the wind. The frozen landscape was not unlike a desert. Julian was overcome by remorse, he trembled with it, and it wasn't his father's death that made him feel as he did, but the death of another man. He felt near to tears; he felt that he and Horace were as they had been a long time ago—one brother a child, the other already nearly an adult.

"Horace, there's something in my life I could never speak about to Pa; I'd like to tell you."

Horace held up a palm; his smile returned. "Don't," he said. "Not tonight."

2

In Baghdad, Patrick Graham met the man Clive Wilmot had sent him to see. Furtive Arabs, obviously terrorists, gave Patrick an address in the worst quarter of the city. They made him repeat the directions over and over again, as if they were putting him under discipline as a member of their organization, instructing him to knock twice, then once, then twice again on a certain door. They demanded that he arrive at precisely fourteen minutes before midnight—if he was so much as a minute early or late their leader would break the rendezvous and there would be no second chance. "Come alone," they whispered; "we'll *know* whether you're alone."

Patrick found his way without trouble through the unmarked streets. The crowds parted before him, a lone foreigner in a place where he did not belong. Patrick guessed that the poor of Baghdad must know who was following him; the terrorists walking behind him were Mao's fish, swimming in the sea of people. He entered a building. Its masonry was twisted like a human body distorted by an untreated childhood disease. Patrick climbed the narrow staircase, pausing at one of its turnings to look at the lighted dial of his watch. He was early. He stood on the landing, letting the seconds go by, and gazed out the unglazed window, narrow as a rifle port, that looked onto the warren below. Half of Patrick's lifetime had passed since the day he realized, shattered, that most of the world lived, and had always lived, as these people did: sleeping, coupling, giving birth, gobbling food, dying, in the open streets. He did not

23

see actual human forms, only their shadows thrown by guttering cooking fires. He smelled the half-spoiled food and open drains and bodies rotted by sickness. Men and women and children shrieked in anger or merriment, their voices breaking against the crumbling buildings like surf against rocks. Only the power of speech made it possible for them to live without hope; had they been dumb they would have fallen on one another like wild animals for the meat.

Patrick mounted the last drunken flight of stairs and knocked, as he had been told to do, on a door. No one answered, but he pushed open the door; it was hung on broken hinges and it squealed over the concrete floor. Someone struck a match and lit a candle, and Patrick saw Clive's man sitting on the floor inside a ring of light. The smell of melting wax and human sweat was very strong. The man on the floor was a Palestinian terrorist of the old type: fugitive, threadbare, emaciated; his incurable political fever had eaten the flesh from his bones. Maddened eyes glittered in the sockets of a skull covered by a tissue of polished tan skin. He sat with his back pressed against the scabrous wall. Someone who had followed Patrick up the stairs pulled the squealing door shut behind him.

Insects and small animals scuttled away from the candlelight. The memory of the East Village, where he and Caroline had loved each other in their youth, struck Patrick in the stomach like a fist. The apartment in which they had lived had been as much like this room as was possible in America. In order to link their destiny, their very consciousness, to that of the wretched, Patrick and Caroline had tried to join themselves physically to them, to live with rats and insects and the diseases these creatures carried, to be made weak and sick by a bad diet. They had even called themselves by the names of the hunted. Patrick's revolutionary name had been Ahmed; Caroline's, Fat'ma.

"I am called Hassan," said the man on the floor.

Patrick remained silent. So far as he knew, no outsider had ever seen this man face to face and lived. Hassan was the head of a terrorist organization known as the Eye of Gaza; he hadn't been sighted—in the sense that the Eye of Gaza had not claimed credit for a new outrage—in years; many believed him dead. This implacable man had been responsible for hundreds of murders, scores of bombings, dozens of kidnappings. In one month his followers had exploded five airliners filled with passengers over Israel. The terrorists made each pilot fly low over Tel Aviv and Jerusalem as they broadcast their messages to the world over the plane's radio, and then mercilessly blew it up. The debris, fragments of the machine and parts of human bodies, had fallen into the city streets and onto rooftops.

All this happened at a time when security measures were so strict that the authorities believed it had finally become impossible for a terrorist to smuggle any sort of bomb or weapon aboard a passenger flight. But Hassan had outwitted them. A Palestinian surgeon had found a way to implant plastic explosives inside the bodies of the terrorists of the Eye of Gaza. Several ounces could be packed between the muscles of the thighs; the terrorist, his fresh incision deadened by a local anesthetic, could walk onto the plane and into the cockpit, and there detonate himself with the charge from a battery in an electric watch. These living bombs, spewing blood and slivers of bone and gobbets of flesh, were enough to bring down any airliner. How they did it baffled the counterterrorist police until one of Hassan's walking bombs was recognized by chance in the airport at Cairo and shot dead before he could explode the charges within him. The autopsy on his body, intact except for the head wound that had killed him, revealed the secret. It was very nearly the only secret about Hassan that had ever been betrayed.

Hassan said, "Do you know who I am?"

"Yes," said Patrick.

"Good. I know something about you—that you were once called Ahmed in a romantic period of your youth. I know other things as well."

"I'm flattered."

"Are you? Twenty-five years ago you wanted to join the revolution. Now you wear a watch that costs more than one of those people down in the streets holds in his hands in a lifetime."

Patrick had remained standing. He felt a movement behind him and realized that whoever had shut the door had come into the room before doing so. A man moved into his field of vision. He had a Kalashnikov machine pistol in his hands and the candle's tongue flicked over its blued surface. Patrick recognized the outmoded weapon, its vicious snout and curved magazine, from a thousand photographs, as he might have identified the flintlock on the shoulder of a statue on a New England village green; it was a homely revolutionary object.

"That is a comrade," Hassan said; "he's here to protect you. No harm will come to you from us."

Hassan was speaking in an almost inaudible voice, in the rippling English of an educated Arab. It didn't matter how loudly they spoke; the building was abandoned and empty, no one could hear. If the terrorists decided to fire a whole magazine from the

Kalashnikov into Patrick's body and leave him dead in this room, no one would hear that either. Someone might come and take the watch from his leaking corpse after Hassan and the gunman departed. But no one would hear.

Patrick was terrified, but when he spoke the words came out of him clear and loud. Nothing ever affected the strength of his voice. "I am looking into the death of Ibn Awad," he said.

"So I've been told."

"It's been suggested to me that you may be able to help me."

"What do you want to prove?"

Patrick didn't answer. Uninvited, he sat down on the floor opposite Hassan. At Patrick's sudden movement, the gunman shifted his feet, but relaxed at a gesture from Hassan. Hassan and Patrick were looking directly into each other's face now. The candle burned between them. Patrick noted every detail; he could bring this scene alive in words during a broadcast as vividly as the camera could have done it.

"The truth is quite simple," Hassan said. "Ibn Awad was murdered on the orders of the American President."

"President Lockwood?"

"Lockwood, yes." He made an impatient gesture. "They're all the same. Don't you realize that—that they are all the same? Or have you smothered Ahmed and become Patrick Graham, a rich and famous man—become just like them?"

"You can judge what I am for yourself. I know what the realities are. I know the truth when I hear it."

"And did you hear the truth when Ibn Awad was assassinated?"

"I heard what the whole world believed to be the truth at the time."

"Then you don't know a lie when you hear one."

"I saw the document Ibn Awad had written out in his own hand, ordering his own death."

"A forgery."

"Then where is the forger?"

Hassan's teeth gleamed. "If he were my forger, he'd be dead. I suppose the one the Americans used is dead, too."

Patrick's fear was fading. In a way, even in this place, he was on his own ground. He was used to testing men, pushing them back with his voice, making them reveal themselves and the facts.

"The document, Ibn Awad's suicide note if you want to call it that, was sent to the imam of the great mosque in Mecca. Surely he is trustworthy?"

"Priests can be trusted to believe what they want. The imam wanted to believe that Ibn Awad had done this bizarre thing, this insane thing—had his favorite son kill him, knowing that his son would be executed for the crime and they both would go to hell forever—because he wanted to save Islam even at the cost of those two souls."

"You call it bizarre. You're right. It's too bizarre *not* to be true."

"You're a clever man, my friend. If one wants to deceive a clever man one must act in a clever way. The Americans were clever. They killed Ibn Awad, then forged a suicide note that was so unbelievable, so absurd, that the only choice clever men had was to believe it."

Hassan was utterly relaxed. He reached down the neck of his jibba—it was made of unbleached cloth and was much patched—and scratched his chest. Patrick opened his mouth to speak but Hassan held up his palm to stop him.

"I'll tell you what I can tell you," he said. "Then you can go away."

"I have a lot of questions."

"Ask them of the Americans. We hear that you go to tea at the White House. Put down your teacup and ask President Lockwood questions."

Hassan leaned forward. As he came closer to the flame it cast darker shadows in the deep hollows of his face and his polished head looked more than ever like a skull.

"Two facts," he said. "First fact: I saw Ibn Awad only hours before his death, in his tent in the desert of Hagreb—the very tent in which he was killed. We made plans to meet the next day. Ibn Awad was going to give me an important gift at that time."

"What gift?"

"It was buried in the desert, only he knew where."

"What gift?" Patrick insisted.

"Something to give the Eye of Gaza its greatest victory. Ibn Awad believed in our cause. He was a great Arab."

"He was a saint, not a terrorist."

"In his understanding, the Eye of Gaza killed in the name of God. We killed bad Arabs who had betrayed their people and their religion. We killed Jews. What did Ibn Awad want above everything else? To cleanse Islam. He saw the Eye of Gaza as God's instrument to do that."

"Ibn Awad was secretly connected to the Eye of Gaza? He was giving you money?"

"He was going to make us a great gift. The Americans learned about it. They killed him to prevent our having what he was going to give us."

"How did the Americans find out? Who told them? And what

was this gift that it should make them kill the holiest man on earth?"

Hassan had been holding his skeletal hands clasped in his lap. Now he spread them in resignation. His yellow nails looked like bits of gnawed bone.

"Prince Talil's father trusted him utterly. Talil trusted the Americans. As for the nature of the gift—ask the Americans. Perhaps they found it. I could not, though I searched very hard."

Hassan's hands were still suspended before him. He clapped them together twice, tiny explosions in the stifling room. "Ibn Awad," he said after the first clap; "Prince Talil," he said after the second. "The Americans killed them both."

"But I saw Ibn Awad's note. It was examined by every expert in the world. It was compared to Awad's handwriting by computers and by humans. The handwriting on the document sent to the imam in Mecca was genuine."

"Was it?" asked Hassan. Patrick had to strain to hear what he was saying. "Here is a second fact," Hassan said. "Ibn Awad, the emir of Hagreb, *could not write*. As a child he was thought to be an imbecile. He very nearly didn't inherit the throne because he couldn't learn to write. His tutors—priests, naturally—assumed that he couldn't learn to read either, so they didn't bother to teach him."

Patrick was stifled by the odor of bodies in the close room. Hassan was watching him; in the Arab style he made no effort to conceal the crafty pleasure on his face as he waited for Patrick to challenge what he had just told him. Patrick, instead, continued to stare, and made a gesture with his fingers, beckoning more information out of Hassan's mouth.

"What made Ibn Awad seem an idiot as a child was later on regarded as a sign from God—his family and the priests thought God had meant to keep him innocent. Ibn Awad was a very intelligent person, some would call him a genius. He memorized the whole Koran, by having it read to him. If he heard a thing once, no matter what it was, he never forgot it."

"But he couldn't write, or read."

"Correct. But this was no sign from God. Modern people like you and me know it was a disorder with a scientific name. This inability to write is called dysgraphia. It's caused by a lesion on the brain. Perhaps he had a childhood fever or an injury at birth."

"What proof have you of that?"

"Ibn Awad had other medical problems. Prince Talil had him examined by American doctors. They discovered the lesion. Find the records of their examination. Surely that's not beyond a man of your skills and connections?"

Hassan stood up. He brushed the grit from the skirts of his

jibba. They had been sitting on the stone floor for a long time, but Hassan showed no sign of discomfort though his bones, poking through his leathery skin, must ache. Patrick's shanks, his spine, his whole body gave him pain.

"Go to Hagreb and ask questions. Go back to Washington and ask questions," Hassan said.

"I will, don't worry."

"Worry? I have no reason to worry. The revolution will happen in its own time whether you're still strong enough to help it or not." Hassan leaned over and cupped the candle with both hands; the fingers were sinewy and his sleeves fell back to reveal corded muscular forearms; this man who seemed so fleshless had killed with his hands more than once.

Hassan blew out the candle. In the dark he said, "Ahmed. I wonder if that person—that believer—is still alive in you?"

Alone, Patrick waited until he could hear no noise outside the door. Then he lit a cigarette and smoked the whole thing down to the filter, inhaling lungful after lungful of hot smoke. He did not think about what Hassan had told him. He had had to learn not to let his mind work too quickly. It was best when he had been startled, when he ceased to believe one thing, and began to believe another, to keep his head empty. All around him in the dark the little unclean creatures rustled and he concentrated on that sound and on the scorching smoke going in and out of his throat and lungs.

When he went into the street he found that the Eye of Gaza had withdrawn its shadowers. He was pawed by beggars all the way back to his hotel. Children touched his genitals and snatched at his watch while their ragged elders pointed and laughed. Patrick wanted to break into a run, but he controlled himself. At last, emerging into a broad lighted street, he found a taxi.

Patrick's hotel room was cooled to a temperature thirty degrees below that in the streets. He could still feel the beggars' hands on his skin. He stripped off his clothes and took a shower, soaping and scrubbing, rinsing and scrubbing again. He called room service and ordered breakfast. A large glass of water came with it, filled with the tubular transparent ice cubes that only an American machine could have produced. Patrick took the glass to the window, cranked open the sash, and threw the water and the ice cubes out. The heat and smell of the ancient city came in.

The air-conditioned room, the food on its heated plate, the ice cubes, awakened in Patrick the hatred he had felt all his life for his country, inventor of devices that no one needed but that every human being—even Hassan, even the silent guard ready to die for

29

Hassan, certainly the beggars who had frightened Patrick with their sores—envied and coveted. Patrick himself, born poor, had done so.

" 'They're all the same, don't you realize that?' " Patrick heard the echo of Hassan's sibilant question.

The window remained open; he was sweating. Smelling himself, he smelled Hassan in his filthy jibba. His mind, trained to miss no useful detail, remembered Hassan's queer fastidious gesture—how he had brushed his gown when he rose from the verminous floor. After all was said, what was it that Hassan wanted? For what had he plotted and tortured and torn the life out of strangers all through his bloody life? He used code words to explain the horrors he was driven to: freedom, revolution, justice, homeland. But what did he want? He wanted a country—and what was a country if it was not a machine for making the men who invented it rich?

3

Stepping from the shower, Julian heard the waking call of a veery, and went to the window to see if he could catch a glimpse of this shy woodland bird. He watched the damp ground beneath the willow in the garden corner, but had no luck. Jenny had seen eggs, two delicate greenish ones in a ground nest, and had tried to transcribe the thrush's song for the piano: twelve falling notes. Usually it sang at evening. Back at the sink, he opened the medicine cabinet, putting his mug and brush and razor neatly in their places, and then snapped open the tube of pills. His blood pressure, 200 over 120 before treatment, was alarming to Julian's doctor, but not to Julian. His condition led to heart attacks, cerebral hemorrhages —quick, private deaths like his father's. Julian, in his rational way, took the pills, six each day, faithfully; the medication reduced his blood pressure to 130 over 80, a normal reading. Of course, only the symptoms were controlled; the condition itself remained, concealed deep in Julian's body.

Julian had learned early that his own death was not a matter of great interest to him. Three times he had almost died: at fifteen, when he swam out too far in the Seine; at twenty-one, when his Phantom was crippled by flak over Vietnam and he was pulled, bleeding, out of the sea by a rescue helicopter; and, the last time, a year or so before, when Emily, angry after a quarrel, drove her car through a guardrail and over an embankment on a seaside road in Maine. Each time, after the briefest of struggles, Julian had been ready to let life go. On every occasion his last thoughts, or what he imagined to be his last thoughts, had been of others.

At his first near-drowning, he had been seized by an undercurrent so strong that he thought some big animal had pulled him beneath the surface of the Seine. He fought upwards, towards a patch of sunlight on the muddy surface of the river, and as his head broke water he heard his mother's voice calling from the bank. The sound of it, so gay, so unsuspecting that Julian was going to die while she watched, filled him with unbearable sorrow. He struggled, fought the current, sank and rose, wept with the effort to escape. He reached safety a long distance downstream from where his mother was, coming ashore in a grassy meadow where a herd of black and white cattle, let out to graze after their morning milking, quietly regarded his dripping figure, working their jaws and switching their tails. He remembered the deep silence of the moment after the roar of the water, and that of his own blood, in his ears.

His mother waited for him in the moored dinghy. For a breakfast picnic she had brought their thick chewy sandwiches of fried eggs, and sweetened coffee in the cloudy wine tumblers. They sat facing each other in the gently rocking boat as they ate; his mother wore a faded bikini and a wide straw hat that left her face, except for her shining teeth, in shadow. The food, the sun, the motion of the boat—and, he supposed, years later, the escape from death— gave Julian an erection that he could not hide. His mother smiled and left him, walking up the steep bank, its wild grasses cropped like a lawn by farm animals. He put up the sail and took the dinghy out alone, and in a short while he saw her, fully clothed in her jeans and smock, working at her easel on a hilltop. She could never have known that his arousal had nothing to do with her. She died before Julian was old enough to tell her why this had happened to him.

That was his most painful regret when he was shot down in Vietnam, crash-landing his jet in the sea. By that time he retained no vestige of religious belief, but some part of his mind that had remained behind in childhood (during chapel at Exeter he had often tried, while praying, to transmit messages to his mother in France, as if God were an antenna) attempted to send assurances to his dead mother that he had never wished to desire her sexually; it seemed vital to Julian that she understand that, and that it was possible she might do so through the intensity of his last thoughts. Otherwise, as he hemorrhaged into waters that were the same temperature as his blood, he felt nothing but a sort of giddy good humor. He had no idea how many Vietnamese he had killed in sixty sorties with napalm and high explosives and rapid-fire miniguns. Hundreds, he supposed. It seemed to him a comedy of justice that his hidden, dumb victims should at last have killed *him*, bringing down his complicated airplane and his whole complex American organism, educated at enormous expense, with a primitive weapon —perhaps a heavy machine gun, clumsily aimed by human hand and eye, that was no different from those used by the Western powers against bewildered Asians in the Boxer Rebellion. Dying, as he believed himself to be, Julian imagined the celebration his killers must be having in their burning encampment, the heart-bursting joy they must have felt on seeing the black trail of his burning machine falling beyond the horizon.

But once again Julian survived. Rising from a drugged sleep in a naval hospital in Hawaii, he found Horace standing at his bedside. Julian's injuries weren't serious—broken bones and cuts—but he had less control than usual over his mind because of the morphine he had been given, and so he told Horace how it felt to die by water. "You had no will to fight against death?" Horace asked. Julian shook his head; he wanted very much to see his brother's features, but he couldn't because Horace was standing with his back to the window and it was a bright day, so that his lanky body was outlined by brilliant sunlight. Horace's face was in shadow, as Julian's mother's face had been hidden by the shadow of her hat in the dinghy long ago. "No. It's very peaceful to feel the person going," Julian said. Horace stroked his younger brother's hair, rubbed a knuckle over his cheek, scratchy with a two-day beard. "It's all that time you spent with Pa," he said. "I know he thinks that nothing matters, that humanity is a junk species. But he may not be right, Julian. Next time, struggle a little, have a little curiosity about the future, try to live. You can be damn sure our father would take his full three times going down before *he* drowned."

Horace had always tried to teach Julian to struggle against the pessimism in their father. That was why Julian had gone into politics. Even in school, he had begun to want to believe in the goodness of man. Julian didn't like the idea of sin, of blame, of responsibility. Especially, he couldn't attach those words to the poor and the exploited: whatever they did to attack their horrible lives, even if murdered, they had a right to do. Surely Julian, bleeding to death in the Gulf of Tonkin, had put this conviction to the test: his final thought before he lost consciousness was this: *Good for you.* The thought was addressed to the yellow men who had shot him down, scrawny and superstitious and deceived even by their own ruler who had fed a whole generation of them into the meat grinder of Western technology. Ho Chi Minh had killed these peasants to fulfill his own idea of himself as the greatest

32

Vietnamese of all time. Julian and his fellow aviators had killed them for sport, like German officers at the turn of the century hunting Bushmen instead of gazelles in South-West Africa; but the Vietnamese had killed Julian out of hatred and fear, and to Julian they were, therefore, the only true human beings involved in the cycle of slaughter.

Julian's choice of a political career was his one conscious rebellion against the values of his father's life. Julian stood next to a President who was trying to change society, who was reckless in his belief in the goodness of man. The two of them thought it was possible to destroy the hateful stupidities of the past. Neither Lockwood nor Julian believed in change—they believed, instead, in the imminent discovery of man's goodness beneath the grime and the scars of his history. Man had only to *be* himself to save himself. A hundred years earlier, the two of them would have sailed for the Congo with a kit of medicines and a crate of Bibles. The cool intelligence of Elliott Hubbard had mingled with the romantic impulsiveness of Julian's mother to produce, in their son, an idealist.

Nothing in his life surprised Elliott more, or amused him as much. Even in the 1950s, when he was saving romantic leftists, Elliott had had contempt for politics. He looked on belief as poison. "You're old enough to look around at what's happening," Elliott said at table one night in the sixties, when Julian was in his late teens. "Do you think you've lived so far in a sane and stable world?" Julian shook his head. "Unlucky boy," his father said; "but how do you think you would've liked *my* boyhood? Irishwomen singing in the kitchen, the honest dead ball in the major leagues, steamy horseshit in the streets, a wonderful aroma. The American elms were still alive in New York, the sky in West Stockbridge was full of barn swallows; I used to spend whole days trying to shoot one on the wing with my slingshot. The medieval hierarchy prevailed: God, seraphim, angels, saints, kings, nobles, peasants, animals, plants, earth, water, stones; every idea and every creature in its place."

Julian had stopped eating in order to listen.

"That was your great-grandfather's view of the universe," Elliott said. "In his mind, he was one of the nobles; he wanted to teach me how to be one, too. He had cotton mills in which he killed children. Their parents, immigrants from Europe, were his accomplices—they'd breed big families and send them into the mills at the age of eight, then confiscate the wages. The children would get tuberculosis from breathing the mill dust. Once when I was at the Harbor for Christmas, down from Exeter for the holiday, I walked by a very pretty girl on Fenn Street—she may have been fifteen. I've never seen such rosy cheeks as she had. She was Irish;

in those days Americans could tell who was who. She was in front of the mill, on her way to work. She was coughing blood into a snowbank, scarlet gobs of it. It made me see the real color of money. You should, too, Julian."

Julian put down his fork with a clatter. He was reading a lot by that time, and he had begun to think that it was wrong to be rich. "What has any Hubbard ever done to make up for that girl?" he demanded.

His father pressed his lips together in a smile. "I can't speak for the others," he said. "I've saved a lot of my friends who've let the kind of conscience you seem to want for yourself carry them too far. In the fifties I kept Sam Rodgers—you know him, he writes things—out of jail for perjuring himself about the identities of people he'd known in the Communist Party. Sam was never really much of a revolutionary. The Communists humored him because he was a source of money. They made their girls sleep with him the way they'd send them up to Harlem to hand out leaflets, for discipline. Back in the thirties he'd have what were called 'Red Gets'—fund-raising parties for comrades fighting in Spain. He used his father's mansion on the North Shore, filled it with Bolshevists— it was a delicious joke. Sam Rodgers came to me again last week. His son, a few years older than you, is a true believer like his father, but no more anxious to go to jail for his beliefs than old Sam was fifteen years ago. The youngster has received a draft notice. Sam wanted me to get the kid out of the draft without getting him into trouble with the law. Therefore I sent Sam and young Sam to a lawyer who specializes in Selective Service law—he can get any young man whose father has two thousand dollars for his fee out of the draft. Sam's son will not be inducted in November, as scheduled. Think what that means, Julian. This boy won't have to compromise his conscience, he'll never have to kill an innocent Vietcong or himself be killed by one. But think further. Does the fact that this youngster has evaded the draft mean that the government will take one less young man in November? No, it does not. It means that some Negro or some poor white will be drafted in his place, and *that* young fellow will kill or be killed in the dirty war my friend Sam Rodgers has saved his son from. I pointed this out to Sam. Would you like to hear what Sam said to me? Sam said, 'Then what I'm doing for my son is politically correct. The black or the poor white boy who goes in his place will come back from that God-damned war a revolutionary!' That, Julian, is the beauty of idealism—it always finds a way to make others pay for its pleasures."

Nevertheless, Julian believed it was possible to be an honorable man. He joined the Navy when he graduated from Yale. He wanted to be a pilot, but he had difficulty being admitted to flight school because he measured forty inches from seat to head, an inch above the limit for flyers who might have to eject from jet aircraft. Julian went to his father for help. "If you were willing to get Sam Rodgers's kid out of going to war, you ought to be willing to get me into it," Julian said. Elliott sympathized; he himself had parachuted into France with the OSS when he was far too old for the work, and had needed the intervention of friends. Influence was applied; Julian was remeasured. The medical officer who signed the form shrugged. "I advise you never to pull that ejection lever, son," he said. "You'll leave your skull or your ass in the cockpit." It was that advice that saved Julian's life when his Phantom was struck by ground fire: he crash-landed in the sea instead of bailing out.

Caroline and Julian met at his father's house when she was a freshman at Vassar; Julian was then in his third year at Yale. She was a granddaughter of one of Elliott's friends. Caroline had lovely changing eyes with deep blue irises and glistening whites. They gave her face—she had classical American features and an astonishing ivory skin and gleaming black hair—a dramatic look of intelligence and deep emotion. Julian told her so. "It's a trick of the light," Caroline said; she was a pretty girl who didn't like to discuss her looks.

Julian soon found that she was more than that. They were standing together near the fireplace, away from the older guests. This was a Christmas party, and Horace was at home. He came and stood with them, holding a glass of brandy in his long fingers. Julian introduced him as a banker. Caroline, with a great white smile, took the glass from Horace's hand and threw its contents into the fire; a tongue of blue flame shot into the room and singed the long skirt she wore. Julian pulled her violently out of danger. Her hair flew.

"That was an asinine thing to do," Julian said.

"I don't like the stink of money," she said. Caroline was a very small girl, but she did not seem to realize that Julian and Horace were taller than she as she glared up into their faces far above her own.

Horace looked her up and down. She was wearing hundreds of dollars' worth of clothes from Bergdorf's and a young girl's jewels— a topaz pendant, an emerald-chip ring. "Is that entirely rational?" he asked.

"Rationality is the enemy of consciousness."

"I see." Horace was just back from Israel. He had seen a busload of children blown up by a terrorist's bomb on a road near

Jerusalem. He described the little torn limbs on the pavement smeared with blood, and women shrieking as they sorted through the dead searching for their sons and daughters.

"Savagery is the highest morality if it brings change," Caroline said. "The past must be smashed, a clean new international class of youth, united to the oppressed, must arise."

She had marched against the Establishment, screaming obscenities. She told them of her experiences, how she had been radicalized. At her first demonstration, a black girl, beautiful and serene, caught Caroline's eye because she was wearing a dress. All the whites, male and female, were in overalls and chambray shirts, bandannas and work boots. Suddenly the black girl turned her back to the police, lifted her skirt, grasped her ankles, and urinated—a long thick yellow stream, arching in the bright autumn sun. The outraged officers rushed the students. "We all had Baggies filled with our turds. We *pelted* the motherfuckers!" said Caroline. She was not quite nineteen.

Horace took his glass from her hand and went to get himself another drink. Julian went away, too, and Caroline remained where she was. She was too pretty to be left alone for long, and as the party went on, Julian watched as men approached her, smiling, only to leave her moments later with the stunned eyes she had hoped to inflict on Horace and Julian. When she left with her parents, she walked across the room with hand outstretched to say good-night to the brothers. Horace put his brandy glass in her fingers and Julian laughed aloud. She drained the glass. The cognac brought tears to her eyes. With her wonderful smile she said, "Fuck you."

Soon afterwards, Caroline began to call Julian on the telephone. She always called after midnight, to talk for hours in a low, insistent voice. Julian would lie in the dark with the receiver on his pillow, dozing as her voice penetrated the distance between them. She required no response. Julian thought at first that Caroline was mad, but then he saw that she was merely dazed by the atmosphere of her times: the words, endlessly repeated, that didn't mean anything; the television images, ceaselessly rebroadcast, of the dead in Vietnam—broken dolls, seeping red televised blood. In her boarding school intonation she spoke over the telephone of highs and lows, ups and downs, orgasms and male sexual failures, napalm and torture. She had a single emotional pitch: the wholesale death of human beings in Vietnam and the extinction of the blue pike in Lake Erie brought her to the same level of frenzy.

After some weeks, they met in New York. Caroline borrowed an apartment, cluttered with dirty clothes and unwashed pots and dishes, and, taking Julian there, she made him her lover. She bled; she was the only virgin he ever had. Julian, so much larger than she, was afraid of hurting her and drew away. "Think of your own fucking pleasure and leave me to mine," Caroline cried, seizing his slippery member in both her small hands and driving it into herself. She wanted to be deflowered by her own will and act, she told him afterwards. She told him, too, that she loved him. Julian was as astonished by that as he had been by her virginity. He could no more answer than reply to her monologues over the long-distance telephone.

Usually Julian let Caroline talk while he himself remained silent. She had mastered a vocabulary, but she had no ideas, only passions. She didn't understand her love for Julian and tried to force him to explain it to her. "Make me understand!" she cried. "Passion is the whole answer," Julian replied, quoting her. Julian's political passivity, or what she took to be that, drove her into a frenzy. He cared nothing for her causes. Caroline beat him in her fury. Her fragile fists, thumbs clenched inside curled fingers, pattered on his chest and face. Sexually, she devoured him. They made love on the grass in public places and in her parents' bed, in her room at college while her roommate slept three feet away in the other cot and in the deep leather chairs in the boardroom of the Yale *Daily News* with Britton Hadden looking down on them from his unctuous portrait. Caroline loved risk. She wouldn't use contraceptives. She aborted three of Julian's children, never telling him of her pregnancies until after the fetuses were dead. She took drugs that were supposed to intensify orgasm, snapped ampules of smelling salts under Julian's nose as he ejaculated. Once, in an empty subway car after midnight, she had fellated him, hiding the action with the spread curtain of her long gleaming hair. Julian watched as the amazed faces of people on station platforms flashed by the windows of the speeding express.

Julian realized that she was trying to kill her sexual inhibitions. He himself had none.

On his final leave before reporting aboard *Enterprise*, then on station off the Vietnamese coast, Julian took Caroline out to dinner in New York. He wore his khakis, she was in her disguise—bib overalls, work boots—as a member of the working class. He had to smuggle her into a room in the Dorset Hotel. In bed, with her frail body joined to his enormous one in a narrow single bed, she had screamed, *"Don't die! don't die! don't die!"* She rolled off his body, and folding herself into a miserable package with her head between her knees and her arms locked around her thighs, had sobbed un-

37

controllably for a long time. Then she told Julian that she had joined a revolutionary cell while he was in flight training and, only two weeks before, had aborted a baby belonging to one of the other members. "These are committed people, they've gone beyond the counter culture into the ultimate reality of total violence," she told Julian. "They're the North American Tupamaros. You'll hear about me, but you'll never see me again. I've become another person, secret from you forever."

Caroline put on her clothes and left. It was the only time in all their lives together that she had been satisfied to make love to him just once. Years later, Julian learned that the child she had gouged from her womb belonged to Patrick Graham.

4

Patrick Graham shut the window in his Baghdad hotel and took another shower. Shortly afterwards, dressed in a fresh suit, he boarded the first available flight to Beirut. In that glistening city, in another hotel, he was able, with the aid of a pill, to sleep through the afternoon.

He dined that evening with Horace Hubbard. Horace had been in Beirut for a long time and he did himself well. His apartment, reached by a private elevator, occupied the entire top floor of a high glass tower, and he had made the rooftop into a garden, with huge trees growing in tubs and many kinds of roses. The table had been laid in the garden: white damask and blue china and silver as thin as an old voice; a fitful wind blew in from the sea, and the perfume of the blooming flowers came to their nostrils from time to time like a puff of scent left by a woman passing in the darkness. A small fountain splashed beyond the candlelight; Patrick had seen it in daylight on a previous visit and knew that it came from a Roman bath that Horace's great-uncle had excavated in Cappadocia.

Horace spread his napkin on his lap. Patrick began to ask him questions about Ibn Awad.

"You knew the old fellow pretty well, everyone says."

"He was a valued customer of the bank," Horace said. "Years ago I saw quite a lot of him before the oil came in in Hagreb. In his last years, he was pretty solitary."

Horace was vice-president of the Beirut branch of a private New York bank called D. & D. Laux & Co. He was also, as men like Patrick knew, the head of American intelligence for the entire Near East; this was the most important post in the Foreign Intelligence Service after that of Director of Foreign Intelligence.

"Ibn Awad *did* send Prince Talil to live with you for years while the boy was educated," said Patrick.

"Hardly to live with me. I helped Talil to set himself up in a house in Beirut and the family consulted me about tutors. We brought people from Harvard and Oxford—professors on sabbatical. They all found Talil an exceptional young man."

"I saw them cut his head off."

Horace's butler, a displaced Taiwanese who spoke neither Arabic nor English, came in with a silver tray: Horace's version of the deaf-mute of more barbaric times, thought Patrick. Patrick took a piece of veal and some peas. Horace, a less careful eater, helped himself to larger portions. He made no reply to Patrick's last statement apart from a quick movement in his eyes.

"What *was* your relationship with the Awad family?" Patrick insisted.

Horace finished chewing and took a sip of wine. It was Horace's idea of courtesy, Patrick knew, never to betray surprise. He showed interest in everything that was said to him, and he had trained himself to give the impression that the man he was dealing with was obviously more intelligent than he himself. When Horace said an interesting thing, he did so with a faint smile of apology.

"One doesn't have a relationship with a royal family," Horace said now with one of those smiles. "One is either admitted into the presence or not; one is either useful or not. I was one of their bankers." Horace put down his glass and looked about him at the foliage ruffled by the breeze. "I suppose they regarded me as a sort of day servant."

Patrick laughed. "Was the Awad family as grand as all that, Horace? Up to the time old Ibn Awad was persuaded to let Universal Energy drill for the last deposits of oil in the Near East, he was a tribal chieftain out of the past, counting his wealth in horses and eating sheeps' eyes."

"That's true. But his blood went back to Mohammed. Horses or oil didn't come into it. Ibn Awad knew just who he was. But of course you knew him, too—better than I did, probably. I remember those amazing television interviews you did with him. It was you who made him into a world figure."

"Nonsense. He did that himself, simply by being himself. I just brought cameras and microphones to him."

"He had force of character, all right. But you talk so well, Patrick." Horace raised his bushy eyebrows. "You made him play beyond his game. I never heard him so eloquent."

Patrick hadn't touched his food; he seldom ate. The table, for him, was a workbench. In his own house he could let course after course go cold on his plate while he asked questions of his guests. He heard their most telling answers, sometimes, in their jokes and their silences. He heard something valuable, now, in Horace's flattery.

To Horace he said, "And now Ibn Awad is dead and Hagreb is a hellhole. I wonder how he'd feel. His life, his teaching, seems to have come to nothing—worse than nothing."

"I imagine he'd be confident that Islam will triumph in the end. He took a long view of life."

"It was you, wasn't it, who talked him into letting Universal Energy in?"

Horace shook his head. "Patrick, you have an exaggerated view of me. I'm just the manager of a small bank. The fact is, nobody could talk Ibn Awad into anything. He made up his own mind, in his own way and in his own time. He waited twenty-five years before letting the first drilling rig into Hagreb."

"Why did he do it?"

"He told you, on that broadcast of yours. He decided he could use the money from the oil to propagate the faith. That's pretty much what he did—the mosques, the radio transmitter, the pilgrimages."

"I don't mean that. I mean *why*—all of a sudden, after years of refusing, he decided to let Universal Energy—O. N. Laster, that whole oily crowd, *Mallory's* men!—come in."

The Chinese returned and poured more claret; Horace watched the ruby liquid trickle into his glass and answered a question the man asked in what Patrick supposed was Cantonese.

Horace turned to Patrick and said, "I don't think Ibn Awad was quite so sensitive to the shades of moral difference among oil cartels as, for instance, you are, Patrick. You ask why he did what he did. I understand the decision came to him in a dream."

"In a dream? How do you know that?"

"He told me so. Ibn Awad often had dreams and visions. That's why he stayed so much in the desert—he saw things when he was alone out there."

"Saw things?"

Horace, sipping Pomerol, looked around at his garden again. "I may be saying too much. The man is dead."

"He *saw* things?"

"And heard them. It's a common experience of mystics. Ibn Awad would go out into the Hagrebi desert alone and fast and pray, and he'd encounter God and His angels."

Nothing in Horace's manner suggested that he saw anything unbelievable in what Ibn Awad believed he saw and heard in the desert. He took another mouthful of food.

"Do you think Ibn Awad believed he was the Mahdi?"

Horace was thoughtful. "Maybe. He never said so."

"A lot of other people said so."

"I know. He did fit the description—a purified man out of the desert, a great teacher burning with faith. Types like that don't come along very often."

"And are dangerous when they do."

"Well, the world's never very glad to see messiahs, is it? They all seem to die untimely deaths."

Patrick pushed his untouched plate away. "Do you believe," he asked, "that Ibn Awad actually had himself killed by Prince Talil?"

"That was the explanation at the time."

"But do you believe it?"

"Why shouldn't I?"

"You knew him better than anyone."

"I don't deserve that compliment. But I did know him. It seemed, to me anyway, perfectly in character for him to do what he did."

"Why?"

"Why did he do anything he did? God spoke to him."

"You're suggesting he was mad."

Horace sighed. He let a moment go by, turning his wineglass by its stem. "I don't know what constitutes madness. Ibn Awad was fixed on a single idea, the rebirth of Islam. He killed himself for the idea, I guess, to show the world how much he believed in it."

"Would he have killed others?"

Horace gave Patrick a mild look. "He killed Talil for it, surely. And he loved the boy above everything in this world."

"Everyone seems to have loved Talil. The crowd was weeping, grown men were sobbing in that square in Hagreb City, when he was executed. Talil himself was absolutely serene. Did you ever really look at Talil? His face in profile was like Alexander's on a coin."

Patrick thought for an instant that he had lost Horace's attention. The other man's eyes wandered away.

"You ought to be glad you didn't have to see Talil's execution," Patrick said in his hardest voice. "He was a stranger to me, and even so it was bad enough." Horace's gaze turned back to Patrick. He still wore his expression of polite interest. "Something startling

41

has been suggested to me in the past few days," Patrick said. "I don't know what to think about it."

Horace waited for him to go on. His brother Julian had this mannerism too; he never encouraged others to speak, and somehow this made them talk all the more. Patrick wasn't saying more than he intended to say, but he did not like this trick of the Hubbards'. They watched to see how far into their privacy you'd dare to come. They were the old rich. Their money, their possessions, their manners, were warning signs. Would you know enough to recognize them?

Patrick leaned across the table. His movement made the goblets touch and ring. "Is it conceivable to you, Horace," he asked, "that Ibn Awad could have been involved somehow with terrorists?"

"Terrorists? What terrorists?"

"I don't know. Imagine the worst case—that he had some connection with—oh, the Eye of Gaza."

In the silence before Patrick spoke, Horace had picked up the wine bottle in its wicker basket. Still holding it, waiting to pour, he looked steadily at Patrick.

Patrick said, "I want to be frank with you, Horace. I'm beginning to fear that Ibn Awad was murdered—that he had nothing to do with his own death, that the whole thing was staged. That someone else was behind it. I think someone killed a holy man, and killed Talil, too."

"The Eye of Gaza?"

"No. Worse than that."

Patrick knew all the signs of a liar—the unblinking eye, the smiling lips, the confidence surging into the voice, the hand that was a bit too steady. Horace showed none of these; he just looked interested, but at a loss—as if Patrick, as a guest in Horace's club, had started a political argument with one of the members. He put down the basket with the bottle in it.

"Well," he said, "anything is possible. But this is quite a leap of intuition, even for you, Patrick. Who on earth have you been talking to?"

"Sources."

"I hope for everyone's sake they're reliable sources." Horace relaxed in his chair and gave a dry laugh. "You may turn out to be the Mahdi instead of poor old Ibn Awad. If you can convince people around here that he was slaughtered by the infidels you'll certainly be the cause of a holy war."

The Chinese returned and cleared the plates. Horace offered no dessert, but pushed back his chair and put his napkin on the table. He led Patrick down the stairs into a sitting room. It was the highest room in the city—no window in Beirut had line of sight on Horace's apartment. One whole wall was glass, and Patrick, knowing that it must be bulletproof, stepped fearlessly up to it. He could see the line of surf along the beach, and cars, dozens of them, in the streets. This was a sight seen now only in Arab countries. The Near East, because of its oil reserves, bulged with cars and gold, as America once had done.

Horace offered Patrick a Havana cigar. The humidor he held in his hands was a beautiful old thing, inlaid with rare woods and mother-of-pearl. Patrick commented on it. "It belonged to my grandfather," Horace said. There was a Pissarro on the wall and a hunting carpet that must have been two centuries old, and a Constable, with its unmistakable fleecy English clouds. Horace hadn't had to buy anything in the room. Patrick, who'd had to pay for everything he owned, knew that. Horace was smiling easily at Patrick, holding the open humidor. Patrick selected a cigar and Horace cut it for him. Patrick put the blunt end into the flame of a wooden match to start it burning before he placed the tip between his lips. He sucked the cigar to get it going.

"Horace, there was something else I wanted to ask you."

Horace, lighting his own cigar, welcomed the question by opening his eyes a bit wider.

"Do you happen to know," Patrick asked, "whether Ibn Awad was illiterate?"

Horace exhaled a mouthful of smoke and watched it drift away. "Illiterate?" he said. "Now that, Patrick, is not a question I would ever have felt comfortable putting to a man in Ibn Awad's position."

Next morning, as his SST crossed the ocean, Patrick found himself thinking of Caroline. He had trained himself over the years not to do this, but he had slept badly after he left Horace and he had taken two tranquilizers in the hope of having a nap while the plane took him back to Washington. It was a piece of music coming over the earphones that triggered Patrick's thoughts —the *Trout* Quintet. One night, when they were having a revolutionary meeting with the members of the cell they had both belonged to and when they feared, as they always did, that the FBI or the CIA had planted microphones in their hideaway, Caroline had astonished him by sitting down at a battered piano that some earlier tenant had left behind and playing, with a perfect touch, an hour of Schubert; the music was supposed to muffle their words so that the listening devices couldn't pick them up. Patrick hadn't known until that moment that Caroline could

43

play. She surrendered secrets to him in the way a frigid woman permits caresses—at bad moments, when it suited her purposes. Thus she told him of the one moment in her life, beyond any others, that had formed her politically. When she was fourteen her parents had taken her, on her birthday, to Lutèce. Something about the restaurant—the glittering decor, the fawning service (her father was an extravagant expense-account spender), the rich unrecognizable food glistening with sauces, like a king's vomit —put Caroline in a state of rage. She attacked her parents for living as they did while the poor suffered in the streets of New York and all over the world. Her mother said: "We give ten percent of our income to charity. All our lives, even before it was fashionable, we've fought for Negro rights, we've hated discrimination and injustice. We *believe* in causes." Caroline laughed in her face. She went on taunting her parents, and they went on drinking cocktails—two kinds of French wine, champagne with dessert, cognac with their coffee. Caroline glared at them, refusing to eat the treats they ordered for her. With each new dish she hissed, "Hypocrites!" Her mother wept, but Caroline's father made her stop. At last they went outside. Caroline's father went to get their car. In a doorway on Fiftieth Street, her mother noticed a female derelict, chattering to herself and hugging her skeletal body in the cold. Caroline's mother, without so much as a glance at her daughter, removed her sable jacket and gave it to the old woman. The derelict, bony elbows and hips under a shapeless black dress, awakened from her torpor and seized the jacket, examining it like a rat that has come on a bit of good food, and then gathered up her shopping bags and the beautiful fur and scuttled away into the dark. When Caroline's father came back with the car, the women told him what had happened. At first he said nothing, just drove out of the city in silence. But when they were halfway to Westchester he pulled the car off the Saw Mill River Parkway into a darkened gas station, carefully set the brake, and then, his face contorted in the green glow of the speedometer lamp, turned towards Caroline's mother, who had fallen asleep beside him, and drove his fist with all his strength into her stomach. The next day he reported the jacket stolen and collected the insurance.

Then Caroline told Patrick about Julian. This happened on the night Julian left for Vietnam. Patrick had known for years about the love affair, but the idea that she would come to him from this lover, this man who was going to Asia to do murder, caused something to break in Patrick. They were lying on a stained mattress on the floor, with the streetlight coming through the sooty panes of the uncurtained window; all the other members of the cell lay about them on the floor in the same room, sleeping or talking or smoking dope. Patrick raised his hand, clenched his fist: he had never struck a human being, but he wanted to kill Caroline. Instead, he raped her. She lay naked, unsmiling. He fell on her, grappling with her unresisting body. No woman had ever excited him as she did. Making love to her, he would shudder and cry out; he felt that his heart was emptying out of his body and into her. When he came to himself, her eyes were open. They always were. He rolled away. Caroline began to masturbate. He heard her in the dark. He could not open his eyes to watch. He heard her quickening breath.

He heard her whisper: "Julian."

On the plane, in the darkness behind his eyelids, Patrick listened to Schubert; he smelled the room where he had met Hassan. He smelled Caroline again.

5

Caroline never wrote to Julian while he was at war, and for years after he returned he saw nothing of her. They had no friends in common, so he met no one who had been in touch with her. Finally, the last American left Vietnam, and though the war there continued, Vietnamese killing Vietnamese with foreign weapons, the conflict ceased to interest Americans. Julian did not understand this; he remembered the vivid fragments of all that had happened to him: the fires, imperial red and black, in the midst of the green carpet below his plane, the landscape blurred by speed before him but preternaturally clear behind; he remembered especially the sleepy joy of the moment when he thought he was dying in the sea. What had made his generation of Americans shriek through a tantrum, split the night with the untreatable anger of the insane —and then fall silent and never mention the war again? Julian did not know; no one would talk to him about it. His father said, "The last white man has died. It's as simple as that."

On the night that Elliott made that remark, Bedford Forrest Lockwood was dining with a large group of men in the house on Ninety-third Street. Lockwood was then a United States senator. Julian, still limping from his wounds, had just come back to the city after spending a month alone at the Harbor. Elliott placed his son and the senator side by side. Lockwood questioned Julian throughout supper, and afterwards in the sitting room, about his experiences in Vietnam.

Lockwood phoned at six the next morning to offer Julian a job as a legislative aide. Julian had nothing else in mind and he wanted a job at which he could work hard.

"I'll come, Senator," he said, "if our conversation about the war is over."

Lockwood laughed. "Don't worry. Your father was right as usual. No one is interested anymore."

Soon Julian's brain and his capacity for work made him Lockwood's closest aide. He learned and learned; finally he knew as many secrets as any American had ever known.

He never learned how many human beings died in Vietnam. No one but Julian thought the exact number was important. Of the millions who perished, as Elliott had pointed out, only a few thousand were white; and few of them had been friends of Sam Rodgers and his son.

Julian had been in Washington for a long time when, dining one night with another girl in the Cantina d'Italia, he heard Caroline's voice in the booth at his back. He finished his food. On the way out he passed by Caroline's table. She caught his hand in hers. She said, "Kiss me." Julian touched her cheek with his lips and she lifted his hand and held it against her face, shaking back her wonderful long hair. She was wearing scent and a linen suit, with pearls at her throat. A red fox fur jacket lay beside her on the banquette. Despite her years of political rage, her face was still the untouched face of a young girl. When last Julian had seen her, she had talked in Movement argot; now she had her own clear accent back. She introduced the man with her. He wore a cashmere blazer and a shirt with an open collar, and a gold chain around his neck. His hair had been styled and it lay on his skull like a peruke. It was Patrick Graham.

"You don't remember," Patrick said, "but we were at New Haven in the same years."

"Of course I remember. You quit the Yalie Daily over Che Guevara. I hope you're not still unhappy over that."

Patrick had written a piece for the News about the death of Guevara in Bolivia, reporting that peasants in Andean villages were displaying newspaper photographs of the slain revolutionary in their huts in place of the customary cheap pictures of Jesus. Julian, as managing editor of the paper, didn't believe this story and refused to print it. Patrick, after listening in furious silence to Julian's decision, had resigned. Julian remembered now that the waxen peaceful face of Che's bearded corpse did resemble traditional renderings of Christ's exalted features after the Crucifixion.

46

"Poor Che," said Patrick Graham. "No—I'm not mad at you. I've lost too many points of principle since."

Caroline said, "Patrick's been anchor man at a station in New York, but he's with the network now. He's going to cover the Senate, so you'll see each other, I guess." Caroline had been working in New York at the same television station as Graham.

"I think we were in Vietnam for a while at about the same time," Patrick said to Julian. "I went over for a wire service. The thing I finally realized was this: we, the press, were making the war sound *sane*. Every act committed in Vietnam was a crazy act, and every day thousands of reporters would sit down at typewriters and reduce that insanity to sentences, paragraphs, whole stories—making it sane so that the folks back home would be able to believe that the unbelievable was happening to them and their country. But they never believed it."

Patrick spilled a glass of wine and paid no attention to what he had done; he was truly agitated. Julian remembered, suddenly, the other man's capacity for moral outrage, his clenched stubborn face when he had quit the *News* over Guevara. Graham had loved Che; he had been inflamed by Julian's refusal to believe that the Bolivians loved him too.

"Did the war seem crazy to you, too, Julian, up in your Phantom with the bombs and guns hanging on it?" Patrick asked.

"Yes," Julian said.

Caroline took Julian's girl away; some of Patrick's spilled wine had run onto her dress. While they were gone, Patrick looked hard into Julian's eyes.

"I used to see you and Caroline at Yale," he said. "I know what was between you. But she and I are lovers now. We have been for a long time. It was me she came to after you saw her that last time in New York. We are always going to be lovers, Caroline and I."

"How nice that both of you know that," said Julian. He meant it.

The next day early, Julian picked up the telephone in his office and heard Caroline's voice. "I'd like to see you," she said. "Patrick is away on his first network assignment. We could have dinner."

At the Old Angler's Inn that evening, Caroline told him what had happened to her. The revolutionary cell hadn't worked out. "We planned kidnappings," Caroline said. "We tried to make a bomb from a diagram we saw in some heavy breather of a magazine—the one black who was in the cell called it the New York

Jewview of Books. He made all of us toe the anti-Semitic line, he was a very sensitive cat. But in the end we never *did* anything except smoke dope and yell. What the men wanted was sex. You were supposed to share everything, bodies too, with the family. Especially the black guy. He had that line, it was already too old to get results, that every white chick owed him a fuck in payment for all the times his female ancestors had been banged by rednecks. It turns out he was penetrating us in more ways than one—he was our very own FBI informer." Caroline took both Julian's hands—he had forgotten how tiny her own hands were—and laughed, as in the old days. "I was only with them a month. It was so boring. It was so hopeless. I got a job in television, my father was deliriously happy to help. It was my original idea to work my way up through the network hierarchy, and then thirty years hence when the revolution came, seize the transmitters and announce my true identity—Red Caro, secret leader of the underground. But the work they gave me was so God-damned interesting, and I got so hooked on office politics—you know, beating out some other woman for a promotion, making it to the top without ever taking even one foot off the floor—that I went to bed one night, and when I woke up I had turned from a cockroach back into the perfect honey you see before you—good manners, proper clothes, poise. Put a dress on me, Julian, and you can take me anywhere."

Patrick fled the cell, too—Caroline was the reason for his being there—and in time he found her. She borrowed one of her father's suits and a shirt and tie, and got Patrick an audition at the station. "As soon as they saw him on camera they grabbed him. He's been a tremendous success. You see how handsome he is, he leaps right off the screen like Clara Bow, and he has that voice. And, God, does he want to be a star!"

After dinner, in the parking lot, Caroline embraced Julian. On the way home she kept stopping her Volkswagen beside the Potomac to kiss him.

An hour later, they were in Julian's bed, Patrick betrayed and forgotten. Their sex life resumed at the same screaming pitch. Caroline, straddling Julian's depleted body, threw back her tousled hair and lifted her clenched fists above her head in triumph. "It's like walking by an open window and hearing a song you've been trying to remember for years and years," she said.

The story of her life with Patrick spilled out of her as she lay in Julian's arms: "He loves me. He asks only to love me. He begs to be permitted to love me, it's like being trapped in some Russian novel. He tried to kill the black guy in the cell for sleeping with me and the black guy beat him to a pulp—he'd been in prison, I never before saw anyone who knew, really *knew,* how to hurt people physically. It's maddening to be loved the way Patrick loves me. There's nothing *wrong* with him, understand, he has all the moves. But he's never given me an orgasm. Not once. The tension! You can't imagine what it's like."

When Patrick returned from his first network assignment he found that Caroline had moved out on him. He couldn't find her; he searched for her among all her friends and none had seen her. She might as well have gone underground again. Finally he called Julian's apartment and heard her voice on the phone. He hung up without speaking, and that evening waited for Julian outside the Senate Office Building. When Julian emerged, Patrick seized his arm and propelled him across the avenue and onto the deserted west lawn of the Capitol. Graham, who had been so neat and groomed when Julian last saw him in the Cantina d'Italia, was disheveled. His hair was in disorder, he wore a sweaty shirt with the points of the collar turning up, his jacket and pants were wrinkled. Chest heaving, fists clenched, he confronted Julian. Patrick was, of course, the much smaller man, but Julian thought at first that he meant to attack him. Patrick was violent, uncontrolled, raging—the old wild self Julian remembered from Yale. He lived by a system of resentments. He believed that men like Julian, whose family had buildings named after them on campus, were joined to others just like them in a secret circle, a sort of universal Skull and Bones, to control Graham's life, to break the heart of mankind.

Julian believed in the honesty of Patrick's emotions. He didn't know how to deal with him. He knew that he could overpower him physically with little effort; he didn't want to hurt him. Caroline had hurt him enough. "You take what you bloody want, don't you?" Patrick screamed. Julian realized that Patrick saw in his recovery of Caroline some form of droit de seigneur. Graham had loved Caroline for five years and he knew, at last, that he had brought her to bed for nothing. He had thought that her politics, so much like his own, were a surer basis for love than the attraction of manners and class and position that Julian had to offer. Julian looked down, unspeaking, into Patrick's distorted face; he wanted to put an arm around the other man's shoulders to comfort him: he understood so little.

Winter was beginning in Washington, it was dark in the early evening and chilly. Patrick, raw-eyed and breathless, wore no coat. Behind him, on the roof of the Capitol, the floodlit flag whipped in a strong wind. Though he was shivering violently, he did not seem to feel the cold; he felt nothing but his loss. "I want to say one thing to you, Hubbard," he said. "I hate you! I know that solves nothing, but I want you to live with the fact. You don't care—I know how people like you think. Who the hell am I to you? But remember: *I hate you*. I always have. I hated you when you were napalming kids in Vietnam, I hated you when you got yourself next to Frosty Lockwood, who's the best guy in the Senate and oughtn't to be contaminated by your God-damned kind. I hated you at Yale when the professors overpraised your rotten short stories because of the glorious old Eli name at the top of your paper. I hated it when you made managing editor of the *News*—and made it on talent, you bastard. But I'm not going to shit you with class conflict and politics. I really hated you because for years I had to watch while you fucked the girl I love. Now you're doing it again. You couldn't wait a week after you saw her with me again. You *stepped* on me! You cocksucker, I wish you'd die!"

Patrick raved on, a torrent of profanity and abuse. Traffic flowed up and down Capitol Hill as the working day ended, a rattle of breath through the diseased lung of the city. Patrick's broadcaster's voice, trained and strong, penetrated all background noise. Julian let him talk. Patrick was weeping. At last Julian put a hand on his shoulder. Patrick went on; Julian increased the pressure of his hand, he looked into Patrick's face. It shone with tears. He wanted to say: I admire you, Patrick, all that feeling, that wonderful lack of shame. What's wrong with Caroline that she can't love you? But instead he just stood there and took it, and after a while Patrick stopped shouting. He drew in great broken breaths. Then he did something Julian hadn't seen since he used to follow Lipton, the gardener, around the lawns of the Harbor, in the years before his mother left for France and they used to spend summers all together in West Stockbridge. Patrick turned away, bent at the waist, and blew his nose on the grass, closing first one nostril and then the other with his forefinger and expelling long, viscous ropes of mucus.

Julian handed Patrick his own clean handkerchief. Patrick wiped his cheeks on it and cleaned his nose. Then he flung it to the ground. The wind took it and it went skittering down the steep lawn, a little playful patch of white vanishing into the darkness.

Patrick said, "It's over now. But Julian, I meant every word I said."

"I'm sorry," Julian said. "Would you like a drink?"

Patrick turned away. It was an unmistakable gesture of disgust. But then he turned around again and followed Julian out to the curb, where they found a cab, already loaded with other passengers. The two men sat crowded together. Patrick drew himself away. Julian's body had been with Caroline's, had been inside it, so recently, that Patrick imagined he could smell her hair and skin in the overheated air of the cab.

They had a single drink at the Federal City Club, and in its tranquil atmosphere, standing at the bar with men he wanted to know, Patrick was transformed into his new, self-controlled personality again. As they left, Julian paused at the bulletin board to read the list of candidates for membership.

"You ought to belong here, Patrick," he said. "It's not a bad place. I'd be glad to put your name up."

For an instant, Patrick's face twisted and he looked like an enemy again; but then he nodded. "That's nice of you, Julian," he said. "It's *like* you."

6

Caroline and Julian were married in the spring in the chantry at Saint Thomas's. It was a white wedding. Caroline's mother provided the details for a long notice in the *Times*; the writer listed schools and colleges, clubs and occupations, grandparents and even more remote ancestors, including a forebear of Caroline's father who had been among the signers of the Declaration of Independence. It was noted that the bride was called "Caro" by her friends, and that both the groom and his half-brother, who acted as best man, had been awarded the Navy Cross, in different wars.

Patrick did not attend the wedding. Later that year he was transferred to London. Julian, by that time, had arranged for his membership in the Federal City Club. The two men never spoke of Caroline again, though they often saw each other, and, when Patrick returned from England a few years later with Charlotte as his bride, the two couples frequently met socially.

The marriage was happy for a long while. Caroline, who had destroyed so many fetuses, was a long time conceiving their son Elliott, but carried him to term without difficulty. Two years later she gave birth to Jenny. After that, she had herself sterilized. She hated contraceptives. "I know what it is now to see a living child," she told Julian; "I couldn't do what I did before, I'd keep seeing human faces like Elliott's and Jenny's." Caroline remained a voracious lover. That she lost none of her desire for Julian did not surprise her. It amazed Julian, he had never had the gift of being excited by sexual experiences once they were over. He did not resist the feeling of responsibility for Caroline that her lust reawakened in him. He was passionately interested in her. Caroline seemed to Julian, as she had always done, to be alive in a dimension that was inaccessible to him. He did not love her, but he observed her love for him, saw how much pain it gave her and how much pleasure, and he envied her—more, he entered her person, lived his emotional life through her. The intensity of her feelings set up echoes in his own emotional field. Sometimes, when making love, a faint rash, like a dusting of freckles, would appear on Caroline's chest. Her interior life, breaking through the surface of her skin, made it possible for Julian to see the reality of love. That was the key to himself, Julian realized: he lived in others. He was always trying to complete himself by hiding himself in others. He required a host.

Caroline discovered the joys of mainstream politics with the thrill an astronomer might feel on finding that a row of planets, identical to those in the known solar system, existed on the opposite side of the sun. Lockwood was the first conventional politician she had ever known. He astonished her with his intelligence, his decency, his honesty. Lockwood was a Kentuckian, the son of a man who had spent his life working in an ammonia plant in a wasted town on the banks of the Ohio River. Lockwood escaped his father's fate because he'd been born with the ability to run one hundred yards in less than ten seconds, and this earned him a football scholarship at the University of Kentucky. He became an All-America back, and that feat made his name famous in his home state. He was gaunt and tall, with a sad, creased face and a bulbous nose saved from clownishness by many fractures on the football field. He had a charming smile and a gentle manner, and he had been elected to Congress, and then to the Senate, and finally to the presidency, defeating an incumbent President by the narrowest of margins, simply by offering himself, as he was, to the voters. And, in the most recent ten years of his career, by listening to Julian's advice.

Lockwood and Julian, over this long period of time when they were almost never out of each other's company, entered into each other's mind. They became the two working parts of a single organism. Caroline, meanwhile, was having her babies, living (as she afterwards told Julian) at second hand through the slow rise of her children to the powers of speech and thought, and meanwhile watching the climb of Lockwood to the head of affairs. It was only very late that she realized that Julian had been absorbed by the President.

She could not live with the symbiosis after she saw that Lockwood was the stronger of the two parts—the ideal host for whom Julian had been searching all his life. She had imagined that it was Julian who was the real person in the relationship, that Lockwood was the star and Julian the writer-director of the great film that was their life. Caroline believed, of course, that she had created Julian before Julian created Lockwood. She had given him his ideas. The defection of Julian's spirit to Lockwood was a worse crime against their marriage than adultery.

She told Julian to choose: Lockwood or his marriage. "But, my God, Caro, I can't," he replied. "I won't. Lockwood is the best human being who's ever been elected President of the United States. For a quarter of my life I've done nothing but work to help him get where he is. So have you. You've always wanted the world to change in a certain way, to become more decent. This man will make the necessary changes." They had their conversations now in the sitting room, not in bed, and Caroline, drinking a whole martini at a swallow, had replied, "Nothing changes. Ever."

She never raised the subject again, and Julian went on with his work.

Soon after Caroline confronted Julian, there was a White House evening to thank the theatrical people who had helped in Lockwood's campaign. The administration was still only a few months old, and the good feeling about it had not yet begun to dissipate. A popular singer who had raised a great deal of money for Lockwood begged an invitation for a man called Leo Dwyer. He was a rich novelist who was said to get his lurid plots and characters from gossip magazines and from what he overheard at parties in Beverly Hills. "You've got to do it for me, Julian," the singer said, "otherwise that God-damned midget will put me in his next book."

Leo Dwyer turned out to be a jovial man with an enormous curly head on a flyweight's body. He wore a maroon tuxedo made of a luxurious material that Caroline later reported to be vicuña. Julian seated Leo at his own table, and introduced him to the President. Julian urged his wife to dance with the little man, and she stayed with him on the dance floor all evening. As a youth, Leo had been an instructor in a dance studio. When he moved to music, as when he talked or used a typewriter, there was nothing ridiculous about him.

Within a week, he and Caroline were having an affair. Within a month, Caroline asked for a divorce.

"Leo wanted to be here with me to play this scene; he thinks he's doing you a great injury by stealing me," Caroline said. "I thought he'd better not be, in case you *did* think so, and decided to hit him. He's more my size than yours, you know." Caroline wore a faint smile as she spoke, and Julian returned it. She hadn't had his full attention when she started speaking, and she was almost all the way through her speech before Julian had realized what she was saying. He was used to hiding his reactions, to give himself time to avoid mistakes in doing Lockwood's business. "I've lived with *you* all these years without hitting you, Caro," he said; "Leo Dwyer is in no danger." Caroline took Julian's glass out of his hand and made him another martini; he thanked her for it, in his usual quiet voice, when she brought it back to him.

Caroline gave him the full details of her romance with Leo. "I felt a thrill for him on the dance floor, he has a body like a jockey, Julian—imagine what a change that was for me," she said. "Leo's the first lover I've had since we've been married—does that astonish you?"

It did not. Julian himself had never accepted any of the women who had offered themselves to him on many, very many, of the hundreds of nights he and Lockwood had traveled the country together. He knew it was possible to stop feeling desire for one person, even a person one loved, and transfer the desire to another, renewed and intensified. His mother had not even gone to another man, but to solitude.

Julian didn't ask Caroline for an explanation, but she wanted to invest the moment with ceremony. "I told you before, Julian, that you'd disappeared into Lockwood and what that meant to me; you chose what you chose, and that's all right," she said. "Now I've chosen too. I don't want anything from you, not even the children; I couldn't protect them. I want to be by myself, with Leo, as much as possible for the rest of my life. With my parents, at school, in the Movement, in politics down here, even at home since I had Elliott and Jenny, I've been in a crowd. . . ."

She went on giving details, all unnecessary. Julian knew what she felt. She had never kept anything from him from the moment they met. He felt very tired and a little drunk; emotion and gin mixed badly in him. Watching Caroline—her gestures, the lifted shoulder, the hair pushed back from the eye with her tiny hand on which his mother's diamond glittered—Julian felt the long years of her wifehood, of their oneness, emptying out of him. It was a physical sensation, as in that hour after he crashed in the Gulf of Tonkin more than twenty years before. Caroline's happiness, her glow of satisfaction as she freed herself from him, seemed right to Julian.

But he felt the loss. As Caroline was inflated by joy, something left his own person, pumping out of a wound he couldn't see. He could bear the pain, it was never so bad as one feared, but he knew he'd never get back what he was losing, that he'd never again be quite as he had been before.

Before Caroline left, she and Julian had one last dinner with the Lockwoods, who slipped through the media cordon to come to the house in Georgetown. Lockwood brought wine from the White House stock, and Caroline and Polly Lockwood cooked the dinner, Caroline having come down from her parents' apartment in New York for the occasion. The meal passed in silence, and by evening's end the women were showing signs of tears.

They had been friends, and they had made Lockwood and Julian friends. Polly had lost babies in her young womanhood, and she loved Caroline's children. She spent long afternoons with them and long mornings with Caroline, and the cupboards were filled with toys that Lockwood himself had brought on Christmas and at birthdays. Caroline had shown him her sweet side always; if Jenny and Elliott were all Polly had for grandchildren, Caroline was all Lockwood had ever wanted as a daughter: pretty and mild and bright; she played the piano for him, the plaintive mountain songs he loved to sing. They all knew the friendship had broken when the marriage broke.

Leaving, Lockwood kissed Caroline on the lips. "Godfrey," he said, "I'm crying too. Julian is the only one here who knows how to keep a dry eye. It must be those fancy schools he went to." Two Secret Service men stood in the small hall with them, faces blank, eyes unfocused: they had to be watchful only in public moments. It was too late to return to New York that night, so Caroline slept in the guest room. The next morning, before she flew to Santo Domingo for her divorce, Julian carried her bag downstairs and found her in the hall, making some last adjustments in her appearance. Seeing him behind her in the mirror, she smiled and, still the unselfconscious wife, lifted her skirt and fixed a twisted stocking. Julian smiled too, at her solemnity that he had always loved so much, at her impatience with her own prettiness.

He wanted to kiss her, but he knew she wouldn't permit it: Caroline was an honorable woman, committed now to Leo Dwyer, whom she was going to meet in Las Vegas two days hence for a wedding among his friends. Caroline and Julian never even shook hands again, and that morning, after half a lifetime of incessant questions and speeches, she left him without uttering a word.

For a long time, Julian was content to be alone. His Sundays with the children gave him pleasure, and now that he did not have to engage in long conversations with Caroline in the evening, he took up his father's practice of reading to the children at bedtime, and he read them the same books. Elliott liked *Kim* and *The Jungle Books* well enough, and Jenny, having outgrown poems about Christopher Robin, listened impatiently to these stories, leaning against her father's shins in her bathrobe while Elliott lay in bed, his eyes fixed on his father's face. Their favorite novel was *Little Big Man*, and Julian read it twice, starting over as soon as he had finished. He was never late coming home when he was in Washington; he and the children dined together every night. Most nights, he returned to the White House after they were asleep. When he was away, he telephoned. The Secret Service was always with Elliott and Jenny, watching.

By the time Emily came into the house as Julian's new wife, the children knew her well; she had been their father's only female companion for more than a year. Emily was a journalist, and a gifted one. She wrote profiles for the Style section of *The Washington Post*, long pieces filled with information about the eccentricities of famous Washingtonians. She specialized in what she called invisible men—quiet presidential assistants like Julian.

Emily had been introduced; she, too, was the granddaughter of one of Elliott Hubbard's friends. Julian agreed to an interview, thinking that the ordeal would take no more than an hour. But Emily was a leech—she dogged Julian's movements, waited in his office, asked him to dinner, startled him with intensely personal questions, all the while scribbling in a pad. Emily had been described as an admirer of Lockwood's, but during her investigation of Julian she kept her political feelings hidden. She asked him about his sex life: "You're never seen with girls since your divorce. Why?" Julian, tired of her questions and tired of her despite her lovely physical being, replied, "Miss Barker, to be frank, most of the women available in Washington are your age; and girls your age are about as memorable as so many *New Yorker* covers."

Emily printed the quote and it created a little storm. "My idea was to make every other female under thirty too angry at you to give you the time of day," explained Emily. Like Caroline before her, she chose Julian, seduced him, herded him by her dependency into marriage. After they began sleeping together, she followed him to Maine, where he had accompanied Lockwood on a political trip.

At a party, Julian paid attention to a woman his own age, small and dark and taut, as Caroline had been. Someone told Emily of the resemblance between this woman and Julian's ex-wife. Emily coaxed him into her rented car and started a violent quarrel. Weeping and shouting, she drove through a guard rail and over a high coastal bluff. The car turned lazily over and over with their bodies suspended inside it by safety harnesses, headlights sweeping through the limbs of pine trees, the radio playing Chopin. Emily's tawny hair lifted and opened like that of a girl swimming; her wet eyes turned on Julian with longing. She made no attempt to protect her face; her hands instead reached for Julian. They landed, uninjured, in a clump of pines, the motor still running, Emily's feet pressed convulsively on the brake. They were upside down, hanging side by side in their seat belts. Emily uttered a deep sob. "That's as close as I ever care to come to dying for love," said Julian. They were married a month later.

Julian's children, used to having strangers in their lives, made room for Emily with no fuss. Julian kept their routine as it had always been; Emily became a part of everything except the Sunday morning outings. At dinner, she told them stories of her interviews, and she and Julian vied to make the children laugh with their accounts of the most eccentric interview of the day.

Emily kept her own name for professional purposes, but few did not know that her husband was Julian Hubbard. She wanted no reflected power. Nor did she want the bother of being guarded. She went about the city and did her work without escorts. Jenny worried about her. Shots had been fired twice at Caroline, and Julian's life had been threatened times without number. Jenny had been with him once, riding her bicycle along the towpath while Julian and Elliott ran in the early morning, when the Secret Service, loping ahead of them, discovered a man with a machine pistol lying in ambush, and shot him dead. The children saw his body. Julian made no attempt to shield them, there was no use in it. They lived in an age of terror; powerful men like Julian were kidnapped and tortured and killed every day. To be murdered by a fool who knew you only from photographs was a very modern fate, one that Elliott and Jenny had always known about.

Julian was saddened by the things that Jenny knew. She had lived her whole childhood as a fugitive because of her father's position in the world. How could she realize that there had once been a time when money and influence, and especially political power, made people safe? All of Jenny's life the reverse had been true. She and her brother, huddled near the little fire of political decency that her father and President Lockwood had lit, were surrounded by a ring of beasts, snapping and growling just beyond the feeble light. Terrorists and kidnappers were as much a fact of Jenny's existence as death by typhoid and tuberculosis had been a hundred years before for the girls who went to work at Jenny's age in the Pittsfield mills. Julian's father had put that linked image —Jenny and the doomed mill girls—into Julian's head; the old man had liked the symmetry of it. Julian did not. He feared for his child in a world where madmen thought that *he* was the madman for trying to keep the ideas of order and justice alive and working. In his heart, Julian was not sure that he and Lockwood and the others who believed as they did could succeed in the end. But he was sure that Lockwood was almost the last wholly sane man in politics.

Sometimes Julian spoke of these things to the children. Ideas didn't interest Elliott very much, but Jenny's little face, framed by her mother's sable hair, shone with solemn intelligence. She loved music and flowers (her room was full of plants). She had formed the habit of going to vespers at the cathedral, where she went to school. "I like the *stony* smell of the church," Jenny explained to Julian. Now he went with her whenever he could; though he was no more a believer than he'd ever been, he, too, liked the atmosphere of the cathedral, its emptiness.

There was in Jenny something that reminded Julian of his spinster aunts and great-aunts, all of them dead now. Of all the people he had ever known, only his aunts and Jenny had accepted Julian for what he was, and loved him uncritically. Jenny, like these ancestresses who had lived among potted flowers and cats and photographs in old dark houses emptied by the deaths of their parents, saw him with absolute clarity. Jenny could never have the life that the aunts had had; yet Julian wished that she could have known, for a little while at least, their innocence. Julian remembered these women as shining with intelligence and modesty, as never being at a loss for the right English sentence, as treasuring the things that belonged to the family—the mills equally with teacups, brought home in the China trade by ancestors whose names and voyages they knew by heart.

In spite of all that she knew that they could never have known, Jenny was like Julian's aunts, as passive, and as alert, as Emily Dickinson. Caroline had seen this too, and fought against it. When one of the great-aunts died, a particular favorite of Julian's, he and his father listened after the funeral to a long harangue by Caroline about the dead woman's wasted life: she had been all the things that offended Caroline—a virgin, a lady, a Christian; even a Daughter of the American Revolution. Caroline's speech was really addressed to Jenny, then six years old, who was seated with her mother on a sofa in the house on Ninety-third Street.

At last Elliott Hubbard held up a hand. "You must bear in mind, Caroline," he said, "that Julian's Great-aunt Ella was born in a time in which it was not considered bad form to have good manners. If you were dead today instead of Aunt Ella, and she were sitting there in one of her changeable silk dresses, she would say the only thing she ever said about you, because it was a good thing—that you have beautiful eyes and a love for Julian that's wonderful to see. Then she would have made tea, and begun calling you 'dear Caroline.' The dead were always dear to Ella; their faults died with them."

Sometimes, listening to Jenny read or watching her as she patiently practiced a difficult run at the piano, or seeing her eyes dance as she listened to foolish talk but kept her peace, Julian would fancy that the shade of one of the aunts had passed into the little girl. It was they who had taught Julian what to love in women. Who would teach the man who was waiting for Jenny?

8

Patrick Graham returned from the Near East on a Saturday night, and the next morning Julian woke at dawn as usual. He dressed himself in old corduroys and a faded Yale sweat shirt, the last one made of pure cotton he had ever been able to find; he and Elliott and Jenny were going for a hike in the woods that morning. As he laced his boots, the light on the speaker phone blinked—it had no bell. The automatic recording device was on, and Julian pressed the key of the machine to listen to the incoming call without having to answer it. It was always possible that Lockwood was calling, and if he was, it was important; the President knew that Sundays belonged to Elliott and Jenny, and he had intruded only half a dozen times in all the years he and Julian had been together.

Julian knew the voice that came over the speaker at once. It was Patrick Graham's. Julian switched on the phone. "Yes, Patrick," he said. Graham, who had been speaking to the tape recorder, stopped in mid-sentence. When he resumed talking, this time directly to Julian, he had taken some of the resonance out of his voice, and Julian could hear the voice Patrick had had at Yale, before he trained himself to speak into microphones.

"Julian," Graham said, "I know it's Sunday morning, and I'm sorry to break in, but I wanted to catch you before you took your kids out." Graham paused to light a cigarette—the speaker amplified sound more than an ordinary phone, and Julian could hear the snap of the lighter. Before he began to speak again, Graham coughed convulsively on the smoke, and when he came back on the line, his voice had been roughened; Julian wondered why a man in Graham's line of work would use cigarettes.

"I wondered if you and your Emily would drop by for a drink this evening about five," Graham said. "Wear whatever you have on, there'll be no one but Charlotte and me."

Julian hesitated. The Grahams lived only a block away on O Street, in a much grander house than Julian's, and Julian had often gone there, though never with pleasure.

"I just got off a plane from Beirut," Graham said. "I spoke to Horace. I spoke to some others, too, in Baghdad. The subject was Ibn Awad. It's time, I think, to speak to you about what sent me out there."

Graham began coughing again; evidently he was holding the telephone away from his mouth because the dry barking sound came weakly through the speaker. Julian waited until he thought Graham had the phone at his ear again.

"Five o'clock," Julian said, and broke the connection. His mind began to worry the problem Patrick's call had created, but he stopped himself: Sunday belonged to Jenny and Elliott.

Julian woke the children on his way downstairs, and in the kitchen fried eggs for himself and Elliott and Jenny and made sandwiches with French bread. This was their regular Sunday breakfast, as it had been Julian's and his mother's, along with coffee mixed with sweetened hot milk. He packed cold meat, cheese, a loaf of bread, some apples, and a thermos of lemonade into a rucksack, and then the three of them went off in Julian's small car, the Secret Service vehicle tailing behind. They traveled south, across the Potomac into Virginia, rolling along the deserted back roads just after sunrise. This was their only ride of the week in their own car; Julian had the same ration of diesel fuel as anyone else, and it was just sufficient to take them to a forest. Franklin Mallory, when he was President, had followed a policy of unlimited burning of fossil fuels, arguing that their maximum use was necessary to reach the next stage of technology in which new fuels would be invented and exist in plenty. Lockwood had preferred to conserve the earth's dwindling resources. Under him, the skies were clear of smoke again, and traffic ceased roaring through America; on any day, in the largest city, Americans could hear the unstifled sounds of nature again.

In a forest near Leesville they walked quietly for several hours, and saw a wood thrush, a gray squirrel, and in a swampy place the tracks of a white-tailed buck. They ate their lunch on a hilltop under a red oak. Julian and Elliott played with a ball while Jenny gathered wildflowers. On the way out of the woods, walking behind them, Jenny sang: *I'd rather have one kiss from the gypsy's lips than all your silver and gold.*

Julian stopped, waited for her, and put an arm around her shoulders. "That's an old, old song," he said. "Where did you hear it?"

Jenny's face was hidden by her unbound hair and she shook her head so that her father could see her. "Mummy used to sing me to sleep with it," she said.

When Julian returned with the children, he found that Emily had decorated the house for a celebration—paper streamers, fresh flowers, candles. The children were in on the surprise and they watched their father—Elliott with bursts of delighted laughter, Jenny with her solemn smile—to see if he could guess the occasion. He could not; they had to tell him it was Father's Day, celebrated a week late because he had been traveling the Sunday before.

Emily had chilled a bottle of champagne, and as the four of them drank it, the children gave Julian their present. The gift dazzled Julian. He took pains unwrapping it; the silver paper and the ribbon had been put on with great care. Inside the package he found a scrapbook, the wooden cover made by Elliott. On opening it, he saw that Jenny had mounted on each page a different dried wildflower: lady's slipper, wild columbine, gaywings, spring beauty, showy orchis, wild pink, meadow rue—all the blooms he had taught her to know and she had gathered season by season on their Sunday outings. The faint woodsy smell of each dead blossom rose from the volume as they turned the pages together. Julian lifted the little girl onto his lap and kissed her.

Emily told him later that his eyes had been filled with tears. "It was wonderful," she said, "you love Jenny so. I long to see you look at *our* child in that way."

9

"Isn't the evening light lovely at this time of year?" asked Emily. She and Julian walked hand in hand along O Street, on their way to the Grahams', and the late afternoon sun fell through the trees ahead of them in a series of diagonals. Within these shafts of light, Julian saw the colors of the quiet street—pale greens of new leaves, mellow pinks and yellows of old brick. He smiled and Emily thought it was for her. She squeezed his arm.

Emily kissed him, tugging his head downwards to her lips. Two Secret Service guards walked ahead of them and two behind, and two across the street.

Julian rang the Grahams' doorbell. It was an old-fashioned bell pull, not an electrical device. The heavy glass and grillework door had been brought from England, and Patrick had found in Paris two enameled blue and white house numbers which, side by side, showed the four digits of his American address.

Patrick himself opened the door. He drew Emily inside and kissed her on the cheek. He and Julian nodded to one another. They never shook hands. Patrick walked ahead of Julian into the living room with his arm around Emily's shoulders. Emily had known him before she knew Julian. "Journalists run in a pack, didn't you know that?" she'd said to Julian, explaining her friendship with Patrick. "Patrick's sort of regarded as the dominant male of the local baboons."

Patrick had grown handsomer with age. He had a reputation among young women as a seducer. Julian had never known of this until Emily told him about it. The news surprised him; knowing how desperately Patrick had been able to love Caroline, he had supposed that he must now love Charlotte just as much.

Charlotte was at the bar, and by the time Julian entered the room she had a drink for him. She knew what he wanted without asking. Charlotte put a hand on Julian's sleeve. He liked this woman very much, liked her way of showing no emotion except amusement and her pose of saying whatever came into her head while, every moment, she kept her head. Patrick led Emily to the other end of the room, his arm still about her. He was showing her a new painting. The canvas, a winged nude, was displayed on an easel.

Charlotte, her slim figure bent back like a strung bow, watched her husband and Julian's wife together and then turned to Julian. "What is this fascination your wives exercise over poor Patrick, do you suppose?" she asked. "It was hellish all those years you were married to Caroline, Patrick staring across the room at her with spaniel eyes. Now he leads Emily straight to the nearest nude and gives her little pats. Do you mind?"

Julian smiled. "Not if my wives don't."

"I rather think Patrick wishes you *would* mind. Really, some-times I think it's you he wants to fondle, Julian, instead of your women. You're the last man in America—in the *world*—Patrick is truly jealous of. Don't let on I told you that."

They watched Patrick and Emily coming back to them. Patrick shrugged to settle his jacket back on his shoulders. He was wearing just the right things for a Sunday afternoon at home: a tweed jacket, flannels, knitted shirt, and the buckled oxblood boots that were in fashion that year. Patrick had always had a sense of costume. In the old days in New Haven he had worn dirty jeans and lumberjack shirts and broken shoes. He had had a beard then and reeked of unwashed skin; now his cheeks shone from the razor and he smelled of cologne. Charlotte had done a great deal for him; she had taught him some subtle things about dress, and he had picked up her upper-class mannerisms. When young, he had been surly; Charlotte, unable to change his character, had shown him how to be rude in a way that flattered people, and gave them the idea that it had been a natural thing for him to wed the daughter of an earl.

"How do you like Patrick's flying nymph?" Charlotte asked Emily. "I should think she'd have found the missionary position rather uncomfortable with those great wings folded up under her. Patrick is making a collection of Victorian nudes. He's found this wonderful man named Alan Stone who climbs into attics and finds them for him." Emily and Charlotte kissed.

Charlotte turned to Julian. "Did you watch Patrick's show last night?"

"I'm afraid I missed it."

"He keeps on saying dreadful Mallory may defeat your wonderful Frosty Lockwood in November. Say it isn't possible, Julian."

The forthcoming election was only four months away, and Graham had already said on television, many times, that the re-election of Lockwood was in jeopardy. Julian knew he was right, and knew that Graham's pounding on the point on his weekly show was really designed to awaken Lockwood's supporters to their danger. But the President's admirers didn't like to be reminded that Lockwood had made so many enemies, even if they were the right enemies.

"I'm worried about you people," Patrick Graham said. "Lockwood will be renominated all right. But you've seen the polls. I think the party is afraid he can lose in November."

"To Mallory?"

"Fascism isn't dead."

"Come on, Patrick." Julian was not going to run the chance of being quoted as agreeing that Franklin Mallory was a fascist.

"If Mallory is able to run the kind of campaign he's talking about, combining vision with viciousness—nobody's his equal at that—he may damn well be the first President since Grover

63

Cleveland to serve two nonconsecutive terms," said Patrick. "That's his new witticism. He goes around the country asking people if they can name the President who served between Cleveland's two terms. Can you?"

"Harrison," said Emily.

"Smart girl. *Which* Harrison?"

"I'm not that smart," Emily said. She giggled, but Patrick was dead serious.

"A line like that can do a lot of damage," he said. "It makes men laugh, it forms a connection between two Presidents nobody remembers and Bedford Forrest Lockwood."

"Does he talk to you?" Julian asked.

"Mallory? Sure. He's a very professional fellow, doesn't let his grudges show. I may have killed him off last time, but this time he may find a way to make me help him. That's how his mind works."

"Perhaps he isn't altogether wrong, Patrick. You're the equivalent of a neutral power. If you found a scandal in our administration, would you hide it? If Mallory doesn't think so, knowing your sympathies, then you ought to be flattered."

"Do *you* think I'd cover up for you, Julian?"

Julian believed, after all the years he had known him, that he could read Patrick's moods; Graham wasn't a man who tried to conceal what he meant. Tonight Patrick wanted to semaphore some tension in himself. He didn't require an answer to his question; he went on with what he wanted to say, hardly pausing to draw breath.

"I'd say this, Julian. I don't think you realize how hard Mallory can hit you."

"You think he can win with a witticism about the two Harrisons?"

"I think he can win on an issue, if he finds one. He's not some survivor of the primaries who has to pussyfoot. He's the maximum leader of a fanatical political party. He's the former President. To a lot of people he never stopped *being* the President. That includes a lot of the media. He'll be coming back, in a lot of people's minds, to pull Excalibur out of the sacred stone. Frosty has made a lot of enemies."

Charlotte fluttered a beringed hand. "I must say I have to depend on you wise men to remind me what a demon Franklin Mallory is supposed to be," she said. "When I see him on television, much less when he used to press my flesh in the old days, I go all squishy. He makes everything so simple. Perhaps he does have hooves—but like Pan, with that white hair and that glowing skin and those hypnotic eyes. Don't you agree, Emily?"

"Yes, but all the same, he'd put all of us into one of those prisons he built in Alaska, wouldn't he?"

Patrick took Julian's empty glass from his hand and put it, with his own, on a table. Patrick never had more than one drink, and he knew that Julian didn't either. He enjoyed drawing attention to his remarkable memory for small details.

The doors to the garden were open and Patrick, with a nod to the women excusing him and Julian from their company, led the way outside. In the house behind them Patrick and Julian could hear Charlotte's English voice rippling with mirth and Emily's American one, throaty and serious.

Patrick had converted the ground behind his house into a small-scale replica of an eighteenth-century formal garden; the original owner had been an early minister to France who brought the plans for the garden back from Paris but lacked the money to build it. Money was no problem for Patrick; his contract with the network was worth millions, and he earned almost as much again from books and documentaries. He had hired an architect to work from the old drawings. The architect had built in an American backyard a garden designed as a park. To keep the proportions correct, everything had been made small—the fountains and statues were a quarter their expected size, the walks were mere strips of gravel, the shrubs and trees were dwarf species. Patrick's garden was one of the rare places where Julian was conscious of his tallness. A man of normal size seemed large here. Julian loomed like a giant.

The two men sat down on a low bench by a fountain. Patrick lapsed into a silence. Julian, watching the fountain, said, "You say you saw Horace in Beirut?"

"Yes. He's well."

A mild wind was blowing and spray from the fountain pattered on the gravel at their feet. Patrick got up and Julian followed him to another bench on the opposite side of the fountain.

"I'd hoped Horace could help me," Patrick said, "but he chose to be polite."

"What did you want?"

"I'm not sure. Reassurance, perhaps. Horace was a great friend of Ibn Awad."

"You said something about Awad on the phone." Julian felt a spot of cold, like an ice cube lodged in the gullet, forming in his chest.

"I'm developing an interest in Awad's death—in how he died."

Julian said nothing. Patrick lit one of his cigarettes. Even in the open air, it smelled very strong. Patrick inhaled and turned aside to cough up the smoke.

"I have to ask you this, Julian. Did you or Frosty Lockwood have any foreknowledge of the death of Ibn Awad?"

"Foreknowledge?" Julian widened his eyes. "Exactly what kind of a question is that supposed to be?"

"It's an easy question," Patrick said, "if the answer happens to be no."

The smoke from Patrick's cigarette was blowing away from them. It must come from the Near East; the burning tobacco had a peculiar smell.

"Let me show you how to answer, Julian. I have a suggestion from one usually reliable source, corroborated by a second source, that Ibn Awad did not, as the world has always believed, order his own death. My sources say he was murdered. They say, further, that President Lockwood had a hand in this murder."

Julian controlled his voice. "And you're prepared to entertain that as a possibility, knowing what Lockwood is?"

"It's my job to examine possibilities. Four years ago, in this garden, Julian, you gave me a piece of paper that seemed to incriminate Franklin Mallory in a plot to steal half of Canada. If I hadn't entertained *that* possibility, maybe you and Frosty would be living happily today as private citizens."

"Lockwood is not Franklin Mallory."

"I can tell the good guys from the bad guys, Julian," Patrick said. "In my heart, I think Lockwood's the best human being we've had in the White House since Kennedy. But as a reporter, I'm paid to be suspicious. I'm telling you I'm suspicious."

Julian returned Patrick's look in silence. There was danger here. When Patrick had the bloody bone of a fresh story in his teeth, he could growl over it. The old vengeful beast still slouched in him.

"Do you really think, Patrick," Julian said, "that Lockwood, or any President, could survive even the suggestion that he'd been mixed up in an assassination?"

"No."

"Then you have a simple choice before you. If you go on the air with such a suggestion about Lockwood, Franklin Mallory will defeat him for the presidency in the fall."

"Are you telling me what I've heard is a lie?"

Julian blew a long breath through his nose and looked at Pat-

66

rick. The other man's eyes, squinting against the smoke, were un-readable.

"You stand silent?" Patrick asked.

"Dumbstruck. People do lie to journalists, Patrick, even jour-nalists as eminent as you. Wasn't it you, just a moment ago, who told me that Lockwood has made enemies?"

"You're saying Frosty's enemies are retailing this lie?"

"I don't know. We don't follow his enemies around or tap their phones." Exasperation sharpened Julian's voice. He got to his feet. Beyond the brick wall surrounding the garden he heard the crackle of radios as his Secret Service guards talked to one another.

"Perhaps I should go on with this story of mine a little further," Partick said. "Then we can talk again. It may come to a point where I'd want to talk to Frosty."

This repetition of the President's nickname irritated Julian. What right had Patrick to use it? To Patrick, Julian said, "I doubt that your researches will ever carry you to that point."

"I hope not," Patrick replied, rising from the bench. "Really I do." He dropped his cigarette into a marble bowl filled with sand, and drew a line in the sand with his index finger. "The mysterious desert," he said. "You remember what a force Ibn Awad was, Julian?"

"They seemed to think a lot of him in his part of the world. But Hagreb is a very small country."

"So was Galilee. You know, I followed Awad on those pil-grimages of his, when he was praying at all the great mosques of Islam. He'd walk barefoot into the Muslim cities—Damascus, Bagh-dad, Cairo, all of them—and people would just rise up out of the dust and follow him. The streets would be choked with humanity. Yet the babble would die. There was silence—total silence. Thou-sands would follow Awad to the mosque to pray—they'd be all over the ground outside, a great sea of the poor."

Julian listened, studying Patrick's tone. He was speaking in a conversational voice. He seemed to be moved by the memory of the events he was describing. Julian waited, unspeaking, for Patrick to take him inside. Patrick, with a shrug, let him find his own way back.

Charlotte, when she returned from saying good-bye to Julian and Emily, found Patrick walking around his little garden, smoking again. She waited until they could no longer hear the Hubbards' footsteps on the brick sidewalk or the crackle of their bodyguards' radios. Then she spoke.

"Was it a success?"

"A stand-off. Julian's reaction was what you'd expect—he won't dignify such an accusation with a denial."

Charlotte made herself a fresh Scotch and milk. She sank onto the bench where Patrick and Julian had been sitting and, reaching beneath it, turned a valve that shut down the fountain.

"My hair will go funny in the mist," she explained. Patrick was frowning; he liked the fountain. "Emily is a delicious girl, don't you think?"

"Yes."

"She's quite mad about Julian, you know."

Patrick gave his wife a look. Her eyes were bright above the rim of her glass and her skirt was spread beautifully on the bench; Charlotte's clothes always behaved perfectly for her. Patrick made an impatient gesture and Charlotte came back to the subject.

"Do try and remember," she said, "that Clive Wilmot can be a swine. He may just be having you on for the hell of it, or he may be playing a deeper game."

"A *deeper game?* Do you say that, actually still use those words?"

"Joke. But Clive's no joke."

"Neither is Julian."

Charlotte drank, daintly. "I do wish you could see some humor in Julian," she said. "He's really rather sweet, the way he loves that great booby Frosty Lockwood. But of course you love Lockwood as well."

"Love Lockwood? For twenty years I've hoped he was the enemy of my enemies, that's all."

"And you don't love Julian at all, do you? You're a very human chap, Patrick. But the past *is* the past, and Julian can't help Caroline being Caroline any more than you can. It's well to remember that."

"I remember a lot more than just Caroline." Patrick wasn't able to go on speaking. This only lasted for a moment. "Julian symbolizes something I hate."

"Yes, but you two *have* been useful to one another." Charlotte gave one of her dazzling smiles. "He may not be what you've always wanted. But think about the alternative." Her smile brightened. "One *can* live without love better than one can live in chains in Alaska."

Patrick's head was in his hands, but he was listening to Charlotte. He had never acted against her advice without doing himself harm. He pinched out his cigarette and with its dead end drew a design in the white sand—the helix within a circle that had been

68

the symbol of the revolutionary army he and Caroline and the others had wanted to be born in the East Village. They had never got beyond designing the symbol, and now here he was in a toy garden that had cost enough to arm a battalion of guerrillas, chatting with a wife who had the blood of Stuarts running in her veins.

"The past is the past—you're absolutely right," Patrick said. "But no one ever forgets it. Coming back from Baghdad, something happened to me. My old self was shocked back to life. I don't know what caused it—coming face to face with poor Hassan, maybe."

"*Poor* Hassan? My dear Patrick! He's the greatest murderer of his age."

Patrick glared; Charlotte looked down into her glass.

"I remembered what it was I used to love," Patrick said. "I used to love an idea. There was a time when everyone I loved loved the same idea."

"And that's why you loved Caroline?"

Patrick didn't hear. He wanted to say aloud what was on his mind. He lived by the sound of his own voice. Unspoken thoughts had no reality for him. He had to bring words out of his subconscious, hear them vibrate; this was necessary to him in the way a painter must see color on a canvas or a poet lines on a page in order to know what lies within him, hiding.

"The idea was this: that people like Julian—people like your family used to be, Charlotte—had done enough harm. That it had to stop."

"You still believe that?"

Patrick pointed a finger at her. "Yes. I'd forgotten how much I believe it. No harm ever comes to Julian and his kind. They take over everything with a smile. We even gave them our idea because we hadn't the power to make it work. Gave it to *them!*"

"They haven't done so badly with it."

Patrick didn't listen. "Julian thinks he can control anything. Lockwood, me, himself. Perhaps some harm ought to come to him, so he'll know the taste of it."

"Oh, dear," said Charlotte. "I don't like the sound of *that.*"

10

A dozen Thoroughbred yearlings, fleeing from some alarm that had rung in the nerves of the herd, galloped wildly around the pasture, their bright hides flowing together like that of a single

69

radiant animal. Lockwood watched the colts with pleasure as he and Julian stood together by the white board fence that enclosed the paddock. The President was as tall as Julian, but rawboned and weather-burnt. He wore his country clothes—scarred boots, old whipcords, a battered Stetson—and he smelled of horse and crushed grass; a moment before, he had kneeled in the dew to handle an ailing foal, and the knees of his trousers were stained green. It was early yet. Lockwood and Julian were just beginning to feel the sun on their shoulders, and a haze lay on the wooded hills that encircled Lockwood's farm in the Bluegrass of Kentucky.

Julian had just told Lockwood about Patrick Graham's suspicions about the manner in which Ibn Awad had died. It was Julian's helicopter, lifting off for the return trip to Washington, that had frightened the colts. Now, as the noise of the machine receded, they stopped running; the herd divided itself into individuals again and resumed grazing.

Lockwood turned his back on the animals and gazed at the porticoed mansion, standing some distance away on a little hill at the end of an avenue of flaunting oaks. The sight of the house, white and ancient, gave Lockwood peace. More and more, as his first term drew to a close, he came here in order to be alone. No reporters were permitted to follow him; no member of the Cabinet or congressman or senator had ever flown down for consultations. Julian came and went as the need arose.

Lockwood himself didn't really belong here, as much as he loved the place with its colony of barns, its long marches of white fence, its Southern voices calling and laughing in the quiet. Polly's family had built the house before the Civil War, naming it Live Oaks for its avenue of trees, and her father, ruined by his love for horses, had lost it when she was a girl. Lockwood, when he was still a senator, bought it back for her and used what little money he had to make it look again as it must have looked a century before, when there had been famous parties here. Paintings of belles in ball gowns, Polly's aunts and cousins, had been hung on the walls again, and Polly had found most of the old furniture in the houses of her relations, and returned it to its rightful place. She'd brought the gardens back.

Lockwood said, "You mean Patrick intends to go after us on this?"

"That's what he was saying to me."

"Have you done anything?"

"I spoke to Jack Philindros. He's the authority on this question. I asked him to fly down here this morning."

Lockwood nodded, and looked to the northern horizon, as

70

though searching for an approaching helicopter. Philindros was the Director of Foreign Intelligence. He wasn't a man Lockwood saw very often.

"Can we talk to Patrick, explain?"

"He'd never understand," said Julian. "It was hard enough for you to believe what we had to do. It's taken me years to accept it. How could a man like Patrick Graham possibly grasp all the shades of judgment that went into that decision?"

"He isn't stupid. Anyone who knew the truth would understand."

Julian didn't reply and Lockwood gave him a bleak smile. It was always the President's first instinct to tell the truth. Julian believed in silence and in the possibility of controlling men and situations.

The colts began to gallop again and the earth quivered beneath their hooves. Julian felt it through the soles of his shoes. Lockwood turned to watch; he couldn't get enough of the sight of horses. Julian, with his aviator's eye, saw the sun flash on the perspex of an approaching helicopter, and in a moment heard the clatter of its engine.

"That's Philindros," he said.

"Has he been down here since that night?" Lockwood asked. Julian shook his head.

"Then he'll see changes in the place."

The President started the long uphill walk across the lawns to the house. When he moved he lost all his awkwardness; he was still an athlete at sixty. As he walked, he watched Philindros's helicopter settle with its rotors winking onto the landing pad.

Philindros had come prepared for everything except the questions Lockwood was asking him. The operation against Ibn Awad had lain quiet for three years. Why should it now start talking in its sleep? Philindros gave Julian Hubbard a hard look; the man might have told him what was in store at five that morning, when he ordered him over the telephone to fly to the farm in time for breakfast.

He and Julian were seated with the President on a lawn enclosed by high hedges; masses of climbing roses, white and lavender, had woven themselves into the evergreen. A cloth had been spread on a round table, and a black man, not one of the Navy's Filipinos who had served every other President, laid out breakfast for them. Philindros had no appetite for the hot cakes and fried ham, but he did have a great thirst. A large pitcher of fresh orange juice stood before him, losing its chill. Philindros wished that Lockwood would take some juice so that he could wet his own throat. Lockwood showed no interest in the juice, or in his food either, and Philindros would not touch his breakfast before the President had done so. He was not awed, merely patient and polite; Philindros had always made it a rule to let a superior make the first move in any situation. Now, after listening to the President's long list of questions, he cleared his dry throat and spoke in his usual measured way.

"Mr. President, if the history of intelligence activities in this country tells us anything, it is this: there is no such thing in an open society as a secure espionage apparatus."

"Jack, I'm not interested in philosophical principles," Lockwood said. "We're discusing a specific case."

Philindros had never seen Lockwood so sharp-edged. He and this President, Philindros's third since he became Director of Foreign Intelligence, hardly knew one another. Lockwood had been content to let the intelligence service run itself. His two predecessors had been ravenous for information, especially about the quirks of other heads of state; Lockwood accepted briefings, but seemed to make his own judgments of men. Philindros had been appointed to a ten-year term, and no President could relieve him before the end of his term or keep him after it expired. The head of intelligence had ceased serving at the pleasure of the President as one of the reforms that followed the great CIA scandals of the seventies.

Philindros had been a young officer in those days, and he remembered very well what had happened. The old CIA had been laid waste, its reputation twisted and its spirit destroyed. Brilliant men, loyal officers who had thought themselves the most trusted men in America, had been sacrificed in cold blood by the reformers. Philindros had spent his whole career haunted by the ghosts of his ruined friends. They had never understood why no one had seen the obvious truth: that the attempts at assassination, the overthrow of governments overseas, the betrayal of allies, the perversions of the Constitution, had all been ordered in secret *by Presidents*. Presidents had misused the intelligence apparatus, and then put the blame for what happened on the apparatus they had corrupted. The men of the CIA, trained to trust no one, had put their trust in princes, and paid the price. Philindros knew it, and never forgot it.

Lockwood reached across the tablecloth and poured juice into Philindros's glass, and with a wave of his hand urged him to drink and eat. Philindros drained the glass and felt the chill and sweetness spread down his throat and into his chest.

72

"Do we in fact have a specific case yet?" Philindros asked. "All Julian really seems to be reporting is a series of hints and veiled statements made by Patrick Graham during a social encounter."

"Julian thinks it was more than that."

"Why?" Philindros addressed the question to Julian.

"I've known Graham since we were in college. He could hardly have made it plainer that he was giving me a warning."

"A warning that he knows—or pretends to know—that the United States government was involved in the death of Ibn Awad? It's not impossible that he could know that. But, Mr. President, it's very, very unlikely."

Lockwood offered the plate of fried ham. It seemed to Philindros that the President was making these hospitable gestures for a purpose—to show that he wasn't unnerved, that he was in control. There was, Philindros thought, a cold man beneath Lockwood's shell of charm and humane talk. The presidency had toughened Lockwood. He knew how to defend himself now. He had learned how to sacrifice men in order to save his policies and his own reputation. Some Presidents came into office because they were ruthless; all were ruthless before they left.

Only a man who was a perfect bureaucrat, without politics, could survive such men. Philindros had made himself into the perfect bureaucrat, and he had weeded out of the FIS any man who was capable of loving a President for his politics. No one in Philindros's FIS would make the mistake of loving ideas or men, as the CIA had loved liberalism and its leaders. Philindros loved the truth—the bare bones of it put back together by intelligence and logic—and he had trained his men to be like him.

Julian said, "Is it so unlikely that Graham could have picked up the truth, or part of it, Jack? He certainly has all kinds of sources."

"In theory there *are* no sources. The President is secure by definition, and we assume that you and I are, too. Only one other person in my shop knew about the operation—the FIS man in the field who carried out the actual recruitment of the assassin. He, too, is secure. And, as we know, the assassin is dead."

"He could have talked before he died," Lockwood said.

"We know he didn't. Talil was held in the emir's palace for the entire forty-eight hours between the time he killed his father and the time he was himself executed. We had transmitters in every room of the palace; we have tapes of every word spoken."

"Every word?"

"Yes, sir. He stuck to the cover story to the end. He believed

73

the assassination was his own idea. He was handled very skillfully by the case officer."

Lockwood, as he listened to Philindros, had poured syrup on his pancakes and cut the stack into neat squares. Now he put down his knife and fork and fixed Philindros with a steady gaze.

"So was I," the President said. " 'Handled,' as you call it."

Philindros was at any time a man of deliberate speech and movement, and now his body and voice were absolutely controlled.

"Sir, with all respect, I won't hear that said. You made your wishes plain. FIS carried them out. We had certain information, and certain means to act. You made the decision. We executed it— not, I may say, without misgivings on my part and great pain to our man in the field."

"Pain?"

"There was a strong personal attachment between Prince Talil and our man. It went back many years. He—our man in the field— fought your decision."

"Fought it? How?"

Philindros blinked, his first involuntary movement since the conversation began. It was a sign of embarrassment over what he said next. "By suggesting alternatives. It's always been the policy of FIS, and, in recent years, of the White House as well, to prevent violence—and particularly, to prevent assassination."

"Could you have prevented this assassination?"

"Perhaps. Time was very short. Would you have run the risk of testing alternatives?"

The President's eyes, dark blue and filled with sympathy and intelligence, were his fine feature, the equivalent of Eisenhower's smile or Kennedy's easy wit. Even on television they seemed to take the person who was looking at Lockwood into their depths. Much had been said and written about their warmth, but as he looked at Philindros they were very cold.

"Let me ask you this, Mr. Director," Lockwood said. "Why did you decide, on your own, that I shouldn't be apprised of these options at the time we discussed removing Awad?"

"Mr. President, it was Julian Hubbard's judgment that you didn't want to know the details. It was a painful decision for you. Julian made it plain that it was my job to carry it through without making small talk about the methods. If that was an error I apologize. It was an attempt to be sensitive to what I took to be your wishes."

"That was all?"

Philindros returned Lockwood's gaze with expressionless brown eyes. "Mr. President, no—that was not all. The Awad matter was

74

the first time in my experience that American intelligence had been instructed to kill a human being. Candidly, sir, it was the last order I ever expected to receive in my term as DFI. It's not a pleasant thing to be made a party to murder. I detested giving it. I detest the memory of it still."

For once, Philindros did not defer to the President; he let Lockwood be the first to break eye contact.

A fly settled on Lockwood's pancakes and fed on the syrup. Lockwood didn't disturb the fly, though he watched it with close attention.

When Ibn Awad was murdered in the Hagrebi desert, Lockwood had been in the presidency for only four months. Already he was very tired. He had just lost his first big fight in Congress to undo some of Franklin Mallory's cold-blooded work. Lockwood had asked for the repeal of a law, enacted during the Mallory Administration, under which every schoolchild in America was screened, as a matter of routine, for signs of a criminal personality. The idea of drawing blood from children and counting their chromosomes, of examining the electrical patterns in their brains—of classifying them like so many laboratory animals—filled Lockwood with horror. "If we treat our children as suspects, how can we be free—how can America remain what it is?" he cried in a television address to the nation. But Lockwood had lost. "Do people want a police state?" he asked Julian. "They want to be safe," Julian replied. "I thought they elected me because they saw the danger of being safe at any price," Lockwood said. Then he had come down to Live Oaks to have a weekend of peace.

The time was late April, the foaling season. Lockwood was in one of the barns with Polly, sitting up with a mare in labor, when the scrambler phone rang at ten in the evening. Julian answered. Philindros identified himself. His voice was soft, and Julian had trouble hearing him. He asked him to repeat. Philindros was requesting an immediate meeting with the President.

"Can't you tell me?" Julian asked.

There was a short dead moment on the sound-free line. Then Philindros's murmuring voice said, "No. It's something that only the President can act on."

Julian hesitated. Lockwood certainly did not want to be disturbed. But Philindros had never behaved in this way before. Julian told him to come, and ordered a helicopter for him.

The farm lay at the limit of helicopter range from Washington, and it was midnight before the radarmen reported the approach of the White House ship carrying Philindros. Julian met him in a

Jeep at the landing pad, which was concealed by a screen of cedars. Lockwood's greyhounds had leaped into the back of the vehicle—they rode everywhere with the President—and as Philindros approached they stood up on their spindly legs, arching their backs like big exotic cats, and barked shrilly. Philindros stopped in his tracks, his quiet eyes fixed on the animals. "They're just pets," Julian said; "get in." The dogs settled back, side by side on their haunches in the narrow back seat, for the ride back through the aromatic wood. Even in the dark, Julian saw, Philindros noted the cameras and sensors that watched the Jeep in its progress towards the buildings of the farm.

In the barn, they found Lockwood and Polly kneeling, one on either side of a newborn foal. They were cleaning its eyes and nostrils as the mare, still down herself, watched with white-ringed eyes. Julian drew Philindros away from the stall as the mare heaved to her feet and Lockwood put his body between the animal and his wife. A Secret Service man dressed as a groom swallowed audibly and went into the stall. Lockwood spoke to the mare and she quieted.

Polly Lockwood came out of the stall. "It's a colt; the President's already thinking of the Derby three years from now," she said. "We'd better have a bottle of champagne ready for him when he comes up to the house." She smiled at Philindros and showed him her hands, still slippery from the foal, to explain why she didn't offer them to him. In her long years as a political wife, Polly had learned never to be surprised to see anyone. Philindros congratulated her and gave her the shadow of a bow. He had odd, very careful manners, as though he had passed most of his life in solitary confinement and remembered only dimly how human beings were supposed to treat each other.

They went outside. It was a starry night, but clouds were forming in the west and they smelled rain in a little breeze that had just begun to blow.

In the small sitting room that had been fixed up as a place for Julian to work they drank a toast to the foal. The presidential telephones were here, and the other necessary machines. There was no desk—only some chairs and tables and a pair of sofas by a fireplace. Lockwood sat down and pulled off his boots. He swung his feet onto the low table between the sofas. Bits of straw were stuck in the yarn of his red socks.

Philindros was, as always, freshly groomed. There wasn't a wrinkle about him despite the late hour and his long ride from

Washington in a bucking helicopter. His clothes were dark and his dark hair was brushed as flat as a schoolboy's after a morning bath. There was no shadow of a beard on his smooth olive skin. Philindros was odorless; he brushed his teeth with table salt and used an unscented soap.

Philindros looked from the President to Julian and back again. A flicker of expression showed that he wasn't certain if he should begin to speak while Julian was still present. Polly had left the windows open and her white organdy curtains billowed into the room.

"Close those, will you?" Lockwood asked. Before Julian could move, Philindros went to the windows and pulled them shut; the sashes, swollen by the spring damp, squealed in their frames. "Sit down, Jack," Lockwood said; "Julian hears everything I hear. It may save trouble in case you ever want to read my mind if I happen to die suddenly." Lockwood grinned; he was still drinking champagne. Philindros did not return the smile.

"Mr. President," Philindros began. They had to strain to hear his voice, and Lockwood, whose normal conversational tone could easily be heard by fifty people in an open field, impatiently beckoned him closer. It was useless to ask Philindros to talk louder; he couldn't. When he did speak, he spoke in spare language and directly to the point; this came of a lifetime of telling men, even great men, facts he was sure they did not want to know. Philindros never carried a briefcase, never referred to notes. He was able to recall, in as much detail as required, anything of importance that his service knew.

To Lockwood, he now said, without preamble, "We have a fully confirmed report that two nuclear weapons will be delivered to the terrorist group called the Eye of Gaza before midnight tomorrow, Washington time."

Lockwood's face tightened. He took his stocking feet off the table and pulled his body upright. Philindros, holding the President's gaze, went on without a pause. His voice was as neutral, and almost as rapid, as the heatless green lettering on a computer screen.

"These weapons," Philindros continued, "are physically small, about the size of an ordinary suitcase, and are easily portable by one man. They can be detonated by a timing device, by a radio signal, or—the likeliest method because it's the most certain—by a terrorist on a suicide mission throwing a simple switch. These are ten-kiloton devices, made to be dirty, and big enough to destroy a small city or make a large one uninhabitable for years."

Philindros paused. This was one of his shy courtesies. He looked at Lockwood with intensely interested eyes; he wanted Lockwood to ask questions.

Lockwood said, "The terrorists don't actually, at this moment, have these bombs in their possession?"

"That's correct, sir. But they will have them in a matter of hours if our information is correct."

"Do you have any doubt that it *is* correct?"

"No, sir."

"You say the bombs will be handed over to the Eye of Gaza. Who will hand them over?"

Philindros cleared his throat. His voice came out a trifle more strongly. "The emir of Hagreb, Ibn Awad," he said.

"*Who?*" Lockwood had his own mannerisms. When something truly astonished him he reached in his pocket and found his reading glasses. He did that now, and with the glasses on his nose peered over the tops of the lenses as though the use of spectacles made it easier for him to understand the spoken word.

The FIS had reported, not once but several times, that Ibn Awad had plutonium in his possession and was presumed to be fabricating low-yield atomic weapons. Half the petty dictators in the world were doing the same. For years there had been a busy black market in fissionable plutonium centered in the Low Countries, and no one had been able to shut it down, though every police force and intelligence service in the world knew about it. Like the heroin trade, the plutonium market was based entirely on the profit motive. Therefore it could probably never be controlled; it had been running, and returning large fortunes to its operators, since the late seventies, when the possession of nuclear weapons had become a matter of prestige to the scores of small nations around the world who could afford them. The bombs were easy to make, and they were just as great a deterrent to aggression by small country against small country as they had been in the case of the superpowers. The black marketeers understood that their one unforgivable crime would be to furnish fissionable material to terrorists, and they had never done so. Now Ibn Awad was on the verge of doing the unthinkable.

Lockwood said, "Why?"

"Ibn Awad," Philindros replied, "has had a sign from God. An angel appeared to him in the desert and told him to destroy Israel by fire."

Lockwood leaned towards Philindros, and, whipping off his glasses, stabbed at Philindros's leg with them. "God? An angel in the desert? You're telling me this man is insane."

78

Now Philindros, just for an instant, did show surprise. How could Lockwood not know this basic fact? He shifted his gaze to Julian.

Julian, nodding, said, "Philindros's people have been reporting for some time that Awad is—well, unbalanced, sir."

"This is a medical certainty?" Lockwood asked.

"Yes. In October of last year, Awad was physically ill—he needed surgery to remove a cancerous prostate. An American medical team was flown in. They did a complete work-up and diagnosed him as an acute manic-depressive. He loses control over his own behavior for considerable periods of time."

"I thought this condition was being treated," Julian said.

"It was. The doctors gave him lithium carbonate and he improved. This drug modifies the manic state, which is the dangerous one in people like Awad. But after a month or two he stopped taking the medicine. He said it deprived him of his visions."

Lockwood closed his eyes and put his head on the back of the sofa. He remained in this position, silent, for long moments. The storm was drawing closer and Philindros and Julian turned their heads quickly when the first fat drops of rain struck the window-panes.

"Get back to the bombs," Lockwood said. "Where are they?"

"We don't know."

Lockwood's eyes snapped open. "You don't *know?*"

"We know they're hidden somewhere in the Hagrebi desert. Ibn Awad himself concealed them somewhere the last time he went out alone."

"Only he knows where they are?"

"That's correct."

"Nuclear weapons give off radiation. Can't we detect this radiation and find the bombs?" Lockwood spoke slowly, as if to a backward child.

"Not in time. The Hagrebi desert looks small on the map, but it contains fifty thousand square kilometers, and half of that consists of rocky mountains honeycombed by deep caves. We have no satellite in orbit capable of scanning for the very weak type of radiation these bombs would emit. A search by aircraft would take days, even weeks, and would involve massive intrusion into Hagrebi air space. Ten thousand men on foot and in vehicles would need six months to comb the area. That, of course, would require that we invade Hagreb."

It was raining hard now against the rattling windows and Lockwood, flushed and glaring, put his face within a few inches of Philindros's in order to hear him.

"What *do* you know?" Lockwood demanded. "Do you know the targets?"

"The primary targets are Jerusalem and Tel Aviv."

"Can we deny the terrorists those targets if the worst happens and they get their hands on the bombs?"

"Almost certainly. We could just tell the Israelis what we know. They'd have a ninety percent chance of preventing the bombs from going off inside Israel. But they'd have to flood the country with troops and police, search every person and every room and every vehicle. When Hassan Abdallah saw that happening, he'd know the reason why."

"And?"

"He'd hit another target, probably a city in the West with a large Jewish population."

"You mean New York? Miami?"

Philindros nodded and drew breath to list the other possible targets. Lockwood held up his hand to silence him.

"We couldn't keep them out of the United States?"

The answer was obvious. Even Philindros saw no need to reply. Lockwood knew as well as he how many miles of unguarded coastline and unpatrolled border surrounded America, how weak were the powers of the police, what panic would result if the media got hold of this story.

"Can we catch Hassan Abdallah?" Lockwood asked. "Can we neutralize the Eye of Gaza?"

"In a word, no. The Eye of Gaza is the last relic of the old Palestinian terrorist movement. The FIS code word for it is 'Snakehead'—the body has been cut off, but the fangs remain. It has no political objectives—even Hassan knows that the idea of a Palestinian state is dead. He goes on killing anyway. The Eye of Gaza is a revenge operation, blood for blood. Hassan and his followers are hysterics, and their purpose is to go on killing Jews forever. That's what drew Hassan and Ibn Awad together; I don't know where the line between political hysteria and religious hysteria lies."

"Forever? This Hassan thinks he can go on forever?"

"Literally forever, yes. Hassan only recruits the children of terrorists who have died for the cause. Each terrorist's first duty, before he goes on a mission, is to breed a child to replace him. All missions for the Eye of Gaza are suicide missions, so the child is told from the time he can understand that his father or mother was a hero who was killed by Jews and imperialists. Hassan makes sure his people interbreed with other nationalities, usually while they're students in foreign universities. A lot of his babies have been fathered on American and German and English and French females. Then they have their mother's nationality, and can grow up in a democratic country where the police won't bother them. Sometimes both parents are ordered to die—the father when the child is very small, the mother when the child is in his early teens, to reinforce the psychological impact. Then the child passes into a 'family' which is really a cell of the Eye of Gaza. He hears nothing but the details of his parents' deaths, and the duty to revenge them, from then onward."

"Don't they lose some of the kids?"

"A few. Some refuse to play the game and have to be killed. The rest are trained for their mission. A mate is found for them while they wait. They are trained by the cell members—a terrorist's skills are simple, and only need to be used once. They see their baby born and know they'll be avenged. They're given their mission. They carry it out and die."

"Hassan invented this system?"

"Yes. In his way, he's a genius. He's created an organism that, in theory, cannot be destroyed. It goes on metastasizing forever."

Philindros remained as he had been from the beginning of the conversation, seated on the edge of the sofa with his back straight and his hands resting quietly in his lap. It had stopped raining.

Lockwood pulled on his boots. "Let's go outside," he said.

There was a rule that the floodlights must be on when the President was outdoors at night, and as soon as Lockwood emerged from the house the switches were thrown. The light was so intense that it affected senses other than sight; Julian imagined that it made a noise, a humming like an insect, that was just beyond the range of human hearing. The lights had been designed to eliminate all shadows, so there could be no patch of darkness in which an assassin could lurk. All colors appeared as black. Human faces looked like overexposed photographs. Julian realized, with the little shock this always gave him, that Lockwood's lithe body was made up of ugly parts—huge hands with bulging knuckles and nails the size of coins, heavy legs, a neck that was corded by tension and too thin in proportion to the great rough head. In bad moments, though nothing might show in Lockwood's face, his body lost its athlete's grace; for the moment, he was no longer the natural runner, born with the instinct to make the perfect move without conscious thought.

Lockwood, with Julian and Philindros following, walked between two long rows of lilac bushes. These were in bloom, and the conical blossoms sparkled with rainwater in the brilliant light. The men came to a large round lawn surrounded by a ring of gravel. To Philindros, Lockwood said, "This is where the hunt used to form—is that the right verb, Julian?—when Polly's people had Live Oaks. It must have been quite a scene, horses and hounds and ladies and gentlemen drinking juleps out of silver cups early in the day. They looked rich, but it was all a joke. They were always, all of them, on the edge of losing everything. They never let it show. That was their style." Lockwood stepped off the gravel path onto the spongy turf. He extended an arm and wriggled a forefinger as if he were sketching the absent riders and their plunging hunters in the empty air.

"I suppose we'll have to act," Lockwood said. "The question is, what can we do?" Lockwood was thinking aloud; he didn't require an answer. "Is there anyone in Hagreb who can talk to Ibn Awad, take him a message from me?"

"The ambassador could do that, sir. I don't know how effective it might be. You haven't met Awad; to him, you're a faraway figure without much reality. You have to remember, he's never even been up in an airplane. The United States is as remote to him as the planets are to you."

"You say he's out in the desert by himself. I assume you know where, exactly."

"We have a radio fix on his tent; there's a transmitter in the pole. We think he's going to meet Hassan."

"Follow him."

"The landscape there is as bare as a tabletop. As bright as this." Philindros looked around at the floodlights. "He'd see us. He'd turn back; he'd give the bombs to Hassan another time. We'd lose all we have."

Lockwood nodded, absorbing this information. "Suppose I ordered a plane and flew to Hagreb now. Could you get me to him? Could I talk to him?"

This idea made Lockwood glow. He gave Philindros a triumphant look.

Philindros said, "No doubt you could get to him by helicopter from Hagreb City. I don't know how you could do this in secret, Mr. President."

"Secret, hell! I'll go on all networks and tell the people exactly what's going on, exactly what I'm trying to prevent."

"You mean, tell the truth to the world?"

Lockwood gave his raucous laugh. "Right! What's wrong with the truth?"

Philindros cleared his throat. "The truth works very slowly," he said. "Much slower than Hassan Abdallah. If you go on television before you go to Hagreb, you'll be warning them. You'll be too late."

"If I don't go, they'll do the same thing anyway. The bombs will go off," Lockwood said. "What, exactly, have we got to lose by coming out in the open like decent men?"

Philindros took a step backwards. It was Julian who answered. "Everything," he said. "In the best case, Ibn Awad will simply deny the plot. What evidence do we have?"

"Jack's report. The bombs."

"We don't know where the bombs are. Why should Awad tell us? He's perceived by the world as a man of peace and healing, a saintly figure."

"We have proof that he's mad."

"We have a medical opinion of American doctors. Who paid the doctors, Jack?"

"They were all staff physicians of the FIS," Philindros said.

"American spies. Who in the world would believe them?" Julian said. "Suppose you should fail altogether? Suppose you go to Hagreb in a blaze of publicity and talk to Ibn Awad, and he then gives the bombs to the Eye of Gaza. A city, perhaps two cities, would be destroyed. We're talking about a hundred thousand dead. On television."

Lockwood gave a shudder, like an animal bothered by stinging insects. "You're assuming I'll fail," he said. "Why should I fail?"

Philindros gave Julian a look of appeal.

"Because Ibn Awad is insane," Julian said.

Lockwood looked from one man to the other and turned his back on them. He folded his arms and bowed his head, and spoke without turning. "What you two fellows are saying is that Ibn Awad and the Eye of Gaza cannot be stopped. We're helpless."

Philindros let a moment pass, waiting to see if Julian would speak. Julian said nothing. He knew what must happen next, and he could have stopped it. He didn't. He never understood why, though in years to come he relived this scene again and again in his memory.

"No, Mr. President," Philindros said, "I don't think we're helpless. I'm doing what the law requires me to do. I'm informing the President of the facts."

Lockwood said, "You never go beyond facts?"

"No, sir. But let me repeat a fact. Ibn Awad is a manic-depressive. Just now he's in a manic period. But he has deep depressions, too. When he's in the depressive cycle he talks openly and often about suicide. He disguises his suicidal urge with rhetoric about sacrificing his life in a way that will glorify God, but suicide is what he means."

"You want me to hope he'll commit suicide? Even lunatics don't kill themselves at their moment of triumph. Ibn Awad is on the verge of destroying Israel by fire."

"Nobody knows that but us—and Ibn Awad."

The meaning of Philindros's words did not register at once. Then Lockwood understood and he took a lunging step towards the other man. The violence of his movement made the coins jingle in his pockets.

"Are you telling me that bringing about Ibn Awad's . . . suicide is among FIS's capabilities?"

Philindros said, "Yes." The simple word alone, without his usual care to follow it with an honorific.

"There *must* be an alternative."

"Perhaps there is, sir. You have all the information FIS can provide. It's your province, Mr. President, to make the decision."

"Kill a man?" Lockwood said. "*Assassinate* somebody?"

Philindros didn't bother to look in Julian's direction. His eyes were on the President.

"You're offering me a cup of poison," Lockwood said.

Something moved in the depths of Philindros's opaque brown eyes. It was gone in an instant. He waited. There was no sign of expectation in his face; his expression was as neutral as his voice.

Julian thought, There *is* no alternative. Ibn Awad, thousands of miles away in the desert, is forcing Lockwood to kill him.

Lockwood looked into Julian's eyes and read the thought. The President cleared his throat. "Mr. Director," he said. His voice failed. He turned his eyes away from Philindros and, with a convulsive movement, nodded his head.

He turned and strode across the grass. The Secret Service men, waiting on the gravel walk, spoke into their crackling radios.

"Mr. President," Philindros said.

Lockwood continued to walk away, taking long strides over the wet ground. Philindros repeated himself. Lockwood turned. Philindros waited where he was and the President returned to him.

"I'm sorry, sir," Philindros said, "but I don't understand whether you've just given me an instruction."

"I think you understand, Jack," Lockwood said.

"No, Mr. President, I do not."

No two men had ever seen each other's face more clearly. The lights emphasized every bitter line in Lockwood's. Philindros had the profile of a Greek statue, nose growing straight down from his brow. In plain words, he told Lockwood how Ibn Awad could be killed. Again he waited.

Julian knew well enough what Philindros wanted from Lockwood, and why he wanted it. So did Lockwood. Some of Philindros's predecessors had killed for Presidents, killed on the basis of a hint, a gesture, a nod of the head. They took the guilt on themselves. But the time when freedom from guilt was counted among the rights of Presidents was over. Philindros was willing to be an instrument. That was his duty. But he would not commit murder without making Lockwood—as a man and as President—the author of the crime.

"I must have a clear, spoken order," Philindros said. "Do you instruct me, Mr. President, to use the assets of the Foreign Intelligence Service to bring about the violent death of Ibn Awad and to gain possession of the two nuclear devices now in his possession?"

Lockwood breathed in and out, one great breath. Philindros wrenched the answer from him.

"Yes," he said; and strode away. His Secret Service guards closed in around him, some of them trotting to keep up, as he hurried towards the house.

Julian and Philindros followed more slowly, and by the time they reached the porch, Lockwood had vanished upstairs.

Polly was asleep and the house was quiet except for its own noises—the creak of timbers, the rhythmic tick of a grandfather clock which sounded louder, owing to some trick of acoustics, in the downstairs hall than in the room, three doors deeper in the house, where it stood. There was a smell of fresh wax on the gleaming pine floors.

"Do you want to use the scrambler phone?" Julian asked.

"No. The message has to pass directly from me to the field man; I'll be in Langley in time." Philindros looked at his watch. "It's only nine in the morning in Hagreb; we have till noon, their time."

"Well, then."

"If the situation changes . . ."

"Will it?"

"I doubt it. If it does, the President will know."

Julian nodded. He picked up an ordinary phone and ordered the helicopter readied. Then he drove Philindros back to the pad. The helicopter blades were turning long before they arrived. Julian stopped the Jeep in the woods while they were still far enough away from the stuttering machine to hear one another.

"Shall I fly down tomorrow to give the President a report?"

"I imagine it will be on the news."

"Yes, but the details . . ."

One of the greyhounds put his paws on the back of Julian's seat and, snuffling and whining, licked his face. Julian pushed the animal away; it wanted to play and he had to hold its squirming body off with one hand while he finished talking to Philindros.

"No," Julian said. "No details. Not tomorrow, not ever. He knows enough."

Julian's face was as impassive as Philindros's. Only by guesswork could the spy know how much Julian hated him for what he had just made Lockwood do.

In the rose garden where they were having breakfast three years afterwards, Lockwood watched the fly on his pancakes. The insect had trapped itself in the syrup. Lockwood lifted its struggling body on the blunt point of a butter knife and put it gently on the tablecloth. After a desperate effort its gummed wings regained the power of flight.

"Julian was right to do what he did," Lockwood said. "But now, I guess, we'd better have the whole story."

Philindros started to speak. Once again Lockwood held up a hand to stop him.

"Deal with Julian. Give him all the evidence you have on the Awad case."

"*All* of it, sir?"

Lockwood lifted his head. "Something wrong?"

"No, but it's an enormous file, going back twenty years. It would take days to read it."

"Digest it, then. Really only the last days are important, and the evidence of Awad's insanity. And the bombs."

Lockwood rose to his feet. He had left his old hat on the lawn beside him and he stooped to pick it up. He looked at the sky from under its brim. The sun hung on the horizon like a spot of rouge on a powdery cheek. "Gonna have some weather," Lockwood said.

Philindros looked at Julian, and Julian got the President's attention again. Lockwood wasn't pleased to return to a subject he'd exhausted.

"I want Julian to have a good briefing, Jack," he said. "Every last little thing. I may have to defend this."

"I'll have to bring back the man who handled the case. He's still out there."

"Fine. Do it soon. Julian will talk to him."

Lockwood held out his hand. Philindros grasped it, intending to give it a quick pressure. Lockwood wouldn't let him withdraw; he held Philindros's small limber fingers in his own great horny

86

ones and pulled him a step closer. Philindros felt the President's breath on his face.

"I can defend this, Jack, can't I? In public? Everything's as you reported?"

"Yes, but there's a problem, Mr. President."

Lockwood held on to Philindros. Julian moved around so that he could see the faces of both men. Philindros was uncomfortable. He was a small man between two very large ones.

"It would have been better to have accepted a report on this at the time," he said. "We never found the bombs. There's no evidence—no physical evidence—that they existed."

Lockwood didn't speak. Julian said, "Witnesses?"

"Talil is gone, of course," Philindros said. "But there's the man we're bringing back from the field, the one who handled Talil. He'll tell you what happened, and you can be the judge."

"Who is he?" asked Lockwood.

"Horace Hubbard," Philindros said.

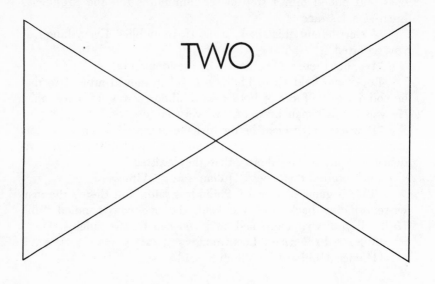

TWO

1

HORACE spent an hour with Sebastian Laux, the president of
D. & D. Laux & Co., while waiting for Philindros to come up to
New York for their meeting. Old Laux had been in the OSS with
Horace's father; he and Elliott Hubbard had been dropped into
Picardy together in 1944. "It was my job to talk French, your
father's to outwit the Germans," Sebastian told Horace, not for
the first time. "We must both of us have been adequate, because
we came through all right. Lots of the younger men didn't—it
takes seasoning to feel intelligent fear. Elliott and I were old even
then, by military standards." He gave Horace tea, from a tinkling
cart that was wheeled in at four o'clock by an employee whose
aged skin was as yellowed and transparent as Sebastian's own.
The two old men, banker and servant, poised over the silver service,
with the afternoon sun falling on them, looked like figures carved
out of Pears' soap.

This tea ceremony was the chief thing Philindros had liked
about D. & D. Laux & Co. when Horace, accompanied by his father,
had introduced him to the place and to Sebastian. Philindros had
admired the look of the old private bank from the outside—it was
a Greek Revival temple in the Doric style, its marble facing blackened by the fumes of centuries; jostled on all sides by the vulgar
glass towers of the financial district, D. & D. Laux & Co. was all

but invisible to the passerby. But it was the elegant old man, pouring tea into Raku bowls and talking of his war adventures, that touched Philindros's love for the right theatrical touch in a cover mechanism. "We slept rough, in the fields, Elliott and I," Sebastian told him; "it was spring, the invasion was coming, we were dynamiting bridges and things; but what I remember after all these years is the smell of the fields in the morning: wild-flowers, Mr. Philindros, a sea of blossoms—there really *are* roses in Picardy!"

Philindros came directly to the point. For many years, Horace had been carrying out his FIS duties, with Sebastian's knowledge, as the Near East representative of D. & D. Laux & Co.; Philindros proposed an enlargement of this arrangement.

Work like Horace's was supposed to have been eliminated by the reform of the intelligence community that followed the investigations of the CIA. Covert action was banished from the charter of the new Foreign Intelligence Service. But the very President who had destroyed the CIA soon believed that he could not maintain America's position in the world, or his own power to make things happen, without the old secret apparatus; dark acts were sometimes necessary, and often good acts had to be performed in the dark. The old covert action staff, renamed and operating under new controls, was revived.

In days past, men like Horace had worked out of American embassies, posing as diplomats. The State Department had always despised them, had felt sullied by their masquerade. The diplomatists put up with the spies because at that time only an embassy provided the things an intelligence service must have to operate abroad: secure storage of records, safe communications, untouchability of staff through diplomatic immunity. The computer had solved two of these problems. First, there was no longer any need to file paper; all information could be reduced to electronic impulses and stored in a central data bank. This information could be put beyond the reach of an enemy, could be erased by touching a button. Second, computer-related technology had produced radio equipment that could squirt a million words from one continent to another via satellite in a droplet of electric energy that required less than a millisecond to send or receive. Space was filled with particles of data traveling at the speed of light from computer to earthbound computer. No power had the resources to sort them all out, much less decode them.

Last, the immunity of intelligence agents was impossible to attain in the modern world. No diplomatic passport, no idea of sovereign territory, no flag, meant anything to men like Hassan

Abdallah of the Eye of Gaza. They killed or kidnapped or tortured whom they chose, when they chose. These losses could not be prevented.

Sebastian Laux, wearing a beautifully tailored suit that was ten years out of style, had eaten a strawberry tart while Philindros explained all this. The gold watch in Sebastian's breast pocket, secured by a chain wound through the buttonhole in his lapel, chimed the half hour.

"So you want to take your men out of the embassies and put them into my bank?" he said.

"Yes. We anticipate large profits. There would be no financial risk to you or your stockholders. There would be no written contract, no trace of our agreement. Of course, a measure of control over the bank's character would pass out of the hands of your family. Horace has suggested that that might trouble you."

The walls of Sebastian's office were hung with oil portraits of earlier presidents. Many looked remarkably like Sebastian, their faces had a kind of pinched merriment, and half of them had his Christian name. There was also one especially fine screen of the Momoyama period. First-born sons had been bank presidents; younger ones had been missionaries and collectors.

"My family opened D. & D. Laux & Co. in 1820," Sebastian said to Philindros. "They're all dead but me and my sisters, and as the three of us are very old and unmarried, control of this banking house will pass out of our hands whether we're troubled about it or not. Bless Horace—he's turned into a pretty good banker; and he is my godson—but the Laux blood has run out."

Philindros, therefore, bought out D. & D. Laux & Co. He opened branches in Brussels for Europe, Beirut for the Near East, Tokyo for the Far East, São Paulo for Latin America, and Johannesburg for Black Africa. The bankers who had always run D. & D. Laux & Co. for the benefit of the Laux family went on doing so. The business brought in by the dynamic young staff Philindros put into the branches made the bank richer than ever in its history. The computers and communications in New York were handled by Philindros's technicians. Abroad, the banks provided men like Horace with all they needed: a reason to exist and travel, a reason to own elaborate data processing equipment and powerful radio transmitters and lock them up in massive vaults, and a reason to be secretive. Bankers were expected to be secretive. It was a more efficient system than the old one that had tied the CIA to the embassies, and a much more imaginative one. Besides, it gave Sebastian Laux a whiff of Picardy.

* * *

The old servant, trembling, passed around the cakes and departed. Sebastian poured. He sipped from his bowl, taking in a lot of air with the hot liquid; Sebastian was a connoisseur of teas in the way that other men have a palate for wines. He pursed his lips and identified the leaf from which the tea had been brewed. "It's hard to get passable green tea from Japan; most of them fertilize with chemicals now," he said. "You've got to use oily fish and night soil to get the proper taste. Your man Percy Andrews brings me the right stuff from Tokyo when he comes to New York. He's a silly sort of bird, Horace—he went to Princeton, can't spell, none of them can—but he knows tea and he knows banking. I hope he's as good at your side of the work."

"He is."

"Good," said Sebastian. He nibbled at his strawberry tart, holding it, as he had held the tea bowl, in both hands, like a squirrel.

Horace felt affection rush into his chest. "Our side of it hasn't been a worry to you all these years?"

"Of course not. It made the bank more private than it ever was, and that's a very good thing. Then, you fellows have brought in ten times the business we had before. My only worry is my age." Sebastian sucked more tea into his mouth and tapped himself on the breastbone. "This clock will stop someday soon. I'm older than your father was, you know. I want a good man taking my place in this office—you. You're the nearest thing to a relative I've got. I keep on telling your inscrutable friend Philindros that. He listens in silence."

"Maybe he doesn't think quite as much of me as a banker as you do, Sebastian."

"That's not it. He thinks any fool can be president of a bank, but it takes real brains to do what you do. He wants you as *his* successor. It's a great mistake to be too good at anything, Horace." Sebastian touched his bloodless lips with a napkin. "When I left college I wanted to go to Montparnasse and write unpublished poems and have mistresses. I dreamt of rose-lipt maidens in a garret. But my father died young and the family glued me to this chair, and here I've been for sixty years."

"Except for the roses of Picardy."

"Too brief an escape. Ah, well!"

Sebastian poured more tea and offered another cake. The silver pot, thinned by a hundred years of polishing, could have been pierced like rice paper with a stiff forefinger.

2

At five, Sebastian departed. After walking him to the door, and putting him into the hands of his guards, Horace made his way across the long Hamadan carpet that covered the floor of the main hall. Years before, when camel's hair was still obtainable, worn bits had been rewoven and now it showed splotches of brown in many shades, like a diseased lawn. Beneath the building lay the vaults, and beyond the door that led into the FIS safe rooms, D. & D. Laux's traditional tones of mahogany paneling and oil portraits and Persian carpet gave way to gray steel and pastel paint and fluorescent light. FIS people were always on duty here, tending the computers and the radios. Day and night there was invisible but heavy armed security. The technicians were simply locked in the main vault; they could summon help or, in the worst emergency, empty the computers of all data, long before any attackers could blast their way into the safe. The release of nerve gas could prevent that, in any case. Horace used the same arrangements in Beirut.

Philindros was waiting inside a smaller vault, in a cubicle called the "talks room" that was used for meetings of this kind. He shook hands with Horace without rising from his chair. Horace sat down. Between them on a steel table was a chromium tray bearing a chromium thermos jug, filled with water, and two plastic glasses. Philindros wasn't interested in Sebastian's afternoon tea for himself, but for its lulling effect on others. He hardly ever came to the bank.

"I think we may have a flap building up over Ibn Awad," Philindros said. He had stated no reason for summoning Horace home in his cable to Beirut, merely instructed him to be present in this place at this time; that was normal procedure, and it hadn't surprised Horace.

Horace showed no surprise now, nor did he interrupt, while Philindros told him all that had happened in his meeting the previous morning with Lockwood and Julian.

"Your brother is going to be uncomfortable when you see him tomorrow," Philindros said. "I told him yesterday, for the first time, that you had been the case officer on the Awad project."

"He hadn't assumed that already?"

"Evidently not. He may have taken it for granted I'd have the good taste not to use his own brother to commit official murder." Philandros did not employ euphemisms.

"He thinks my involvement gives you some sort of hold over the President?"

92

"Yes. And of course, it does."

Horace took in this information as Philindros knew he would; it was a fact among others. He and Philindros knew each other as well as either of them could be known. They had come through the shambles of the CIA together because they were then too young and too junior, but only just, not to be purged. Both knew well enough that Lockwood would play any card in his hand to save himself if he had to defend the assassination in public. Philindros had taken away his trump. He could not imply, as Kennedy had done after the Bay of Pigs, "It's my responsibility, but it's *their* fault." Not when the brother of the President's closest aide had put the gun into the assassin's hand.

"How did Patrick Graham ever get onto this?" Horace asked.

"I don't know. It's a pity we don't know who he saw in Baghdad."

"Yes. Had he come to me first in Beirut I might have been able to keep an eye on him. But he didn't."

"You got no hint from him?"

"He mentioned the Eye of Gaza."

"Hassan?"

"Patrick was still panting when he came to me in Beirut. We know Hassan slips in and out of Baghdad. The Iraqis won't touch him. It's possible."

"How could Hassan, even Hassan, *know* anything? He never got the bombs; he never got near Talil."

"If there *were* any bombs. Lockwood knows we couldn't find them?"

"Yes."

Horace scratched his cheek. "Who could have put Patrick Graham and Hassan Abdallah together?"

Philindros pointed to the computers, the long whispering row of them, on one of the television screens that covered one wall of the talks room. "We're scanning. The source may pop up."

They discussed the history of the operation. This was not information that could be put on the air and into the computers. When everything was done verbally, when there were no records, even trained men like Philindros and Horace Hubbard sometimes forogt to tell one another things that later turned out to be vitally important. Horace went over his part of it—the subtle handling of Prince Talil, the painstaking physical and technical arrangements he had made to assure that he alone controlled events.

"This is by way of rehearsal," Philindros said. "You'll have to tell your brother all this."

"All?"

"That's the President's order. I want it carried out. Nothing omitted."

Horace received this instruction with outward calm. He could not imagine how Julian would weather this tale—the brutal narration of detail upon detail. Julian would have to accept that he and Lockwood had been responsible for doing murder. Horace knew Julian had always believed Lockwood incapable of such an act; the whole world, even his enemies, believed him incapable of it. Horace already knew that he, Horace, was a murderer; when he entered on his vocation he began living with the realization that he was prepared to become a murderer. Could Julian admit such a thing about himself, about Lockwood? Had they thought about it? Had they watched the news of it on television, even? Horace doubted it, from what he knew of men who were in love with power. It was one thing to hear a man you loved as a second Lincoln give an order to kill a man halfway around the world. It was another thing to be lifted up to the coffin and forced to put your bare hand on the corpse.

Horace loved his brother, but all his life he had been exasperated by people who thought as Julian did. Julian believed that some men did good in the world and others did evil, and that he had joined the right side. Julian, all his life, had wanted to see the world perfected in one man—first their father, now Lockwood.

Horace, on the other hand, perceived that nothing ran unmixed in men or causes or nations. Evil was permanent and it was everywhere. What mattered was that it should be channeled, tricked into working for your own side. That was what an intelligence service was for. That was why Horace had spent his life in espionage.

"Are they panicked by this?" Horace asked.

"Not yet. But the political conventions are next month, and the election—the last American presidential election of the 1900s, think of it—takes place in November."

"They suspect Mallory?"

"They didn't say so, but he's the usual suspect when anything threatens them," Philindros said. "If Mallory's found a way to use Graham as a cat's-paw, after what Graham did to him four years ago, then Lockwood and Julian *ought* to be worried."

"Is that possible?"

Philindros tried to go on speaking but he was able to utter nothing more than a hoarse croak. He shook his head in annoyance. His throat had closed; this always happened to him when he had to talk for any length of time in an air-conditioned room. He poured

94

water from the thermos and drank, throwing back his head so as to bathe the whole parched lining of his throat.

"Who knows?" he said at last. "Your brother is our best hope of finding out. He's always had a string on Graham. Maybe he still has."

Philindros knew the interconnecting histories of most powerful Americans. He didn't keep files or run investigations; that was forbidden. He merely listened and observed and remembered. He had made himself, a man who came from outside the elite, an expert on the power structure of the United States. He was capable of electrifying insights; Horace thought that he must be the descendant of a line of undiscovered geniuses, unlettered men who had been locked away in the Greek mountains by poverty or the Turks, and that their genes had finally come into their own in Philindros's subtle and elusive mind. Jack Philindros, Horace knew, believed that the CIA had died because of a hidden but fatal weakness. Its men, the most brilliant ever brought together in one organization, understood every country in the world except their own. They never studied the United States because they never imagined that it could become an enemy and attack them. When the onslaught came, they were helpless to defend themselves. Philindros would not let that happen to his FIS.

Philindros, intense, leaned towards Horace; he even lifted a hand. "I wonder, Horace," he said, "if your brother realizes that there's not going to be any way out of this for Lockwood. Even if they hush Graham, the other side will find another outlet. You see that, don't you?"

"Oh, yes. Julian will, too. It may take him a little time."

"And in the meantime, he'll look for a solution."

"I suppose he will. Wouldn't you?" Horace made a gesture that acknowledged their long friendship. "Wouldn't I?"

"Yes. But if all else failed, you wouldn't fall on your own sword to save Lockwood."

"You think that Julian might?"

Philindros shrugged. He stood up and turned the combination lock that was mounted on the inside of the door of the talks room.

"I'll leave you now," he said. "Talk to your brother. Think some more. You'll have to stick around as long as the White House wants you."

Philindros, having unlocked the door, stood for a moment in silence, watching the row of television screens. The image of a tall woman wearing a long starched coat, like those worn by physicians on hospital rounds, appeared on one of the monitors. She was standing by a computer unit, and she put her hand on its metal surface and cocked her head, as if listening for some particular sound. For the first time, Philindros smiled; his teeth were as perfect as an actor's.

"There's Rose," he said.

Rose MacKenzie was the officer in charge of the night operation. She was a two-interest person. Electronics was her vocation; she could hear distress in the hum of a computer, and fix the trouble, in the way an old-time mechanic diagnosed breakdown in the cough of a flivver's engine. Her other interest was Horace Hubbard; they had been lovers and colleagues for a long time; she'd been with Horace when Talil died. That's how they spoke of the Awad operation: as the time when Talil died.

Philindros pressed a button and the lens of the closed-circuit camera zoomed in on Rose MacKenzie. She heard the change in the tone of the equipment—few others would have done so—and lifted her face. It was a spare face, freckled; her bright hair was pulled back tight for work; her ears were quite large. Her wide mouth curved in a smile.

"I think she knows you're here," Philindros said. "She's doing the scan on Hassan and Graham. No one else could. You can talk to her about all this as much as you like. She was with you in Hagreb, after all."

He raised a hand in farewell and left. Horace looked at Rose's screen, and she was still there, grinning into the camera. Her lips opened and formed a word. Horace read the silent syllable: "When?"

She couldn't see him and he couldn't answer her through twenty feet of steel and reinforced concrete. Rose was locked in for the night.

Horace refused the car that awaited him in the garage, and went into the street alone. Dark had fallen, and Hanover Square was empty. He walked west towards the Hudson through the deserted streets to the building where Rose lived. She'd phoned ahead; Condon, her security man, was expecting him.

Horace put his key into the lock of Rose's apartment and, as the bolt clicked, heard the quick thud and patter of many sets of paws as her cats leaped and ran to hiding places. Horace's body was in New York, but its nervous system was still in Beirut, where the sun had been down for seven hours. He did not call Julian. He had a glass of brandy and got into Rose's bed. She had made it with the several books she was reading—two inscrutable mathematical texts, the score of *Don Giovanni, Cakes and Ale*—still scattered inside the covers. Horace went to sleep at once.

Very early in the morning, he felt Rose's long body, the skin still cold and the hair a little damp from her walk in the rain, pressed against his. He put an arm around her.

"Us first," Rose whispered. "Then, my God, what I have to tell you!"

Rose could never sleep after lovemaking, and she leaped from the bed when they were done. Her hair was dry now, and it flew as she hurried from the bedroom. Horace put on a dressing gown and followed her to the kitchen. Rose had brought lox and cream cheese and bagels with her and she was on her knees in front of the cluttered refrigerator, removing small dishes of leftovers and putting them on the floor.

"Somewhere in this fridge there's a bottle of sparkling Vouvray," she said. Rose found the wine at the back of a shelf and handed it to Horace to be opened. They ate the delicatessen food from the paper it came in.

"You were going to tell me something," Horace said.

"Ah. I woke Jack to tell *him*. He told you I'd been scanning for traces of that thing you're working on. I started with other computers in Beirut." Rose was a famous tapper; she could find a way, using her superb computers, to read the contents of any other computer in the world. She took another bite of her bagel. At the corner of her mouth there was a little spot of cream cheese and Horace reached over and wiped it off with his fingertip.

"And guess what?" continued Rose. "I found that a computer out there—the main data bank of Universal Energy—knew some things that only our computer was supposed to know."

"How can that be?"

"They tapped us, obviously. They have a lot of our stuff on Ibn Awad; and it's ours, all right; it's in our handwriting."

Rose drank sparkling Vouvray. She made another sandwich and cut it in half, part for Horace and part for herself. She was interested in phenomena, not in their implications.

"But I thought our equipment was untappable."

Rose chewed and swallowed. "What man has made," she said, "man can understand."

97

3

Horace had never visited his brother at work, in fact had never been inside the White House. He was surprised by the smallness of Julian's quarters; there was no more than enough room for both their long bodies in Julian's office, already crowded with a large desk, a file safe, a wall of books. Julian was the second most powerful man in the United States government, yet he worked pressed against a smudged wall in an office that didn't even have a door leading into a corridor; Horace, hidden deep in the body of the same government, occupied an office in Beirut where kings and emirs and billionaire sheikhs, who often came there, would feel themselves in a space large enough, and rich enough, to befit their presence. Julian, like Sebastian Laux in his old suits, needed no display to signal who he was.

Horace took the one visitor's chair, a soft leather easy chair whose worn springs sagged beneath his weight. His head was much lower than Julian's, which was framed by the high back of a swivel chair. Julian's desk was clear, nothing on its polished top except a telephone, a pen stand, a blotter; and a large framed photograph that Horace, who could see only the back of it, guessed must be Julian's inscribed picture of President Lockwood. The one clear wall was crowded with framed photographs. Horace, looking at these while Julian finished a telephone call, saw that they were not the posed pictures of politicians that he might have expected to find, but a collection of family portraits. Their father was there in a naval uniform and in a Sunfish with Julian; Horace himself appeared as a captain of Marines and in an Exeter letter sweater; there were others—their grandparents; aunts and cousins; Julian's children with their mother; Emily; Lipton, the gardener at the Harbor, who had been thought tetched by the great-aunts but who, as the boys knew, was made dreamy because he chewed the leaves of the marijuana that he grew in the greenhouse. Horace hadn't seen, or thought about, most of these faces for years.

Julian had no smile for his brother. "I suppose you've talked to Jack Philindros," he said.

"Yes, on my way here."

"Horace, you and I are going to have to work together on this. Before we go onto a professional footing I want to say something to you as your brother."

Horace nodded, looking upward into Julian's steady eyes. His brother was sitting bolt upright, fingers laced on the desk before him.

"Jack Philindros may have some idea he can use the fact that you and I are brothers against the President. That will not happen, I promise you."

Horace could hear the clatter of a secretary's typewriter through the thin wall behind him. Julian was making no effort to moderate his voice; Horace wasn't comfortable. He responded in a lower tone.

"Why should you fear any such thing? Nothing has happened yet. Patrick Graham has raised some dust. He may know nothing."

"We'll come to Patrick Graham later. I'm speaking to another problem. You. More accurately, you and me. You know as well as I do what your involvement means."

In Julian's voice there was a rasp of anger, the tone of a man looking for a quarrel. Horace spoke softly.

"It means," Horace replied, "that I was the FIS resident in that part of the world. It means that I had the necessary access to the target. It means nobody else could do it. That's all it *means*. You're talking about how it *looks*. That's a different matter, and I see your point."

"You didn't see it three years ago, when you were given that order?"

"Of course. But I'm under discipline. What I'm instructed to do, I do."

"Without question? Without examination of the consequences?"

"Consequences," said Horace, "are not my problem. They're the President's problem and yours. You both have brains. I assumed you knew what you were doing, that you had examined the options, as they used to say thirty-five years ago in this house, when assassination was a new toy."

"Don't compare us to those people."

Beyond Julian's rigid body, framed in the window at his back, were the lawns of the White House. The sprinkler system was on. The sun, shining through the playing waters, created rainbows. Horace watched the colors in the dancing spray, collecting his thoughts; he wanted to give Julian time to reflect on what he had just said. He and Julian were not thinking of the same people. It made no difference. Those who had sat in Julian's place—possibly in this same mean room just down the corridor from the Oval Office—justifying the attempts on Castro and Diem and the rest might well have felt just as Julian did. They were very old men now. They had spent what was left of their lives arranging for the blame to fall on others, preserving their President's myth.

"You think Jack Philindros tricked the President—that I tricked

99

you, Julian—by not telling you I was involved in Awad's murder?"

"You and Philindros both. Horace, I didn't even know you were in the FIS until I learned it by accident, in this job. Now, to learn this about you . . ."

"About me? Didn't President Lockwood give the order, with your advice and approval?"

"Perhaps. But to use my brother, to make me responsible for sending you out to kill . . ."

"Julian."

Horace leaned towards his brother, put a hand on the edge of the desk. He saw that the silver frame on Julian's desk contained two photographs—Lockwood on one side, Elliott Hubbard on the other, both men frozen on film at about the age of fifty-five, both outdoors with the sun shining on their faces.

"That night in New York, after Pa died, after Emily had gone upstairs," Horace said. "You began to tell me something. Do you remember?"

"I remember. You stopped me."

"I thought it must be this business. I didn't know how you could *not* know about my part in it. There was no point in talking about it; the thing was done."

"It might have been better to talk then than now. We were never more brothers than we were that night."

Horace raised his hand, a shadow of the gesture he had made in their father's dining room the winter before. "We're not responsible for each other," he said. He settled back into his chair. He told himself to be careful: he was so used to handling men in their moments of weakness, and this man was his brother, and the President's assistant.

"Philindros might not believe that," Julian said.

"He would. He knows the world wouldn't. Jack has a long memory, Julian. He knows what happened in the past in affairs like this one. He loves the FIS. He loves this country. He doesn't think they can exist without each other."

"So he'd destroy the country to save the FIS?"

"Is that really your question, Julian? If you want to know if he'd humiliate a President to save the FIS, the answer is yes. That would just tie the game, a generation after the last time a President put the blame on us for what *he'd* done. We couldn't survive another scandal."

Horace spoke in the tones of a reasonable man. To him, the case was obvious. All at once, Julian realized that Horace was bound by ties of brotherhood to something that he loved more, perhaps, than he loved his family. Julian swiveled in his chair and

100

looked out the window as Horace had done a few moments before. A pair of Zeiss field glasses that Elliott Hubbard had brought back as a war trophy hung by their worn leather strap on a hook screwed into the sash. Horace guessed that Julian watched birds in odd moments, perhaps while he chewed a sandwich during a hurried lunch, his mind still on the President's work. Horace was pleased by the thought of Julian identifying some unusual species in the White House shrubbery and noting the sighting in his field book. "I never stop seeing the boy in Julian," their father had said to Horace after the three of them had lunched together on Ninety-third Street to celebrate Lockwood's election to the presidency. Neither did Horace: his brother's outgrown younger face was always visible to him in the craggy features of the grown man; he heard the lighter voice of the child in Julian's baritone. Julian swung around to face him again.

"Our hope is to contain this story," he said. "Our expectation is that we won't be able to do so. In that case, I want to keep the damage to the President to a minimum."

Horace nodded.

"Tell me everything about your part in this," Julian said.

4

The Awad situation was only one thread, though a scarlet one, in the fabric of Julian's day. Horace told his story—what had actually happened—in minute detail; what he had felt played no part in his narrative. In his profession, emotions were not discussed; that was its only privacy.

There were incessant interruptions. Julian's telephone rang relentlessly; he was pestered by members of the staff whose problems could not wait, by senators who could not be ignored, by political workers who were planning the last details of the party's convention in New York. Julian had had the bold idea of renominating Lockwood in Mallory's own city, to dramatize the changes the Lockwood Administration had made there. A young woman with a pencil thrust in her hair came in and, ignoring Horace's presence, perched on a sliding pile of documents that filled the old green sofa beneath Julian's family pictures; she had a Mallory story.

"He's going to ask for a constitutional convention if he can lie his way back into the White House," she said. "Can you imagine? A few small modifications of the Bill of Rights, a minor rewording of the other Amendments. They say he has a plan to institutionalize everyone who's committed one violent crime for life; all those kids he's marked down as criminals would be put away before they could do harm; anyone with an extra chromosome would be sterilized. They talk of a vast new prison in Alaska, on the North Slope, *underground*, Julian—just one way in, a steel hatch in the tundra, and no way out. Can you believe it?"

Julian listened patiently. "Research it," he said; the girl went away.

Horace, a lover of women—their tempers, their bodies, the force of their love and hate—watched the girl's fine back disappear. "Is Franklin Mallory really such an ogre?" he asked.

Julian grunted. "It does no harm to have smart people like Mary, there, think so. Mallory wants to take this government back. But we're going to keep it."

The reason Julian's office was so small became apparent; he had sacrificed size for proximity to the President. It was separated from the Oval Office only by one tiny room used by Lockwood as a place to change clothes and take cat naps. At the sound of a buzzer, Julian would disappear through a low door, frameless and set flush into the plaster wall. Once or twice Horace caught glimpses of the President; near the end of the day, Julian responded to a knock on the door and when he opened it Lockwood stood on the other side, naked to the waist, removing the laundry's cardboard from a fresh shirt. Lockwood saw Horace but made no acknowledgment of his presence.

By the day's end, Horace wasn't sure that Julian had absorbed anything that he had told him.

"I have a feeling that I've been shouting into the wind all day," Horace said.

"I've had no trouble hearing you."

It was six in the evening. The typewriters had ceased; untended telephones rang in deserted offices. Lights seldom burned at midnight in Lockwood's White House. By six o'clock he and his staff had already worked twelve hours; the President believed a man who couldn't do his job in that length of time was inefficient. Lockwood came in to say good-bye to Julian before he went upstairs to join Polly; again, he ignored Horace.

"Why don't you go over to O Street by yourself?" Julian said. "We can have dinner. Emily and the kids want to see you. The guest room is made up for you."

"What about you?"

"I have to do my diary. It's something I never neglect."

Horace's solemnity vanished. "Pa again." Elliott Hubbard had kept a journal for fifty years, writing a full page on vellum paper in

102

a calfskin volume each night before he slept. Julian got his diaries from the same company in New York, with the year stamped in gold leaf on the spine.

"Pa had you burn his, did he?"

"Yes; I did it at the bank—the facilities are there," Horace said. "It was quite a load. I wonder what was inside. If he told all he knew about everyone he knew, a lot of secret history went up in smoke."

Julian smiled. "I don't know who'll burn mine. Jenny, I think."

He showed Horace the way to the garage. Then he went back to his office, opened his safe, and got out his diary. He held it in his hands for a moment, liking the compact weight of it and the texture and scent of its leather cover. He enjoyed the discipline of keeping the journal; it gave him fluency in his real work. Julian, like his father before him, never had a writer's block; sentences, paragraphs, pages of English leaped out of him. He took up his pen, and after a long interval of thought, began to write.

I find this difficult to write. I've sat for a long time with the ink drying on the point of the pen, remembering over and over again, like a film run backwards and forwards, that day when I lay drugged in the hospital in Hawaii and Horace, against every rule I thought he had, leaned over and kissed me as he said good-bye. He had just told me to love life and want it.

Today my brother and I have come together because I made a murderer out of him.

Of course Philindros knew what the effect of using Horace would be. He has the right sort of name, Philindros: there is a Greek cunning in him. It is his profession—it is in his blood—to know what the rest of us have forgotten: that the simplest tricks, the oldest, always work best. I can never sacrifice Philindros, never advise Lockwood to sacrifice him or the FIS, unless I am willing to sacrifice my brother as well. Never have I been so utterly outwitted, never so stung by surprise.

Philindros let me know what a fool my job has made of me; I am the only man permitted to touch the king: I really had come to believe that this made *me* untouchable. The magic of Lockwood's person would keep enemies away. Now Jack Philindros, a man so low in my estimation that I didn't trouble to understand him, has made me the instrument by which he can, if he will, strike down the two men I would protect with more ferocity than my own children: the President and Horace. *There is no way out of this dilemma.* I have accepted that.

Horace has spoken to me openly of his life in the intelligence service, and especially of his role in the assassination of Ibn Awad. He's held nothing back; Horace is a man in whom duty reacts like an enzyme. He's told to kill a holy man, revered throughout the world as a saint, and does so. He's told to spill secrets that he had meant to keep locked away in his darknesses until he died, and does so. No matter what the truth may be, he faces it. In some odd way that is almost frightening to me, Horace is able to turn me at will from his brother into The Assistant to the President; on signal, he no longer sees Julian, he sees a man with a legal right to know all secrets.

He tells me these secrets, the terrible sets of facts that make up his hidden life, with a complete lack of emotion. His voice loses pitch, his face loses expression. He might be Philindros's twin. I keep watching him for signs of himself, traces of him as a boy, expressions that will strike some note that I've heard in him before, or heard in Pa or someone else in the family. Nothing. For almost thirty years Horace has been a man that none of us who loved him even knew existed. *Our* Horace has been the actor. Philindros's Horace has been the real man.

I dramatize; I exaggerate. It's true that Horace kept his real existence hidden from everyone outside the FIS—except, it seems, our father. Pa's connections within the intelligence world never eroded: once in, always a part of it. That old saw is true. They went on trusting Elliott Hubbard until the day he died. It was he who made the purchase of D. & D. Laux & Co. possible through his comradeship with old Sebastian on one side and the fact that he was Horace's father on the other. Apart from the man who was President at the time of the purchase, and the heads of the intelligence oversight committees in Congress, only Pa and Sebastian, outside of the FIS, knew what D. & D. Laux was in reality. Only they, outside the FIS, knew about Horace. Even I did not guess until I came into the White House and was told by Lockwood what Horace's bank did as its main business.

Otherwise Horace would never have told me. It is no temptation for him to tell; he lives in secret as easily as a trout lives in running water.

Why do I reach for metaphors? In fact there is nothing more unnatural in Horace's living as he does than there is in my life. Horace's life seems strange only because I have not been able to imagine living it. And then there is this: I desire to believe his life bizarre. Do I think that will make it easier for me to accept that it was I, as I'm a part of everything Lockwood does, who made Horace kill? That he *wanted* the order we gave him? He never wanted anything less.

Having unburdened myself of the foregoing, I want to set down, so that I can see it on the page and make it real in my mind, what Horace has told me about the Ibn Awad affair. I cannot capture his tone, but what I write is faithful to the substance of his experience.

Hagreb, because of its oil reserves and its geographical position, was a natural target for U.S. intelligence activity. The Hagrebi were an autonomous tribe, but no one thought of them as a nation until the oil wells came in; the wells only came in because Americans—Universal Energy, Lockwood's enemies—found a way to bring very deep-lying pools of oil to the surface by pumping heated gases into them. For years Ibn Awad would not permit exploitation of the oil. He wanted to keep his people—fanatically orthodox Muslims—in the desert and in the past, living according to the uncorrupted teachings of the Prophet. You must move with the times, some Texan told him. "The times are unclean!" retorted Ibn Awad.

Horace overheard that. He had an idea. Horace is of course a speaker of Arabic, an Islamic scholar. Horace made friends with Awad. The process took years. Horace, knowing Awad's hatred of machines, had always to arrive on horseback at the emir's encampment. There were no cities in Hagreb, only the wandering tribe in the empty desert and their tents.

Horace would have the tents photographed by space satellite; their location would be beamed to him through his computers at the Beirut branch of D. & D. Laux & Co. The resolution of the pictures was so fine that Horace could sometimes see Awad himself, actually recognize his face, in the enlargements that the computers made. After tracking Awad with a camera that floated hundreds of miles outside the earth's atmosphere, Horace would ride out on horseback to find him in his tent on his speck of desert. Horace would bring gifts. He and Awad would speak; Horace is a great amateur of the Koran and it pleased Awad to have scripture spoken aloud to him. Awad's other passion was the history of the Hagrebi; Horace learned this by heart too, though it was not written down.

Awad believed that the Hagrebi were chosen by God to carry His message out of the purifying desert and into the corrupted world. This is not, Horace says, an uncommon delusion among desert patriarchs (or any other people for that matter); Awad differed from all the rest in that he thought, as late as the final decade of the twentieth century, that the Word could be heard by human ear, and that it could bring salvation.

We wanted the oil. The point of leverage was Awad's religious obsession. "Is it pious to refuse?" Horace began to ask Awad. "Perhaps the greed of these oilmen is the instrument of God to send you forth out of the desert to purify Islam."

Finally (the process of persuasion took Horace years), Awad permitted the wells to be drilled. Soon he was depositing royalties amounting to several million dollars a week in the Beirut branch of D. & D. Laux & Co. Awad immediately hired American engineers to design and build the electronic minaret that was called Radio Hagreb. In its shadow he built the largest mosque in the world. Around the mosque, Hagreb City—skyscrapers and hospitals, schools and stadiums, gardens and parks irrigated with desalinated water pumped overland from the sea—rose out of the sands.

Awad came to his new mosque to worship from time to time but continued to live as he'd always done, in a tent in the desert. He spent almost his entire waking time in prayer. Horace kept up his visits to the desert, but he seldom saw Awad. More and more, Ibn Awad was beyond the reach of influence or even simple friendship. The corruption he had foreseen for the Hagrebi when the oil came in was all around him. He withdrew from it. Even the crown prince, a loutish boy in his twenties called Kamal, was wallowing in drink and drugs, women and boys on trips abroad, though he took care to live carefully when he was near his father in Hagreb.

Awad had only the two sons. His wives and concubines had given him a flock of female children. It was unlikely, as he had abstained from sexual intercourse for years, that he would ever have more heirs. Most of his hopes he placed in Prince Talil, the only child of the youngest of his wives.

When Horace first knew Talil he was a very young boy, and Horace was the first person from the outside world he had encountered. From the start, even before Horace had any ulterior purpose, there was an attraction between them. Horace and Talil spent long hours together, talking, hunting. Horace, with his afterglow of the life outside, must have been like a lamp in that dark medieval Bedouin world. Talil studied by Horace's lamp. (I did the same, at fifteen.) Naturally, as Horace foresaw, Talil came to want more than Horace could offer on his occasional visits. Talil persuaded Ibn Awad that he should have a modern education. Awad gave his son to Horace, and Horace set up in Beirut what amounted to a university with a student body of one. Using Ibn Awad's inexhaustible funds, Horace brought the best teachers from everywhere in the world. Talil knew the Koran front to back before he came to Beirut; at the end of three years he knew as much as most specialists about Arab history and Islamic culture, and more than most American Ph.D.s about Western civilization. He was expert in the theory of oil production and marketing. He spoke English and read French and German. Through Horace he met the most influential men in the Near East, Arab and outsider alike.

When Talil went back to Hagreb, he found his father insane. Ibn Awad spoke to the prince of conversations with angels. He heard voices in the desert, and the voices insistently repeated two things: purify Islam; kill the Jews. He spoke like a madman only in private; in public, and in his radio speeches, he was the saintly figure and voice the world still believes in. Radio Hagreb, along with the example of Ibn Awad's ascetic life, won the old man an enormous following among the Arab masses. They were ripe for him: the moneyed young were sickened by the excesses of their parents, the poor were enraged that they had remained poor in the midst of an ocean of money.

Awad made Prince Talil the head of his bodyguard and his prime minister. To him alone he confided that he was planning to cleanse Islam through the use of terrorists.

Talil turned to Horace for help. He saw that his father's illness could be controlled if he could be brought under treatment; but Awad would not leave the desert.

A team of FIS doctors was flown to Hagreb. They saw at once what Awad's problem was, gave him lithium carbonate, and brought his psychosis under control. As we know, Awad refused to continue the treatment because the medicine took away the visions and voices he saw in the desert.

Before long, the voices told him to destroy Israel by fire. He had agents buy the necessary plutonium and find the required technicians. He made his bombs.

Horace had known for some time that there was a connection between Ibn Awad and Hassan Abdallah of the Eye of Gaza. Rose MacKenzie, a kind of magical technocrat who worked with Horace, had learned to read the messages that Awad sent to the Eye of Gaza in the form of prayers broadcast at certain hours, in a certain sequence, over Radio Hagreb. The broken code told Horace that the bombs would be handed over as Philindros described to the President and me that night three years ago at the farm.

"Never did I suggest to Talil that he should kill his father," says Horace. "We examined one way out after another; we saw that none would work. I suggested kidnapping, a Swiss clinic. There would have been an uprising in Hagreb. Finally Talil said, 'I will have to kill him.' That was what I had wanted him to say . . . trained him to say. I advised him not to do it. He came back to me again. And again. Finally I received the order from the President. At that point, and not before, I told Talil that he must kill his father. You have to understand, Julian, that he loved the old man. Imagine yourself murdering Pa—an insane Pa, dangerous to the world, but your father all the same. That was Talil's situation, and I—you and Lockwood and I—put him into it.

"Talil was wearing the robes of a royal prince—gauzy white with a purple headpiece. It was night. He had just come from a reception at the palace. We were alone in the desert. There was a very bright moon. Talil sank in his robes to the ground, so limp with anguish that I imagined for a moment that his body had left his clothes; he was just a heap of bright rags on the sand. He yipped like a dog. This boy I had created *yipped*. That was the most intelligent sound he could make."

It was Horace, of course, who brought Talil, step by step, to murder. Talil thought the idea was his own, that the guilt was his own; Horace, manipulator of hidden controls, knew better. It was Horace, too, who suggested the bizarre faked suicide note. In it, as the world knows, Ibn Awad informed mankind that he had ordered Prince Talil to kill him as a sacrifice to his faith. At the time, I half-believed this story myself (Horace knows *my* secret weaknesses); I thought Awad in his madness had saved Lockwood and me from doing murder. But it was only Horace's cleverness that saved us, for a few years, from suspicion.

107

Talil's execution wasn't part of Horace's plan. He wanted Talil, his instrument, on the throne of Hagreb. Talil was a man who could influence the Arab world for a generation to come. He believed Horace to be his best friend—more than that, his second father. Yet when Talil was beheaded, Horace was able to weigh up the benefits against the loss. Unblinking, Horace said to me, "It did occur to me that Talil was the only witness to American involvement."

Still, Horace was puzzled. Had some unseen enemy altered the suicide note of Ibn Awad? He had Rose MacKenzie run the computers day and night, analyzing and reanalyzing the new material in the note that condemned Talil to death.

"The explanation," says Horace, "was very O. Henryish—real life often is. Talil had *himself* executed; perhaps he went into madness with his father before he followed him into death. Rose compared the suicide note with all samples of Prince Talil's handwriting in the computer. There was no doubt Talil had written it himself. Ibn Awad was illiterate—Talil had always done all his writing for him. After we said good-bye, Talil simply added another paragraph. It was his own death warrant. It read: 'My beloved son Prince Talil begs that he be executed according to God's law for this act of patricide. I have instructed him to kill me, and he, in his great love for me, has obeyed. May the sacrifice of our two lives wake Islam; may God forgive my son and me for doing His work as we have done it. If He should punish us forever, we accept the fire as the sign of His love for our souls, and of our love for His Word and His people.' "

Talil could kill his father, he would let no one else do it. But he himself refused to live afterwards.

"*Imagine killing Pa.*" I could not have done what Talil did, and lived myself. How does Horace, who loved Talil, live?

Julian closed his diary, capped his pen, and locked away what he had written. His eye followed his hand as it reached for the switch on his desk lamp, and saw his father's picture. He turned off the lights and went home.

5

Emily lunched that day with Charlotte Graham. They were alone, and before they ate they had an apéritif. They were seated side by side in the love seats where Charlotte and Patrick had been when Clive Wilmot began everything, only two weeks before.

"These chairs are Delanois, aren't they?" Emily said. "And the *duchesse brisée*, too." She indicated the chair and the long footstool on which Clive had sprawled while telling his tale.

"How clever you are," Charlotte said. "Not many people know a Delanois from a Black Forest clock—but then you have rooms full of the stuff, too, don't you?"

"Not all that much, and it's a bit newer—Empire, mostly. I did art history at Bryn Mawr and stayed up all night swallowing pills to memorize all the names. This *is* a lovely room."

The furniture was remarkably fine—French and Italian and a few German pieces, marquetry tables and commodes. Charlotte had replaced the blocked windows with pier glass; two of the mirrors were possibly by Matthias Lock.

"The room was supposed to be rococo, you know," Charlotte said, "but Patrick had his Persian carpets. I suppose that's all right; but then he developed this passion for hanging nude females about. They all have moon-colored skin, d'you see, and great hams. It does give an effect—what would one say?—of dykes in a china shop."

Emily couldn't imagine why Charlotte had wanted to give her lunch. It was a very good one, served by a tall pale boy younger, even, than Emily. Willowy, thought Emily, as the slender footman served them cold soup and sherry, grilled sole and Montrachet; she had read the word but until now had seen no one in life whom it described. "I do hate thin wines," said Charlotte. "Men think they have to shrivel their tongues with those dry things, but they aren't here to watch, are they?" She spoke to the servant. "Go away now, ffoulkes, we can pour the rest for ourselves."

"Your ladyship."

Charlotte ate with gusto and went on talking about furniture. Emily wondered if she really had such a passion for it, or if she feared it might be Emily's only subject.

"You know," Charlotte said, when she had got through her food, "I'm a great reader of those pieces you do in the *Post*. How can anyone as young as you be so wise about people?"

"I'm not wise, the people I write about are. I just follow them around and take notes like mad. It's all quotes and straight description."

"But you *capture* them! I remember poor Julian. You wrote he had eyes like Boswell's, assuming that he had burned the notes for his *Life* of Johnson."

"Did I write that?" Emily didn't smile. "Those were sad days for Lockwood and Julian, just at the beginning of the administration. Lockwood had pardoned Glick, that lawyer Mallory had hounded into jail for defending terrorists, and the whole right wing was down on him. Everything was going wrong. They had a horrid fight on over repeal of Mallory's program to give free heroin to addicts without even trying to rehabilitate them—let them shoot up and die was Mallory's idea. 'Administrative murder,' Lockwood called it."

"I remember all that. And of course, Caroline had just run away with that dwarf."

"I don't know that that was such a blow to Julian. But who knows what Julian felt? In any case he's very attached to Lockwood, as everyone knows, and secretive—he'd tell me *nothing*. I kept provoking him, asking why they failed to do good in the world when they talked such a good game." Emily picked up her wineglass and looked through the amber liquid at the sun pouring through a round window set high in the wall. "I'm afraid Julian got awfully fed up with me. Lots of people do. I'm a pest when I'm doing these profiles."

"No one who looks as you do, my girl, is ever a pest."

Charlotte rang and ffoulkes came back to clear away the plates and give them strawberries. Once again Charlotte got busy; she ate the berries, as an Englishwoman would, with a fork and spoon, pausing after chewing each one as though she wanted to forget the flavor of it before being delighted by the next.

"You know, Emily, I am finding you rather sly," she said at last.

"Sly?"

"I know the *Post* has given you Patrick as a subject. Are you going to do him?"

Emily was astonished; she had got the assignment only that morning, by telephone, and hadn't yet approached Patrick. How could Charlotte possibly know?

"You'll think me a meddler," Charlotte said, "but I suggested it to Trevor when he dined here last week. He rang up this morning to say they'd asked you to do it. I'm so glad."

"Why?"

"Why am I glad, or why did I suggest it?"

"Both." Emily was faintly annoyed. She never mixed social things with professional ones. She never even discussed her work with Julian; she had never discussed it with anyone.

"I'm glad because you're so very good, and I don't think anyone has ever written about Patrick as he really is—he's built up this persona, you know, and all anyone sees is hair and flashing teeth, and all anyone hears is the voice from the burning bush. I think you'll get underneath all that and rehumanize him. And that's why I suggested it."

"Patrick may not think that's such a wonderful thing."

Charlotte laughed. "My dear, he'll be delighted. I think you ought to go to San Francisco with him next week to watch the convention nominate Mallory."

Emily had drunk hardly any wine, and now she put a finger on the rim of her glass as ffoulkes approached with the bottle.

"ffoulkes, do take these fruit plates."

"Your ladyship."

Emily said, "I'll have to speak to Patrick. But San Francisco would be the place to do the piece. That's what interested the paper —Mallory and Patrick, toe-to-toe again."

"Yes, I could see they'd like that. Pump it up, I would if I were you. Patrick loathes the man. They're rather alike, Patrick and Mallory. So bright, so beautiful, so . . ."

"Yes?"

". . . so unlike Julian. So unlike One. D'you ever read Nancy Mitford? I suppose no one does now, but she was rather funny about English society. She adored snobs, the poor dead things. In her books, or maybe it was just one book, she had a prancing queer who called himself One, with the O capitalized. 'Not like One, the Germans'; 'Not like One, those American divans—everyone sits in a row and the ennui makes One fall off.' Those aren't Mitford's exact words, but that was the sense of it. That's Mallory's trouble, he knows he's not like One; it's Patrick's trouble too."

Emily looked in wonderment at Charlotte's animated face across the table. This woman seemed to think it was all right to speak as flippantly about her own husband as she would gossip about an acquaintance.

"You see, the thing about Patrick," Charlotte went on, "is that he's always lived rather at second hand. Really, he wants to be President—or, at least, he wants to be Julian. He wants to *run* things, not just describe them and attack them. He doesn't have what he wants, poor chap."

"He seems to have quite a lot." Emily let her eyes wander around the opulent room, and finally rest on Charlotte herself.

"Yes, One would be satisfied, but not Patrick, I'm afraid. It's all disguise; he wanted to be born higher. He thinks it means something. I keep returning to Julian. In Patrick's eyes, your husband just stepped effortlessly through doors into the room where the secret of life is kept in a box. Poor old Patrick has been scratching at the door all these years. He can't know there is no box."

Charlotte shrugged and gave a helpless smile.

ffoulkes returned. "Coffee, your ladyship?"

"In the drawing room."

ffoulkes withdrew. "Why does he keep on calling you that?" Emily asked.

" 'Your ladyship'? It gives him a giggle. He would have been a marquess, his people were much grander than my family, had there always been an England. These young chaps, handing the plates around, pretend what's happened to them is a great joke. The Russian nobility did the same for the first generation or so. *Noblesse oblige*, you know. In five years he'll paint his face and go off on a yacht with some Arab."

Charlotte, her Scotch and milk in her hand, took Emily back into the drawing room, where ffoulkes gave them coffee. They talked some more about decor. Charlotte's long hands flew with her voice; Emily, a quiet girl who never wore jewelry in daytime, counted her hostess's rings. Because of her lineage it was assumed Charlotte had brought the family jewels with her into marriage, but Patrick had purchased everything she had.

"There *is* this," Charlotte said suddenly. "I'm talking to you in this way because I have a bit of a conscience, Emily. There's something new going on between Patrick and Julian."

"Going on?"

"I mean Patrick wants to know something and Julian won't tell him, or isn't ready to. Patrick gets awfully cross about such things."

"That's nothing to do with me, Charlotte. On assignment, I'm Emily Barker; I have no Hubbard connection."

"How intelligent. Do make Patrick understand that. He might think you were the door to Julian, you know."

Emily gave Charlotte a long, solemn look. Christ, these Americans are such lovely creatures, thought Charlotte; or is it only that she's young?

"I mean, Patrick *does* require feeding and grooming and you're awfully beautiful," Charlotte said. "If you're going to spend a week with him three thousand miles away from Julian, you can expect sudden moves."

"*Liaisons dangereuses?*" Emily laughed. "Is that a worry to you?"

"Darling! No. Respond as you like. But you *are* so sweet, and Patrick—well, he *will* think he's more than a match for you."

Charlotte lit a cigarette, Emily watching until she had it going.

"But not for Julian."

"That," said Charlotte, her words mixed with a long plume of tobacco smoke, "is the question." She laid a hand on Emily's. "So many enemies, darling; it's all such a waste. Do let's be friends, you and I."

Emily had shopping to do, and she slipped away from the Secret Service man to go to the market. In the cab, riding home, she wrote down everything that Charlotte had said to her in her notebook.

Emily thought no more about Charlotte. People spoke to Emily all the time as if they were mad. Only Julian had never done that; she could lay her hand on him and feel the rhythms of sanity in the flow of his blood and the steady working of his lungs.

She hadn't menstruated in thirty-five days. At night she put her fingers against Julian's heartbeat; she knew that the baby's heart, when it came to life, would feel the same as his through her own skin.

6

Horace was examining the portrait of his grandmother—the painting was bathed in the glow of a spotlight affixed to the ceiling—when Emily came into the house on O Street. She carried a string bag filled with fresh vegetables and clutched a stack of books and file folders against her breast. A bulging purse was slung over one shoulder, a camera bag over the other. The large round glasses that she wore when she worked had slid down to the tip of her small nose, and on her neck was the faint shine of perspiration.

"You look like the world's most beautiful infantryman, with all that equipment hanging on you," Horace said.

"I just want to drop it, and drop myself into a bath," said Emily. She held up her cheek to be kissed. Horace gave her a hearty smack, and with a forefinger pushed her glasses back to the bridge of her nose. She grinned at him.

Horace had liked Emily from the start. There was a cheerful note within her that he admired; she was more like the oldest of his nieces than a sister-in-law. He would never have done to Caroline anything so intimate as to push her glasses back into place. Julian's first wife had liked to establish a current of sexuality between herself and all men, and she hadn't spared Horace. He'd never had any doubts that Caroline would have taken any man it pleased her to have.

Emily was a different matter. Horace looked at her, and looked again at the portrait of Jennifer Hubbard. "I never realized it, but you and Grandmother favor one another. I wonder if Julian sees that."

"Rot," said Emily, pointing her chin at the woman in the portrait. "*That* is the face of a woman who never in her life carried her own groceries."

113

She dropped her purse and her bundle of papers on the sofa and went into the kitchen. Horace, catching a jumble of papers as they slid off the smooth cloth of the cushion, saw the name "Patrick Graham" written on a file folder with the broad black tip of a felt marking pen. A handful of notes and press clippings fell out of the folder. Horace put them inside without reading them.

Julian had already gone upstairs to shower and change, and Emily followed him, leaving Horace with the children. Elliott told his uncle that he wouldn't go away to boarding school the next year, though he would be the right age for it. It was impossible to protect him at Exeter as he was guarded at home by the Secret Service.

"That's why we're here so much and with Mummy so little," he said. "It's not legal for the Secret Service to watch us when we're in our mother's custody. I don't know why."

"I like it this way," said Jenny. "Leo always takes us on his boat to secret destinations. We observe radio silence. There's no one near you, nobody can find you—I love the sea. Leo gets Secret Service men on their vacations to come along and pays their expenses. It's very smart of him, I think."

"You admire Leo?"

"Like anything. He's never serious—is he, Elliott?"

"A laugh a minute," replied Elliott, with a wary glance at Horace. He wasn't sure how his Uncle Horace, a fierce defender of Julian, felt about Leo and Caroline.

Horace pressed the children for details; he was curious about Leo Dwyer. With the profits from his novels and the films that were made from them Leo had bought a yacht from the estate of a Greek billionaire. He and Caroline lived aboard, always in the sun; they put into port sometimes to see friends; once they had dined with Horace in Beirut, and he had found Caroline, her ivory skin burned nearly as black as that of one of the fellahin she had once longed to be, free of her political obsessions at last. Leo had no interest in politics except as material for his books, no interest in men and women for their looks or money, but only for what they were behind their masks. Horace had liked him at once and saw why Caroline did; he was exactly what he was. "Leo has an acute case of total good will," Caroline had told Horace. Evidently it was contagious —she had even kissed her former brother-in-law.

"At first we thought Leo was weird," Jenny said. "He took us swimming on the boat, it has a big pool aft. He was so small, and all covered with hair." The children, used to the smooth bodies of the men in their own family, had been repelled by Leo's grizzled pelt; tufts of graying hair sprouted from his shoulders and his back as well as his chest. Leo saw the trouble. "Some guys, like your Pa, are higher on the evolutionary tree. Look at you, Elliott—you're already taller than I am; you'll be a skyscraper. Think of the advantages of being two feet taller than your stepfather."

Leo played Marco Polo with them in the pool. He taught Elliott to cheat at cards; he had little evening dresses made for Jenny in Paris, and, dancing with her to the music of a tape recorder, taught her forgotten numbers like the rumba, the tango, the cha-cha-cha; he spoke of his experiences, while he had been waiting for fame, as a dance instructor at a studio in his native New York. "It gave ugly girls a sense of confidence to start out with me," he explained; "the ganefs handed them on to handsome guys in tight pants when it came time to sign up for the full course of lessons—twenty dollars a week for the rest of your natural life for half an hour alone in a room with Romeo."

"Mummy really *likes* Leo," Jenny said to Horace. "But I think she still loves Pa."

"You mustn't hope for that. There's Emily now."

"Emily loves him madly, *madly*," said Elliott. Jenny flushed; that was what he'd wanted. Both children were used to the healthy appetite Julian's wives had for him. For Jenny, of course, her mother's sexuality was one thing; Emily's was another. She never got into her father's lap anymore, or kissed him to wake him up— Emily did these things; Jenny didn't like their having a new meaning.

At dinner, all traces of their frantic day had vanished from the faces of Julian and Emily. They wore clean clothes—Julian a seersucker jacket, Emily a flowered frock that left her smooth shoulders bare. She had a glow that no shower could account for, and Horace wondered if Emily and Julian had taken time to make love while he chatted with Elliott and Jenny. He hoped so. In any case, Julian's mood had changed. He was once again the bantering person he'd always been within the family, listening with a smile deep in his eyes to Jenny's account of a painting lesson, questioning Elliott about a game of baseball he had played that afternoon. They were leaving in a week or two to join their mother at sea, depending on when Leo finished a screen treatment of one of his novels. They didn't know where Leo was taking them this time; he always guarded the surprise. The children excused themselves and left. "Antarctica," said Emily in a whisper. "Can you imagine? Icebergs, penguins, Spitsbergen, noble Scott and nasty Amundsen. I wish *I'd* had a stepfather like Leo, but my mother stuck like glue to Daddy. I'm just like her. From bridal bed to double death-bed, that's my life's journey."

They had lobster salad. Horace took the last bite from his plate. "Pa's sort of meal," he said.

"Don't you like cold things, Horace?"

"Of course, and this was wonderful. Lobster has vanished from the Mediterranean, you know—killed by pollution and gone forever, they say."

"What brings you to Washington?" Emily asked.

Horace smiled. "Dark doings for D. & D. Laux & Co. I don't think I'll be here long."

"Perhaps I'll keep him in town for a while," Julian said. "I'll need the company." Julian took a dripping bottle from the ice bucket beside him and, stretching his long arm, divided what was left of the wine among their three glasses. "Emily's off to San Francisco, she tells me."

"I have to cover the convention—or, rather, cover a man who's covering the convention," Emily explained. "One of my profiles. I'd like to do you, Horace, but they'd hang me for conflict of interest."

"I thought you only did silent, powerful types like Julian."

"Like brother, like brother."

Emily's remark brought Ibn Awad into the room. Two murderers relaxing at twilight. Horace and Julian exchanged a look, and in his brother's eyes Horace thought he saw guilt move, then vanish, like a small animal at the mouth of its burrow. Emily noticed nothing.

"That's the *other* party's convention. I'll be regarded as a spy in Franklin Mallory's camp. They know whose wife I am."

"They're a floating police state; they know everything," Julian said. "There'll be microphones in your mattress, Emily."

"Oh, I hope they send you faked tapes! I want to see you mad with jealousy, thinking of nothing but me, tempted by all those rich old men and muscular bullies in Mallory's party."

"Not to mention Patrick. Emily's been assigned to do a story on Patrick Graham. Why does the *Post* think he's interesting?"

"Because he *is* interesting," Emily said. "He's the man who knows everything. This town is filled with eager attendants, pumping secrets into Patrick's ear. . . . That's not bad; I'll use it in the story."

Emily giggled. She loved these assignments, a week of living pressed up against a stranger's life. She heard astonishing confessions off the record; her subjects gave her information in confidence about themselves that they feared to see in print. By binding

116

her to secrecy, giving her the trust that only a friend could have, they protected themselves from exposure. It wasn't necessary. Emily was a kindly writer—and in the end she always surprised some more vivid secret from her subjects than any they volunteered about themselves. There was no bottom to her curiosity. Like all good reporters, she could be astonished by the commonplace. In Emily's eyes nothing was so extraordinary as the normal.

"I should think the interesting thing would be Graham's encounters with Franklin Mallory," Horace said. "After all—with all due respect to Lockwood's appeal and your genius, Julian—it was Graham who swung the election against Mallory four years ago. Have they seen each other since?"

Julian did not volunteer what he knew. Emily was able to find out whatever she needed to know without tapping him as a source. Even before they had married, there had been no pillow talk between them.

"Charlotte says yes," Emily replied. "Evidently Mallory had them up to dinner in New York, and couldn't have been nicer. She says she expected a noseful of cyanide spray when they stepped off the elevator. Instead, Mallory told her Patrick was the best journalist in the world."

"I hope Mallory was being true to his character when he said that," Julian said.

"How's that?" asked Horace; it was almost an interruption.

"Insincere."

Horace paused before he spoke again; at the best of times he didn't like to discuss American politics. As things were now, he had better reasons than ever for keeping up the strict political neutrality Philindros drilled into all his people. Horace *was* neutral; he cared little who was President; it was the bureaucracy that was the living organism.

"Insincere?" he said. "I'd have thought Mallory was one of the most sincere men who ever won the presidency. He said what he was going to do, and did it—or as much of it as could be done in this country. He means what he says and does what he means."

"I suppose you'd say Hitler was sincere," Julian said.

"Of course. I wouldn't say Mallory was like Hitler."

"Wouldn't you? Both created a mythical monster—Hitler the Jews, Mallory the humanitarians—'humanitarians' means Lockwood and you, Emily and me, but it also means the blacks and the poor. Hitler gassed defectives; Mallory passed a law to have anyone whose IQ falls below a certain norm sterilized on the birth of their first child. Hitler made a frontal attack on religion; Mallory tells us we must be 'rational.' . . ."

"Are you so religious?"

"No. But I don't mind if others are. People can be as irrational as they like—that's called free speech and thought."

"He hasn't used Hitler's thuggery."

"No. He didn't begin in the streets. He began among the elite. Who are Mallory's people? First of all, the colossal rich, men like O. N. Laster of Universal Energy, but he keeps them well hidden. They only come out in the night when he tries to steal Canada. Second, the educated disgruntled. We have two million men and women under thirty-five in this country who have advanced academic degrees and can't get jobs. Mallory with his space program and the rest of his gadgetry *gave* them jobs—he harnessed their education and intellectual ingenuity in the way Hitler harnessed the physical brutality of the Brown Shirts. He made someone of each of them. No, there's no thuggery—people aren't beaten with truncheons, they're just quietly castrated as soon as they produce one drone to replace them, or quietly put away forever in a federal prison if they commit a crime out of desperation, or quietly deprived of a living if they believe in the perfectibility of man. That's not thuggery, Horace, is it? It's all quite rational."

"It seems to have an effect on *your* rationality."

Julian swallowed the rest of his wine. "Fear tends to do that," he said.

Quiet descended on them. Nobody had expected this outburst, least of all Emily. She put her hand over Julian's.

"Mallory's not going to win," she said. "He's a lovely cynic— but *too* lovely."

Julian ran his thumb over the back of Emily's small golden hand. "That sounds like one of Charlotte's brittle witticisms."

"It is. I confess."

"Have you been talking to her a lot?"

"Just at lunch today. It was her idea that I should do the piece on Patrick. Isn't that interesting?"

Julian and Horace exchanged yet another look.

"Yes," said Julian.

7

"The obsession with the invisible is the curse of mankind," said Franklin Mallory.

Patrick Graham was taking no notes. He wanted Mallory relaxed. This was a conversation, not an interview. Patrick would have Mallory on his show two days hence. If he could discover now what Mallory really intended, he might be able to maneuver him into revealing himself before the cameras later on.

Patrick and Emily were in Mallory's suite in the Fairmont Hotel in San Francisco. Although this was Patrick's interview, Mallory's remarks were addressed mainly to Emily. As she had foreseen, he knew exactly who she was, and of course she had her looks. It was plain to Emily that Mallory was having fun with Patrick, baiting him with these sardonic pronouncements that were a parody of Patrick's own speaking style. The woman who was Mallory's chief assistant, and who was known to be his lover as well, watched the byplay with an amused smile on her lips.

"Frosty Lockwood is obsessed with the invisible," Mallory continued, "and so is that whole crowd of dreamers he represents. All that talk about the spirit of man, the destiny of America, brotherhood. They're missionaries, armed missionaries. They want to save man from himself, reveal to him the mystical good that lurks within."

Patrick Graham found it difficult to smile at this man. He thought Mallory was a maniac, but he sensed his appeal. There was political electricity in him. Patrick was more than half afraid that Mallory might be the first of the new Americans, a man who had burst into a new era that only he understood, because he was in the act of creating it. The country had been through a lot. Its heroes had been murdered, its resources bled, its money and idealism debased. Mallory looked like its rescuer.

We're so much like the Germans at the time of Weimar, thought Patrick. He had had the thought before. He knew it was trite. But he dealt in worn simplicities—only worn simplicities could be understood on television.

"And what are you obsessed with, Mr. Mallory?" Patrick asked. He would not call Mallory "Mr. President."

"Nothing. I'm *interested* in life on this planet. Life as it is, as it always has been, as it always will be so long as the human species is in charge—defined by our nature, limited by our limitations. I am interested in reality, Patrick, and I'm going to run for President again, and I think I'm going to be elected President again, on the platform of reality."

"Such as stealing Canada?"

"A case in point." Mallory's brilliant eyes turned on Emily again; he made his argument to her, knowing that Patrick of all people was unconvincible. "The United States and Canada are a natural unit—our technology and capital and population, their space and natural resources," Mallory said. "Canada has no authenticity as a political entity. It can't support itself or even defend itself.

119

The British designed it as a colony to be exploited. When the British Empire expired, naturally an enormous power like the United States absorbed Canada economically and culturally, and dominated its consciousness. Why not join the Canadians to us politically as well? It would have been good for Canada and good for the United States. We have that headache over energy and minerals, you know, and there are an awful lot of those things under the tundra."

"And you think we ought to swallow Canada like an aspirin to cure our headache?"

Mallory laughed. He had a boisterous laugh, one of his most human qualities. "I suspect we'll hear that phrase on TV before November," he said. "I envy you your silver tongue, Patrick. Also your gift for leaving out the essential fact. We weren't going to march in and take the Canadians' country away from them. I thought the whole episode would go down in history as a noble success—the first time ever that one country had been joined to another, at least on such a scale, through the consent of the peoples involved. It's not without grandeur, this idea—even you'd have to grant that, Patrick."

"Napoleonic, sir. Yet the American people saw it as a deception. That's why you were defeated."

Patrick shifted in his chair, throwing his ankle onto his knee, staring for an instant at the gleaming leather of his hand-sewn shoe. Emily noted the gesture; it was usable, a little window opening on Graham's inner person. On television, he would never have permitted himself so visible a reaction to a man who offended him. In private, he didn't think it worthwhile to conceal what he felt.

By some trick of Emily's sensibility—she knew what it was, it was the condition induced in her by thousands of hours of watching television—people like Mallory and Patrick and Lockwood seemed as eerie as ghosts when seen in the flesh, when touched, when apprehended with all the senses. Sometimes she failed to remember that she had three senses in addition to sight and hearing. Now, only three feet away from Mallory, she could smell him—like Julian, he had the scent of cleanliness, the soapy aura of a recent bath; mixed with this was the faint pungency of pipe tobacco, an odor she loved. She had not yet touched him; she examined his neat ear and wondered with an inward giggle what it would taste like. Mallory had a well-made face, regular and American, pink and unlined except for the creases that laughter had left around his eyes. He had silver hair and heavy eyebrows, a combination of features that made him vividly photogenic. His voice was dry, uninflected, and in this hotel sitting room it didn't carry well. That surprised Emily; amplified through microphones, Mallory was a powerful speaker. She had expected his words to ring in private as they did in public; Lockwood's certainly did. Perhaps Mallory didn't set off the same resonance in her as Lockwood did. She, too, thought Mallory and all he stood for were bad and dangerous.

"Can you really attack what Lockwood's done?" asked Patrick. "The polls show his policies have a lot of support."

"Not as much as my policies had four years ago," Mallory replied. "Public opinion is a great clumsy beast, Patrick. One good sting on the ass can turn the whole creature around."

Patrick reacted strongly to Mallory's last sentence—almost leaped. Mallory watched, eyes glittering with amusement. Emily made a note in her book; these two *knew* something, and whatever it was, they were hiding it from each other.

Patrick said, "Your ideas haven't changed in your years out of office?"

Mallory's eyes moved from Patrick's face to Emily's and back again. "No," he said. "I'm afraid you're going to be in for four more years of cold rationality if I'm elected, Patrick."

Emily, in a flash, understood something essential about Mallory; she had never seen it before, but the tone of his voice, so much flatter than she was used to, and the amused disdain in his eyes when he spoke to Patrick, brought the truth home to her. Horace was right—Mallory was an honest man; he believed absolutely in what he said and did. More than that, he had the power to make millions agree with him. No wonder Julian feared him and Patrick could hardly bear the sound of his voice. They knew that it was only luck that the people hadn't chosen Mallory over Lockwood four years before. A tiny percentage of the vote, only two hundred thousand people, had swung to Lockwood on an emotional issue. What if it swung back?

"It's a simple matter," Mallory said. "Either Frosty's right about the way the people are and how they think, or I am. We'll see in November."

Mallory's assistant rose to her feet. Patrick, after an instant of hesitation, got up, too. "Susan," he said, "shall I call you about setting up the broadcast?"

Susan Grant, as sure of her ground with Mallory as Julian was with Lockwood, answered without glancing at her employer. "The President can't work in a studio, Patrick," she said, "and we'd rather have your clutter somewhere else than in this suite. You're staying in this hotel, aren't you? Can't you set up in your room or somewhere else in the Fairmont for Thursday evening?"

"Yes."

"Call me with the room number an hour early so that we can set up security."

"Only an hour?"

Susan Grant's face was already turned away; she had considered their business done and was already on the way to open the door for Patrick and Emily. She paused. "Our security people can do everything they need to do in an hour, Patrick."

Emily, observing this exchange, was startled to feel Mallory's dry hand slipping into hers. She turned her head and gave him a look of spitting female warning, and then saw that he had meant nothing by what he'd done. He gave her hand a little squeeze, and even in that pressure she could feel his wiry strength. He let go her hand.

"Can you take a minute off from work?" Mallory asked. "I wanted to ask you how the President is. You've seen him recently, I guess?"

"About three weeks ago, Mr. President." Emily saw no reason not to call Mallory by the title that was his by right. "He seemed the same—full of life, relaxed. He told me a lot of funny stories about his football days."

"Did he? Athletes have a lot of fun. They all seem to be comedians. Certainly Lockwood is."

"Do you and he know each other?" Emily flushed. "I mean, have you met and spent time together? That was a silly question."

"Not at all. It was a good question. Yes, we do know each other, and pretty well. We were in the Senate together, and we were friends, Polly and Frosty and my wife and I, long before either of us ever thought about ending up as we have. The friendship lasted, especially for the girls. We saw each other often until Marilyn died—in New York at our place and in Washington at theirs. After my wife was gone, I had them to dinner with me in the White House a few times, but I guess we ran out of things to say to one another. Polly couldn't really keep us off politics without Marilyn's help."

A smile, startling in its sweetness, lit Mallory's face. The man was remembering his wife. Emily felt tenderness for him; she wanted to slip her hand back in his. Patrick called to her from the doorway. Mallory's smile vanished—it did not amuse him that Graham would suggest in this way that his time was more valuable than that of a former President of the United States.

"When you see Frosty again," Mallory said, "I hope you'll give him my best. Tell him—this is important—tell him to call me if there's anything he needs from me. Will you do that?"

"Of course I will, sir."

122

"Good. He'll trust the messenger, I think. It's hard for men in our position to get word back and forth, you know. It's hard, too, Mrs. Hubbard, to run for the presidency against a friend. I like Lockwood so much."

Mallory gave a little nod, smiled again, repeated the nod. He held out his hand and Emily shook it. Mallory's eyes were now cleared of whatever tender memory she'd seen in them a moment earlier. The look he gave her was one she was used to seeing: it was the half-smile of a male who wishes he had the time, or room, for a woman who is about to walk away forever.

In the corridor, Patrick was silent. Closed-circuit television cameras surveilled him and Emily as they walked to the end of the hall, where Mallory's security men took back the unobtrusive badges they'd given them when they entered. Emily, used to such things at home, knew that the badges deactivated the alarm systems. One of the bodyguards inserted a key in a control panel, and an empty elevator opened before them. He rode with them to their floor and let them out.

"Opinion?" Patrick asked.

They were inside his suite. His producer was busy on the telephone, and the crew played cards on the white cloth of Patrick's breakfast table. They had piled the dishes in the hall outside.

"Of Mallory? Yours first, Patrick."

"Mine is no secret. What did your first glimpse tell you?"

"I came away surprised. You've all made me think he's such an ogre. Actually, he's awfully nice and bright. Charming, in fact."

Patrick lit one of his innumerable cigarettes and dragged hungrily on it; he hadn't smoked in Mallory's presence. Emily had never known him to abstain before, and she noted the detail.

"You sound like Charlotte. I think she'd have gone to Munich and hung around that restaurant where Hitler came to eat spaghetti, hoping to catch his eye. Women want to breed with tyrants; if they have to, they hide inside an ideology, the way Queen Pasiphaë did with the wooden cow for the Cretan bull, to beget the Minotaur."

"Oh, Patrick, bullshit," said Emily.

8

Susan Grant was the only person who was ever alone with Mallory. They had become lovers a year after Mallory's wife died. Susan was the second woman he had known sexually. Though many women had desired Mallory and he knew it, he had wanted no one but his wife while they were married, and no one since except Susan.

Mallory and his wife had first made love when they were fifteen, in a pine grove on a hillside above a country fairground in New York State. They had simply left the fair and climbed the hill, taken off their clothes, and lain down on a bed of fragrant pine needles, lustrous and brown like Marilyn's spreading hair. In their amazed pleasure they heard the distorted noise of the carnival below, cheap mechanical music and the shouting of the barkers above the hum of the crowd, and saw the garish lights glowing in the night sky.

They married at twenty. Working as a secretary, Marilyn put Mallory through college and the Harvard Business School. At night she studied with him, and though she had no degrees her formal education duplicated his. In Mallory's years in business and politics, even in the presidency, his wife had been his only true assistant. Until the week she died, without warning, of a pulmonary embolism, they had given each other everything that either wanted, sexually and as loving friends. When Marilyn died, she left Mallory alone; thirty-five years of reckless lovemaking had never produced a child. He learned from her doctor that she had been taking birth-control pills almost since the night they claimed each other's virginity above the fairground; the pills' side effects had produced the blood clot that killed her. Mallory could never decide whether Marilyn, surreptitiously swallowing a substance that deprived them of sons and daughters, had been selfless or the opposite.

To Mallory, though to nobody else and least of all to herself, Susan Grant resembled Marilyn. The likeness wasn't physical. Susan was a cheetah of a girl—tall and blond, with a narrow boyish body, firm and small-breasted, with wide hazel eyes. She was all one golden color, hair, eyes, skin. Marilyn had been small and soft and pink. The two women were similar in their minds and emotions: crackling with intelligence, quick to be roused to passion. Susan had everything Marilyn hadn't: a well-to-do father, degrees from Smith and Harvard, a place of her own in the world as an associate professor of economics at Columbia.

She had come to the White House with a group of economists to talk to Mallory about the economic effects of his policies. He was then in the second year of his presidency; Susan was thirty-one years old, Mallory fifty. She detested his politics. So did all her friends. They thought they saw what he meant to do to the country. Susan wanted to see the man close up. Even so, she lost friends by the mere act of stepping into Mallory's presence. Only the week before, he had appointed his fifth Supreme Court justice in the course of a single year: two had resigned, one had died, two had been killed by terrorists. Nobody who hated Mallory could believe that blackmail and assassination had not been involved.

During the meeting, Susan caught Mallory's eyes upon her more than once. His gaze made her uncomfortable, but she met it squarely. As the others left, Susan, as the junior person present, was last in line. Mallory slipped his hand in hers, the same gesture he would use years later when he spoke to Emily.

"Miss Grant," he said, "I wonder if you could dine with me here tonight at eight. Would that inconvenience you?"

She was disarmed by the charm of his smile, the apology in his eyes. She did not see a ruthless man who had seized control of the Supreme Court, but a man of startling appeal. Looking at him, she felt as she always felt when she saw her name in print without expecting to do so: her heart leaped; what would come next?

"I'd be glad to come," Susan said. "I can take the last plane to New York."

When she returned to the White House, Mallory met her in an upstairs sitting room and, taking her hand again, led her to a west window to look at a spectacular sunset: shafts of brilliant sunlight and boiling purple thunderheads. Mallory began at once to speak to her as if he had known her all his life. There was no fencing, no initiation rite of polite questions. Later she learned he was that way with everyone. If he decided that another human being was worth knowing, he wasted no time knowing him. The other's past meant nothing to Mallory: he was interested exclusively in his own relationship with the person. More than anyone Susan had ever met, Mallory lived in the moment in which he found himself.

She had dined with him twice at the White House when one night, very late, the doorbell rang in her apartment in New York. She looked through the peephole and saw Mallory standing outside. It was February and he was wearing a sheepskin coat and a knitted hat that concealed his famous white hair. She let him in; there was no sign of the Secret Service anywhere; she wondered how he dared to be alone.

He pulled off his cap and his hair was tousled. Susan was in her dressing gown. Mallory put his hand—the flesh so cold that he couldn't have come in a car, he must have walked up Broadway past the night hunters to find her—he put his hand on her flat stomach. The gesture didn't surprise her. She had expected it sooner or later and she had planned to step away from it. No President could tumble her like a shepherdess unless she wanted him as she would want any other man. Susan hadn't thought that she could want this intense bleached man with his hard mind. But she hadn't anticipated that he would come to her like this, dressed like a mortal, his flesh chilled by the wind. She moved closer and kissed him, and then took him down the long, echoing hall into her study, where no lover had ever lain with her before.

Mallory shut the door behind them. Susan felt the same half-fear, half-thrill that she had felt when their flesh had first touched: what was next? She sat down in the only chair in the room, the one drawn up to her cluttered desk. Mallory, smiling, took off his clothes where he stood and left them in a heap on the floor. There was only the light from the street, but Susan saw that he had the hard body of a boy: a wedge of muscles. He began to kiss her, gently. His body was still cold from the outdoors and this made him seem more of a stranger. She accepted his mouth but did not respond. She turned her head away; she thought that she couldn't do it. Mallory put his hands over her eyes, as if gentling an animal. They remained so for several moments. She put a hand on his chest and felt the chill of the wind again. Mallory took his hands away. She saw him smile. He opened her robe and began to kiss her again. Except for those moments when he covered her eyes and changed her mind, he never used his hands. She had never known such a lover; she might have been touching herself, he knew her pleasures so well.

For about a year, Susan took the seven o'clock shuttle from LaGuardia each Friday, spent the weekend with Mallory in the White House or at Camp David, and returned to New York on Monday morning in time for her ten o'clock lecture. Susan was an experienced woman, but she had never had an affair that left her so hungry, in the days between Monday and Friday, to return to a man. One Tuesday, while Susan was listening to the confusions of a graduate student in her office at Columbia, Mallory called her on the telephone. His voice was brisk: "Susan, can you come down here tomorrow and see me at two in the afternoon? Good. Thank you."

She canceled a lecture and flew to Washington. Mallory met her in an office in the Executive Office Building that she had never seen before. It was fitted out with his own furniture and pictures; it wasn't a large room, and there was nothing on the door to indicate that this was where he actually worked.

"I wanted you to come, Susan, because I have something to ask you," Mallory said. "As you know, you and I are very compatible; we see things in the same way. . . ."

My God, thought Susan, he's going to propose. Marriage was

the last thing she wanted. She knew nothing would divert him.

"Susan," said Mallory, without pausing, "I want you to resign your professorship, or take a leave of absence. I need you by me all the time, here in this house. I want you to become my executive assistant. The job has always been vacant. I never needed to fill it when Marilyn was alive. I never thought I could fill it until I found you."

Susan and Mallory gazed gravely into each other's eyes for a long moment. Then she exploded a laugh. "Franklin, you've got it all backwards," Susan said. "You're supposed to make a female your employee first, *then* make her your mistress. That's the accepted sequence."

Mallory didn't take the joke; he waited for her answer. "Will you do it?" he insisted.

Susan felt something go dry within her. She knew she had wanted him to ask the other question—she could have said no to that because it was the lesser temptation.

"Do you really think we can work together and sleep together?" she asked. Mallory took off the wedding ring he still wore and laid it on the low table, next to Susan's sharp knee. "I've done it before," he said. "I think you'll find it makes everything better."

And so she had. Mallory never again wore the ring Marilyn had given him, but the ceremony of its removal was as much of a wedding as he and Susan ever had. It was, in the end, as much as Susan wanted. Their life together was one of constant stimulation. They made policy during the week and love on the weekends. Mallory had admitted her into his person without reservation: they were one mind as well as one flesh.

9

After Patrick and Emily left them, Mallory and Susan Grant wasted no time talking about them. They never let any incident spill over into the next segment of time.

Mallory's mind, when it wandered, was not on any of the questions Patrick had raised; those were matters, as Patrick was a man, he could deal with in his sleep. He had something else to think about—something he, and he alone, had done. At eight o'clock that evening, it would happen—the world would see it; Mallory's name would be linked to the event in the way that the names of Ferdinand and Isabella were joined to the discovery of America. Mallory was going to change history, change the way man saw himself. Even now, though his own television screen was unlighted and mute, the images and the excited voices of commentators filled the air; the impulses carrying their voices and images were passing through Mallory's very body.

He had paused in his work for a moment, and Susan must have sensed what was passing through his mind because she touched him, something she almost never did during the working day. He smiled at her, and, in a gesture even more rare, kissed the hand she had laid on his shoulder. There were hours left to wait.

At seven o'clock Susan dismissed the secretaries. Mallory had that in common with Lockwood: he didn't believe in unnecessary night work either. Franklin and Marilyn Mallory had made themselves millionaires by the time they were forty, with a fast-food chain that had spread all across the country. The Mallory's fast food was the fastest of all, and the one nobody had thought of before them: eggs. The stands by the highway that sold omelettes and egg sandwiches, fried and scrambled eggs, egg soufflés and egg surprises, were in the shape of an egg. Mallory's political enemies naturally called him the Egg King.

It was evident to Mallory when he and Marilyn were young that two competent people, working ten hours a day as a unit, were superior to one person working twenty hours alone. He had always organized his staff in two-person units, from top management down to kitchen help. In Mallory's campaign for re-election, Mallory and Susan Grant were the prime two-person unit, as they had been in his White House; dozens of others supported them. Paired workers, sharing jobs and rewards in absolute equality, developed very strong bonds to each other and to their leaders. The system worked as well in government and politics as it had worked in business—and, before that, as Mallory said, among Spartan infantry. Those incomparable soldiers, willing to die together if necessary, had always been lovers too.

Susan, after making the call that shut down all the telephones in the suite except the confidential line, went into her bedroom. She washed her face and hands and loosened her pale hair, brushing it out until it hung to her shoulders. When she returned to the sitting room, she found Mallory shaking cocktails; he liked only one sort of drink, a vodka gimlet weakened with cracked ice. He poured one for each of them and brought them to a table in front of the sofa.

As he handed Susan her drink he leaned down and they touched each other for the second time that day—a soft kiss on the lips. Susan touched the tip of his tongue with hers, then stepped back and smiled. Mallory had put some Mozart on the tape deck while she was out of the room; he liked music played a bit louder than she did, but she had got used to it. They sat down together on the sofa, close together, her hand lying loosely in his, thighs touching, and drank their gimlets. They were waiting for eight o'clock. Vaguely disturbed by each other's body, but as peaceful after the exhausting day as they might have been after making love, they watched through the window as the great nickel sun of summer went down through tendrils of fog into the Pacific.

Almost four hundred million miles from earth, a pioneering force of thirty human beings, fifteen men and fifteen women organized in a hierarchy of pairs, had landed that day on Ganymede, the largest of Jupiter's moons. Franklin Mallory had put them there. He had launched their expedition into space before he left office so that Lockwood was powerless to call it back to earth.

On the floor of the convention, projection screens had been erected so that the delegates could see the landing. The television images, delayed thirty-five minutes in their voyage at the speed of light over the vast distance between the two planets, were as always more brilliant than the true colors of life. The cameras on Ganymede were able to capture, even from a distance of almost seven hundred thousand miles, only a portion of the unimaginably huge disk of Jupiter. But from the rubbled landing site on Ganymede, everyone on earth could see the boiling surface of the planet, thirty-five times as bright as the full moon seen from earth, the eruptions in its atmosphere—storms that were larger than earth and older than the human race. The earthly mind had been projected onto the surface of another astral body.

Franklin Mallory had done this. He and Susan Grant, still in their quiet room with the feeble lights of San Francisco outside the window, watched the transmission from Ganymede. After a long time, the networks began intercutting shots of other watchers: the silent rows of delegates on the floor of the convention that was going to nominate Mallory for the presidency for a third time later that evening; silent crowds in public squares; presidents and dictators and the last kings left on earth. Many faces, like Susan Grant's, were wet with tears. For once there were no interviews. Men with microphones stood silent in the silent crowds.

From Ganymede came another image: the glittering mother ship *Humanity* setting like a heavenly body over the horizon of Jupiter's moon. *Humanity* transmitted one final picture of the landing craft, an ovoid sheathed in gold foil lying on Ganymede's barren plain; and then this alien object, the shape out of which all warm life on earth had emerged, was lost from view.

"You might know," said Patrick Graham, watching from the

floor of the convention at the Cow Palace with Emily by his side, "that Mallory would make the landing craft in the shape of an egg. The Egg King's ultimate commercial message." Emily took out her notebook and wrote down Patrick's words. He expelled breath through his nostrils in annoyance; Emily was learning that few people like being reported upon less than reporters do.

Jupiter's image vanished from the television screen. Franklin Mallory said, "Those were the loveliest moments of my life."

He wiped away Susan's tears with his fingers. The landing on Ganymede had been planned as his valedictory—had he been re-elected four years before, *Humanity*'s destination and Mallory's last hour in the Presidency would have been reached at the same time. Now *Humanity* would carry Mallory back into the presidency. It was his achievement, and the symbol of his idea of man's destiny.

Mallory and Susan went by helicopter to the Cow Palace. Awaiting Mallory on the podium was the only other presidential candidate the party had ever had. He was an uncompromising old oilman who had run on Mallory's ideas before the country was ready for them. Twice he had gone down to defeat to make Mallory's final victory possible. Now he struck the gavel twice and filled his lungs.

"My fellow Americans," he cried in his sonorous Texas basso, "the *true* President of the United States!"

Mallory entered alone, with no further ceremony. He walked quietly across the wide stage, arms hanging loose at his sides, his white hair catching the light. He glanced courteously at the throng of delegates and spectators, all on their feet and chanting his name, as calmly as he might have raised his eyes from his work to acknowledge the arrival of a familiar visitor in his office. Scenes of the landing were being replayed on the big screens suspended from all sides of the hall.

Mallory stood easily behind the podium and waited for the noise to die. It ceased after many minutes, when Mallory, without making even the simplest gesture, spoke his first word.

"*Humanity*," he said, and when the murmur died, said the name of the ship again. "*Humanity* has reached the moons of Jupiter. Years ago, when I named that ship and set her course, I had a purpose in mind. I want to remind men and women everywhere on earth, the race for whom *Humanity* was named, what that purpose was. It was to renew the idea that anything is possible.

"Anything, that is, except to go back. That is not possible. Mankind can never be what it was at any time in the past. It must be what it is at the hour in which it is living. It must accept that it will change and be something new in the future. Man is changing. He must change. He cannot say no to that fact.

"*Humanity*, the finest machine man has yet constructed, has made the greatest voyage in the history of living things, and it has taken the eyes and minds of mankind with it. We are all on Ganymede.

"Yet this is only the first step on our journey. The hardship and the glory lie ahead of us. We are going to take our own evolution into our own hands.

"Those who want the past to return may not have it. What is it they want? To live by mysteries. Superstition, starvation, the hateful separation of mankind into hostile colors and sexes and religions. The supremacy of emotion over reason. Murder. War. Savagery. Crime. They may not have it.

"There are no mysteries. There is only what we don't yet know. There is only life. If men and women as frail as you and I can sail in that fragile craft, which we call *Humanity*, into the face of Jupiter—a body four times as far away from us as the sun—if they can do that, putting away fear, putting away jealousy, leaving behind warmth and gravity and air and water, what can mankind not do? We can do anything. I promise you, in *Humanity*'s name, we shall."

Mallory stopped speaking as abruptly as he had begun. The atmosphere in the convention hall was split by the cries of the delegates. They leaped onto their chairs, fists upraised, and shrieked.

Patrick Graham stood among them with his camera crew. Emily, writing furiously in her pad, studied Patrick's smooth face as it turned and watched, the famous features white with emotion. All around him were faces drenched crimson by feeling.

Where Patrick was struck dumb by Mallory's performance, these people were given voice—a single voice, chanting in unison the three-syllable name of their hero: "Mal-lo-ry! Mal-lo-ry!"

Graham was the opposite of these people; it wasn't just a matter of politics, it was physical. *As if his body were composed of different atoms from theirs.* Emily scribbled: *matter and anti-matter, silicon and carbon.*

In the broadcasting booths above them, Emily could see the faces of the commentators, as agitated as those in the mob; their mouths moved in attempts to describe the scene, analyze what Mallory had said, understand what he had released in these people.

Mallory himself, standing quiet and unsmiling at the podium, did not show the least sign that he was surprised that his speech, with all its appeal to reason, should have touched off this storm of

131

emotion. His eyes roved over the crowd. Emily had the feeling, irrational as the hypnotic repetition of Mallory's name, that Mallory was looking directly at her. He was hundreds of feet away, he couldn't possibly have singled her out of that hopping, shrieking mob. Yet looking up at him she believed his eyes were locked to hers. Did everyone there feel the same? Emily dipped her head to write that down on her pad.

Patrick said something to her but she couldn't hear him; he was mute inside the roar of Mallory's people.

Swallowed, wrote Emily. Patrick looked like a man who was disappearing down the gullet of some great beast. That was the image his cameraman transmitted over the network, and in its way it was as telling as anything the audience had seen that night.

10

Emily remained at the convention until the balloting for the presidential nomination was completed. Mallory won the vote of every delegate from every state, with the chairman of each delegation echoing the words of the old Texan who had introduced Mallory after the landing on Ganymede: "Alaska proudly casts all its votes for the *true* President of the United States, Franklin Douglass Mallory of New York! . . . Mr. Chairman, Washington is unanimous and casts all its votes for the *true* President of the United States! . . ."

Patrick Graham roved the floor, taping the brief interviews with delegates that he meant to use as a montage to introduce his live talk with Mallory at the end of the convention. Mallory's people were calm and happy; not even Patrick's taunting questions or the memory of what he had done to them in the last election could rouse them to reckless answers. He grew sharper: he wanted drama, a glimpse of the primitive mind of this crowd of Pavlovian believers. Nothing worked. Emily wrote in her book: *O Patrick where is thy sting-a-ling-a-ling?*

At two in the morning she and Patrick drifted out of the hall while the delegates joined hands and sang "America the Beautiful." The scene was transmitted through the space communications system to the crews of the American ships moored in Jupiter's gravity.

On the way to the hotel, Patrick slumped in the back seat beside Emily, smoking. Gagging on the fumes of his cigarette, Emily rolled down the window. She put a hand to her long hair to keep it from blowing against Patrick's face in the narrow back seat of the car. They were close, and it required effort to keep their bodies from touching; Emily faintly remembered the wide comfortable cars of her childhood. Everything had been bigger then—houses, cities, distances, portions of food. There had been more lights; windows white with them in the night. It wasn't only growing up that had changed her perspective; the scale of all material objects had been reduced in her short lifetime because Earth was running out of materials, and therefore no one really had wealth anymore. Money meant little: there was less and less that could be bought.

At the Fairmont, as they left the elevator on their floor, Patrick gave Emily an undisguised look of sexual invitation. She had been expecting it. All through the week, she had seen desire gathering in him; his eyes were often upon her legs and breasts. Charlotte Graham had warned her. No warning had been needed. Emily was used to having her male subjects suggest bed when her research arrived at a certain point; she supposed they felt penetrated and wanted to do to her physically what she was doing to them emotionally.

She didn't let Patrick even ask the question. "I'm feeling ill," she told him. "It's no sleep and all that noise in the Cow Palace. And your cigarettes. I warn you you're going to suffer in my piece for blowing smoke at me." Emily kissed Patrick on the cheek and swatted his head lightly with her notepad. He shrugged and left her without saying good-night.

Emily woke at dawn, violently ill. She ran to the bathroom and knelt, retching. Afterwards, brushing her teeth, she felt fine again and wondered why; always before, being sick had left her limp and disgusted. She switched on the light over the mirror and looked at herself. Her sleepy face glowed; she might just have come in from a walk in the woods with Julian. She wore one of his pajama jackets, the one he had hung up behind the bathroom door on the morning she had left, and she lifted the striped cloth of the loose sleeve to her nose and inhaled a trace of her husband's odor. Emily grinned at herself in the glass and raised her clenched hands above her head: the same gesture of triumph made by all those thousands of Mallory people the night before. She went back into the bedroom and punched out the area code and number of the telephone that rang on Julian's desk without going through the White House switchboard.

"Julian? I have morning sickness."

Julian's laughter came over the line. Emily heard a thud and knew that he had put his feet on the desk. He was settling back to talk to her for more than his usual measured minute. Emily loved the telephone; Julian, for a man who lived by the instrument, seemed to despise it. He didn't trust it to convey the nuances of face-to-face conversation or the precision of the written word. He refused to exchange endearments over the Bell system. When he told Emily that he loved her, he had to touch her. She was sure that Julian wasn't going to let her talk about the baby. She had turned in too many false alarms.

"Start thinking of names for your child," she said. "Give me a list for each sex. No—I want it to be Julian if it's a boy."

"Horace. We never name our sons for ourselves, and we already have an Elliott. Emily if it's a girl. That's the complete list."

"I don't get a vote? I'm just the incubator?"

"Exactly." Julian listened, chuckling, as Emily went on about the symptoms of pregnancy for several more sentences.

"I tried to call you last night," he said at last.

"I was at the Cow Palace, watching Patrick suffer. We didn't get back to the hotel until two-thirty or three. I've barely slept."

"Patrick is suffering?"

"Hardly the word. He can't bear it. He thinks he's been transported to the Nuremberg Rally by time machine. . . . Don't quote that, it's for my profile."

"Is Patrick going to like you writing such things about him?"

"Mmmm. Rules of the game."

"Patrick is really upset?"

Emily described the look of Graham among the triumphant delegates, his disgust with Mallory during their conversation in the hotel suite.

"How did *you* like Mallory?"

"Julian, he's as marvelous in his way as Frosty Lockwood. The same magnetism—only more so, I'm sorry to tell you."

"I don't think I'm going to enjoy this article of yours much more than Patrick. Mallory marvelous? Really, Emily."

"Look, love," Emily said, "I'm not a Lockwood voter this week, I'm a reporter on assignment. I have no loyalties—only eyes and ears. Mallory has *force*. Didn't you see him make that speech last night?"

"Yes, and saw the Jupiter extravaganza. Of course he can turn people who respond to his kind of gibberish into whirling dervishes. It's politics by circus."

Emily yawned. "It's six o'clock out here," she said. "As soon as the first doctor opens I'll take in a sample of my waters. I'll be home tomorrow or the day after with the results."

"Is Patrick really so edgy about Mallory?"

"Patrick?" Emily was annoyed to go back to Patrick as a subject. "Of course he is. He's worse than you. He thinks poor old Mallory's the Antichrist."

"You don't?"

"I mustn't have evil thoughts about anyone, Julian. I'm among the blessed."

Julian broke the connection. Horace, seated once again in the worn visitor's chair, had heard the whole conversation over the speaker phone. He made no comment.

Julian turned his back for a moment and gazed through the bulletproof glass onto the lawns. " 'The *true* President of the United States,' " he said. His lips twisted in disgust and he wiped them hard with his knuckles before letting Horace see his face again. "It's possible," Julian said, "that if Patrick feels as Emily says he does, he can be dealt with."

"Is Emily a trustworthy source?" asked Horace.

"When she's working, yes. She sees right into people. It amazed me, the amount she knew about me after a week. She wrote things that I recognized to be the truth about myself, but hadn't perceived before."

"That's quite a gift in a journalist," Horace said. "It must be an uncomfortable thing in marriage."

"No. It only works when she has no emotional attachment. As soon as love entered the picture I became a mystery to her. Odd. I don't understand it."

"How *are* you going to handle Graham?"

Julian's face closed. Even his brother had no business in this chamber of his life.

The two of them had spent hours discussing the assassination, Julian probing for details and more details. As they talked, a change had come over Julian. He had got used to the stench of the dissecting room, the flaccid body of the subject on the slab, the sight of diseased organs. Where, in the beginning, he had covered his mouth and nose with a handkerchief and stared in horror, he now grasped the scalpel firmly and laid open the abdominal cavity, naming the muscles and guts as he slashed them, calling on Horace's greater skill when it was needed to find a nerve that was not quite where it should be. Julian had lost his revulsion, and then his fear. Horace wasn't so sure that he would ever overcome his foreboding. Few did: even the professor of anatomy, munching a fresh pear as he observes the excision of a tumor, knows in his subconscious that only a weak arc of electricity, the voltage in the brain, separates him—hungry and hearty and rubicund—from the gray mutilated cadaver.

135

"The President might talk to Patrick," Julian said.

"That's quite a risk."

"Letting Patrick fester is a worse risk. Lockwood's instinct is always to tell the truth."

"That can be a perilous instinct. The world remembers what Ibn Awad seemed to be when he was alive. If Lockwood tells the truth, he'll have to speak ill of the dead."

"He knows that."

"Does he know it's suicidal?"

Julian didn't want to speak about Lockwood's feelings. On the other hand, he needed help from a mind like his own. There was no other mind like that, now that their father was dead, except Horace's.

"I'm not sure. I'm not sure he cares. It's possible he thinks he's not worthy to be President anymore."

"Because he prevented a holocaust?"

Julian hit the top of his desk, hard, with his bony hand. "Where's the proof of that? Where are the bombs? Where is the evidence? Lockwood has no case except that he acted in blind faith on the suspicions of the FIS."

"He acted on a certitude. Jack Philindros doesn't report suspicions as facts."

Julian's telephone flashed. For once he ignored it.

"Horace," he said. "You've got to find those bombs for me."

Horace sighed; they had been over this before. "You have the whole trail of proof," he said. "The purchase of the plutonium. We have the man who sold it, and he'll talk to Graham. We have the technicians who made the bombs; they'll talk to Graham. All these people work for money. You have—"

"I have nothing unless I have the bombs. The actual *bombs,* Horace, physical, tangible evidence that Ibn Awad truly had them, and truly meant to blow up Jerusalem or New York with them."

The telephone was still blinking. Julian threw a switch and talked to a man who had just learned that Susan Grant, Franklin Mallory's assistant, had met O. N. Laster, the president of Universal Energy, in a borrowed empty house in San Francisco; there were photographs of the two of them entering and leaving the house separately. Susan Grant had been wearing a black wig. Julian listened impatiently. But when he responded, his voice was courteous.

To Horace, though, he muttered, *"Fool!"*

"I thought you didn't run surveillance on your opposition."

"We don't. I can't control every zealot in the party. That man is a skulker. It's his hobby. It was a man like him who . . ."

Julian stopped. Horace had no need to know where the information about Mallory's plot to steal Canada had come from, or how it had got into Patrick Graham's hands. Not even Lockwood knew that.

Julian came back, tenaciously, to the subject of the bombs. "There must be some way," he said. "Horace, damn it, you and Philindros got us into this."

"We didn't think you'd have to defend it in public."

"Do you think we can?"

"No."

"Well, we're going to have to. There *is* a way. All I want, Horace, is a straw for Patrick to grasp. He'll swim the Atlantic for Lockwood, you heard what Emily just said on the phone. But I have to give him something he can hold on to."

"I've given you all we have, Julian. The truth."

The President buzzed for Julian. He stood up. "What I want, what I need, is *better* information," he said to his brother. "I know it must exist. Go where you have to go, do what you have to do. But, Horace, get it." He put his hand on the door leading into the Oval Office.

"Don't you feel any responsibility for this man?" he asked. "Don't you see what losing Lockwood would *mean?*"

Julian went through the door. While it was still open, Horace heard the President's voice and his brother's—Lockwood's loud, Julian's a murmur. Horace knew what he had known all along: that Philindros was right. Julian would ruin himself, ruin their name, ruin the FIS, for Lockwood.

"I'm damned if you will," said Horace to the closed door into the Oval Office; and, smiling at Julian's secretary as he passed through her clamorous office, he sauntered out of the White House.

11

Emily never accepted food or drink from a subject; it was a reporter's principle. But now she had all she needed about Patrick Graham. There was no further need to watch what he did, record what he said; he was just an acquaintance again. She could write the story. When Patrick asked her to dine with him on their last evening in San Francisco, she accepted.

Emily knew, too, that there was almost no chance that Patrick would try again to have her; they were taking a midnight flight to Washington, and before they left for the restaurant they checked out of their rooms at the Fairmont and sent their bags ahead of them to the airport. Before she left the hotel, Emily tried again to reach the physician to whom she'd given a sample of her urine for a pregnancy test. She left the name of the restaurant Patrick was taking her to with the answering service.

The restaurant was French. Patrick was well known there; the owner sent wine to their table and the chef served the entrée himself. It was something he had invented for the occasion, and he stood near the table in his kitchen whites, watchful while Patrick took the first taste.

"Exquisite, Claude," said Patrick.

"So kind, Mr. Graham. May I name it for you?"

They were speaking in French, but Emily understood what they were saying—or, rather, construed the meaning of their simple words by comparing them to the ones she remembered from schoolgirl Latin and French.

"I'm honored," Patrick replied. "But will you name it instead for the lady?"

"Done. Loup de mer jolie Madame."

The chef bowed and Patrick told Emily in English what had happened. She thanked the chef, who kissed the air an inch from her hand. Waiters in black tail coats alighted in flocks at their table; dirty dishes were wafted away, crumbs were brushed up as soon as they fell on the linen cloth, each sip of wine was replaced as it was taken from the glass. Patrick joshed the waiters. He enjoyed the fuss. Emily stopped herself from getting out her notebook. This was private, off the record. The scene did not please her; Julian would never have allowed this sort of attention to be paid to him. No one who knew him would have tried. Julian didn't even like to be recognized in public places, and the headwaiters they knew had learned not to address him by name when he came in. Julian's way, Emily knew, was as bad a pretension as Patrick Graham's, but she preferred it.

There was something attractive about Patrick. She understood why he had all the girls he wanted. His fame might be an aphrodisiac, but there were things about him that would have coaxed women into his bed if he had been unknown and poor. Emily herself cared little for looks in men, and Patrick's handsome face, his perfect clothes, his well-kept body meant less to her than they might have to another woman. He had beautiful hands with long tapered fingers, and the good sense not to spoil them with rings.

The quality in Patrick that moved Emily was his shyness. He fought to hide it, but it came to the surface all the time. Charlotte was right. For all his fame and success, Patrick wasn't quite sure of himself. At some time, thought Emily, he must have lost something that he loved and wanted very much. He feared that it might happen again. Emily imagined that Patrick must be a desperate lover; he would want the woman to like him best of all the men she'd known. There was no glimmer of this trait in Julian; he had never had a woman until she loved him. Who, then, was incomplete—Julian or Patrick?

Patrick spoke to Emily about paintings. Most of his conversation was about objects, and she had never, in her research, quite managed to break through this barrier. He didn't like to talk about people; the men and women he met and interviewed in his work were the raw material of his profession. He lost interest in them as soon as he was through with them. Julian had said once, when he and Emily were walking home from a dinner party at the Grahams', that Patrick and Charlotte had no friends apart from one another, only contacts; Julian thought that was the nature of life in Washington. It was the nature of life in the modern world; somehow, before Emily was born, people had got separated from one another. Before Julian she had never felt attached to any other human. Even her lovers broke away from her during the very fall into pleasure, she could feel them go into themselves, into a blackness where she couldn't follow. As a child, and even now, she loved books and films about simple people in old America, going west in wagons, making farms in the wilderness, facing hardships, loving a little knot of family.

Patrick broke her train of thought. "That's a handsome Sargent, the young woman in the field of black, that you and Julian have," he said.

"Julian's grandmother. Her first husband killed himself when she was twenty-three, no one ever knew why. She was still in mourning when the picture was painted. She married a Hubbard afterwards, and had Julian's father by him."

"She was as romantic as she looks, then."

"Yes. The Hubbards went in for tragic romance in their palmy days."

"Do you have things like that in your family history?"

"Everyone does. In our family we call suicides and people who run away with other people's husbands 'the fools.' A name will come up. 'Ah,' we'll say, 'that was one of the fools.'"

Patrick was given a note by one of the waiters; he read it, then glanced down the row of tables. Near the end, alone, sat Clive Wilmot.

"Speaking of which."

"Of which what?"

"Fools. Clive Wilmot wants to join us for coffee and cognac."

"Should I know him?"

"No. Waiter, please tell the gentleman that we're sorry but we have a plane to catch."

But it was already too late to escape. Wilmot, carrying a bottle of French brandy in his hand, was approaching their table. In his wake came the nervous headwaiter, protesting.

"Glasses, man," Clive said. "Three of those great balloons to put the brandy in."

"It's all right, Jean-Pierre," Patrick said. "Clive. I didn't expect to see you here."

"My dear Patrick, you never expect to see me anywhere. That's my value to your life. I introduce the element of chance. I might be anywhere, spying, breaking in on trysts. Lovely girl you have tonight. Eyes as blue as a Swiss bank note. That's meant as a great compliment. One adores what one doesn't have. As water is to a thirsty Hottentot grubbing for roots in the sands of the Kalahari, so are Swiss bank notes to the Englishman. I *am* an Englishman, my dear. That excuses everything."

Patrick didn't introduce Emily. Clive sat down opposite them in a chair brought by one of the waiters and put his elbows on the narrow table. It tipped towards him and Patrick, with a deft movement of both hands, saved his wineglass and Emily's from spilling.

"Marvelous, you Yanks are all such athletes," said Clive. The glasses came and he poured brandy into them. "This isn't bad stuff, considering where we are. Bought it with secret funds, Patrick. Be warned—it may contain a drug to control the mind. You'll tell me everything—after the first sip, this young woman's name, let us say."

"Emily Barker, Clive Wilmot."

"Howdeedo. Are you a San Franciscan? No? Too bad. I had my first topless shoeshine in San Francisco. Can't forget it. Aureoles and nipples like hypnotic pink eyes at the ends of those great gyrating globes. Where is she now?"

"Have you been observing the local madness?" Patrick asked.

"The convention? Your man Mallory? Yes. Have to keep up the British end, you know. Cable home my keen insights. There's fear of Anschluss in Whitehall. Today Saskatchewan, tomorrow Kent and Cornwall. Will you elect that man again?"

"Anything is possible."

"I do hope so. We haven't had a real lunatic running a first-class power for ages. I mean, madmen like old Amin don't count, do they? Or Qaddafi or even Ibn Awad. Uganda and Libya and Hagreb don't come up to much. Besides, all those chaps are gone.

140

Sanity everywhere. Too boring. Here's to Franklin Mallory. Long may he rave."

Clive lifted his glass to his lips. He closed his eyes tightly while he drank, like someone at the instant of greater pleasure. His lids opened and he stared at Patrick. Neither man spoke.

Emily said, "You're a journalist?"

"No."

"Clive," said Patrick, "that's very good. Can you keep all your replies that short from now on?"

"What, then?" asked Emily.

Patrick replied for Clive Wilmot, speaking in a light tone of voice, smiling. After a week of minute observation, Emily knew the signs that he was annoyed and wanted to hit a target.

"Clive is a secret agent," he said. He paused, then whispered, "*British intelligence.*"

"Are you really, Clive?"

"Patrick likes to glamorize his friends. Always lying them up—makes *him* look better, you see. I work in the embassy in Washington. Perhaps I do skulk a bit, hoping people will believe Patrick's thrilling stories about me."

"Why do you have the Colgate toothpaste in your breast pocket?" Clive had succeeded in amusing Emily.

"To hide microfilm in, you know. Also to brush my teeth. Hygiene's most important here. My predecessor had baize teeth, very British; no one in America could bear the sight. . . . I say, Patrick, when are you going to use that story on Ibn Awad?"

Patrick called for the check and signed it with a gold fountain pen. He ignored the waiter's thanks for the enormous tip. He pushed his untouched brandy glass away with his forefinger, one inch across the white damask.

Clive said, "I mean, you went all the way out there and spoke to the right chap, didn't you? And didn't he tell you Awad had been done in? First-class source, Hassan. Knows all."

"Clive, this is not the place for this conversation."

"No? Ah, the young lady. Probably doesn't know who old Awad was, much less why your chaps wrote finis to him. Just another raghead, eh, Emily?" He gave her a broad wink.

"Why doesn't Patrick like you?" Emily asked.

"Doesn't he? Can't think why not. Gave him the scoop of his life. Lean closer. My breath all right?"

"Clive," Patrick said. "Really I have to leave. Get up and let us out."

"You see," Clive said to Emily, "there was this man called Ibn Awad, the emir of Hagreb. Filthy rich, you know, oil. But mad."

"I know who Ibn Awad was."

"Do you? Brava. Did you know he was murdered by your President? Diabolical plot."

"Which President?"

"The one you've got now. Lockwood? Holy sort of chap himself. But he rubbed out old Ibn Awad. Patrick knows it. Right, Patrick?"

"What is this man saying?" Emily demanded.

Patrick Graham shoved the table. Its opposite edge struck Clive Wilmot's chest. The headwaiter sprang to the back of Wilmot's chair and pulled it backwards. Clive remained seated and was dragged back over the carpet.

"Absolute truth. Patrick loveth not the truth. Pity," Clive said.

"We have a plane to catch," Patrick said.

Clive put both hands firmly on the table, trapping Patrick and Emily on the banquette. "Spare me a moment," he said. From the inside pocket of his sagging jacket he produced a long envelope. He offered it to Patrick. "Do take it," he said. Patrick did so, and heard the snick of a camera; he didn't look up, he was so used to being photographed; but Emily did, and saw a man who had emerged from the men's room a moment before put a tiny camera in his pocket and walk purposefully out the door.

"A bit of light reading for the airplane," Clive said. "I think when you spoke to Hassan he mentioned something about a strange disease. Dysgraphia, is that the name?" He turned his haggard face in appeal to Emily. "Do you know that word?"

"No."

"Pity. Old Patrick does. Look inside, Patrick, old chap. Do."

Patrick opened the clasp and looked into the envelope. He saw a computer printout.

"The medical file. The bit about the lesion on the brain occurs about midway through; I've drawn a red line under it."

Clive gave Emily a brilliant smile. "You wouldn't care to leave at once for Tahiti, would you?" he asked. "You *do* have hundred-franc eyes."

"Where did this come from, Clive?" Patrick demanded.

"From a lover of truth, like yourself." Clive Wilmot stood up, smiled once more at Emily, and pulled the table away. "Happy flight," he said. "Say a prayer for poor old Ibn Awad. Who knows, he may hear you up in heaven, though I don't suppose he's much of a one for listening to Americans, now that he knows everything. Do you believe that, Emily—the dead know everything?"

Patrick took Emily's arm and led her away. The headwaiter was whispering in Wilmot's ear. The Englishman searched his pockets for money. He took no further interest in Graham or in Emily. Emily looked at him closely, pausing to do so while Patrick tugged at her arm.

At the door, the owner spoke her name.

"Mrs. Hubbard, the telephone."

She took the instrument from his hand, listened, thanked the caller.

"Patrick," she said, "is that man really with British intelligence?"

"Yes. He's the head of it in Washington. Julian will tell you."

"Then why was he saying that? Is it true?"

Patrick Graham shrugged. "Julian would know," he said. "Ask him."

12

During the flight to Washington, Emily sat alone, many rows away from Patrick's seat in the smoking section. She refused the drinks the steward offered her and wrapped herself in a blanket, her legs curled beneath her. The flight would take hours: no SSTs flew over the United States under Lockwood. She couldn't sleep. She opened her purse to find a tranquilizer, then remembered that she mustn't take them anymore, because of the baby. The phone call in the restaurant had been from the doctor. Her pregnancy test had been positive.

Emily had always expected that she would sense a quickening within her when at last she heard that news, but as the wind of the jet's passage whined at the cold black window in which she saw her whitened face, she felt nothing at all.

From the airport Emily went straight to the White House. Julian's day was just beginning in the hushed West Wing, but Horace was already in Julian's office. He gave her the single chair and stood leaning against the wall. Emily's hair was unbrushed and separated into lank strands. Her eyes were red from lack of sleep and there was a sickly pale ring around her lips. When Julian's secretary brought coffee, the cup rattled on the saucer in Emily's hands. The smell of it made her ill and she ran from the room with her hand over her mouth.

"You *do* have morning sickness," Julian said. He had gone out into the corridor to wait for her outside the lavatory.

"Yes, I do. The test was positive this time."

Julian put his arms around her. Her body was rigid, withdrawn. When he kissed her, tasting the sourness that lingered in her mouth,

143

her lips didn't move against his. Her eyes behind her glasses were watchful; he hadn't seen that look in them since the first week they'd known each other, when she was studying him for her newspaper piece.

"Come back to the office," he said. "I'll have Horace go away."

"He can stay. I haven't come to discuss secrets of the marriage bed."

In the office, Emily gave Julian no chance to speak to Horace about her pregnancy. She told them both what she had heard in San Francisco from Clive Wilmot.

"Does this man know what he's talking about?" she asked.

Julian looked gravely across the desk at Emily. She was sitting upright, a narrow figure in the wide chair; the fine hair at her temples was damp with perspiration after the effort of her retching.

"Did Patrick believe it? Did you?"

"Patrick wouldn't confirm or deny. I certainly don't want to believe it. Murderers? Lockwood? My husband? Julian, tell me."

"Emily, really. Why are you so upset about something that was said by some mad character you don't even know?"

"Wilmot plays the madman. But his eyes aren't crazy at all. He was doing what he did for a purpose. It shook Patrick."

"And you."

"Jesus Christ, yes! Five minutes afterwards I hardly understood what the doctor was telling me when he said I was pregnant."

Horace asked questions. Emily told him all that had been said: Patrick Graham's trip to the Near East, his meeting there with a man named Hassan.

"Hassan?" said Horace, alert. "Where, exactly? What country?"

"They didn't say. Horace, why are you the one who's grilling me? Do you work here now?"

"Horace knows that part of the world," Julian said. "He's trying to help."

Emily looked from one brother to the other. She had never before seen Horace without the faint smile, like Julian's, that always danced in his eyes. Now Horace looked like a very hard man, someone who was too cold to let anger or any other feeling show.

"Julian," she said, "you don't want to discuss this with me, do you?"

"Not now. I knew that Patrick was chasing this rumor."

"Have you spoken to him?"

"In passing. He's not our enemy, Emily. I'm not terribly worried."

"Then you don't understand Patrick. He's a reporter before he's anything else."

Again Julian and Horace were silent. Emily saw that she was an alien here; her husband and her brother-in-law were not the same people when they were in this house. Her body relaxed. The energy that Clive Wilmot had put into her with his accusations drained away. She realized how tired she was—her back ached, the muscles in her thighs were sore, her feet in their flimsy shoes bothered her. She wanted a hot bath and a long sleep. She'd done too much in San Francisco. Anxiety for the baby stabbed at her, and then guilt that she hadn't thought enough about this small life for which she'd waited such a long time. Julian saw the change in Emily. He held out both his hands as if to grasp Emily's, though they were too far away from each other to be able to do this.

Horace broke in. "The envelope Wilmot gave to Patrick," he said. "Can you describe it?"

Emily sighed. "It was a long brown envelope with a clasp at the flap, you know the kind."

"What was in it?"

"I didn't look. Wilmot said it was a medical report. He said that this Hassan Patrick had interviewed had mentioned it."

"Anything else?"

"Wilmot mentioned a disease, asked me if I knew what it was —dys-something."

Horace was looking at her with his pale bright eyes, distant as the sky in a waterless country. She wanted to tell him whatever he wanted to know.

"Wilmot said something about a lesion on the brain. He said he'd underlined it in red."

The smile came back into Horace's eyes. Emily had always thought that the sight of her gave Horace pleasure. Now she wasn't so sure—she'd seen how easily he could put out the light in his face. He put on good humor like a disguise. Julian, too. They were both, in their silence, lying to her. She knew it.

"I'm so glad about the morning sickness," Julian said. "Celebration tonight at the Cantina?"

Emily nodded. Julian always wanted to go to this restaurant when he was happy. It was the best in Washington.

"I'll call Joseph and make the reservation," Emily said. She took Julian's face between her hands when he came around his desk, and kissed his lips.

The Secret Service took her home. The children weren't there. She turned on a tape machine to break the silence. Lying in the tub, she had the frightening idea—it came and went in an instant— that the baby could read her thoughts. She stopped thinking about Julian and what he might have done. With her head cushioned on a folded towel, she dozed, her slight body half afloat in the soapy water.

13

Jack Philindros's plain black shoes were together on the carpet and his hands were folded in his lap. He looked, Julian thought, like a parson waiting for the choir to finish a hymn. Horace had been sent away before his chief arrived. Julian told him what Emily had reported about the encounter between Patrick Graham and Clive Wilmot in San Francisco.

Philindros said, "Wilmot has always been too reckless. But even knowing he's the source, FIS can't surveille him while he's still in the United States. It would be illegal. Do you want me to notify the Bureau? Of course, I'd have to tell them *why* they're tailing Wilmot, but if that's what the President desires . . ."

Giving the FBI so much as a scent of the case was the last thing Julian desired. Mallory had seeded the Bureau with his men when he was in office; it was the natural place for them.

"What we desire, Jack, is to find out two things—how Wilmot knows what happened to Awad, and why he told Graham about it. He must be acting as somebody's agent. Is he being paid? Is he a believer of some kind?"

"Clive is not a believer," Philindros said. He made no other reply to Julian's remarks. Julian had been giving a command. He didn't know if Philindros understood that. He chafed under Philindros's stolid caution, his polite refusal to see another man's intentions until they had been spoken aloud. Julian was used to dealing with people who thought as he thought, who acted as they knew he would act.

"I'd like your advice as to how we can discover these facts, Jack," he said, spacing the words.

Julian wanted Philindros to hear the annoyance in his voice. The other man registered nothing; in his measured, soft tones he answered Julian at once.

"Assuming that you reject domestic surveillance by the Bureau, and want FIS to deal with the investigation," Philindros said, "then the best thing would be to somehow send Wilmot out of the United States. Panic him in some way. Follow him abroad, track him to his source."

"Is that possible?"

"Yes, but difficult. He's vulnerable, but he's British. We've

146

always felt we should be . . . *correct* with the British. Would you countenance an operation against them—a deception?"

Julian used a gesture he found useful with Philindros—he beckoned with a forefinger, as if Philindros's words were figures small in the distance that must be called closer. Nevertheless, Philindros waited until Julian nodded.

"Then if you'll give me a few days, and give me back Horace for that period, I'll work out some possibilities."

Julian named a time the next day when Philindros was to come back.

Philindros said, "Can I take Horace with me now?"

"He's downstairs. You can meet him in the garage."

Philindros was already standing; he'd risen from the chair without touching the arms; most people struggled and heaved in its depths to get to their feet. Philindros had extraordinary muscle tone; he ran twenty miles a day and had climbed some unnamed peak in the Himalayas on his last vacation.

Beneath a James Joseph Cerruti oil of two work-thickened old Italians playing cards in an American tenement yard, a table at the Cantina d'Italia was set for Emily and Julian. Champagne cooled in a silver bucket. Julian touched Emily's hand under the table. On coming home two hours before, he had found her asleep and wakened her to make love. She never failed to leave Julian filled with tenderness; from the start Emily had been something new to him. Caroline in the acts of sex had seemed to snarl over her shoulder at the male like a lioness, and this strangeness was exciting; other women had wept in Julian's arms or lain under him like stones. Emily danced and glowed, breathing gently during her excitement, sighing afterwards like a bride in wartime holding a photograph to her breast. But today she had held him away from her, and risen quickly from the rumpled bed.

Emily ate very little. She said she feared sickness in the morning. She drank sparingly of the wine Julian had ordered to celebrate the baby's conception. Julian found her looking at him several times during dinner. That afternoon, with her supple muscles still gripping his emptied flesh, he had opened his eyes and found Emily's eyes, wide and wiser than he thought they could be, staring at him. It was only a matter of time before Emily began to ask more insistent questions. Curiosity—a compulsion to know people and events for what they really were—was Emily's curse. She studied, burrowed, questioned, observed; she practiced her writing as a girl with an ear for music might spend eight hours a day at the piano.

147

"Julian, is Horace something besides a banker? Is that why he's spending all this time with you?"

Julian turned his gaze on her. The Hubbard twinkle, thought Emily, remembering how suddenly it had vanished that morning from both brothers' eyes. Now it went out again.

"You won't answer because you won't lie to me, is that it?"

"Because this is not the place. Emily, Horace truly is a very good banker. And he's my brother."

"But that's not where the truth about him ends."

"Where does the truth about you end? Are you my wife to the exclusion of everything else?"

"Before everything else."

Julian nodded. "Believe me, Horace is my brother before everything else."

For a long moment Emily watched her finger as it traced a pattern on the starched tablecloth.

She said, "Julian, why don't you tell me Clive Wilmot was lying?"

Emily looked up quickly; sometimes, she knew, she could catch the reaction to the shock of a question before it could be hidden. But in her husband's face she saw nothing at all.

At home, Emily, after her long afternoon nap, couldn't sleep. She went downstairs in her dressing gown; before she left she leaned over the bed, her big round glasses golden in the lamplight, and gave Julian a chaste kiss on the forehead. Since they left the restaurant she hadn't spoken to him at all. Julian turned out the light and drifted in and out of sleep. Each time he woke he heard the clatter of Emily's typewriter drifting up the stairwell from her workroom in the basement.

Julian woke at four and Emily still wasn't beside him. He found her downstairs, stretched out on a sofa, covered by his camping coat. The acrid smell of woodsmoke rose from the waterproof cloth. He went back to bed.

Three hours later, when he came into the kitchen fully dressed, Julian found Emily at the table with a cup of coffee held between her hands as though she were warming them on a winter's day. Outside, the sun of late July beat down on the garden. The skin of Emily's face bore creases from a wrinkle in the sofa pillow, and her eyes were still dull after her long night of work and sleep. When Julian leaned to kiss her she offered her cheek but didn't respond in any other way.

"Look," he said. "I know how troubled you are."

Julian touched Emily's tousled hair. He heard the engine of his car starting, precisely on time, at the back of the house.

Emily wouldn't look at him. Her glasses were on top of her head; she slid them down over her eyes, pulled the untidy stack of manuscript pages that lay on the table towards her, and began editing her story about Patrick Graham.

Julian left her so. As he went out he heard Jenny call down the stairs, and Emily answered. When speaking to the child, her voice was as free and musical as ever—like his mother's, answering a question before she went away again into one of her paintings.

14

Charlotte Graham pointed with a bony shoulder into the chattering crowd at the cocktail party. The gesture was not quite a shrug.

"That dark lady by the window," she said. "How small she seems, Patrick, how like a wren, a waif! Ah, she sees she's been recognized. She takes a tremulous step backwards in her simple black dress, like a chanteuse pawed by applause."

Patrick handed Charlotte his drink, wrapped in a sopping napkin, and crossed the room to Caroline. She stood alone by a sheet of curved glass that ran the whole length of the room, two stories high. Beyond her, distorted by the glass, were the buildings of the United Nations with their floodlit crescent of tiny flags out front. Farther away, twisted like melted chocolate, were the East River bridges—dark shapes in the Lockwood Administration, which allowed no wasteful bulbs to burn on their old girders.

"Why are you alone?" Patrick asked.

Caroline looked up at him out of the same ivory face that he remembered. The eyes were as full of movement, the pianist's hands as still.

"Leo has gone to find me a glass of wine."

Everyone was in evening clothes. The woman who was giving this party for President Lockwood had a sense of theater. She had been an actress on the musical stage before marrying a popular composer. Patrick looked over the room filled with men in dinner jackets and women in jewels and long gowns. When he turned again, Caroline was looking out the window.

"Can you see as far as the East Village from that window?" he asked.

"Ah, Patrick—still the romantic. *This* has always been Camelot." She indicated the gossiping fashionable crowd.

Caroline had a way of standing, one foot slightly ahead of the other, as if ready to step into anything. Whatever jokes Patrick's wife might make about her, Caroline never shrank.

She wore a dress that was the same shade of black as her hair and even had the same lights in the fabric. A necklace of star sapphires mimicked her eyes. Leo must have given it to her; Patrick knew Caroline had left all her old jewels behind, because he had seen some of them on Emily Hubbard.

Everyone in the room knew who Caroline was—knew, rather, who she had been. Julian hadn't come yet, but he would. He and Lockwood, inseparable, were at the Waldorf, working on the last version of Lockwood's acceptance speech. Suzie Stanwood, the hostess, had announced that. The President would be there not later than ten.

"Frosty had better not be much later than that," Suzie said, standing on the piano bench with her hand on the shoulder of her husband, "because Harvey's written something for him as a surprise, and our friend and host the composer falls asleep promptly at ten-thirty."

Harvey, like many successful songwriters, wrote one tune supremely well. From show to show he changed the tempo of his music and sometimes transposed whole bars, but fast or slow, backwards or forwards, his tune was always the same tune. Only a trained musical ear could detect this, and he sent people whistling from theaters. He'd had the luck, too, to have a clever lyricist whose name nobody could ever remember. And he had Suzie. Singing softly of love, she could bring people forwards in their seats to catch the subtleties of her tremolo—or, with her perfect diction, she could shoot words into an audience like darts from a blowgun.

Leo Dwyer appeared in an iridescent silk dinner jacket, a goblet of white wine in one hand and his own darker drink in the other. His face broke into a grin at the sight of Patrick. He wiped the palm that had been holding Caroline's sweating drink on his woolly head, and shook hands.

"Patrick! Never miss your show when we're ashore. I thought you won the round with Mallory. Caroline didn't."

"Caroline has always judged me pretty harshly."

"Patrick let Mallory talk too much," Caroline said.

"That was the beauty of it," said Leo. "Let him babble. It's the best thing you could have done. I mean, germ warfare, oil spills, infanticide for the blacks, tax bonuses for people who have babies with high IQs, gobbling up the whole hemisphere! You could smell the carrion on his breath."

"That must be from one of your books, Leo."

"Listen, I haven't got the imagination to create a character like Mallory. He opens his mouth and little devils march out—you've seen those statues in Japan?"

Leo put a hand on the small of Caroline's back and let it slide carelessly over her buttocks. Patrick was able to watch this caress with detachment; Caroline's being touched, entered, smelled in her heat by this man didn't disturb him. He wondered why. Caroline had the look, which he had never seen in her before, of a woman satisfied with the physical side of her life. Julian had never touched her in public, but she had always looked at him when his attention was elsewhere like a bitch in heat. At Leo, she wrinkled her nose. It was a parody of wifely flirtation. This was so out of character—Charlotte's turning a cartwheel would have surprised him less—that Patrick snorted with laughter. Caroline gave him a questioning look.

"I like the look of you two together," Patrick explained. "Young folks in love. It's appealing. I told Charlotte about you after we had dinner on your boat last year."

"Yeah," said Leo, "well, I tell you, Patrick, prostates are failing left and right in my age group. If mine goes I want to get the benefit of its last ounce."

Leo's words, delivered in his fast shrill voice clicking with the dentals of his native New York, were distinctly heard by all around them. Faces turned, then turned away again as one.

Lockwood had entered the room, with Julian just behind. The President's head with its shock of hair and its great pulpy nose floated far above the crowd. He and Julian were inches taller than all but a few of the other men. Women clutched the arms of men for support and pulled themselves up on tiptoe.

The hush created by Lockwood's entrance lasted only seconds. Suddenly Leo began to clap. The others turned, startled; Suzie Stanwood's outraged face snarled at them. Leo had spoiled the illusion that Lockwood was just dropping into a familiar house. To save Lockwood the embarrassment of seeing Leo humiliated, Suzie and then all the others began to applaud.

Lockwood stood nodding, smiling, seeking out faces in the room. Then he held up his hands and the noise stopped.

Lockwood began to talk. The guests in their rich clothes fell back, as if to give him air. Lockwood's whole lanky frame was visible now. He looked odd in a tuxedo; his clothes never fit him particularly well, and though his outfit was a new one, the collar stood away from his neck. The trousers bagged. Julian, standing behind him, wore a very old dinner jacket that lay, as his clothes always did, unwrinkled on his body. There were signs that finger-

151

nail scissors had been used to trim the frayed satin of its lapels.

Lockwood said very little. It was a speech of thanks.

"I know how much you all paid for Suzie and Harvey's very fine tea and crackers, and I want you to know it's appreciated; we're poor folks in this administration, and we're glad to have your help, and proud to know every one of you," he said. "Just keep on helping us right to the end. If you've been watching the opposition, I guess you know how much we need you, how much the country needs you."

"Needs *you,* Mr. President," Suzie Stanwood cried. This time the applause needed no leading.

Suzie announced the song her husband had written for Lockwood, and the President stood near the piano with a glass of soda water in his hand, a smile rippling over his battered features, while Harvey played the piano and Suzie sang the words in her glassiest musical comedy soprano. The lyric had just the right touch—affectionate badinage suggesting the deeper feelings Lockwood's supporters had about him.

"By golly, Suzie, I think I'm going to take you along on the campaign and have you sing," said Lockwood, when she was done and the applause died. "I'll just sit in a chair on the stage and smile. We'll win by a landslide."

Suzie reached up and kissed Lockwood, then stepped back, clapping her hands over her mouth in mock surprise at her own boldness. Lockwood, never at a loss for the right gesture, put his arm around Harvey Stanwood's shoulder, led him over to his flushed wife, and, hugging them both, spoke their names in his booming backwoodsman's voice. Then with a nod seeking permission from Harvey, he planted a loud kiss on Suzie's cheek.

The knack of breaking away from people was one that Lockwood had long ago perfected. He gave the Stanwoods one final squeeze, then lifted a hand and plunged across the room, his eyes fixed on a point at the edge of the crowd.

He shook hands with Leo and nodded to the Grahams. Then he leaned down and gave Caroline a tender kiss on the forehead. His hand lingered on her cheek.

"They didn't tell me you'd be here," Lockwood said.

"Maybe they were afraid you wouldn't come. Hello, Julian."

Julian had taken a step or two backwards when he saw where Lockwood was heading. Now he reached around the President and shook hands with Leo. Leo beamed. To be picked out of two hundred people to be kissed by the President! Julian felt his own lungs filling with the breath of enjoyment, to see how pleased Leo was with Caroline.

152

Lockwood went on talking to her for several minutes, asking about the children, about her new life. The crowd pressed close and listened.

"Polly gives me reports when you two talk on the phone," Lockwood said, "and I have some word from Julian when you see each other. But it's not the same as seeing you. It was *so* nice of you, Leo, to bring Caroline here."

"Well, Mr. President," said Leo, "I guess you could say you brought us together, so it's only fair."

Everyone except Leo was careful not to look at Julian. The little man looked upwards at him, eyes dancing. Julian smiled. Charlotte, like a monkey snatching a grape from the floor of a cage, grinned brightly at this exchange between old husband and new.

Caroline went on with the conversation as though nothing had been said. Patrick watched her, all his old feeling for her rekindled. She had always been invulnerable. When they were lovers he'd had a recurrent dream in which some part of Caroline's body, an arm or leg or sometimes even her trunk, would be cut off. Something would slice through the round flesh, and it would be the same inside as out, the color of ivory. In the dream, there was no blood; she would heal at once. She did the same in life.

Finally Lockwood and Julian moved away. Most of the others drifted with them, so that there were expanses of empty space in the long room at one end, and a tight crowd of people at the other. Patrick and Charlotte and Leo and Caroline were quite alone.

"If this room were a ship we'd turn turtle," said Charlotte.

Julian separated himself from the crowd and returned to them.

"I wanted to say hello properly," he said. "How are you both? Jenny and Elliott are all packed and sitting on their suitcases, waiting for you."

They exchanged dates and times; Caroline and Leo would pick up the children in Washington on the day the convention ended. Leo peppered Julian with questions; he was anxious that the surprise of the trip to Antarctica be preserved.

"Between you and me," Leo said, "Caroline finds it hard, not having the kids all the time. But you two did the right thing, giving you custody. Who but the Secret Service can protect them as long as you're with Lockwood? I want you to know, Julian, I do everything I can to keep them safe. They're like my own."

Julian nodded. Leo had seized his arm in his sincerity.

Caroline watched their reflection in the glass. Now that it was after ten and all the lights of the city were extinguished, the blackness outside made a fun house mirror of the twisted glass. That

153

was the idea of it. It was a work of art that created a kaleidoscope of new works of art. The crowd around Lockwood was reflected as a long crawling creature with a glittering back, the women's jewels, and many short black legs, the men's trousers.

Julian said, "Patrick, come with me to the piano." They walked together to the instrument. A few alert heads turned but no one approached. Julian put a finger on a treble key and pressed it silently; only he and Patrick heard the hammer brush the wire.

"I've looked into that Ibn Awad question since we talked," he said.

"So have I," Patrick replied.

"And?"

"There's some persuasive evidence, Julian. I suppose Emily told you about our encounter with Clive Wilmot in that place in San Francisco."

"Yes. What's his purpose?"

Graham looked away. "I've no idea. You know, of course, that if I don't handle this story Clive will find someone else who will?"

Julian sighed. "Yes. Patrick, I think it would be unwise to jump into this too quickly. I'm checking, but there's a limit to how much I can do while the convention is going on."

"You'll have to do something soon. It's a choice of doing it before the story breaks, or reacting afterwards."

"Yes. That's the standard set of choices."

The cords in Julian's neck were stretched tighter than usual. Caroline had turned around again and was watching him and Patrick.

"I only wanted to tell you that I'll talk to you as soon as I have a full picture of this thing," Julian said.

"I want to talk to Lockwood."

The President had separated himself from the crowd. Twenty minutes had passed since his arrival. He was walking across the room through eddies of laughing people, hand in hand with Suzie Stanwood. Julian struck a series of treble quarter notes on the piano, nine rising followed by nine falling.

"The song of the Maryland yellowthroat," he said. "The President may want to come on the air with you, Patrick. Go slow. Be patient." Horace had been gone for a week. "Wait a little," Julian said.

Lockwood, his face still alight with the long anecdote he'd just told, shook hands with Patrick. Politicians have a look about them when they stop recognizing faces after days of campaigning. Lockwood had it now as he wrung Patrick's hand, squeezed his forearm. Suddenly he realized who Patrick was, and the intelligence came back into his gaze.

"Patrick," he said, "we've got to get together. It's been too long."

"So Julian and I were just saying to each other."

Patrick looked deep into Lockwood's eyes. He saw nothing there but the same clear conscience he'd always seen. The President gave his arm one more squeeze and was borne off into the crowd again.

Patrick turned to Julian. "How much truth are you telling him?"

"About what?"

Patrick reproduced the rudimentary tune Julian had picked out a moment before on the piano. "Why was Horace in your office every day? Where is he now?"

Julian began to turn away. Patrick grasped his sleeve. The hard wool was so old—probably it was the same dinner jacket Julian had had at Yale—that it had a faint sheen of green under the bright light that was focused on the piano. The Stanwoods' whole apartment was lit like a stage set; it was even signed on one white wall with the bold signature of the theatrical designer who had done it for them. The place was on the edge of going out of style; people were beginning to copy it.

"You've been very careful not to lie to me, Julian. Are you doing the President the same favor, you and Horace?"

"Patrick . . ." Julian's bony shoulders shrugged.

"Horace left the country, Julian. Where did he go?"

Patrick's face, usually so smooth, had its old look, like a face inked on a knuckle, with emotions twitching beneath the surface like a joint under the skin.

Lockwood was leaving. Julian shook off Patrick's hand and followed him out the door.

15

Next day, there were more looking glasses in Caroline's hotel suite. She offered Patrick Graham a drink from the tray on a side table, but he refused. Caroline shrugged, and her image was thrown from one mirrored wall to another. She looked like her old self: jeans, a simple blouse, a scarf knotted under her falling hair. Her shoes, Patrick knew, had cost three hundred dollars. She wore a throwaway discount store watch on her wrist.

Patrick took her downstairs to the bar; the food was good, and it wasn't a place where he'd be likely to encounter anyone who knew him.

Caroline didn't look at the menu. For tax purposes, Leo owned the suite they were staying in and her tastes were known. The waiter brought her a spinach salad and a glass of iced tea. She ate the salad without pausing, then sat back and watched Patrick debone a grilled sole. He did it with dexterity, lifting out the spine and ribs in one piece and leaving two plump pieces of white flesh on his plate.

He let the fish go cold. Patrick didn't really like to eat. Caroline remembered that about him, the tiny mouthfuls slowly chewed. An invisible mother seemed to stand by him, muttering encouragement: *Don't you want nice strong teeth? Wouldn't you like wonderful curly hair?* He was deaf to her coaxing.

"Caro, I want to talk to you."

"So I gathered."

"You're the only truly daring person I've ever known."

"Oh, dung, Ahmed."

Patrick was startled. "Out of what dark pocket did that name come?" he asked.

"I don't know. Seeing you. You haven't changed at all, except to get rich."

Caroline reached across the table and snuffed out the cigarette Patrick had left burning in the ashtray. She called the waiter and he took the ashtray away.

"I'm just back from Baghdad," Patrick said. "The people are no better off now than they were in the sixties. It's the same all over the Third World. Hopelessness, flesh dropping off people's faces from untreated disease; bad diet, sleeping minds. Nothing has worked."

"I know that."

"You don't care."

"*They* don't care. Why don't they build boats and come and kill us? Or even kill their own leaders? They've had long enough."

"You know why."

"Yes, and so do you by this time. Patrick, whatever we said to each other when we were young, we always knew that change was an impossibility. It really made no difference to us. We could always go back to being Americans. Face it—we were just fucking around."

"You, maybe. Not me; not in any way."

Caroline gave him a long look, and a grin spread over her

156

face. Within this polished man she did see the boy, posing for her, as for a photographer, in revolutionary's rags.

"I believe you," she said. "You *are* still the same. I see it sometimes on television. When you were on with Mallory last week you burned with loathing for him."

"You don't burn anymore, Caro?"

"I love Lockwood. That's a personal thing. Can he stop Mallory? Not in the long run, Patrick. Nobody can. Mallory is right, you know—he's seen the really vital point about mankind."

"Mallory has?"

"Yes. It's obvious. Humanity is sick and tired of being what it is. It's always wanted to escape from its state of being—into the ocean seas, the Indies, the frontier, the New Frontier, space, the life hereafter, war—anything to kill the boredom. You and I and all the other pathetic asses in the Movement were desperately trying to fly out of ourselves. Why do you think angels—and devils, too—have wings? Behind all the religion and all the bullshit about how wonderful we are—'humanity' is a word meaning instinctive goodness, the one quality humanity lacks totally—the real fact about this race is its incurable self-disgust. Mallory *sees* that."

"I won't believe that."

"Of course you won't. That's why you always hated Julian, apart from the sexual competition. He was different from you and me. Ahmed and Fat'ma—I mean, Jesus! We had to see things through filters—drugs or illusion. Julian at least looked at them as they were."

"Julian? Do you think he saw *you* as you were?"

"Oh, yes. That's why he never loved me. And that's why I loved him, you know—because he wouldn't love *me*. He refused to think that loving me was important. To Julian, our marriage, and our love affair before it, was like Russia. I was the invader. I'd advance and advance like Napoleon or the Wehrmacht, leaving scorched earth behind me. Julian was the imperturbable Russian general. He just kept on retreating. In the end, he knew I'd march into the winter and freeze to death."

Caroline's eyes were bright; in the darkened bar their glistening was like a lighting effect—where did the light reflected in them come from? Patrick had never heard her talk so much. Her speech when they were living together had to be pulled out of her; days would go by while she read or watched hours of television or practiced yoga in utter silence.

Even later, after she and Julian had married, she seldom spoke to Patrick. When she did, it was usually to hurl some bitter wit-

157

ticism. In Washington, she'd had a certain fame out of that; he feared her at his dinner table.

Patrick realized that the only subject that had ever truly interested Caroline was Julian. Everything else bored her. Anger, all the old injury and sense of loss, rose in Patrick; then it left him. He felt free; never before had he been with Caroline without having in his heart some fragment of hope that she would come back to him and love him. He'd seen at last that that could never happen.

"It's Julian I wanted to talk to you about," Patrick said. "You know him better than anyone. Does he fear anything? Does he want anything?"

Caroline laughed. "Are you planning to blackmail him?"

Patrick waited for her answer. Caroline saw that he was serious, and she gave him a smile he remembered—the amused tolerant grin of one who is obliged to explain the obvious.

"There's no fear in Julian," she said. "You have to want things for yourself—love, money, power—and care about losing those things in order to feel fear. There is nothing Julian wants that ordinary people want. He wants to be what he is; he would kill, probably, to remain what he is."

"You really think that?"

Caroline was impatient; she wanted to finish what she had to say; she held up her hand to stop Patrick from talking. "Yes. The thing about Julian is this: he controls and uses everyone as a matter of instinct. He is stronger than anyone else because he needs nothing. He doesn't even need sex. That's what drove me crazy with desire for him, I smelled it on him the first time I saw him. I thought I could change him; other males had been after me practically since I was born. Not Julian. He doesn't *know* he's a bastard. I never mattered to him, you'll never matter to him. Lockwood matters to him only because he's the means of Julian doing what he really wants to do. Julian wants to do good. He wants to solve human problems. There are people who believe, actually believe on the intellectual level, that mankind at some time in the deep past could talk to the animals and somehow lost that magical power. Julian feels that way about the masses. He wants to rediscover a way for his kind to talk to their kind. He wants to talk to the poor and the hopeless and the stupid. He knows he hasn't the gift, he's evolved too far. He thinks Lockwood can do it, the way mystics in India talk to monkeys. Of course it can't be done— no one has ever been able to talk to monkeys. But Julian will never stop trying. He'd destroy anyone who interfered with the experiment."

158

Patrick reached across the table and took both of Caroline's hands. She pulled sharply away but he tightened his grip. He saw in her the same fleshly suspicion he'd noticed in Emily in the hotel in San Francisco. Both women assumed that he wanted sex; but he was finished with desiring females that Julian had already had.

He said, "Julian has committed murder."

In a few sentences, squeezing the limber bones in Caroline's hands at the points in his narrative where the punctuation belonged, he told her about Ibn Awad. As the last word issued from his lips, Patrick let go of her hands.

Caroline let them lie on the table as if they were, because he'd touched them, no longer parts of her own body. She laughed at him again, until she lost her breath. It was she, this time, who took Patrick's struggling hands and squeezed them.

"Oh, what a joke," she gasped. "That Julian should have to do *that* for you, too!"

16

Horace Hubbard had visited Rose MacKenzie in her apartments all over the world, and he loved what they said about her. Rose lived her professional life in perfect order. In the vaults of D. & D. Laux & Co., among her computers, everything—lucite, stainless steel, silicon—was utterly free of dust, touched only with tools and gloved hands, sterile and functional. Her flat was something else again. Horace found his way from room to room among chairs piled one on top of the other, drunken heaps of books, discarded items of clothing dangling like vines from the chandeliers and the plumbing.

Horace had returned that day from two weeks of hard work in Europe and the Near East. He had carried back with him a tape cassette, and now he brought it into Rose's bedroom and slipped it under the pillow before he got into bed. Rose had cooked curry, many kinds of it, and the aromas of their dinner lingered; an ancient air conditioner wheezed in her bedroom window, but it couldn't cope with the choked atmosphere of the flat. Horace liked the apartment, it relaxed him; Rose's jumble of useless possessions made it seem, against what they both knew was logic, that danger could not penetrate these rooms. There was too much good humor in them.

Rose lay on her back with the base of a wineglass resting on the red fleece between her legs. She watched Horace put the cassette under his pillow. She'd asked no questions in the hours

159

they'd been together. Now she said, "You ran Clive down, did you?"

"I think so. It was just a matter of staying behind him after Jack had done his part of it."

"Does Jack know?"

"Not all of it. We meet at dawn in the talks room. He may want you, so stay sober."

Rose dug Horace's ribs and he recoiled. He was naked, too. They had not yet begun to make love; perhaps they wouldn't. In bed, Horace and Rose had the leisurely ways of old friends. That is what they were; though they had known each other sexually for twenty years and there was love between them, neither made any claim on the other. What they did for each other—cooking meals, making gifts of wine, saving jokes, watching one another's professional flanks—they did for the pleasure of it.

Neither ever had to be uncertain about the other's reaction to anything—after all their years together in the same peculiar profession they knew each other's mind. Spy must love spy as a dancer can only really love another dancer. All others are fat and clumsy.

"Sound?" asked Rose.

On the television screen at the foot of the bed, President Lockwood had just entered Madison Square Garden to make his speech accepting renomination. For many minutes, politicians had gestured soundlessly on the tube, making their introductory speeches. Rose pressed a button and they heard the crash of stormy applause as Lockwood came onto the stage with Polly's hand in his.

These delegates were very different from the ones who had nominated Mallory in San Francisco. No more than half of Lockwood's people were white, and those who were tended to be very young or very old. This dappled crowd, black and brown and yellow faces among the white, seemed to give off the shine of joy and good will. It was happy, exhausted, loud; affectionate towards Lockwood. Mallory's convention had been smug, self-controlled, deadly patient; and, towards Mallory, worshipful.

Horace asked Rose if she saw these differences too.

"I'd like to run those two sets of adjectives through the computer," she said. "They're a semantic history of political attitudes in the United States."

Rose held up her empty glass and Horace filled it from a bottle of Orvieto; droplets of ice water fell on their bodies. Rose shivered; Horace held the dripping bottle above her, and ran it down the length of her torso. She plunged her hand into the ice bucket and then clapped it over Horace's genitals. Rose liked this sort of play; she had almost no interest in politics. She switched off the sound and started to take off her glasses.

"No," Horace said. "I want to hear."

Lockwood had not yet begun to speak. In the President's face, Horace saw the signs of strain; anyone who did not know what Horace knew would see this as the natural wear of office. Lockwood never spoke from a text. He *conversed* with audiences; when, shuffling and dry-throated, he began a speech, it seemed that he had just spent a long time listening to what everyone else in the room had had to say, and now wanted to talk for a while himself. After long stretches of muddy plodding, eloquence would burst from time to time like a star shell.

"Well," Lockwood began, "in spite of everything, here we are. The family has gathered. Four years ago, some said there wouldn't be another gathering of this clan. But brothers and sisters are held together, and brought back together in spite of everything, by ties of love. We love one another in this party, and in this country, and in this world from which so much misery remains to be lifted.

"That's what we have to say—that we know how to love. That's what we have to offer—invisible gifts of the heart, spoken in the heart's inaudible language."

Lockwood spoke to his exultant followers of new sacrifices, of new gestures of friendship to enemies, of new gifts of food and energy to the poor in America and abroad.

"Let us go to the world, an America with clean hands, saying, let there be peace; let there be food; let there be freedom. Let there be good sense and gratitude, so that if the worst comes to the very worst, and everything is extinguished on this planet—the lights of our cities, the flames of our furnaces, the sparks of our machines—if all that goes out, and nothing burns here except the little fires in the darkness around which the human family began, then, my fellow Americans, we will have lost nothing. We will instead have found ourselves once more."

Rose, one ankle crossed over the other, sipped wine and listened.

"We'll have found ourselves once more, all right," she said. "Some of us will be turning on spits over those little fires in the darkness. But, God, I like Lockwood. He kisses me right on the primitive brain."

Rose switched off the television set. Lockwood's face, superimposed on his joyous army, smiled one last time and then shrank and vanished.

Before the point of light had disappeared from the blackness of the deadened screen, Rose was kissing Horace erect. He needed more help than usual, but Rose was skilled and patient, and once he was roused he remained so for a long time. He had drunk a lot that evening. Drink, he had been told, left other men flaccid; it made Horace rampant. Even when he was young, alcohol had had the effect of delaying his ejaculation; now he required as much help from Rose to finish as to begin, and even afterwards he would drift, still swollen, towards sleep.

All during the act—while Rose straddled his body or turned her back to him, moving and muttering, her whole capacity for sensation concentrated on the places where his body entered hers— Horace had been unable to focus on what was happening between him and this familiar woman. Other impressions kept registering— the title of a book lying open on the floor; a highlight in a painting, splotched and reckless like one of Julian's mother's pictures; and from outside, the re-echoing double shriek of a police car, like the heartbeat of a machine that has enough intelligence to hunt.

Horace was trying not to think about Lockwood. Or Julian. He had no primitive brain to be kissed.

In the cassette under his pillow was the key to Lockwood's fate, and therefore to Julian's. Lockwood, political ideas, the presidency —these meant nothing to Horace, who knew how little they meant, how soon time erased such things.

Once, when he was a young officer, Horace had brought in a piece of information that the man then occupying the White House had not wanted to believe; it contradicted everything the President's most trusted advisers had told him. He cared nothing that Horace had made a man die to get the information. (Thousands died every day; one of this President's advisers, a brilliant academic, had said that the total number of Americans killed in Vietnam was only equal to the number killed in highway crashes in the United States every year. "Hell," said the professor with a sardonic grin; "we can afford that; it's small change.")

So they had not believed Horace. But what Horace reported was going to happen, happened. Now that President was gone, vanished utterly from the public mind, as Presidents do as soon as they walk down the White House steps and hear "Ruffles and Flourishes" for the last time.

Horace was still there.

17

Horace and Rose got out of her crumpled bed at three in the morning. Downstairs, a car waited; Philindros was inside, at the wheel.

"What do you have?" he asked.

Horace told him and held up the tape cassette to show that the longer version of the story was on it.

Philindros told them what had happened in London; Horace hadn't seen him since they left Julian's office two weeks before and went their separate ways.

"The Brits were terrified when I showed them the pictures," Philindros said. "They haven't had a really horrendous scandal in twenty years. They managed to hush up the trouble Wilmot got into in Baghdad. This was more of the same. They wanted to dismiss him at once. I had to plead with them just to show him the pictures and open an investigation. That would mean prison. Wilmot couldn't face that. I thought that would make him run."

"It did," Horace said. "We had a hell of a time keeping up with him. He's really not such a bad operative, you know."

"Why is he *doing* this?"

"Money. He thinks he can escape being what he is if he has enough of it. 'Poverty is like a woman you realize you can't bear for another day,' he told one of his contacts—you'll hear it on the tape; 'one day, if you're British as I am, and the product of the sort of people who bred me, you know you simply cannot get into bed and do your duty even once more.' "

Rose said, "There may be more to it than that. I never understood why his sister was killed in Baghdad. Who would do it, unless it was a random thing? There was a lot between those two. Byron and Augusta? Some of the Brits in Baghdad thought so."

Philindros wasn't a man to believe in incestuous relationships unless there were motion pictures showing the brother and sister in the act of copulation; but he never dismissed a possibility from his calculations.

"Wilmot was mad with sorrow at the time," Rose said. "She was a beautiful girl and the only relative he had left. Even if she was just a little sister, Jack, her death might be a motive."

"It might be." Philindros settled into the corner of the seat and said nothing more. When they arrived in the garage beneath D. & D. Laux & Co., Julian Hubbard was already there, standing in full view beside a parked car with two FIS security men by his side. Philindros wouldn't let the Secret Service know of this place. Even Julian had never been here before, and he didn't quite know why he was here now. He strode across the concrete and spoke to Horace.

"Why now? Why here?"

"Your hotel room didn't seem quite the place, Julian. Mallory's people probably have transmitters sewn into your underwear."

And, before Julian was allowed to enter the talks room with
Horace and Philindros, Rose shut him in a transparent booth and
her computers scanned all the frequencies on which a transmitter
secreted on his person might be broadcasting. Julian didn't undergo
the ordeal with good grace.

In the talks room, he soon forgot the inconvenience. Horace
pressed the cassette into a player. They began to hear Clive Wilmot's jittery speech. The cassette was a condensation of many
hours of conversation, in several cities, with a number of different
people.

First came Wilmot's encounter with his masters in London,
who wanted to know why he had let himself be photographed
with two hairy male lovers in the same bed. These were the pictures
Philindros had flown to London and put in the hands of his friend,
the head of the British service—quietly, without comment, as a
gesture of fraternity. Wilmot's homosexual partners were members
of the KGB; Philindros had got the photographs from an agent
inside the Soviet embassy in Ottawa. Wilmot had been entrapped
while on a visit there by the local Soviet station chief, an old-liner
who still believed that Westerners could be blackmailed with
evidence that they had performed acts which were even now considered disgusting in the puritanical U.S.S.R.

"'I mean *Ottawa,* hidden cameras, one-way mirrors, in this
day and age!'" Wilmot said.

"'And before that, Baghdad. Why, Clive, do you expose yourself and this service to these hideous embarrassments?'

"'It was a cold night, I was alone. How can it matter, my dear
fellow? KGB or no KGB, it was squirt squirt and good-bye. A bit
of tail in a strange city.'

"'Precisely.'"

To Philindros, Julian said, "I didn't know this was quite the
sort of thing you had in mind when you spoke of our countenancing
an operation against the British."

Philindros ignored the rebuke. Julian held up his hand. They
had come to a portion of tape on which Wilmot was talking to an
Arab. Philindros switched it off to ask a question.

"Do we know who this is?" he asked.

"Hassan Abdallah. We have his voice print in the computer."

It was the final section of the tape that caused Julian to listen,
deep in thought, with his eyes closed. Here the voice responding
to Wilmot's, first on a telephone and then in face-to-face conversation, was American.

The two men were discussing, in detail, the death of Ibn
Awad. Horace's name was openly spoken. Secrets that ought to

have been locked in the FIS computers were discussed: the death warrant from Lockwood, the meetings between Horace and Prince Talil, the forged suicide note that sent Awad to his death, the alteration in the note that resulted in Talil's execution.

The man with the American voice reassured Wilmot: his money would be paid as soon as the full story of Awad's assassination on Lockwood's order appeared in the United States. Patrick Graham, because of his known loyalty to Lockwood, was the preferred outlet. Only in the last resort could another reporter be used.

" 'Graham wants more evidence,' " Wilmot's voice said. " 'He wouldn't buy Hassan; I wouldn't myself—old Hassan's not really a witness one can produce and be proud of, is he?' "

Wilmot was desperate for the money. Of course he saw Philindros's hand in the delivery of the photographs to his own service. He expected dismissal. His chief had long wanted to rid himself of Wilmot in any case; the pretext that he might be a Soviet agent would serve as well as any.

Philindros rewound the tape and took it out of the machine. He handed it to Rose. "One copy," he said. She returned in an instant with the extra spool. Philindros put the original in his pocket.

"The American voice," Horace said, "belongs to O. N. Laster. It's amazing that Wilmot is dealing directly with him. Usually the presidents of outfits like Universal Energy don't run this kind of errand themselves."

"Laster wants Lockwood defeated and Mallory back in the White House," Philindros said. "It makes sense. Mallory's in favor of unlimited use of fossil fuels. Lockwood has cost Universal Energy billions in oil and coal and gas revenues. They had a big piece of the fusion power development contract."

Philindros touched the tape in his pocket through the black cloth of his jacket. He lifted his chin. Horace answered the unspoken question.

"They've tapped our computer system. There's no other way they could have all that data."

"But FIS has its own communications satellite; it's supposed to be unbuggable," said Julian angrily.

"Unbuggable by the Russians or the Chinese or the Japs. Not by Universal Energy. They have the blueprint. They own the electronics company that manufactured the satellite."

Julian absorbed this information, and understood it. He asked no more questions. He glanced at some photographs showing Wilmot in the places where the conversations took place.

"There's no picture of him actually with Laster?"

"Even better. We have voice prints," Horace said. "It was a bit difficult to get the two of them on tape; we had to insert a transmitter into Clive's tube of Colgate." He smiled; so, for the first time in Julian's experience, did Philindros. These men were pranksters at heart.

"You say voice prints are just as reliable as photos?" Julian asked.

"More so. You can put on a putty nose and a false beard before someone takes your photo; you can't escape your vocal tones—they're like the whorls in fingerprints. You can be sure that the men on this tape are Laster and Wilmot."

"I want to be sure of more than that. I want Franklin Mallory's fingerprints on this money Wilmot is so anxious to earn," Julian said. "Maybe his prints are on other money in the past—was it the Eye of Gaza that killed two members of the Supreme Court? Was it . . ."

Horace tried to stop his brother, but Julian was aroused; he was snapping out orders to Philindros as if he were a Navy rating.

Philindros said, "There are difficulties."

"Overcome them. Years ago, there were difficulties with the CIA. Men who were loyal to the President then were put into a special unit. The Director didn't need to know what was happening. There must be men in FIS who are loyal to Lockwood; cull them out of the herd, give them to Horace. Go away, Jack. Cover your eyes."

Philindros said nothing.

"That incident, in the end, destroyed the CIA," Horace said.

Julian threw his hands apart in impatience. "You've got Wilmot and Laster. I want Mallory," he said.

Philindros interrupted. "Julian, there are certain requirements you cannot put on the FIS," he said. "When we began this investigation it was clearly a counterintelligence problem. If the President's role in Awad's death was known outside our government—"

"Wait a minute," Julian said.

Philindros increased the volume of his voice and went on speaking.

". . . *If the President's role in Awad's death* was known outside our government, then clearly that meant that the FIS had been penetrated. We had a duty, and a legal right, to find out how and by whom. We've done that. We've repaired the leak. Our operation is over."

Julian stared, dumbfounded, at Philindros. The man was displaying emotion. Two spots of red appeared on his olive cheeks; he

166

pressed his lips together to keep them from trembling; his hands were hidden. His throat was dry and he cleared it repeatedly.

"Jack, I don't quite follow you," Julian said.

"Then I'll be more specific. This has become a domestic political matter. You will not use the FIS for domestic political purposes. It's against the law. It's wrong. I won't help you further in this. Neither will any other officer of the FIS."

Julian looked to Horace.

"You can have a copy of the tape, of course," Horace said. "Jack agrees that's within the President's power to demand."

Philindros pushed the duplicate cassette across the table, and a manila envelope containing the photographs of Wilmot.

"Be sure to have Horace hold the cassette when you go through the glass booth on the way out. Otherwise the tape will be erased," Philindros said. "There's a magnetic field designed to do that."

Julian's tone, when he replied, was elaborately polite. "Horace is accompanying me?"

"I don't see why not," Philindros replied. He poured ice water into a plastic cup and drank it. "Your brother is retired from the FIS as of the close of business today. He can go where he wants, help whom he pleases."

Julian looked from Philindros to Horace and back again. "You don't seem to understand," he said. "I'm speaking for the President."

"But I do understand," Philindros replied. "You're speaking for the head of your party. You're speaking for a political movement. The FIS talks to people like you all over the world, supports them, seduces them. But it doesn't do so in the United States."

"So you're giving me Horace, and that's all?"

Julian thought he saw something, a glint of amusement, in Philindros's glance, but he couldn't be sure.

"Horace ought to be enough," Philindros said.

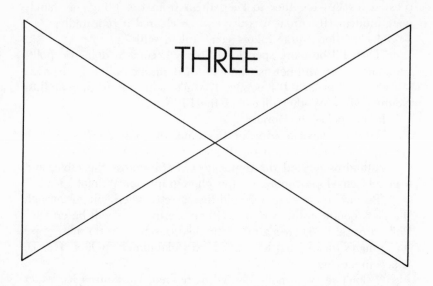

THREE

1

JULIAN had waited until he and the President were back in Washington to tell Lockwood the facts Horace had discovered. He didn't mention Horace's retirement. Julian was not Philindros; he was Lockwood's man and it was his job to tell him what he had to know, keeping from him the things that might trouble him—or put him in the position of having to choose, someday, between telling the truth or a lie to someone like Patrick Graham.

As the last syllable of evidence fell from Julian's lips, Lockwood made up his mind.

"There's only one thing to do, Julian. Tell the truth. Put out the story. No cover-up, no excuses. That way lies quicksand. The people will understand."

Julian was not so sure about that. He said nothing to contradict Lockwood; the President knew as well as he how damaging this scandal was going to be. As it was, Mallory was only two points behind in the polls. This could very well put him ahead. Nothing, then, could bring victory to Lockwood except a furious campaign, travel, speeches, exhortations, explanations. If Lockwood's people saw him often enough as he was, they might by election day be persuaded once again that he was what he'd always seemed to be. They might forget what he'd done to Ibn Awad.

"Of *course* this was O. N. Laster's work," said Lockwood. "It *had* to be him or someone like him. They want Mallory back. His barons are plotting to restore the monarchy, smother parliament, grind down the poor. I wonder how much Franklin knows about this. Half of that Canadian business was the work of the conglomerates, greedy for oil and all the rest. Franklin could have been a great man if he'd got in with a different crowd."

Horace's information about the connection between Clive Wilmot and Universal Energy meant that Patrick Graham could be given the story; permitted to break it. In his hands, the emphasis would change. Sinister forces would be proved to be working against Lockwood. The reason they were doing so could be made secondary.

In the weeks since Patrick had first voiced his suspicions to Julian, a change had come over Lockwood. He now believed that he could not, in fairness, be held responsible for the death of Ibn Awad; the old visionary *had* somehow killed himself. Mallory and his ruthless backers had set the whole thing up, contrived a trap.

"I wouldn't be surprised if it turns out that Universal Energy was in this deeper than we know," Lockwood said. "Doesn't energy include plutonium? They've built half the nuclear power plants on earth, damn them, and they have their hands on half the nuclear experts in the world. Why couldn't they have made those bombs for Awad?"

He was pacing the floor. "You can't dismiss that possibility, Julian," he said, pounding a fist into a palm.

Julian waited for him to sit down again.

"There are difficulties," he said. "Remember, we don't have the bombs. We don't know where they are. There's no physical evidence."

Lockwood waved the objection aside. "There's our word." He picked up the tape recorder and the documents and brandished them. "There's all this."

"Your word has always been good. That's mainly what we have going for us. But however much Patrick Graham wants to believe you, however much your supporters want to believe you, Mallory is going to bite back."

"Then we'll suck the poison out. Patrick'll do it when it comes down to it. Where he leads, the rest of the media will follow. That's why we've got to give him the story, and do it quick."

"I can speak to him tonight, brief him."

Lockwood nodded. "Good. Leave the part about the bombs to me. Send him over here for coffee at six o'clock in the morning."

"Do you want me with him?"

"No. Just Patrick and me—and the truth."

That night, in Julian's study in the house on O Street, the evidence was laid out: a psychiatrist's report on Ibn Awad; documents with the headings clipped off that could only have come from the FIS, detailing Awad's involvement with the Eye of Gaza.

Patrick Graham read each document under the saffron glow of Julian's old gooseneck lamp. Julian sat quietly in the shadows, his attaché case open on his knees. Like a fisherman drawing a big catch near the boat by casting entrails on the water, Julian was chumming. The real bait wasn't yet on the hook. Patrick awaited it. He had been through other scenes like this one with Julian.

Julian gave him the photographs of Clive Wilmot in London and Paris and Beirut. They were numbered and captioned, keyed to the conversations on the tape recording. Julian produced a small cassette recorder from his bag, switched it on, and handed it to Patrick. He made him listen to it through an earpiece, as though the hidden listening devices of Mallory's apparatus might be a danger to them even here.

When Laster and Wilmot spoke of using Patrick, and of their reasons for wanting to do so, Patrick's lips tightened for an instant. He listened impassively to the rest.

The tape ended and Patrick rewound it and popped it out of the recorder. He placed it atop the stack of papers and photographs on the bare surface of the desk. Like all of Julian's desks, this one was completely uncluttered.

"What am I supposed to conclude from all this, Julian?"

"You'll have to form your own conclusions. I told you I'd give you the facts when we had them. I'm doing that."

"All the facts?"

"I haven't finished."

Julian went on in his precise way. Patrick had never heard him speak an incomplete sentence or an ungrammatical one. Julian had a weakness for old-fashioned usage: supper instead of dinner; dinner instead of lunch; looking glass, not mirror. He almost never used even the mildest profanity.

Patrick realized what it was about Julian that he had never before been able to classify: he didn't merely speak, he recited. He was always rehearsed. In all his conversations with Patrick, he had been speaking for others: at Yale for the invisible men who could shut down the *News* if it went too far; in the outburst of Patrick's jealousy and heartbreak, for Caroline; now for Lockwood.

"You're telling me that the President of the United States ordered the assassination of Ibn Awad?" Patrick said.

"In law and conscience there is such a thing as justifiable homicide."

"And you think this stuff makes a case for justifiable homicide? Killing a man—a *saint*, Julian—because he has a bit of a neurosis? And maybe, just maybe, because he's had some connection with the Eye of Gaza?"

"Yes, and I hope you'll think so, too, when you have the complete picture, when you've talked to Frosty"—Julian used the nickname for a purpose, to remind Patrick of all Lockwood had been to him—"when you've thought it through. It's Frosty who will have to make the people understand."

"He's going public?"

"Of course. What else would you expect him to do? You've known him half your life."

Patrick riffled the papers Julian had given him; they were fresh from the copying machine and still gave off its faint acid odor. "You've left things out," he said.

Julian gave him an inquisitive look: Horace's mannerism.

"The medical report isn't complete. You didn't give me the physical part."

Julian reached into his briefcase. "Oh. Is that interesting to you? Awad had a malignant tumor of the prostate; that was removed. A mild case of high blood pressure, traces of childhood ailments. He'd lived in primitive circumstances."

"Traces of childhood illnesses. Nothing about a brain lesion that left him unable to write? Therefore making it impossible for him to have written that famous suicide note?"

Julian handed Patrick the papers. "I believe that's mentioned. Is it important?" He knew Patrick could not admit not knowing something if it was presented as a well-known fact. "Was it a *secret* that he was illiterate? I thought everyone believed that was one of the admirable things about him—how he could keep the whole Koran in his head, along with all the business of his emirate. I believe he dictated to scribes—usually to Prince Talil, when important documents, secret things, were involved."

Julian let a minute go by. Patrick, defeated by his bravura, said nothing more. Then Julian put the real bait in the water. "There's more. I haven't told you everything, Patrick."

"Then somebody had better."

"Yes, I agree. The President himself wants to fill you in on the rest. He'd like you to have coffee with him, upstairs in his

171

study, at six tomorrow morning. You know the way in. He wants to speak to you alone."

Patrick could not let himself appear to be mollified. "He won't speak to the cameras?"

"After he's spoken to you, why not? But have coffee first—that's what Frosty wants. And I don't suppose you want to go on camera cold."

Julian rose to his feet. It was part of his loyalty to Lockwood never to use air conditioning, and it was sweltering in the room.

"Would you like a big envelope to put that stuff in?" he asked courteously.

Patrick filled the manila envelope—he noticed it wasn't government issue, but of a kind available in all stationery stores—then juggled it on his palm, as if guessing its weight.

"I assume there are no restrictions on my use of this material," he said.

"What I give you is background. The President will give you quotes."

Julian walked down the stairs with Patrick. The treads creaked under their feet, a faint squeal under Patrick's weight, a louder one under Julian's. At the door, two Secret Service men waited to escort Patrick home; Julian had asked him not to bring his own security people; he wanted no outside witnesses to Patrick's midnight visit.

"I don't understand any of this," Patrick said.

"Tomorrow you will, after you've talked to Frosty."

Graham stood for a moment with his head down. Then, without speaking, he lifted the manila envelope Julian had given him in a gesture of farewell. He turned and walked out the door. Julian and Patrick had not shaken hands in years.

Next morning, Lockwood had no difficulty in conveying his anguish first to Patrick and then to the camera. It was genuine. Patrick felt it, and he knew how the camera would magnify it.

Lockwood's mobile face reflected the suffering his terrible decision had cost him. Equally, the screen showed Patrick's reactions to Lockwood's off-camera voice. Patrick asked no easy questions. Lockwood responded firmly to the harshest demands for facts. Patrick didn't ask about Clive Wilmot or O. N. Laster; no accusation of a conspiracy should come from Lockwood.

At the end of the interview, the camera stayed on Patrick and the audience could read in his eyes the struggle between shock and sympathy. In a softened voice, Patrick asked his final question:

"Mr. President, I understand, and I think the American people will understand, why this terrible thing happened. Why now of all times, in the middle of a campaign for re-election, have you decided to tell the American people the truth?"

Lockwood's ravaged face appeared while Patrick spoke. His eyes, in which the memory of his awful decision swam, were made even more expressive by the lighting and the angle of the camera.

"Because telling the people what happened, and why—all the terrible reasons—is the right thing to do," Lockwood said simply. "I can only hope that they will understand."

Patrick's face came back. He said nothing. His expression told those watching that they had elected a President who was incapable of telling a lie. At that moment, he believed that, and so did Lockwood.

Patrick spent the day locked in his office, using the telephone, typing the story. O. N. Laster wouldn't speak to him; Clive Wilmot couldn't be located. Patrick did not try to contact Philindros. It would be useless; Philindros never spoke to the press, and the FIS was not the heart of the story.

On camera, Patrick never read from notes or used cue cards. In interviews or commentary, Patrick spoke with a peculiar intensity, as if he had seen the truth at that exact moment. He alone had mastered the technique. Viewers and even some professionals believed that Patrick's performances were utterly spontaneous. In a sense, they were right. He wrote everything down in private and committed it to memory; he could remember hundreds of words, exactly as they appeared on the page. His words simply came out of him, first as letters of the alphabet on a white sheet of paper, then as spoken words. No conscious effort was involved. Once he had uttered them on the air, he forgot them.

Charlotte said that he had mastered self-hypnosis and that was the secret of his success. She alone knew how he worked. It was all instinct, all feeling. That was why his audience believed him.

It was not until Patrick saw the whole show going out over the network that he realized how predictably he had reacted to the stimuli Julian had subjected him to. Patrick really thought that he had forced this story out of the White House, rather than having it planted on him. All day, as he worked, the conviction that he was ending Lockwood's political career and bringing Mallory back into the presidency haunted him. Once or twice he had to stop to fight back tears. But he had gone ahead, putting fact next to fact—remorselessly, as he believed. The realization uppermost in his mind, so keen that it was almost pain, was that Lockwood had at least condoned, and very probably actually committed, murder. The President had put himself beyond forgiveness.

But Patrick's hour on the air didn't leave that impression.

Instead, Lockwood was made to seem almost innocent. Without even knowing he was doing it, Patrick had chosen material and tones of voice and nuances of expression that had the effect of exonerating the President. The real story seemed to be that Lockwood had saved Israel from destruction, and perhaps the world from global war; and that O. N. Laster and the oil interests, using a seedy British spy, had tried to betray a state secret in order to put Franklin Mallory, their puppet, back into power. The real plot, discovered just in time, was against Lockwood.

Ibn Awad's death and Talil's punishment for it occupied no more than a minute of air time, at the very beginning of the broadcast. There were no scenes of Ibn Awad leading his great praying crowds of the faithful, no horrible reminders of the execution of Talil. Instead there were shots of the oil fields of Hagreb, footage of acts of terror by the Eye of Gaza. Still photographs of O. N. Laster's cold features, reminders of his connections to Mallory, were intercut. Patrick's chilling description of his meeting with Hassan in Baghdad and the terrorist's admission, recorded on Horace's tape, that the Eye of Gaza had meant to destroy the holy city of Jerusalem and perhaps even New York, drove the fact of Awad's assassination to the back of the audience's consciousness. What was the death of one man, and a madman at that, against all that Patrick had to tell?

"Great show, Patrick," said his producer as the closing credits blinked on the screen. Patrick strode out of the screening room without answering. From the windows of his penthouse office he could look down on the White House. Despite Lockwood's campaign to save energy, the grounds of the mansion were floodlit for security reasons, and its white paint, more brilliant than any other, shimmered in the darkness.

A presidential helicopter, navigation lights flashing, left the south lawn in a steep climb and turned south. Patrick had no doubt that Lockwood and Julian were inside; and as the whole show—the images he had chosen, the tones of his own voice, the cumulative effect of it—rolled once more through his mind, Patrick had this thought: They are getting away.

He had come back from Baghdad a hunter, and the prey he'd been stalking had led him in a circle and finally, like some wise great cat, had come on him from behind. He saw at last how ruthlessly he had been used. Patrick struck the springy glass of his office window with his fist. It bent beneath the blow and gave out a throaty half-musical, half-animal sound, like that of a temple bell.

"Fool!" Patrick cried to himself.

Julian had told him no lies. He hadn't had to—he had merely relied on Patrick's conditioning.

For years, Julian had given Patrick gifts—first that club membership, then the friendship of men who were Julian's friends because he was born to be trusted—after all, he was one of them, one of that crowd of imperialist liberals who had been running the United States for generations. Finally Julian had given Patrick the last thing he ever expected to have—an American he could believe in: Frosty Lockwood.

Julian, scrap by scrap, had given Patrick a place in life that he was terrified to lose. He had made him his creature.

"Fool," Patrick repeated, whispering.

His phone was ringing. The people who had his private number were calling to tell him what a splendid job he'd done; how well he'd held the line—how he'd made things clear to the people, who were so apt to be confused, who couldn't quite be trusted to think unless, like hounds having a bit of clothing rubbed over their muzzles, they were given the right words to remember and follow.

Patrick used another line to call the girl with the raven hair he'd talked to at the Midsummer party. He didn't even speak his name; Patrick never spoke his name on the telephone, even to Presidents—he *was* his voice. He knew just what the girl's voice would sound like when she heard his on the line.

2

Julian, while he spoke to Patrick, had known that Emily was somewhere in the house. He hadn't seen her all day; they had both had to work late. The children were asleep; in a few days they would be at sea with Leo and Caroline.

After showing Patrick out the front door, Julian called Emily's name. Things hadn't come right between them after her return from San Francisco. She was silent and mistrustful. He'd told her nothing, and he'd been home very little. There had been the convention to handle, and the long wait for Horace's return from abroad had told on Julian's nerves.

Pregnancy made Emily pale and sleepy; Julian found her curled up on a sofa in the evening. She'd stopped drinking for the baby's sake, and though she was still nauseated in the morning she would take no pills to relieve the condition. She ate the right diet, did the correct exercises. For months she had been studying manuals for pregnant women; she knew exactly what to do to make her body give itself over completely to the well-being of the fetus.

Julian found her in the living room, just wakened by the sound of his voice, stretched out in a chair. They kissed. Her dry lips were hot but he knew this was no fever; sleep heated Emily's skin. Julian sat down near her and waited for her to wake completely. Emily smiled as she woke—one of her old bursts of joyful response. Then, in an instant, she was serious again.

"I read your piece on Patrick," Julian said.

"And?" Emily loved praise for her work. She wrote as a kitten played: a pretty bundle of fluff scampering along her sentences, rising on her hind legs to bat a dangling bell with a soft little paw. And then the wee claws and teeth flashed.

"One of your best. I loved the description of Patrick among the freaks after Mallory's Ganymede Address. I'm not sure you've done the President a favor, coining that phrase for it."

"It was supposed to be ironic."

"Irony is lost on Mallory voters, I'm afraid. Did Patrick really make you that extraordinary speech about himself?"

"About his loutish family and his first girl? Yes. I thought it was wonderful. Would that have been Caroline he meant, the girl he loved who didn't want him?"

"I suppose so, unless there was some prom queen before her I never heard about."

"So sad. He still loves her, you know. I saw it in his eyes when he spoke to me about her."

Emily's eyes, so much less changeful than Caroline's, brimmed with sympathy.

"Patrick is like Rhett Butler," Julian said. "He has a weakness for lost causes once they're really lost."

Emily got out of her chair and pointed a finger at Julian.

"Julian," she said, "I'm going to tell you something. You make a mistake, having so much contempt for Patrick."

She went to the bar, poured and stirred, and came back with a frosted glass. Emily made the best martini Julian had ever drunk: Bombay gin and Noilly Prat and one drop of Pernod. Her father had taught her how; he'd belonged to a generation that made a lifetime study of the drink. Julian didn't know why Emily imagined he'd want a martini at two in the morning.

Julian sipped, then put the cocktail on the table beside him

176

and held out his arms. Emily hesitated, then sat on his lap. She was nearly weightless. Emily drifted when she made love, moved over the water like a blown leaf when she swam; her footfall was inaudible. Julian held her as tightly as he dared, pushed back her hair, kissed her soft cheek. His beard scratched her and she moved her face away an inch, smiling.

"Patrick was here while you slept," Julian said.

"To serve a summons on me?"

"No. How could he not like what you've written? Nobody's ever made him seem so human."

"Then why? Charlotte's going to Chipmunk Island, you know. She can't bear the heat of summer, or Patrick's absences in an election year. I think she has a lobsterman on the side."

"Surely one has lobstermen on the bottom?"

Julian reproduced Charlotte's accent. It made Emily laugh. This woman would probably die, like Gertrude Stein, with a mockery on her lips.

"Why was Patrick here in the middle of the night?" Emily asked again.

Julian told her. Before he began to speak, he moved her body a bit farther away on his long thighs so that they could look into each other's face. His hands lay lightly upon her, one on her back, the other on her rounded knee; he didn't feel in Emily the tensing of muscles that he had expected.

He did not tell Emily everything—only what she would learn anyway from the news. He left out Horace and Philindros and the FIS; he said nothing of the night scenes with Lockwood in Kentucky. He spoke in detail about the link between Clive Wilmot and O. N. Laster of Universal Energy.

"Clive Wilmot is doing this for *money?*"

"I guess so," Julian said. "Life is hard for Englishmen of his class. They've had everything taken away from them at home."

Emily fell silent, sitting absolutely still on his lap. His martini remained unnoticed, the ice melting in it.

"Was there no way *not* to have that happen to Awad?" she asked.

Julian didn't answer. Emily's mind was quick again; she had absorbed what he'd told her. Now the questions were beginning to whirl within her. Two or three times he saw her bite back impulses to speak.

At last she said, "You *wanted* him dead."

Emily rose from Julian's lap and went back to her own chair.

"Yes," Julian said. "It would be a lie if I told you otherwise."

"Would it have been a lie if you'd never told me? You wouldn't have told me ever, Julian, if Patrick hadn't been put onto the story by Clive Wilmot."

"No. Some things I'm not free to tell you."

"Is this the sort of thing, conniving at murder, that's called *Realpolitik*? I thought this was what we were supposed to be free of, people like us, and what we were supposed to fear in Franklin Mallory."

"It is. Do you think it's Lockwood O. N. Laster wants to see in the White House?"

"It's Lockwood that killed Ibn Awad. Not Mallory. Not O. N. Laster. Not the interests."

"That's a cruel judgment."

"It's the one the whole world will make as soon as this story is out. Lockwood's an accessory to murder. My God, Julian, so are you."

Emily began to cry. Bright tears squeezed from the corners of her wide-open eyes and ran glistening over her cheeks. She made no attempt to wipe them away. Both her hands were pressed against her stomach.

"Do you know how large your child is?" she asked. "No bigger than his father's finger, but he has eyes and ears and a heart; he sleeps and wakes. *Julian!*"

"There's something you don't know. Emily, will you listen?"

Her wetted eyes had not left his face. There was horror in them. She shuddered. *"Someone has just walked on my grave,"* Julian's Aunt Jennifer would say when that happened to her. Julian had walked on the grave of Emily's child; even now, only weeks after its conception, it was living within her. But she knew that ten or fifty or sixty years from this moment, it could be killed by men it didn't even know, just as Lockwood and Julian had killed Ibn Awad.

Julian told her about the nuclear weapons; about the Eye of Gaza. He didn't dramatize. Such a thing was hardly possible, given the plain facts of the case. As he spoke, Emily watched. Julian showed no emotion, he let no color come into his dry voice.

Emily asked no more questions. For some time she sat quietly, looking into Julian's face. His beard was dark on his cheeks. At length Emily rose and touched a light switch. The lamps over the paintings came on, and she turned out the others. The center of the room, where Julian and Emily were, lay in shadow. All along the walls, the paintings glowed in little pools of light.

Emily picked up Julian's glass, emptied his warm untouched

drink, and made him another. He took the martini from her and drank. She remained standing before him in her stocking feet.

"How many would have died if you'd let Awad live?" she asked.

"I don't know. Half the Jews in Israel. Perhaps most of New York. It would have been a holocaust."

Emily nodded. She touched Julian's fingers, the ones curled around the cold martini glass, and her hand seemed, as it always did, very warm. Julian finished his drink and they went upstairs to bed.

During the night, Emily lost the baby.

Julian had slept badly. He dreamed of Vietnam. He felt ground fire striking his Phantom, felt the huge weight of the machine become real as it lost the power of flight. He jerked into wakefulness. Emily, roused by his sudden movement or possibly already awake, turned nervously to a new position. Once or twice she uttered her soft nighttime groan. Finally Julian fell into a deep sleep.

He woke to the sound of sobbing. Julian leaped to his feet and started out the door into the hall, flying to Jenny, believing she had been awakened by a nightmare.

But his mind cleared at once, and he knew it was Emily who was crying. Light showed around the frame of the bathroom door. Julian tried the door. It was locked. He called Emily's name; only the racking sobs came back. He put his enormous hands against the thin panels of the door and heaved; the lock ripped out of its screws.

All the lights were on. Emily in her long transparent night-gown stood staring down into the toilet.

Julian put his arms around her. He could not force himself to look.

"I just came in. . . ."

Emily gave him a wild look. She gasped, throwing back her head like a diver rising into the air.

". . . I just had a little stomach ache," Emily said. "I thought I'd look for something in the medicine chest when I got up. Then I felt him go. Julian, he just *left me*."

Emily leaned against him and resumed sobbing. This time tears came; she shuddered so that he wrapped her into his body for the warmth, as though it was the cold that made her shake.

Julian looked down. Their child floated in the cold water. It was, as Emily had said, no larger than its father's finger.

179

Later that morning, while Patrick and Lockwood were talking of Ibn Awad, Julian brought Emily home from the hospital and helped her into bed. The doctor had given her an injection; she could barely hold on to consciousness as Julian undressed her. As Julian pulled the sheet over her Emily beckoned him closer, and forming the words but making no sound, she said:

"He . . . heard . . . us . . . talking."

3

Franklin Mallory and Susan Grant and O. N. Laster, the president of Universal Energy, sat together on a long couch in Mallory's hunting lodge and watched a television cassette of Patrick Graham's program about the Ibn Awad assassination. Mallory and Laster were unshaven and they wore flannel shirts and hunting boots with woolen socks, hand-knitted by Ute women from the un-bleached fleece of sheep that ran wild on Laster's ranch.

"I would like to have been in the room while Frosty made that decision," said Laster. He was drinking bourbon and he took a small sip and shook his head over the strength of the liquor and the humor of the image. "What a mixture of guilt and ecstasy! Lockwood must have looked like a Jesuit undergoing fellatio."

Susan Grant turned off the television. "He seems to have handled Patrick Graham pretty well," she said. "Graham's made it sound like a laying on of hands—Lockwood prevented World War III and cured Ibn Awad of insanity."

"That image will change. The thing is to keep the story alive."

"I think we can do that," Franklin Mallory said.

O. N. Laster stared for a moment at the dead screen. "Is it Lockwood's line that he didn't have anything to do *personally* with the assassination of Ibn Awad—that maybe he didn't even know about it till he saw it on the morning news? Or am I imagining things?"

Susan said, "You're not imagining things. He didn't actually lie. But you know what he wants the world to think—the FIS did it; or at worst, he just let it happen. That cover story has worked before. He knows that Pavlov's dogs in the media will support such a version."

Susan's voice was level; she was a technician stating a set of facts. Mallory smiled at the truth of what she said.

"It may not work this time," he said. "We all know, and the country is going to know, that the American intelligence service cannot carry out an assassination without a direct order from the President. If I know anything about Jack Philindros, there's a tape recording of Lockwood saying yes, oh yes! locked up in a very safe place."

"And then there's Horace Hubbard. He's Jack's ace in the hole. The minute Frosty starts blaming it all on the FIS, Horace's name will come out. He's Julian Hubbard's brother. And who is Julian Hubbard?"

"Yes. Philindros grabs as many handles on a man as he can," said Mallory. "I used to wish Jack had some politics, but he doesn't; he's as blank ideologically as a newborn babe. A fellow could *use* a man with Jack's skills."

"You'll only have him for the first year of your new term, Franklin," said Laster. "Then you can appoint some more warm-blooded type. Ten years is a long term; a Director of Foreign Intelligence could do a lot in that length of time, if he was the right fellow."

They smiled, all three. Franklin Mallory wagged his head in mock disbelief at his outspoken friend.

Aspen logs crackled in the huge stone fireplace. Mallory's lodge lay high in the Uinta Mountains in Utah, the loneliest place left in America. At nine thousand feet, the afternoons already had the edge of winter in them; sometimes there was snow in the mornings, even in late August. Mallory owned ten thousand acres of wild country here; he'd bought it when a law was passed by the first Congress controlled by his party—before he was President—making it possible for the tribes to sell off their reservations to those who would explore for energy resources. Mallory had dammed a snow-fed stream and made a lake, built an airstrip, done some timbering, and found a little coal. Susan had taken care of all that, to satisfy the law and the terms of his contract with the Indians.

Far from the lodge, lower down the mountain where aspen and cottonwood and conifers grew more thickly, hundreds of acres had been fenced. The space within the fences had been stocked with game, just as the crystalline lake by the lodge had been stocked with bass and trout and even muskellunge from Minnesota. All were fed like livestock. The fish here were bigger, and easier to catch, than anywhere else. Hunters could bag elk and deer, moose and antelope, cougar and bear; there were pheasant and partridge in the woods, and geese and duck on the lake.

Mallory bred the game for his friends. The walls of the cabin were hung with trophies and the floors were covered with fur rugs. O. N. Laster, that day, had caught the trout they were having for lunch, and in the earlier morning had shot a grizzly bear that measured out at more than eight feet; the guide had been saving it for him on Mallory's orders. O. N. Laster, while he

181

watched the Graham Show, cleaned his rifle, and the acrid odors of gunmetal and burned cordite and oil mixed with those of resinous woodsmoke and bourbon.

Franklin Mallory himself never killed anything. Among the snarling faces of cougars and grizzlies and the antlered heads of gentler species hung tapestries after the paintings of Miró and Picasso and Picasso's great rival, Juan Gris; these reflected Mallory's real taste. The tapestries looked well—almost like the work of savages—against the peeled-log walls among the stuffed beasts. Mallory liked the juxtaposition of Gris and Picasso. Gris, he thought, had been the better and more honest artist, but he had died poor and in obscurity because he hadn't Picasso's great gift; Picasso sensed what the whim of the critics would be, or had their whim at the same time they did. What the public had thought ugly became beautiful as a result. This was the greatest gift a man could have.

"Are you going after Lockwood hard on this?" Laster asked. He was a small man with none of the nervous habits of a small man. He moved with deliberation and spoke in measured tones. The night before he had been sharpening a hunting knife on a stone and he put it down for a moment on its back, so as not to spoil his work; Susan, looking at it with the firelight winking along its surface, thought that Laster was like the knife: honed, with the sharp edge upwards.

"I don't think it will be necessary," Franklin Mallory said. "Bit by bit, the whole thing will get on the record. Lockwood *killed* that pathetic old man. There was no reason for it. It's a simple message."

"Someone has to pound even a simple message home or the voters will forget. You have eight weeks till the election."

"I have a calendar. The media will be fed at feeding time."

Laster put his rifle back together with deft movements. The parts clicked into place with small satisfying noises; the firearm was a perfect instrument. Both Laster and Mallory liked objects that performed as they were designed to do.

Laster carried the rifle up the stairs and racked it with the others at the end of the gallery that ran around the cabin. One whole gable was filled with guns, like organ pipes in the transept of a church.

O. N. Laster was here only for a night and a day; he had flown in from Paris, over the pole, in his own unmarked plane, and the machine had stayed on the ground only long enough to refuel and take off again. He and Mallory and Susan were alone; all the staff had been sent away. Susan was doing the cooking.

"Someone has to ask Lockwood for proof," Laster said. "Where *are* these bombs? It's a reasonable question."

Susan said, "That question will be asked."

"Just as long as it is, and soon. What will he say?"

"I'd say I'd had them destroyed for the good of mankind," Mallory said.

"No one would believe you."

"No, but they might believe Frosty."

"Why should they? They want to believe Lockwood is good for this country, good for the world?"

"You know they do. Two thousand years of Christianity, a century of psychology, three hundred years of political parties have conditioned them to believe that there is such a thing as a savior."

"I believe that, too. His name is Franklin Mallory."

Mallory smiled sardonically. "You might think that if you watched the convention on the night I was nominated. But there are millions of others out there and they weren't in the Cow Palace."

Susan called them to the table. O. N. Laster put food into himself as if he were putting another rifle back together, and then folded his napkin and laid it beside his plate; he'd had no need to use it because his movements were so sure that no food ever touched his lips. Mallory watched him with wry affection.

"Franklin," O. N. Laster said, "I know you don't want to know the details, and I don't want you to know them, but a hell of a lot of planning and expense has gone into this whole thing. It's taken three years. The results so far aren't quite what I wanted."

"You mean your name coming up on the first day?"

"Yes."

"That's the risk you ran. Can they prove anything? Can they actually link you to this man Clive Wilmot?"

"Anything's possible. The man's a fool, playing all sides for nothing but money."

"I suppose he was the only possible man for the job?"

"Yes. He had the access; we had him. Not everyone knows Hassan Abdallah *and* Graham and the Hubbards on a social basis."

Mallory made a sound in his throat. Laster stopped him from saying more. "This is clearly your problem," Laster said, "but I worry sometimes. You have a weakness for Lockwood. I think you'd let him survive. Franklin, it's a mistake to let fools survive. In politics as in zoology, saving defectives defeats natural selection. The body politic goes to hell. Look around you."

"Or above you." Mallory lifted his head to indicate the silvery gibbous moon that had risen in the daylight.

Laster grunted. His company had a thermonuclear laboratory, two-thirds finished, in a high orbit around the moon. Laster was sure—every rational man he knew was sure—that the secrets of fusion power generation could be discovered in that laboratory. Plants could then be built on earth, and unlimited energy would become available to the human race; Laster's unlimited profits were incidental. The laboratory symbolized a step in man's evolution. Lockwood, in his first week in office, had canceled Laster's great project and brought the crews back to earth. The thermonuclear lab went on circling the moon, the cinder of Laster's dream. This wasn't the only thing Lockwood had done to Laster; he thought that Universal Energy and companies like it were, by the nature of their work, a danger to mankind. Lockwood feared changes in the environment, feared changes in man. Laster thought the species would die unless it changed its environment and changed with it—became something else. Man couldn't go on as he was. It was Laster who had given that idea to Mallory; Laster, in his way, was a visionary.

"Bastards!" said O. N. Laster, of Lockwood and those who thought like Lockwood.

Franklin Mallory looked across the table at his friend's unshaven face. It was a rule of the camp that no one shaved or bathed while they were there. Mallory came up here, after victories and after defeats, to breathe the thin air that even in summer never lost the scent of snow, and to feel and smell his own itching skin for a week or two.

"Let's go outside and look at your bear," he said to O. N. Laster.

The enormous hide was stretched on a frame of saplings. The left eye was missing from the grinning head, removed by the single shot with which Laster, from a range of fifteen yards, had ended the animal's life. The fur was unimaginably thick; the fingers could not penetrate it to touch the skin beneath. The inner side was the color of tallow, with traceries of vermilion and blue —exquisite colors.

"Does it please you to kill something like that?" Mallory asked.

O. N. Laster's neat head, like an otter's, turned in a flash. "Of course; but after it falls, the pleasure stops; you forget."

Mallory laughed. "Aren't you going to miss the pleasure of stalking Frosty Lockwood?"

"Someone else will do the stalking. I'm just feeding him, keeping him alive inside his fence, the way you did with this grizzly. There are all kinds of professional hunters, Franklin."

184

O. N. Laster's tone was light, joking. But Susan realized that Laster, somehow, meant to kill Lockwood, literally kill him as he had killed the bear. Would Mallory let him do it? Even she could read nothing in her lover's face. She put her hand on the rich fur of the grizzly.

"Such a beautiful thing this was, alive," she said.

"Maybe, but useless. Endangered species are endangered because they've outlived their time on earth. It's an offense against nature to keep something alive if it can't cope with change."

"Including Lockwood and his kind?"

O. N. Laster didn't answer Susan directly. It wasn't his way to trouble himself with women's questions. The best of them, Susan' herself, were lamed by sentiment. He put a hand on Mallory.

"Franklin's going to win this election," he said. "Afterwards, I predict, nobody is going to miss the grizzlies."

Susan had taken her hand off O. N. Laster's bear, but he stroked it now, smiling at her. It was an affectionate, almost a sexual, gesture.

O. N. Laster's plane came back for him at dusk. Susan and Mallory drove him to the airstrip, Susan at the wheel. They drove back to the cabin. Mallory caught her arm.

"Would you like to sleep on the boat?"

They were so seldom alone. Susan cast off and Mallory took them out. The northern lights were visible for a time.

"From the Strait of Magellan to the aurora borealis!" said Mallory. "Still not such a bad idea a century afterwards."

Susan stood behind him as he steered the boat, with her long body pressed against his. He could feel the warmth of her flesh even through his thick outdoorsman's clothes. They anchored. On deck, the silence was perfect except for the splash of an occasional feeding fish, smashing through the placid face of the lake like a stone through a pane.

They went below and stripped, shivering in the unheated cabin. Soon they were warm inside a goose-down sleeping bag. Mallory's eyes smiled; Susan could read their expressions even when there was almost no light. Susan's muscles contracted. Mallory's enlarged. They floated, in perfect silence, in peace, loving the future as men and women do in these sweetest moments of life.

"Mmmm." Susan was tired. They kissed lazily for long moments; Mallory realized she'd gone to sleep. Softly, he went on kissing her, but his mind was still in the future.

On the day before Patrick went on the air with the Awad story, Horace called on Sebastian Laux.

"I've come to ask for a leave of absence, Sebastian."

"A leave of absence? You're sick?"

Horace told him what he could expect to hear on the Graham Show. "I don't think my name is likely to come up, but after all I'm Julian's brother, and neither of us would want anything to embarrass the bank."

Sebastian waved away the young male secretary, one of Philindros's acquisitions from the Harvard Business School, who started to come into the room with a folder of papers. No one at D. & D. Laux & Co. had the right of free entry enjoyed by Julian into the Oval Office.

"The best way not to embarrass the bank is to go back to Beirut and carry on as vice-president," Sebastian said. "This gnat—Graham, is it?—wouldn't follow you there."

"He would, I'm afraid. Besides, there's Julian."

Sebastian sighed. "Yes, I suppose there is. Take what time you need. Help your brother."

For the time being, there was little that Horace could do to help Julian.

Horace stayed for a few days in Rose MacKenzie's flat; he discovered that several Siamese cats lived in caves in the debris. Dressed in old cords and a tennis shirt, he wandered alone through the unswept streets of the city. He was a student of architecture, and every block or two the front of a lovely building, surviving from New York's great period of a century past, leaped to his eye from the ugly ranks of glass boxes and concrete cubes.

Horace was often accosted by prostitutes of both sexes. A pair of young blacks, as fleet and implacable as Afghan bandits, attempted to rob him; Horace kicked one of them in the groin and broke the other's forearm and left them both vomiting in pain on the pavement. A policeman watched the scene impassively from a parked cruiser; he was eating a hot dog and licking mustard from his fingers. Under Lockwood's policy of giving large federal grants to the leaders of racial minorities, this city, like most other large metropolitan areas in America, had fallen as completely under the control of blacks as in the past they had been in the grip of the white power elite. The black police force neither harassed nor protected the whites who still lived in guarded towers along the

East River and on certain blocks of Fifth Avenue and Park Avenue that were the only ones on which lights still burned after dark. When men like Sebastian Laux ventured out of their sanctuaries, they went like the rich of the Renaissance into the perilous streets of Florence, surrounded by liveried toughs in their private pay.

"I still love this city," Horace said to Sebastian Laux that night in the Millennium Club.

"You don't remember what it was. 'Come back, O glittering and white!'—Scott Fitzgerald. Even *I'm* younger than that era, but the city was still wonderful in my memory."

"Won't it be again, when these people know enough to see its beauty? I've seen metropolis after metropolis rise in the black countries."

"Perhaps. But neither I nor any of mine will live to see it. What's this man Lockwood thinking of? Is he mad, giving money to people so that they can organize crime and corruption?"

"He's an idealist."

Twice a week, Horace met Sebastian at the club for a drink and a chat about bank business; Sebastian wanted to remind Horace that he must someday come back to D. & D. Laux & Co. Now he twisted the bell on the waxed table between them to call for another drink.

"The two greatest idealists of my time were Heinrich Himmler and that fellow Beria in Russia—they even *looked* alike, round eyeglasses on flabby faces. Tremblers," Sebastian said. "Preserve me from true believers. Your father would say the same if he were here."

"I'm sure he would. Isn't Mallory a true believer?"

"Don't know him."

"Julian told me something; Lockwood did all the things you hate so—let the habitual criminals out of jail, canceled the space program, stopped the free heroin, turned out the lights—under the laws passed by Mallory's men when he was in, giving Mallory special powers. Then he started fighting to have the Mallory laws repealed."

"Your father thought *that* was funny. 'There's a lot of fox in Lockwood,' he said. I guess there is, but the hounds are on him now."

That didn't trouble Sebastian. Politicians came and went. But he didn't like the idea of somebody like Mallory blooding his pack on a Hubbard. "Look after young Julian," he said each time he and Horace parted.

While he'd worked for the bank, Horace had lived the life of a tycoon; D. & D. Laux & Co. kept apartments in all the cities where it had branches for the use of its vice-presidents. Horace had never carried luggage when he traveled; clothes and toilet articles awaited him wherever he might go. Sebastian, forgetting that these apartments really belonged to Philindros, offered the one in New York to Horace, but Horace declined. Sebastian saw his mistake, but it took a moment; he wasn't used to not being able to give away whatever was in his name.

Sebastian told Horace one morning about the death of an old man who had been living in the Millennium Club. Horace moved into these rooms. He still had his flat in Beirut; his things were in the care of the Chinese manservant and well guarded.

The old man who had had the rooms in the club before Horace left no heirs. No one took away his possessions: two shelves of first editions; a wall of sketches done by a gifted amateur (the old man's wife); a small case of rare butterflies; trout rods with the line rotted on the reels. Horace, who had nothing with him but the clothes he kept in New York, lived among these objects and ate in the club except on the two nights a week when he and Rose cooked in her apartment and slept together afterwards.

Rose was always cooking. When Horace thought of her he smelled spices; her hair was full of their afterscent. The first time he'd gone to Sri Lanka, when it was still Ceylon, he'd stood in a spice grove, moving from tree to tree, breathing the aroma of clove and cinnamon, nutmeg and cumin.

In New York, for the first time in twenty years, Horace had time to let his mind wander. He thought a great deal about his father; Sebastian Laux, of course, mentioned Elliott Hubbard often. One afternoon, after he had seen Sebastian to the door of the club— the old man dashed down the steps as if he had twice as much life in him as he ought to have—Horace remembered something from Julian's childhood. On a summer's day the three of them—their father, Julian, and Horace—had been walking along a graveled path in a park. Julian at the time might have been three or four; he was skipping ahead of his father and his brother, skylarking. Beyond Julian in the path were two wolfish slum boys very much like the ones who only recently had attacked Horace in New York. For no reason except the cruel fun of it, one of the boys reached down, snatched up a large pebble, whirled and threw it at Julian. The stone hit Julian in the stomach. He shrieked in pain and shock. Nobody had ever hurt him before. Elliott Hubbard had been talking to Horace about the lost beauties of Joe DiMaggio's play in center field. He saw the thrown stone, heard Julian's scream, and in an instant was transformed into a mindless animal. Elliott flung his body at Julian's attackers, howling a curse, as if he were springing from the mouth of a cave. The boys stood their ground for a moment, then turned and ran. Elliott pursued them for a few steps, then stopped, and, with his back to his sons, seemed to reach out and draw civilization back into his skin. When he turned around he had conquered his rage, but he was a drained man. Horace knew that his father would have killed the boy who threw the stone if he could have laid hands on him; he saw that his father knew it too. Horace had already picked up Julian and was kissing him to comfort him. Elliott Hubbard didn't touch his younger child, but he gripped Horace at the nape of the neck. Horace guessed that this manly gesture was meant to tell him that there had been a time, before he was old enough to protect himself, when his father would have killed for him as well.

Horace wondered if Philindros knew, after all his years with Horace, that he might not be able to trust him absolutely where Horace's family was concerned. Horace had only lately realized it, with a shock, himself.

5

Julian, gazing through the Plexiglas porthole of the helicopter as it lifted from the south lawn after Patrick Graham's broadcast, might have seen Graham's angry figure in the window of his office if he had looked for it. But he had no thought of Patrick; Julian, instead, looked westward toward Georgetown. The first cold rain of autumn fell on Washington. The streets, as the helicopter left them behind, glistened in the wetness, and so did the numberless trees of the city. Because there were only two bright pools of light within it, one at the Capitol and the other at the White House, Washington seemed more than ever like a city in a forest. Julian, straining his eyes, tried to pick out the roof of his house on O Street. He knew this was impossible, the helicopter was flying away from it and the dripping leaves hid everything; but Emily was in the house.

Lockwood spoke to him. Julian went back to him. The President sat with his head against the pillowed leather of his chair, strapped in and protected by armor plating as the Secret Service insisted. Lockwood asked the time. Then he said, "Patrick wasn't so bad. What did you think?"

"Better than I hoped; his blood was up."

"You did well to hold him off for such a long time, Julian. It's September. I'll only have to talk about it for two months." He smiled; he looked very tired. "Patrick's turned out well; that's all

189

your doing. I used to wonder what you saw in him. You've got your father's eye for the right man."

Lockwood's voice was weary. He had drunk three glasses of neat bourbon while watching the Graham Show. His eyes closed and he went to sleep.

Julian was riding only as far as Andrews with the Lockwoods; from there they would take a small jet to Kentucky and he would return to the house on O Street. It was Friday—the whole weekend lay ahead, dead news time; a cooling period. The press secretary had been left behind to deal with the clamoring reporters who would be outraged by Patrick's scoop. Lockwood had scheduled a news conference for the following Monday—soon enough to keep the initiative, late enough to let some of the first shock of his confession on the Graham Show dissipate.

Polly Lockwood had been holding her husband's hand. He uttered a sudden loud snore and twitched in his shallow sleep. Polly gently disengaged her hand and crossed the carpeted floor of the ship to Julian. She staggered as the craft pitched in the turbulence, and Julian leaped to his feet to assist her. Her round body was very soft under his hands; Polly had grown plump, but she had the vestiges of her darling girlhood looks and the open small-town manners of a girl everyone had always liked. One imagined her as a cheerleader, as the homecoming queen; in fact she had been at Concord and Radcliffe; she had met Lockwood in Cambridge, when he was a ragged law student. Her bankrupt father wouldn't let her marry her hillbilly at Live Oaks, as she had wanted, during the last week that he owned the place. Elliott Hubbard had given her away in the college chapel. Two days before, in Kentucky, she had killed a horse putting it to a jump she knew it couldn't make; everyone in the hunt knew why.

Polly took Julian's hand in both of hers—no pressure, just the gesture. "Is there anything I can do for Emily?"

"I don't think so. She's slept a lot since it happened; the doctor gave her pills."

"She's not alone?"

"She's wanted to be. But, no—not today. Caroline's been with her."

Polly's face opened in surprise. She seldom saw Julian outside his work since Caroline left; Emily was just too young to be her friend.

"I didn't know Caro was here."

"She's come to collect the Pumpkins." Julian made the old joke with an effort: Polly had always called Elliott and Jenny "Pumpkin" when they were small, and she still did so; she and Jenny had long

190

telephone conversations, and they saw each other still—afternoon tea upstairs in the White House.

"I wish I'd known," Polly said. "I never see her since she went off on that boat."

"Nobody does. She and the children are flying to Buenos Aires. Leo's anchored there. They just have time to get to Antarctica by its springtime. The icebergs are supposed to be a great sight."

"I should think they would be. Leo must be very rich."

"Well, he keeps writing those books. Caroline likes the life— the two of them alone most of the time, except for the crew. I don't know where the children would be safer. Terrorists don't have submarines, at least."

Polly let go of his hand. "Caro left no scars on you at all, did she?"

Julian shrugged. "She and I were never enemies. For Caro, that was something. The only other non-enemies she ever had, besides the children I think, were you and Frosty. And now Leo. You know her. She does as she wants. Why shouldn't she?"

Polly, nodding, patted Julian's hand. "You have a lovely girl now," she said. The helicopter made a steep turn and Lockwood woke. He gave a startled look, then realized that they were landing and closed his eyes again.

Polly said, "Getting over this won't be easy for Emily. She's so young, and she wanted a child so." She turned her face away; she didn't want a reply from Julian. She leaned across the aisle as the helicopter settled towards the earth and said something in Lockwood's ear. He put a hand on her cheek and nodded.

Polly gave Julian's hand a final squeeze and debarked, surrounded by her Secret Service men. Lockwood sent his guards away; they went nervously, and Julian saw them standing close by the dull green body of the helicopter as they waited for the President to emerge.

Lockwood got out of his seat and, in a queer gesture, held out a hand to Julian to help him to his feet, as if the younger man had been enfeebled by some sudden seizure. Lockwood up to this moment had said nothing to him at all about Emily or the loss of the baby; Julian had told him nothing about it.

Neither Julian nor Lockwood could stand fully erect in the cabin and they stooped, face to face, while Julian waited for the President to speak. Lockwood's eyes, when he lifted his face a bit, shone with sympathy. He put his hands on Julian's shoulders.

"You go on home now," Lockwood said. "Give Emily my love." From some lost glen in his ancestry of child-loving mountain folk, the President drew forth what he said and did next.

"It'll be all right after a while, honey," he said; and kissed Julian on the forehead.

6

Julian found the children's luggage piled in the hall when he got back to O Street, and from the living room heard Caroline's voice and Emily's. Music from two record machines floated down the stairs; Elliott and Jenny were playing their tapes as they waited to say good-bye to him.

In the living room, he kissed Emily and said hello to Caroline. The women had stopped speaking abruptly as he came through the door.

"I must say your father's pictures make a difference to this room," Caroline said. "They look larger here, and you've put better light on them."

The women were together on one sofa. Julian sat on the other and stretched his legs. He made a face; Caroline and Emily exchanged a look of understanding: Julian always did that at the end of the day, before he had a drink, as he remembered his body for the first time and his war wounds gave him pain.

"We watched the Graham Show," Caroline said. "Frosty was marvelous. I wonder what the reaction will be."

"I've no idea." Julian pointed at Caroline's empty wineglass; she'd given up spirits after she left him. Now she shook her head no even to another California Chablis.

"Caroline thinks there'll be a storm," Emily said. "Everyone will be disillusioned—but then nobody will be able to live with the idea of Frosty Lockwood as a murderer. . . ."

"A murderer?"

"I don't know what else it's called. Anyway, then—you finish it, Caroline. I can't put it back in your words."

"After a while, everyone will be like Patrick. He was horror-struck when I saw him in New York at the convention. . . ."

"He told you then?"

"Patrick has always told me things I didn't want to hear. He was horror-struck a month ago, but now he's finding reasons to admire what Frosty did. He's a bellwether if ever there was one."

"Dominant male, Emily calls it."

Caroline patted Emily's hand, lying on the cushion between them. "Whatever. The Lockwoods of this world aren't supposed to do such things. Therefore, in the end, no one will believe Frosty *did* do it—or if he did it, they'll believe he did it to save the world. Any jury on earth, if there were a trial, would hang him for premeditated murder. But there'll never be a trial, and he'll make the ten-best-loved list of all time. If he's bad, what are we, having trusted and loved him so?"

Caroline got up, a fluid motion. She looked not much different than she had looked more than twenty years before at Elliott Hubbard's Christmas party; she shook her heavy hair back with the same gesture.

"May I call the kids? We'll have to go if we're going to make the plane."

Julian started to speak. Caroline held up both hands in mock surrender. She had heard all his warnings before.

"We're taking four Secret Service men." She named them; they were all good. "Bob Hanna is coming as a tutor, so they'll be miles ahead of everyone in school when they get back. Leo's got the best pilot for Antarctic waters that money can buy; and he's been cleared for security to a fare-thee-well—Jack Philindros did that for me."

It was Julian who surrendered now. Jenny and Elliott clattered down the stairs when Caroline called; it seemed natural to hear her voice, roughened by a lifetime of argument—such a great sound to come out of so small a body—flying up the stairs again. While Julian kissed the children good-bye, he heard Emily and Caroline murmuring behind him. To his astonishment, they hugged each other fiercely and kissed.

"Everything will be fine, you'll see," Caroline said. Julian went to the car with Caroline and the children, all of them screened by the broad bodies of the security detail. A misty rain had begun to fall again.

Emily was sitting on the stairs when Julian came back in. She was pale—paler than Caroline had ever been after any of her abortions. After the first one, when they were still in school, Caroline had treated him to a big meal in Little Italy; only afterwards, as they clinked glasses when the Spumante had been poured, did Caroline tell him what she'd done that day; in Caroline's mind, in those times, abortion had been a joyous political act. Of course, they had never shown Caroline the baby.

Julian sat down on a stair lower than Emily's, and kissed her. When he'd stripped the bed the morning after she lost the child, there had been no more blood on the sheet than the little spot left, all those years ago in the slovenly New York apartment, by the loss of Caroline's virginity.

"You and Caroline seem to have got on."

"She knows a lot. Do you know what she really said about Lockwood? She said he was safe because he had your brain, there'd been a transplant years and years ago; and you and Horace together were too smart for Mallory, or anyone."

Emily had a feverish look in her eyes. She gave Julian a smart pat on the shoulder, as if he'd come off a football field after making a marvelous play.

"Are you hungry?" he asked.

"No. I want a shower."

Emily went up the stairs, walking gingerly with her legs apart, holding herself (Julian could see the muscles tightening) as if she feared the baby would fall out of her again. He went to the kitchen and made sandwiches and carried them up to the bedroom. Emily was still in the shower; she had bathed a great deal lately—scrubbing her body over and over again and washing her hair. When she came out, wrapped in a terry cloth robe, she didn't speak until Julian took the napkin off the tray, revealing the sandwiches and two sweating bottles of beer. "I'm not hungry," she said again. Julian took the sandwiches away, and ate his own, alone, at the kitchen table downstairs. When he returned, he found Emily where he'd left her, in a chair gazing at a painting on the bedroom wall; it was one of Julian's mother's canvases—distended blue shapes, billows of white, with a tiny aluminum sun, like a tinsel beauty spot on a dead face.

"Would you like to go to bed?" Julian asked.

"Sure," said Emily. She lay down and closed her eyes at once.

On Sunday, Emily accepted everything that Julian suggested. It was cool enough to have lunch in the garden. Julian made a salad and opened a bottle of rosé wine. Emily nibbled the greens and sipped a little wine. She touched the petals of the late roses Julian had cut and put in a bowl at the center of the table. Her eyes were empty. When he spoke to her she answered with a shrug or a glance or a flutter of her narrow hand.

After lunch,, Julian wheeled a chaise longue into the shade of an umbrella—a big colorful parasol with the name of a vermouth printed around its edge that Emily had brought to their marriage. With her hundreds of books, the parasol was her dowry. While she lay quietly, Julian in a chair beside her read aloud from a book he knew she loved. He read only the happy parts.

At nightfall they went inside. Emily walked stiffly within the circle of Julian's arm, but slipped away from him once they were indoors. The Secret Service people were keeping themselves out of sight.

"Emily, you don't want to talk? If not to me, to someone else? It might help."

194

Emily shook her head. She had no friend but Julian. For all her rapport with Caroline, she had never liked other females; she didn't believe in their honesty. Her dreaming look, her gawky limbs, her startling way of reading people for what they were, made her a lovable woman; but they had made her a laughable adolescent. She had never forgot the wounds girls had inflicted on her. No man, she said, had ever done her harm. But they were violent and sly, and almost always sentimental. When she rejected them, it was because they thought that she was more than she was. Only Julian had perceived her true and plain.

All afternoon Emily had struggled with a thought about Julian that she did not want to have. It rose toward the light at the surface of her mind like a predator coming up from the sea. Emily fled from it; but it rose again.

At last it broke into view. Their baby had died because Ibn Awad had died. There was no intelligence in this. Emily knew that. No invisible force existed that punished murder by killing the thing the murderer loved. Still, at the moment the baby died, she had felt the connection. All the gates in her mind that had been sealed by education and logic, and by her love for Julian, crashed open at once. The long past of her sex passed through her like an electric current, all the fear and futility and terrible consequences that females had suffered because men loved ideas, and loved danger, more than they loved women.

Caroline, when they were alone that afternoon, had explained. Emily had asked her why she had left Julian. She couldn't blame her for her answer; she had heard enough about Caroline to know that she always told the truth.

"Leave him?" Caroline had said. "Julian was never *there*. I loved him, so it took me years to realize it. Why do you think he's such a true friend, such an honorable man, such a perfect lover? Julian doesn't even want to live, my dear. He sees that everyone *else* wants to live, some of us desperately, and he's polite enough to help us. But himself? He could die tomorrow with as little emotion as he showed when I went out the door. 'Good-bye,' he said, and gave me to Leo. If that was what I wanted, that was fine with Julian."

They had just watched the Graham Show. "But this," Emily said. "He helped kill a man."

"For Frosty Lockwood. Julian will take the blame if he's asked; I'm sure he's already taken on the guilt."

"But he can kill."

"Of course he can. All of them can."

Shivering and clasping her own body in her arms, Emily got

out of his bed. Julian was asleep. She took another pill and went to Jenny's room. There, among the restful fragrances of childhood, she slept alone.

7

Horace never ate breakfast at Rose MacKenzie's. To ration energy, the Lockwood Administration had banned the heating of water after dark, so Rose's sink in the morning was always stacked with foul dishes. Horace woke before her, and left as the sun was coming up.

The city was empty at that time of day and it reminded Horace of the sweetest hours of his youth. Thirty years before, after leaving a girl, he would walk home past the open hydrants over the shimmering pavement, and with the light of dawn beyond its towers and the fresh smell of flowing water in the air, New York had been the best place on earth. Now there was no hot water at night to wash dishes, and no cool water at any time to sluice the streets. As he sauntered down Fifth Avenue, Horace passed two boys of about twelve who were killing a cat with a strangling cord on the steps of Saint Thomas Church.

At the club, Horace bathed and changed and went down to breakfast. A cut grapefruit and the *Times* were already on his regular table. He opened the paper to the text of Lockwood's news conference of the day before. It was his second since the Awad story broke. Once again, Horace was gratified to see, no reporter had asked a question about the role of the FIS in the "Awad Affair," as the media now called the assassination. The press had been put onto a stronger scent, one they were trained to follow, by the revelations about O. N. Laster and Clive Wilmot. The hunt, pink-faced with stirrup cups and good fellowship and the brisk air of an election-year autumn, was following a drag instead of the live fox. Who in this day would understand such a metaphor? Clive Wilmot would, and Horace hoped that the Englishman would live long enough to see the joke.

The waiter brought Horace a telephone message. After he ate his breakfast, a grilled lamb kidney, Horace rang a private number at D. & D. Laux & Co., and Sebastian Laux's reedy voice came over the line.

"Horace, good morning. That man Patrick Graham rang me at home during the night. He wants you to get in touch as a matter of the greatest urgency. Those were his words."

196

There was a pause while Sebastian fumbled with his reading glasses. Then he read a telephone number in a slow, distinct voice. The old man never wanted there to be any mistake about figures. It was a Manhattan number. It didn't appear in the telephone book under any of the listings for Patrick's network or in any other logical place, so Horace called Rose MacKenzie for assistance. In seconds she gave him an address on York Avenue; it was an apartment in a fortified neighborhood kept by the network for visiting stars.

Horace dialed the number. Patrick asked him to lunch in the apartment that day, and Horace accepted; he declined Patrick's offer to send a car for him. While he waited for noon to strike, Horace looked again at the video cassette of Patrick's broadcast. He wondered if Rose would be able to make anything of the difference in voice pitch between this Patrick and this Lockwood, as compared to how they usually sounded. Horace thought he could detect their new emotional states even with the unaided ear.

Horace was lifted to the penthouse of a glass silo by the East River in a high-speed elevator. Its doors opened into the foyer of the apartment, and one of the Grahams' Old Etonians in striped trousers and a black jacket and white gloves greeted him and showed him in. That year in New York there was a fashion for cluttered Victorian decoration, and the room was crammed with lamps with fringed pink shades, horsehair sofas covered in shades of violet, tables with tapestry cloths sweeping bogus Turkey carpets. Photographs in ornate frames surrounded the candelabra on top of the grand piano, and it, too, was covered with a scarf. It was a room that cried out for dimness, but it was airy and sun-splashed, with glass walls on three sides. Horace paused to drink it all in.

"Looks like a flash picture of a guilty husband caught in bed with six tarts, doesn't it?" called Patrick. He sat in a chair in the far reaches of the room. He made Horace come to him; they nodded to one another, Horace smiling, Patrick solemn despite his joke.

A table for two had been laid near a window and the whole lower half of Manhattan Island was spread out below them in the limpid blue light of early autumn. Patrick took no interest in the view. Horace recalled that he had been the same in Beirut. Evidently Patrick was impervious to anything that was farther away than a face in a studio or a picture on a wall. The English servant poured wine from a crystal decanter; he was silent and deft—he had been well trained, but it was evident that a Japanese had done the training: he smiled too much.

"Julian is well?"

"Busy. He and the President are all over the place, campaigning. But you know that. You've made them run harder than they might have. Awad, I mean."

Patrick vouchsafed a tight smile. Oysters were set before them.

In the fortnight since Patrick's broadcast, Horace had not spoken to his brother. There had been no need. Lockwood and Julian required no help in dealing with a domestic political situation. In the first wave of shock that ran through the country after the news broke, Lockwood had lost twelve points in the polls and fallen far behind Mallory. Rose MacKenzie, tapping into the public-opinion firms' computers for a lark, had told Horace the night before that the gap was narrowing already. Sixty-two percent of the American people believed in Lockwood's "essential decency"; only 49 percent felt the same about Mallory. Horace wondered if Julian had had a hand in phrasing that question for the pollsters, or if he had merely relied on their instincts, as he had done in Patrick's case.

Patrick drank some Pouilly Fuissé and lifted a *belon,* flown down that morning from Nova Scotia, to his mouth. There were three oysters on his plate, a half dozen on Horace's.

"You're very hard to reach," Patrick said. "Are you in touch with your brother?"

"I've been moving around a good deal," Horace said. "There's been no occasion to talk to Julian. I have spoken to Emily. Evidently Charlotte has been very kind to her."

Patrick, having made his pretense of eating, left the rest of his oysters. "Yes," he said. "Charlotte mentioned the miscarriage. Well, Julian has other things to think about these days."

"Thanks to your work, I say again. I don't enjoy seeing my brother embarrassed, Patrick, but I have to admire you. Another scoop. What an amazing fellow you are."

The Old Etonian cleared away the first course and gave them the second. Patrick said to him, "Go away. Don't come back until I ring."

To Horace, who was slicing into the medallion of a lamb chop, Patrick said, "All right, Horace. Cut the shit."

"The 'shit,' Patrick?"

"Do you really think I don't know that the FIS was in this business over Awad up to its eyeballs? Do you really think I don't know that D. & D. Laux & Co. *is* the FIS, that I don't know you are what *you* are?"

"Oh? What am I?"

"What you've always been. CIA in the old days, FIS ever since. The Resident for the Near East. Philindros's trigger finger."

Horace, having cut a neat triangle from the lamb chop, put it into his mouth and chewed it. He swallowed.

"Who is your source for all that?" Horace asked pleasantly. "Clive Wilmot?"

"Clive only knew what everyone knows, Horace. Any shoeshine boy from Cairo to Istanbul could have told me."

"I suppose so. The Arab world has always been full of shoeshine boys who hinted to gullible strangers that they are, in real life, the head of the secret service. It's not always wise to believe them."

"Horace, please. Enough urbanity."

Horace laid his silverware on his full plate, as a gesture to show that he took Patrick's questions seriously. "Patrick, I am able to tell you with perfect truth that I am not in the pay of the FIS or any other intelligence service," he said.

A flush of anger spread upwards from Patrick's perfectly laundered collar to the roots of his hair. Beads of spittle formed in the seam of his lips. Horace had read of such things, but he had never in life seen a man's face distorted in this way. It was a rare thing for Horace to make an involuntary gesture, but he thought Patrick might be having a heart attack, and instinctively he started to rise to go around the table to help him. The scarlet drained out of Patrick's face almost as quickly as it had appeared, and Horace sank back in relief. Not so Patrick. He had got hold of himself, but he could not conceal his rage. When he lifted his water glass in his trembling hand, the ice cubes rattled.

"I want you to know what I think, Horace," Patrick said.

"Patrick, I am anxious to know. This is a very strange conversation."

"Julian—"

Patrick's voice broke on the name, and all at once Horace understood. There was hatred here. Horace knew the emotion well —he had used it often enough to turn one Arab against another, and before that, Koreans and Chinese and Vietnamese and half the dark peoples of the world. He just wasn't used to seeing it in its naked form on an American face.

"I think," Patrick Graham continued, "that you used Prince Talil to kill his father. And then you killed the witness—Talil, who loved you—on orders from your brother."

"On orders from Julian."

Horace spoke in a flat tone. He wasn't agreeing. He wasn't

questioning Patrick Graham any more than he would have questioned a lunatic with a knife who confronted him on one of his solitary walks through the midtown streets. He was merely repeating Patrick's words to show he'd understood his delusion.

"Yes. On orders from Julian. I think all that crap Julian dumped in my lap—the tape recordings of Laster and Wilmot, the stuff from FIS files, the whole bundle—came from *you*, Horace. It had your fingerprints all over it."

"Patrick, I don't know what you mean. On the air, you said pretty much everything you're saying here, although you didn't accuse me of murder. I thank you for that. You told the reasons that Awad was killed—the Eye of Gaza, the nuclear devices. What's different here?"

"I'll tell you what's different here. I know fucking well that you and Julian made Frosty Lockwood do it."

Horace, recovered from his astonishment, listened with his habitual look of interest.

"What you and your brother have done," Patrick said, "is hand this country over to Franklin Mallory. He's going to beat Lockwood. We're going into the long night at last, Horace; we can't hold it back this time. Julian and you are to blame. I want you to tell him something, because he won't return my calls. Tell him I *know*."

"Just that?"

"No, you can tell him this, too—before I'm through, everyone will know."

Patrick stood up. Crystal and china swayed on the table. He looked at his watch, though three large clocks standing in various parts of the room were striking the hour of two.

"I'm due somewhere," Patrick said.

Horace used his napkin and got up, too. The pale servant stood by the elevator with the door open; Patrick must have rung a hidden bell to bring him gliding back into their presence. Music, the *Emperor* Concerto, wafted from the speakers in the waiting cage. Patrick was rooted where he stood, and Horace understood that he was to find his own way across the room. He gave it one more admiring glance.

"I'll tell Julian what you've said," Horace said.

In the plummeting elevator, Horace moved his head to the rhythms of the music. The pianist played with bravura. Horace recognized the artist. Horowitz; he had the same recording in his library at Beirut.

8

"Graham cannot *know* what isn't a fact," said Horace to Julian. "He just wants very badly to believe in this theory of his."

"Wanting to believe something is as good as knowing it for Patrick. He's a man of strong emotions."

The brothers were together in the courtyard of the Maison de la Ville in New Orleans. John James Audubon was said to have lived here when he was making his drawings of American birds. Julian liked that legend. Now it was an elegant small hotel. Lockwood always stayed here when he was campaigning in Louisiana, taking over the whole establishment. The President's boisterous voice came to them from the other end of the courtyard as he swapped stories with a group of politicians.

"The question is," Horace said, "is Graham likely to go out of control?"

"Out of control? Who has any control over him anyway?"

"I thought you had some. Certainly he's run on the tracks you laid for him so far."

"He's influenced by his political convictions. That means he likes Lockwood and hates Mallory. It doesn't mean, as you say in your business, that he's 'under discipline.' "

Julian's voice was weary and his appearance was rumpled— tie pulled slightly to one side, suit unpressed. He had been traveling with the President for days. They would visit two or three states and half a dozen cities between dawn and midnight, then fly back to the White House and make a week's decisions in a day before setting out again on the campaign trail.

Lockwood was running very hard to catch up with Franklin Mallory. The pace exhilarated him. He was feeling better inside himself all the time as he went around the country, publicly mourning the death of Ibn Awad. His remorse was being accepted as genuine. Those who had always loved Lockwood loved him still—some of them loved him even more; he had shown fiber. The case for justifiable homicide was being made.

This phase of the campaign would not last much longer; Lockwood did not want to keep Ibn Awad's name alive; he wanted to invent new phrases, new issues. Bit by bit, as October drew near, he began to speak of the old choice: himself and the humanitarian movement, preserving the planet and the spirit of man; or Mallory and his dark forces, filling the skies with smoke and trifling with nature and man. "I want to lead this great people," Lockwood said; "but what does Franklin Mallory want to do? Is it possible he wants to *train* us? Are we the mere creatures he thinks we are, with just enough spark in us to learn new tricks—is America to become a vast obedience school?" The cheers would then crash in Lockwood's ear. He was speaking words that Julian had written.

If Lockwood was rejuvenated by this, Julian was exhausted. It was he who heard all the warnings of defeat that no one dared address to the President. It was no wonder that emperors, if no assassin found them, lived such a long time. Lockwood was shielded from bores, protected from bad news, tended by a doctor, commanded to eat properly and get the right amount of rest. Julian was the President's doorkeeper. This was a sleepless profession. On many days he ate nothing but a sandwich; often he forgot to swallow his blood pressure medicine and then his patience would grow short. He spent his long days with a telephone at his ear or with a stranger's unwelcome hand on his shoulder.

"Is it possible," Horace persisted, "that Patrick Graham will actually go on the air with this nonsense about the sinister FIS and the evil Hubbard brothers?"

"Of course it's possible. It's been possible from the start."

"Is it likely?"

A wry smile cleansed the fatigue from Julian's face. His eyes turned for a moment towards Lockwood, who was having such an enjoyable time with the senior senator from Louisiana and the governor and his wife and a dozen other politicians just a few yards away in the flowered courtyard.

"It wouldn't be such a bad thing for the President if Patrick did just that," Julian said. "The FIS and you and I would become yet another dark force to blame all this on. Better that than blaming it on Lockwood."

The telephone rang in Julian's room and his secretary came to the door. He went away to talk to whoever had called him. Evidently Julian considered that he and Horace had said all that was necessary on the subject of Patrick Graham.

Horace had boarded a plane soon after his lunch with Graham and come to New Orleans in order to warn his brother again that this man was his implacable enemy. Julian already knew that, and did not care.

"Patrick has these seizures," Julian said to Horace; "he always survives, and so far, I have too."

Julian was used to taking the blame for Lockwood, it went with the job; there wasn't much difference between letting the world think he had written a line in a speech that offended some minority group and letting history believe that he, not Lockwood, was Awad's murderer. The only truth was the great one—that the right idea and the people who believed in it should win out in November.

"Horace," he said, "I know you're worried about the FIS. With Lockwood, a promise is a promise; he isn't going to lay the blame for Awad on Philindros or the intelligence service. But if Patrick Graham decides to do a show in which you and Philindros and I meet on Awad's grave, there's nothing anyone can do about it."

"That's not much comfort. Graham can destroy the FIS and Lockwood would go down with it. Even if he doesn't, what do you think you're going to do without an intelligence service in Lockwood's next term?"

"'Tis time enough tomorrow to be brave,'" said Julian. His voice was light, but he had turned his eyes away.

"Quoting Pa's favorite sayings from Shakespeare isn't going to help," Horace said.

Julian did not hear him. Lockwood was calling to him. He touched Horace's arm, his attention already elsewhere, and said again, before he walked away, "Don't worry about the FIS."

It wasn't the FIS Horace was worried about. He saw that it could be saved. Julian was another matter.

Outside, in the tawdry streets lined with nightclubs named for jazz musicians who had long been dead, Horace found a telephone booth with a working instrument. Someone had covered the foul matter on the floor with a newspaper; a picture of Lockwood, arms raised in greeting to a crowd, covered most of the stained front page.

Horace made two calls. First, he booked a seat on a flight to New York. Next, he put through a message to Philindros to meet him there.

9

An hour after Horace left him, Patrick Graham learned something of value.

The girl who lay naked in bed with him kissed him and said, in an idle after-lovemaking voice, "Didn't Ibn Awad belong to the killable category?"

Patrick might have been hearing Caroline's voice.

"I mean," said the girl, stretching her limbs like a waking animal, "the Eye of Gaza, blowing up Jews, marching into the past at the head of an army of the faithful? After *all!*"

It was only then that Patrick realized what a remarkable job Lockwood had done in raising the consciousness—what an old-

203

fashioned phrase that was to come back to him—of people like this girl. She saw now that Awad had personified brutal and backward forces and it was fitting that his life should be extinguished. Patrick, and those who believed with him, had always thought such men should die by violence. Exultation, not mourning, was the right response.

The mere fact that a man held power did not mean that he deserved to die. Some leaders shone in the imagination. Thirty years and more had not sufficed to heal the wound that John Kennedy's death had inflicted on Patrick and his friends. But any one of them, Patrick especially, would have killed Richard Nixon with his own hands and been proud of the act.

Patrick was not sure that the whole people could make the distinction between a good assassination and a bad one. Even in his own heart Patrick knew that Awad's murder was nothing but an act of terrorism.

"It wouldn't be so worrisome if Awad hadn't been built up as a holy man," said Patrick. "Of course he was a charlatan and a madman; I knew him. But appearance is sometimes more than reality."

"What's the truth about Franklin Mallory?" asked the girl. "*He's* so sane he's scary. I mean, all that talk in that cold, cold voice about everybody being rational."

Patrick shifted his body; the girl lay with her head on his shoulder and her skull was digging into the soft flesh there.

"Let me be allegorical," said Patrick. "Once I had a dear friend, an important man at the network, so I won't name him. He had what used to be called a nervous breakdown and was put into a clinic. After he'd been there for a day or two, a *very* important executive, the man's remote superior, came to see him. The visitor had a package with him, a present. Inside was a special clock, with the numbers running from one to twenty-four instead of one to twelve in the usual way. He plugged in the clock and put it on my friend's bedside table. 'Harry,' he said, 'I hear you're crazy. Years ago I was crazy myself for a while. They put me in this same place. This clock got me out of it. Watch it. Watch it for twenty-four hours every day when nobody is looking. The great thing in a place like this is: *Don't let them see that you're crazy.* If they do, they'll never let you out. They watch you like a hawk for signs that you're crazy. Now, anybody can act sane for twenty-four hours at a time. That's what you've got to do. Keep telling yourself, one day at a time, that you won't let them see that you're crazy. Believe me, it works. You'll be out of here and back at the network in no time.'"

"Did it work?"

"Of course. And that's Franklin Mallory's method. He's watching the clock until he's re-elected—being very, very careful not to let anyone see that he's crazy."

Mallory, indeed, was running a strange campaign. He had made no public appearances since the convention in San Francisco. As Lockwood barnstormed the country, Mallory remained in his mansion on Fifth Avenue. He spoke on television every tenth day, gave a news conference every second Tuesday; Susan Grant spoke quietly to favored reporters.

Mallory was asked again and again about the Awad Affair. "It is a clear case of murder," he said. "The President says he is consumed by remorse. Perhaps that's enough for him; we'll see if it's enough for the people." He was pressed to say more. "I don't have all the facts," Mallory would say, always using the same words and the same hard emphasis; "nobody but Bedford Forrest Lockwood has all the facts, *so far*."

The media, their electrical cables running from throbbing mobile units, clustered outside Mallory's house, interviewing the advisers who came and went in a steady procession. Each had a self-effacing statement to make; all referred to Mallory as "the President"; gradually the interviewers began to do the same, in order to save themselves the irritation of being corrected by the persons they were interviewing when they called Mallory by his own name. At night, ambassadors and foreign ministers and even a foreign head of state or two came in by the garage entrance. They too were caught in the glare of the portable television lights.

Then, too, the pictures kept coming back from Ganymede. In their factual tones, the scientists aboard *Humanity* reported the possibility of new sources of mineral wealth. They had taken asteroids in tow on the journey out, proving that the capture of whole free-falling mountains of what had once been called base metals was feasible. Pairs of men in special ships had descended into the outer atmosphere of Jupiter. These most adventurous of ships were called Mallory Explorers.

Through all these events, Mallory remained calm, fluent, confident. From time to time he let himself be interviewed. Apart from his formula about Ibn Awad, he never said the same thing twice; or at least never spoke in the same words. Lockwood, in the tradition of campaigning politicians, had a set speech; he hammered out the same phrases day after day, in city after city. Of the two candidates, Mallory in his mansion in New York was the more remote, the more presidential. Those men who let themselves be interviewed on the sidewalk by his front door somehow had the king's odor still on them. The Mallory campaign was a great novelty; the fact that it was being done as it was being done was in itself a fascinating news story.

Patrick's girl said so. "The once and future President," she added.

Patrick knew a phrase to be feared when he heard it. He put a hand over her mouth.

"Don't you ever speak those words outside this bed," he said.

The girl, struggling to breathe, for Patrick's hand was very tight against her face, twisted away. She looked at him with fear. He had shown her a lot of himself in their sexual life, but this was unmasked ferocity.

"All *right*, Patrick," she said. "I hate Mallory as much as you do."

Patrick subsided. "It isn't hatred," he said, "it's fear. I'm really afraid for the country."

He turned and smiled at her. She was sitting up, cross-legged, at the edge of the bed. The red marks of his fingers were still on her cheeks, as if he had slapped her. Patrick smiled and touched her with a gentler hand.

"You and I and all our friends would be together anyway," he said teasingly. "Mallory would send us all to Alaska to chop wood. Barbed wire and snow, that's what you must see when you close your eyes and think of Mallory.

"Come here," he said.

The fragile dark-haired girl, hardly larger than an Oriental, moved obediently across the bed. Patrick knew why he sought out lovers who looked like this girl; he'd long ago stopped worrying about it. In the end he left a wound on them—he never did women physical harm, but he frightened them, made them remember him. Sometimes, years after the end of an affair, he would chance to meet a girl he had had in some corner of the network building or at a party, and he would see the mingling of fear and desire in her eyes. If they were alone he would sometimes gently caress her breast, or lift her hand and put it on himself, to show that he would never lose the right. He lifted this little body that was so much like Caroline's and fitted it to his own. The girl opened her eyes wide and stared at him in astonishment. He brought her to a shuddering orgasm, and when she was at its very center, with her hands clutching her own breasts, Patrick, thinking of Caroline, made her speak her husband's name, over and over.

The girl left him. Patrick remained in the disordered bed, smoking. He was glad to be alone; he had always been lonely; there had been no one in his family who was anything like him and, like Goethe as a boy, he had imagined that he couldn't be the son of his lumpish father or the brother of his doughy siblings; some other man—Goethe had wanted his natural father to have been a prince—must have got him on his mother, to pass an hour in a dull town. Certainly his mother had loved him best. "There's no one like you," she told him every night, whispering as she kissed him so that his brothers, sprawled on their beds in the same stuffy room that smelled of sports equipment instead of the natural seasons, would not hear.

There was no one at all like Patrick; there never had been, and sometimes he felt this like a physical pain. Charlotte was with him, she had created a portion of him even, but she was no part of him. No one was. He concealed less of himself from Charlotte than from anyone else; she really did not mind what people were like inside themselves. Was there something to conceal? How natural! She was content to help Patrick build up an appearance, and live by it. She had never pretended to love him. "It only makes trouble between men and women, darling," she said. Asking her to marry him, Patrick said, "I don't love you, I just think you'd make me a useful wife." "I'm *so* relieved; I accept," Charlotte replied. She liked the fact that he had chosen a public place, Kettner's restaurant in Romilly Street with its pink luncheon cloths, to make his proposal.

His words to Charlotte on the day they became engaged were almost the only confession he had ever made to another individual. His mother, dying, had pulled him down into the sour envelope of odors in which her fatal disease had enclosed her and, in a whisper, asked if he loved her. Patrick, believing himself to be lying, said yes. His mother wept, two tears pushing themselves from the colorless ducts at the corners of her deadened eyes, as though it required every bit of strength remaining in her body to give him this sign of her joy. Seeing the tears, Patrick realized that he *did* love her, that he always had; and alone with her corpse, he did something that even now returned to him in dreams: before calling in the nurses, he had closed his mother's eyes and her mouth and composed her limbs, and he had combed her hair with his own comb.

Had that been an act of love? Patrick shuddered, remembering the bloated body with its legs like grotesque sausages in which his existence had begun.

Patrick picked up a phone and called an art dealer who had been trying to sell him a painting; they agreed on a price. Patrick needed beautiful things outside himself to look at. Charlotte, knowing why, sometimes mocked him. "It's *you!*" she'd cry when he carried home a new picture, always more exquisite than the last one he had bought.

10

Philindros's eyes had this peculiarity: pupil and iris were the same deep shade of brown; opaque, unchanging. No signal could be read in them. In the talks room, while he listened to Horace, he stared at the thermos jug, at the watch on Horace's bony wrist, at the light in the ceiling, as though sibyls might be lurking in these objects, waiting to speak to him. Philindros dealt every day in prophecy, and knew how often it could be correct if based on a cool reading of the obvious.

"Graham," he said at last, "seems to be in the grip of conflicting emotions. On the one hand he detests us—and evidently hates your brother; on the other he loves Lockwood."

"Or hates and fears Mallory."

Philindros put the tips of his fingers together. "Same thing. Why exactly does he hate Julian?"

"It goes back a long way. You know the story about Caroline. Other things are mixed up in it—class warfare; Patrick imagines that Julian is some sort of Brahmin. And then Julian has done a lot for him over the years. How many kindnesses can a man be expected to forgive? He may have realized that Julian is the closest thing he has to a real friend in the world. That *would* be a shattering insight."

"Yes. Well, we can't very well let him proceed. Is it possible to make him see that he'll take Lockwood down along with us if he decides to attack the FIS? Is there anyone—some disinterested person—who might be able to talk to Graham?"

Philindros waited for Horace to supply the solution. No more to a subordinate than to a President would he venture a direct suggestion—especially not to a subordinate who was so nearly an equal as Horace. He did not like men who couldn't see for themselves what action must be taken, once the target had been identified and all the known facts about it laid out on the table.

"There is a possibility," Horace said.

He told Philindros what he had in mind. Philindros was not taken aback. He and Horace knew the same simple fact: only a human being could sway another human being. In the end, whatever the brain might whisper, it was flesh that acted on flesh. Always. Horace had last seen this in the Hagrebi desert, with Prince

Talil collapsed at his feet in his splendid robes, cut off at the stem by his grief like some unique orchid by the pruning knife. Both men had used human nature so much to achieve their ends—the ends of their country—that the map of it was in their bloodstream, as the plan of the New York subway system is imprinted on the subconscious of those who grow up in that city. They rode people to their destinations as casually as a commuter took a train, and were as oblivious to what went on inside the rattling car after they got off.

"I'd have to have the loan of your tape," Horace said.

"All right, but your girl must get it back, uncopied, from Graham. Can you trust her to do that?"

"I think so. After all, she'll be protecting someone she loves."

Philindros took a lozenge from his pocket, unwrapped it, and put it into his mouth. In the muffled atmosphere of the sealed room, the candy clicked audibly against his white teeth.

"I hope you can move quickly—even tonight—on this Graham business," Philindros said. "Rose has something new on a related matter." He paused, sucking on the lozenge to strengthen his voice. "We've had a new sighting of Clive Wilmot."

Philindros's eyes shifted to a television monitor. Rose Mac-Kenzie was just coming through the outer security system. She chatted in her animated way with the guards as they verified her voice and hand prints and opened the baffled doors for her one after the other.

"Wilmot's been to see Laster again. We picked him up in Riyadh. He'd been in the desert, lost to sight. Then, all of a sudden, he walked into Laster's office. He wanted to talk."

"About what?"

Philindros shrugged. "We couldn't manage audio surveillance. Laster took him up in his plane and they talked there, making right turns for an hour over the desert."

"I thought we had a man inside Universal Energy."

"We do. *Your* man. But he doesn't make the chicken sandwiches on Laster's corporate jet."

Laster's plane served chicken sandwiches, breast of *poulet de Bresse* on paper-thin wheat bread, with some sort of special dressing that smelled of rosemary and tasted of pepper. The sandwich had a clandestine fame; few had tasted it, but those who did never forgot the privilege.

"We think there was talk of money. We know a little more than that. Rose will tell you."

Philindros while he talked had watched Rose's progress through the vaults. Now she stood outside the door of the talks room. He worked the combination lock and let her in. She was carrying a delicatessen sandwich in a brown paper bag, and the odor of pastrami enlivened the sterile atmosphere of the room. Philindros drank a glass of water. He looked at Rose and pointed at Horace.

"Wilmot, yes," said Rose. "The computer thinks that Clive has Ibn Awad's lost atomic bombs."

Horace laughed aloud in his admiration of her discipline. He had slept with this woman the night before; she had known then everything she knew now. They had talked all evening about cooking. They had played three games of chess, and Horace had lost badly as he always did; nobody had Rose's mind for anything with a mathematical base. She had told him nothing until Philindros gave his permission.

"I *should* say," Rose went on, "that the computer thinks *O. N. Laster* thinks Clive Wilmot has the bombs. Earlier, Hassan Abdallah thought that. I've been scanning every data bank in the Near East, and putting the pieces together. Clive's sister comes into it. I knew she would." Rose grinned. "Intuition; it exists."

Rosalind Wilmot was in a Volkswagen van when she was killed in Baghdad; it was a routine terrorist attack in most ways: cars blocking the target vehicle front and back, gunmen firing, then fleeing on foot through the choked streets.

"They put two hundred rounds through the front windows," Rose said; "probably all but a very few struck Rosalind. They scooped her up with jelly spoons. But—listen—not one round struck farther back than the front door handle. They didn't want to start a fire in the gas tank. There was something in the back of the van that they wanted."

Tucked away in the police computer in Baghdad, filed under the wrong case, Rose had found a report. Two aluminum suitcases had been taken out of the van by the terrorists; an eyewitness two blocks away saw the gunmen stuffing the suitcases into a waiting car along with their hot weapons, and the car speeding away. The cases seemed to be very heavy: it took two men to boost them into the trunk. They had stood, gasping for breath, for a moment in the dusty street before separating and vanishing like whippets.

"Three days later," Rose said, "the Iraqis found the suitcases in a known hideout of the Eye of Gaza. Somebody had poured lead into them; that's what made them heavy."

"Shielding?"

"An amateur might think so. Our data bank says not—that probably no shielding was used. Why would it be? The bombs were going to be exploded by suicide squads. What was a little radiation poisoning to them?"

"But Awad?"

"Well, Awad . . ."

Rose had other data. Clive Wilmot had been in the Hagrebi desert, he'd gone in over the Iraqi border by Land Rover, a week or more before Ibn Awad had ridden out into the same desert to hide the bombs. Rosalind had been with him. "A jolly old camping trip, brother and sister roasting chestnuts around the fire in the velvet desert night," Rose said. "We have the report from the Iraqi border patrol of their crossing; they got back unnoticed."

"When did Rosalind die, precisely?"

"A week after Talil. Ostensibly she was going to drive overland in her Volks, back to England. The probabilities are that Clive was using Rosalind as a decoy. How could he know that they'd kill her?"

"How could he not know?"

Rose spread her hands. "Well, she *was* very beautiful. That's a kind of armor. Perhaps Clive thought they'd just stop her van out on the road and take the cases. Finding them empty, they'd come to him and demand the real items."

"They would have taken Rosalind as a hostage, as something to swap."

Rose was irritated. All this was obvious. "Yes, yes," she said. "But what Clive wanted was money, and if he wanted money he couldn't have thought he was dealing with the Eye of Gaza."

"Universal Energy?"

"I don't know who else. O. N. Laster, on the day before Rosalind died, had five hundred thousand Swiss francs flown down from Zurich, in hundred-franc notes. You have to remember, Laster was listening in on you and Jack; he certainly realized that if he could get those bombs, then Lockwood had no evidence that he had a good reason to kill Ibn Awad."

There was a silence.

"It's logical," Philindros said; "but how could Wilmot have *known?*"

"The Brits can't afford our sophisticated devices," Rose said. "Clive probably *followed* people; and he used to treat Talil's brother, Kamal, to little boys and things before Kamal became emir. That was the excuse for expelling him from Baghdad—the police burst in on Kamal and Clive while they were buggering some *very* small Iraqis. Who knows what Kamal knew? He couldn't have liked his little brother very much, and old Ibn Awad was always telling him to pray when he wanted to—"

"All right, Rose," Philindros said. Rose grinned; Philindros liked his women prudish.

"Where is Wilmot now?" Horace asked.

Philindros let his hand drop flat on the table, making a soft noise for emphasis. "You go alone if you go, Horace; FIS cannot be involved. Not our people, not our money. Can you manage that?"

"We'll see. Where's Clive?"

"I just happen to have an address," Rose said. She tore a strip of brown paper from the grease-stained bag containing her pastrami sandwich—it was the only paper in the talks room—and scribbled on it. Philindros frowned: evidence. Rose caught her chief's look. "Horace will swallow it before he leaves the room," Rose said.

When Rose had gone, Philindros said, "Graham first. The men's room by the post office in National Airport at six this evening?" He meant the tape would be passed to Horace there, at that time, by someone he would recognize. Horace nodded.

"Remember, I want it back," Philindros said.

11

Even before he talked to Philindros, Horace had made a supper date with Emily. He arrived at nine o'clock at the house on O Street with a bag of groceries in his arms. The Secret Service man who admitted him took the sack into the kitchen.

Emily came into the hall and kissed Horace. "There must be a nip in the air," she said, "your cheek is cold."

"I walked from the grocery; it's a lovely fall night. I miss this season, living abroad. October is what makes an American of you."

Emily's smile came more slowly than before. Otherwise, she seemed no different to Horace. She had learned to conceal whatever signs might remain from the loss of her child. No one was interested: it hadn't been a real death to anyone except Emily and Julian.

In the sitting room, after Emily had made them both martinis, Horace said as much about the miscarriage as he thought she wanted to hear: he took the drink, looked down at her, touched her upper arm gently with the tips of his long fingers. "All right now?"

Emily nodded. She withdrew a little and then came back. They drank. Horace, who didn't really like martinis, complimented her on this one. Emily, glad to have something to tell him, related how her father had trained her to make the drink.

"It wasn't that he singled me out to know his great secret,"

212

she said; "he taught half the bartenders in the world to do it. He gave them eyedroppers to measure out the Pernod."

"Resourceful."

"Men are."

In the kitchen, Emily sat on a tall stool while Horace laid out the food he had brought and began to prepare it. He shelled oysters, cleaned shrimp, prepared a small striped bass, seasoned these things and laid them in a pottery baking dish. His big hands were as deft as Julian's, but Emily had never seen a male so much at home in the kitchen, or anyone able to cook, as Horace seemed to do, without thinking about it.

"It comes from years of doing it," he said.

"I have to read recipes as I go along. Even then I always think I've left something out."

Horace made a sauce for the pasta with mushrooms and bits of ham and cream, and dropped little nests of green and yellow noodles into boiling water.

"*Paglia e fieno*, hay and straw, the Italians call this," he said. "I ate it first when I was a youngster in a restaurant in Stresa. Sunset, the snowy Alps reflected in Lago Maggiore. Bring me here to die, I thought."

"Julian only likes plain things," said Emily a little later, sighing after she had eaten the noodles. "What made you such an epicure?"

"I don't know. My mother and I lived in Paris for years after the divorce. She was a gourmand—frustrated women often are. Julian's mother, and Pa also, only ate plain food. It's odd, Emily— Julian's mother—went to France after *she* left our father. I wonder what drove his lost women to that country."

"Did they see each other ever?"

"God, no. My mother would have killed Emily on sight, and Julian's mother lived in a trance. She never knew mine existed. The strangler and the dreamer, I used to call Pa's two wives."

Emily couldn't eat everything Horace had cooked, and she drank very little wine. She told him she was writing a children's book to pass the time. She didn't want to do any profiles for a while. "I don't want to be close to a stranger just now," Emily said.

"The one on Patrick was so good. You ended up liking him, I thought."

"I always do. My subjects don't always end up liking me. You get so close to them, something like love happens. You can't let it go on."

"With Julian you did."

"That wasn't something like love. That was *love*."

213

"Is it still love? I guessed what Julian had had to tell you the night the baby died. Do you blame my brother for the . . . loss?"

These were brutal words. Emily didn't seem to realize it. She looked back without flinching into Horace's alert mild face.

"Yes, it's still love. I can never change." She flashed a smile that cost her something. "Your brother is safe with me, Horace."

"Good," said Horace, "because I'm going to ask you if you love him enough to betray him."

The Empire dining room, silk and enamel, suited Emily's fine looks perfectly. David would have painted her, had she lived in his time, with her head held just as she was holding it now. She was so still, after hearing Horace's words, that the points of the candle flames never wavered in the mirrors of her irises.

Horace paused and took a sip of wine.

"There's something I'd like you to hear," he said. He drew a very small tape recorder from his pocket and shoved it across the table. "Please listen through the earpiece: it's a silly precaution, but I'm used to taking them."

Emily pushed back her hair and fitted the device into her ear, first removing an earring Horace had seen a hundred times, brushing his mother's raddled cheek. Emily listened intently. Halfway through, she closed her eyes. At the end, she switched off the tape, and with the automatic gesture of one who has worked with such machines a great deal, rewound it.

Horace said, "I don't imagine Julian told you quite all that."

It was Philindros's tape of his entire conversation with Lockwood and Julian, on the night in Kentucky that Ibn Awad's death warrant had been sealed.

"No," Emily said. "The third voice is . . ."

"Philindros. He's my chief, you know."

"I didn't know. I thought as much."

"I'm responsible for what happens in my part of the world, Emily. Perhaps Julian held back a little on that account—after all, I was the one who put the gun in Prince Talil's hand. Julian wouldn't want you to think less of me."

"I don't, if that's any comfort to you."

"It is, my dear. It's more important that you don't think less of Julian. He has a quality that some would call admirable—he's like our father, a selfless man. He's selfless enough to let you think —to let the world think, if need be—that he was to blame for this murder. . . ."

Emily flinched at the word. Horace kept on in his even tenor.

". . . That he was more to blame than Lockwood."

214

Emily touched the tape recorder. "But he wasn't."

"Of course he wasn't. He was present, that's all. It's his job to be present, to advise. He has an idea, as I think we both know, that it's also part of his job to sacrifice himself for the President."

"Of course he thinks that."

"Well, he won't do it if I can help it. Emily, it's not necessary."

Horace told her how she could help.

12

The Millennium Club was as secure an environment, especially if two men were discussing money, as Philindros's talks room.

Sebastian put down his pink gin and cackled. "You mean to say these . . . *suitcases* were never found? That that great hillbilly Lockwood can't prove their existence? Why hasn't Mallory *used* that?"

"He doesn't know exactly where the bombs are, either. If he can get hold of them, if his agent—"

"O. N. Laster?"

"Presumably. Who but Universal Energy would invest that kind of money just to throw something away? In any case, if they can get hold of the suitcases, as you call them, and destroy all traces of them, then the question can be asked: 'Just where *are* these famous items that were going to erase Jerusalem and/or New York?' "

Sebastian was enjoying himself. "What a web of foibles your work is, Horace. It always was. *Nothing* went right in Picardy; I thought it was the French. Politically speaking, the Maquis were like a troop of Cossacks in a dark room with one naked woman; but disorder must be a feature of secret work."

"It is. That's our deepest secret."

"But you know where this Britisher is, and you want to get to him before Laster?"

"Or Laster's men. They'll kill him afterwards. He knows that."

"He thinks you won't?"

"I've helped him in the past. Once you buy a man, Sebastian, he's like a respectable woman you've had in one of her weak moments; she may or may not have enjoyed it, but she doesn't forget —especially if you behaved well afterwards."

"This is a lot of randy imagery between godfather and godson. I promised at your christening to look after your spiritual welfare."

215

Horace waved away the old waiter who shuffled towards them; their drinks were all but untouched, though they had been talking for a long time.

"What I need," Horace said, "is your authorization to draw funds—clean bank funds, not FIS funds—before I leave New York this afternoon."

"Surely."

"I'm speaking of a million dollars."

Sebastian drained his pink gin and called the waiter over. "Two more, and have them keep a table for us in the dining room," he said.

They were seated by a window. Sebastian looked out. The street below was filled with trash, blowing before an edgy October wind.

"That's a lot of money to re-elect Lockwood and thereby guarantee that there'll be no resumption of garbage collection in my lifetime," he said. "But, by golly, it's worth it. Let Philindros tell me now you can't be president of D. & D. Laux & Co. after I go!"

At three o'clock, back at the bank, Sebastian, groaning a little, got down on all fours in his office and opened a floor safe concealed beneath a rug; Horace had never known it was there. Sebastian placed bundles of thousand-dollar bills one by one on the desk. Then, fussily, he wrapped the lot in a square package, using strong brown paper and stout cord. Horace put his finger on the knots as Sebastian tied them.

"Homely-looking stuff, done up that way, isn't it?" Sebastian said.

"I don't know when you'll get it back."

Sebastian waved a hand; under the transparent skin his blue veins twined. "Paper," he snorted. "It's the human mind that makes it holy. God bless the hopeless human mind—that's what *they* all thought."

His gnarled hand indicated the portraits on the wall.

13

"The great thing," Horace had said to Emily, "is to make Patrick realize that there was nothing in what Julian did that was meant to humiliate him. It will be very, very difficult for him to accept this."

"What makes you think I can do it? I'm hardly a neutral source."

"On the level of the intellect, you can't. Probably no one can. But we're not dealing with Patrick on the level of intellect. You're Julian's wife. You know a lot about Graham, and what you know is fresh in your mind. He respects you as a professional."

"I've never *used* another person. Patrick is very clever, far cleverer and older and crueler than I. I still don't see why you believe I can do anything with him."

"There's a bit of history you ought to know," said Horace.

He told her about Caroline and Patrick and Julian. Horace knew more about this than Julian. Rose MacKenzie had had computers talking to one another; and Patrick's girls had talked more than he thought.

"The hardest part of this job," Horace said, "is that you're going to have to keep it from Julian. Always. As if you were under oath, as he is, to keep secrets even from the person you love most as a duty to"—Horace smiled; devilish, loving—"something higher."

When Patrick came home, late that night, he found Emily waiting for him in the drawing room. ffoulkes, Charlotte's willowy Old Etonian, left in the house while his mistress was on Chipmunk Island, had let her in. The servant asked Patrick if he wanted anything; Patrick told him to go upstairs. Emily had been there for some time; her finger marked a place a third of the way through a book she had taken down from the shelves.

Patrick sat down opposite her, showing no surprise. He knew what was happening.

Emily wasted no time on preliminary talk; she would no more do that than touch him. She told Patrick, in a flat voice, what Horace had told her the night before.

A portion of Patrick's mind awakened, recorded this information. He was hearing things he would never have known if he had not at last found himself in a position to wound Julian Hubbard. He didn't doubt for a moment that what Emily was telling him was the truth. It was late for anything else.

Nevertheless, she made him listen to the tape. He didn't resist when she took it back, as Horace had instructed her to do.

They sat for some moments in silence. All that was lifelike in Emily's young face, all the play of expression that had teased and roused Patrick in San Francisco, had vanished. This face in its changes reminded him of others from his youth. There had been a childlike prostitute in Bangkok who had been all laughter and invitation in a bar but as still and limp as a corpse beneath him an hour later; as he used her he had remembered the unmarked body of a girl lying beside a track into a Vietnamese village after

217

a bombing raid and how, when she was turned over, all the blood from her body lay in a pool on the baked soil. Lifeless women: a whore, a dead peasant—and, always in his memory, Caroline wearing a doll's porcelain face throughout his unbearable pleasure; Caroline must have seen something in his own face (watching with wild eyes) as she did for herself what he could not do for her.

"What do you want from me?" he asked Emily.

Horace had advised: When the moment is right, come right out with it; make sure he understands.

"I want you to know the truth."

"Why?"

"Because I believe you would never broadcast a lie."

"But you think I might conceal the truth?"

Emily moved.

"That's your choice," she said. "But if you bring Julian down, and the FIS, you'll bring Frosty Lockwood down, too, and all the rest of it as well."

Emily was a natural mimic. Her face, which had been so stony, suddenly formed into an unmistakable representation of Franklin Mallory, as he had looked on the platform in San Francisco, taking the cheers and the chanting of the delegates for his Ganymede Address. Her eyes were contemptuous.

Patrick looked at her—the firm unmarked flesh, the white strong teeth, the straight bones, the speed she showed even when at rest. Emily had been made by men like Julian and her own father who bred themselves, generation after generation, to beautiful women as they bred proven stallions to fast mares, in order to produce a type. Emily knew what Patrick might demand of her as his price for believing her. She wasn't afraid. She could refuse or agree as she chose, and nothing would show on her face or be left on her mind. Lend a man your boat and he might sink it, said the Eskimos; lend him your wife and she comes back as good as new.

But suppose the man is never the same again? Julian's wife was begging Patrick for something. Suppose he forced her to kneel and give him the use of her mouth, like some pig of a movie producer in a novel by a writer so young and clumsy he could not describe the act? Would she tell Julian that? In the canal of his shrunken phallus Patrick felt the faintest of sensations, like the tiny charge of electricity that carries an impulse from one region of the mind to another. He knew he would feel nothing more than that. Emily naked and dancing could not arouse him. He laughed, a burst of sound. He listened to the tape again, to Lockwood's unmistakable voice.

"Dead at last," cried Patrick in a black man's voice. "Thank God a'mighty, I'm dead at last."

Emily could make nothing of this remark; nobody her age remembered Martin Luther King. The phrase made Horace smile, though, when she repeated it to him.

14

The last thing Clive Wilmot owned in the world was a small house, made of a kind of tan stone that crumbled like a biscuit, in an olive grove in Provence. Properly, this house could be said to be on the Riviera. Clive's father had always made a point of saying that it was in Provence. He said, too, that he "went to a public school called Harrow." The Wilmots, according to their genealogist, were remote cousins of the sovereign, and if all the hundreds who took precedence over Clive's father in the royal line had died in a plague and he had ascended the throne, he would have explained to visitors at Windsor Castle that he was king of a place called Great Britain.

The house was built into a steep hillside within sight of the harbor at Cannes. When Clive was a child, the intense blue sea could be seen from the dooryard, where there was a rough arbor made of saplings with grapes growing over it. As children, Clive and his sister often sat there with their parents in the shade at midday, wearing bathing costumes, eating lunch, looking out over the peaceful valley. It was, in those days, all farms and vineyards and other small earth-colored houses like their own.

Now the sea could only be seen on days when there was a high wind to blow away the pollution, and then one realized that the spoiled Mediterranean had changed color, like a blinded eye. The gravel tracks of Clive's childhood were broad black highways. The farms were gone. Ghastly new villas stood, like rows of nudging yellow skulls, where once grapes and jasmine, olives and blackberries had grown.

Just beneath Clive's old house one of these new villas had been built. It had a swimming pool, and beside the pool, sunbathing, lay a girl of sixteen in a string bottom, a mere leaf of cloth covering her pubis; lovely conical breasts bare in the sun. How nice French bodies were when they were young. Pity there were only seven faces to go around for the whole nation. This girl's was the doe-eyed heart-shaped one. For a month Clive watched her sunbathe and swim. She liked his watching, she was proud of her

219

young breasts; like those of the Maja in Goya's painting, they stayed where they were even when she lay on her side. You have about two more years of *that*, my girl, thought Clive.

In other days he would have found a way to have her, or at least make the attempt. Now he wanted no risk, no other human in his life. He bought the few things he needed in the town above his house; it was a *village perché*, its streets so steep and its place among the rocks so narrow that it, of all the things within eyeshot, had not changed in years. He ate alone, went about in old jeans and a torn shirt, and let his beard grow; he drank but little wine, and no spirits.

Clive was hiding. It was a matter of form. Any professional who really wanted to find him could do so, but no one at the moment had the desire. Everyone was aware that he had this house; it was the logical place for him to come if he had no money, and the people who might look for him (all except one) believed that he was broke. The house itself was worth a lot as Clive looked at money, but he had always refused to sell. ("Hold on to the place in Provence," his father had told him in their last conversation. "It's your only chance of going south again someday; perhaps Rosalind will have children and they'll want the sun." The old man didn't know his daughter was dead; he wasn't surprised that she never came to see him in the country house, converted to a depot for the dying, where he had been sent. Why should she? Clive had come through a winter rain to visit the old man; the hospital was as cold and as damp as a school dormitory and as full of nasty smells; his father wore a patched tweed suit under a dressing gown, but no socks; there were round spots of black dirt behind his ankle bones. Old Wilmot was as white as a mime. "I used to come to this house for weekends before the war, when it was owned by a brother officer in the Blues," he said. "Slept with Boy Ransome-Sackett's wife here—hauled her out from between the sheets and had her on the floor while Boy slumbered in the bed above us. Boy was drunk, I could smell the whisky fuming out of him each time he snored. The situation excited the woman; she thrashed about as if she'd been beheaded. I don't know why Boy didn't wake up, he must have paralyzed his brain with all that drink. Eleanor was her name. She had an amazing cunt. You labored to get in—it was like a tight rubber band with a bit of spit on it for the first two inches, but that was all there was to it. After all that shoving, you'd emerge, if that's the word, into a cavern, so that four inches of you was sort of waving about in the dark, touching absolutely nothing, while Eleanor had the base of your member locked in this awful grip. The Tourniquet, she was called. We all recommended each other to try it once, and Eleanor was quite happy to oblige." Old Wilmot went to sleep for a moment, then roused to speak of Provence again. He liked it for its dryness, even the rocks there seemed to be made of compacted dust. Clive, with his love of the desert, had inherited his father's hatred of wet climates.)

Horace Hubbard, at the end of his search for him, had found Clive in the desert, in one of the caves of the Hagrebi mountains. Clive had heard a helicopter, and then saw it—an unmarked craft, fluttering along the face of the escarpment. Unfortunately he had put out his sleeping bag, a bright orange one, to dry in the sun; Clive had fever, sweats in the night. The craft landed as near to the cave as it could, but far down the mountain, and a single figure emerged. Clive watched through binoculars as the man labored up the steep slope of polished volcanic rock, and when he was close enough, recognized him. The helicopter flew away.

At the mouth of the cave, Horace stopped, blowing a bit but smiling his cheerful smile. He carried a light pack and he took this off and sat down on it.

"I have a thermos of cold water," Horace said. "Would you care for some?"

Horace had a folding cup of the kind British war correspondents used to buy on the expense account before going out to cover skirmishes in hot climates. The two men drank; the water was icy; you could feel the chill through the thin metal. Clive didn't ask Horace how he had managed to find him, or what he wanted; the first didn't matter, the second he knew.

"I suppose the suitcases are not too close to where we are?" Horace said.

"Not particularly."

"Well, of course I'll have to have someone who knows about these things look at them before I give you any money. I have a technician in the helicopter. If you have map coordinates, we can simply radio them and they'll go and pick up the things. They won't know who the seller is."

Clive believed that. Horace had no reason to want him dead; he was too valuable a witness.

"What sort of payment are we discussing?"

"I thought a million U.S. would be reasonable."

"Plus a passport, plus a receipt."

"The passport, of course. It's Canadian, I thought you'd be comfortable with that. But a receipt? I'm afraid not, Clive."

Clive pointed to the pack under Horace's haunches. He was

221

asking if the money was inside. Horace nodded. "It's in thousands, but the serial numbers are not in any computer system. You'll have no trouble with them."

Clive really had no choice. He could agree to sell Horace the bombs, or refuse and find out what Horace's contingency plan was. The Americans were sparing in their murders, it was true, but Horace knew all sorts of people, everywhere, who were less scrupulous.

"Done," Clive said. He gave Horace map coordinates, and Horace, after transposing the numbers in his head into a letter code, transmitted them to the helicopter, which was circling beyond the horizon. While they waited, Clive and Horace spoke of films. "Ralph Richardson lost his topee off a rock rather like this one in the Sudan and went blind from the pitiless sun before he could get to the bottom, d'you recall?" Clive said. "*Four Feathers*, of course. 'Guns, guns, guns, the Thin Red Line.' What was the girl's name? Esmé?" They couldn't remember.

The helicopter radioed back. The crew had found the bombs. Horace gave Clive the million dollars, still done up in Sebastian's brown parcel. Clive untied the square knots and looked at the money, then wrapped it again.

"I hope you have some sort of shielding for those cases," Clive said. "The half-life, or whatever it is, of plutonium is supposed to be three hundred thousand years or something. You may have odd-looking children if you sit on the things all the way back to where you're going."

"I think that's all been taken care of. Clive, I don't want to thrust advice on you. However, if I were you, I'd be careful about seeing Laster again. This transaction is going to make him impatient with you."

Clive, weighing the parcel of money on an outstretched hand, grinned.

Clive got out of the desert that night; if Horace could find him, so could others. He crossed into Egypt after a lot of night driving. Using his Canadian passport—Horace had renamed him Percival Cheyne—he flew to Stockholm, and then to Berlin, and then went to Frankfurt in a bus, before taking a train for Cannes. No one had been behind him; no one, after he passed by the unshaven lout who glanced at his passport as he left the Cairo airport, had even looked at his identity papers. He'd left his million dollars in a safe place; no one knew the Hagrebi desert as he did, now that the tribesmen had all gone roistering into the city, and there wasn't so much as a mouse in that parched place to chew at the corners of the green thousand-dollar bills; the money would keep forever in its dry cave, in its tin box.

Now, at his place in Provence, Clive waited. Every Tuesday he took a bus into Grasse and asked at poste restante for his letter. It hadn't come yet. It would; there were reasons for O. N. Laster to make payment as he had promised. After the payment, a lot of people would want to find him—Laster, the Arabs Laster used, the Arabs the Americans used, the Arabs his own peevish service used. At least they were all the same Arabs.

Clive came out of his house on a Tuesday morning with a bowl of coffee in his hand; his thumb was in it, he didn't mind. He took a mouthful to soften the stale bread in his mouth. The girl lay on the diving board. She must be an exhibitionist; even here the sun wasn't warm enough on October mornings to lie about naked. Clive had always had keen eyesight. She didn't seem to be shivering, but the nipples were erect. Excitement or cold?

He went to the back of his house and fetched a canvas bag containing his suit and a shirt and tie. This was his day to check poste restante. If the money came, he'd need the suit to go into the bank, if Laster decided to use a bank. Naturally, he hadn't been willing to let Clive control the way in which the money was delivered; Clive was in no position to insist. In the canvas bag, along with his suit, were a loaded pistol and, besides the Canadian passport Horace had given him, a dead man's Irish passport that he'd kept up to date for years.

They had his letter at the post office. It was handwritten. Clive admired that—one would have thought a man like O. N. Laster, an amateur and a tycoon, would have used a typewriter. But no, he had got some female, Dutch perhaps from the spiny shape of her letters, to write it all out as a love note. The paper was perfumed.

Clive took the letter outside and read it. *My beloved, Please wait for me on the terrace of the Negresco at four this Tuesday. A bottle of chilled Mumm's will warm my heart, already on fire for you. . . .*

O. N. Laster must have dictated the letter after all, it sounded so little like anyone who knew how to talk to a lover. That's what comes of being able to buy all the sex you want, thought Clive; you forget it's involved with speech. It was after eleven in the morning. It would take him three hours to get to Nice by local bus over the old steep mountain roads. He put the fake love letter in his pocket and started out.

Clive stopped in at a café in the old marketplace in Grasse and changed into his other clothes. He had a cup of coffee to pay for the use of the toilet as a changing booth. While he was there he washed up a bit, splashing cold water on his face from the trickling tap, combing his hair and beard. He had lost weight. The thin face within the wild beard looked quite different to Clive from his usual one as he examined it in the foggy glass of the mirror. There was no mirror in his house. His father had broken them all years and years before, during a quarrel when he and Clive's mother were still young. The two of them had been to Nice that night and they were drunk—they often were. Clive never knew why the mirrors needed smashing. No one had ever replaced them. He'd had a pretty mother, a pretty sister; the whole family had always been good-looking: slim rosy women with high tempers, gaunt careless men with Norman noses.

At four o'clock exactly Clive stepped onto the terrace of the Negresco. The oil shortage had done nothing to make Nice quieter; swarms of motorbikes roared on the Promenade des Anglais. Clive ordered a half bottle of Mumm's champagne. The waiter didn't like the look of Clive among the silken people already sitting at the white iron tables.

"Don't open it quite yet," said Clive, when the wine came. "I'm waiting for a friend."

The harbor looked clean and the pebble beach was as un-littered, as washed in appearance, as it had ever been. The wind was offshore, blowing away from the pink and white city the smell of a sea in which nothing but algae and a few blinded fishes could live. Clive observed it all: the palms, the potted hibiscus vivid in the wrong season, the old men sitting with merciless young boys and girls.

A very clean young man sat down at Clive's table. He wore a double-breasted white suit with a magenta shirt and necktie. When he took off his hat, a white fedora, not a single hair on his blond head was crushed or displaced. He smiled, and from the perfect teeth going all the way back to his throat Clive saw that he was an American.

"Ah, Mumm's," said the American. "The sight of it chilling warms my heart."

"From the look of you I'd have thought your heart was already on fire," replied Clive.

The waiter opened the wine and poured it.

The American smiled again and put a flimsy French banknote on the table, tucking it under the ice bucket so that it wouldn't blow away in the fresh wind. Whitecaps were beginning to show offshore. Still the American's hair remained in place; Clive's beard fluttered like a helmsman's.

"In real life I can't abide this stuff," said the American, sipping his champagne.

"Bad luck," said Clive. "What shall I call you, in real life?"

"Hugo."

Hugo had placed a pigskin satchel, as new as his clothes, beneath the table beside Clive's old blue drawstring bag. Clive touched it with his toe.

"Is that *it?*" he asked.

"Yes. The agreed sum. I'll ask you for a receipt."

"You intend to pass it to me here, while wearing that fluorescent costume?"

Hugo examined Clive's own clothes, like an actor who has come into a low bar hoping to observe mannerisms for a character he is going to play, and flashed his teeth again.

"No," he said. "I have a car just around the corner. I thought we could go for a drive whenever you've had enough of this delicious wine."

"Not a very long drive. Me at the wheel."

"Fine. Just up to the Moyenne Corniche?"

"No."

"Then you choose the place."

Hugo turned in his chair, knees together, picked up his hat and his satchel, and walked away. His shoes and his silk socks were white like his suit. Clive followed him across the street and down the sidewalk. Beside a tan Mercedes, Hugo halted and handed Clive the keys. He waited patiently by the door on the passenger side until Clive opened it from inside.

Clive drove along the curving road beside the harbor and turned left through an archway into the market. He ran the Mercedes, horn honking, past the stalls through the narrow streets of the old town. He made a long circuit of the city, one eye on the mirror, the other on Hugo. The American lounged, expressionless, on the tan leather seat. From time to time he smiled at Clive; apparently he had hoped for behavior like this.

"Marvelous," Hugo said, "you're my first spy, you know."

At last Clive pulled the car into a parking place near the old port. All the fishing boats were gone, never to return, and here the viscous sea lapped against the soiled stones of the breakwater like oil in the hold of a tanker.

Hugo opened the catches of the pigskin satchel and handed it to Clive. Inside were neat bundles of pale blue hundred-franc notes, done up in the Swiss style, nine notes lengthwise and the tenth folded in half at right angles to the stack. There were five hundred stacks.

"That's only five hundred thousand," said Clive.

"Well, I'm afraid that's all there'll be today. Mr. Laster prefers that you be paid the second installment after he has collected the merchandise you promised. *This* money is for your, uh, press agent work."

"The merchandise is a long way away."

"That's all right. You tell me where, we'll collect it, and you'll collect the second five hundred thousand. There must be *some* trust between us. I mean, here I am, right on time."

Hugo handed Clive a sheet of creamy thick writing paper, with deckled edges, and a fountain pen.

Hugo said, "Please write: 'Received the sum of five hundred thousand Swiss francs (digits *and* letters, please), and one Mercedes automobile. These good and valuable considerations release the holder of this note, unconditionally and forever, from all obligation, debt, or lien whatsoever in regard to myself, my heirs and assigns.' And sign it, printing your name in capital letters below your signature. Date it, too, please."

Clive wrote as Hugo dictated, in a flowing hand. He had nearly forgotten the pleasure of writing on good rag paper with a fine gold point.

"All that remains," Hugo said, "is for you to give me the information about the merchandise."

"You can write that down yourself."

Clive handed back the pen. He dictated the same map coordinates he had given Horace. Now, of course, the cave was empty, but no doubt Laster's men would be able to read the radiation levels with instruments; they might even think someone had stumbled on the cases and carried them off. It wasn't much of a possibility, but Clive had known intelligent men to believe in more foolish theories. Hugo wrote slowly, in tiny letters, in a limp pocket diary with thin blue pages. He was left-handed, an imperfection—a surprise.

Hugo put his hand on the door. "Have a nice trip. If you'd like to meet me here again . . ."

"No. Two weeks from today, same hour, on the Ile Rousseau in Geneva. You can feed the swans if I'm delayed."

"Very well. Happy motoring."

"You're actually giving me this car?"

"A token of good will. It's registered in the name you used

for mail. I hope that's all right; we deduced you must have some sort of identity document with that name on it."

"It must be gratifying, giving away Mercedes as an afterthought."

Hugo put on his white hat and adjusted the brim; he opened the door.

"Well, it's Mr. Laster who does these things," he said. "It's a way of making the impersonal a little more meaningful. The tank is full. Good-bye."

"Good-bye, Hugo," said Clive, but the American was already walking back towards the center of the city in his white suit.

The shops were letting out and there were a lot of people in the street. Clive watched Hugo closely until he vanished into the crowd. The American made no signals. In those clothes, he didn't need to.

15

Clive left Nice by the least likely road, the deserted old secondary highway that led northeast through the Maritime Alps to the Italian frontier. He drove conservatively, climbing all the time, with the soundless diesel engine lifting the Mercedes higher and higher over the switchbacks, so that the sunset was enjoyably prolonged. There was no pursuit. When at last Clive stopped, with all houses behind him, on a lay-by near the Berghe Gorge, he could see that night had fallen below him in the valley, although it was still dusk where he stood and the rim of the sun was visible to him beyond the hills to the west. Higher up, there was snow; Clive could smell it.

He needed light for what he had to do, and privacy. Obviously there had been no ignition bomb in the car, or Hugo would not have got into it; Clive's violent turns on the crooked streets of old Nice would have jarred loose any sort of percussion bomb balanced on the frame of the car. Hugo had shown not the slightest sign of nervousness during the ride. That left only the possibility of a time bomb. Despite Horace's warning, Clive didn't think it likely that O. N. Laster would stoop to such methods, but now that he had half a million francs, he meant to live cautiously until he spent them.

From his duffel bag he took a flashlight, the cheap square French kind, and as an afterthought, the pistol. He tucked the gun, a flat Walther automatic, into the misshapen pocket of his jacket;

it was always possible that a car might be following along half an hour behind. He wanted to be able to defend his francs. Unaccountably, he remembered what he had said to that glorious girl who had been with Patrick Graham in San Francisco about the color of her eyes. The memory of his remark made him smile; Clive loved wordplay.

Methodically he searched the car for a time bomb, looking first in the most likely places: under the front seats and the back, on the frame beneath the driver's seat, and then along the whole underside, especially near the tank, though diesel fuel didn't go up as gasoline used to do; then in the engine compartment. His light was not strong, but it was good enough. He found nothing. There was only the trunk, the least likely place because farthest from the intended victim, remaining. Before he opened it he had to empty his bladder; he had had to do so for some time.

Clive went modestly behind the car, though no other vehicle had passed and there was no sign of life, not even a bird, in all the scrubby landscape that encircled him. The guardrail was low. Clive unbuttoned and put his knees against it. In the last light of the day (though a beam of sun still shone on a snowy peak above him), he watched his yellow stream arch over the edge of the precipice. He thought, It falls to earth I know not where.

Behind Clive, the lid of the Mercedes's trunk opened inch by inch. Hassan Abdallah, with a cord stretched between his two brown hands, emerged. Clive caught the movement, felt it. He put his hand in the pocket where the gun was, but it had got turned around and he grasped the barrel instead of the butt. He couldn't pull it out. For some reason he couldn't drop the flashlight that he held in his other hand. His fly was still undone and his penis was exposed.

Hassan, moving swiftly, reached up and looped the strangling cord around Clive's throat. Clive was so much larger than Hassan that the terrorist had to put both knees in the small of the other man's back in order to get leverage. Clive struggled, smashing backwards with his left elbow. The flashlight spun from his hand and lay at their feet with its weak beam shining upwards.

The cord sawed painfully against Hassan's toughened palms. Clive, too late, tried to get the fingers of his left hand between the cord and his throat. He tugged at the gun, turning it in his lint-filled pocket, and finally got hold of the butt. He put his finger on the trigger. His sight was beginning to go. He released the safety catch. He didn't know if there was a round in the chamber. He pulled the trigger and the pistol went off, smashing the hinge of Clive's artificial leg. He went down.

Clive knew that the man on his back was Hassan. He didn't understand how this Arab could be killing him. Hassan weighed no more than a skeleton, but he wouldn't be dislodged. The strangler was panting and cursing in Arabic. Clive, on three limbs, bucked and smashed backwards into the side of the car, trying to break Hassan's bones. The cord cut deeper into Clive's throat. He knew he had lost, but it was taking such a long time. His penis dangled, naked. He thought, "The Tourniquet, she was called."

Clive thought, Why didn't he use a wire, the twit? A shepherd brought his sheep through the dooryard in Provence, taking them from one pasture to another, and Clive, a very small boy, watched as they flowed over the slope like an avalanche of dirty snow.

Clive thought, I didn't know there *were* any Americans called Hugo.

It took Hassan a long time to regain his strength. When Clive collapsed at last, he kept up the tension on the strangling cord for several minutes more. Then, sobbing for breath and trembling from head to foot, he took the pistol from Clive's pocket and put two bullets through the Englishman's skull. He got inside the Mercedes and lay on the fragrant leather of the rear seat until he was able to breathe normally again and the strength returned to his twitching arms.

He searched Clive's body, but there was nothing in the pockets that could identify him. Hassan lifted Clive, one limb at a time, onto the low guardrail, and pushed him over into the gorge. He heard the body hit, roll in a shower of gravel, hit again, dislodge more shale, and finally stop. Hassan hoped the corpse was not visible from the road. It didn't matter, really—who was likely to look over the edge or, having looked, to believe that the queer bundle far below was a dead man? Even seeing and knowing, most people would simply drive on. Hassan had these thoughts in English, as though they were transmitted by Clive's ghost.

In the car, Hassan found the pigskin satchel and carried it around to examine it in the headlights. He squatted—this was his natural position, he wasn't hiding or feasting on his catch like a bird of prey—and counted the francs. It was a long time since the Eye of Gaza had had this much money. He had a plan for it.

Hassan didn't know precisely where he was. He decided it would be best to go down, since he knew that the car had been climbing for an hour before it stopped. He turned the Mercedes around and went, very cautiously, down the dark vertiginous road.

He turned on the radio, then turned it off. Western music was monotonous in his ear; harsh.

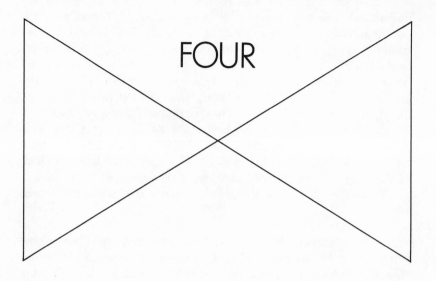

FOUR

1

THE WEATHER was fine all over America in the last week of October, balmy in daylight and crisp at night, aspens golden on the slopes of the Rockies and swamp maples scarlet on the Appalachians. It was a real Indian summer, the first the country had had in several years.

President Lockwood, riding through the towns in an open car, would see, behind the crowds in the streets, men raking leaves in their front yards. In Lisbon, Ohio, on a wide street lined with brick houses, a dazzling girl smiled brilliantly at the President as he passed; she was nursing a baby and drinking beer from a bottle. Lockwood asked Julian if he had seen her. "The American madonna!" he cried.

The girl and her pretty town, so civilized and shady and quiet, remained in Lockwood's mind for a long time. Julian told him there were few votes for him there; Lisbon was Mallory country, conservative, a place proud of its thrift and its dead soldiers. As in most small towns, Lockwood heard no cheers. His strength was in the cities.

Lockwood, as he spoke, was lit by the soft sunlight of autumn and framed by the leaves in their dying colors. Julian roamed the crowds during the speeches, and he sensed a return of good humor and affectionate feeling. It was Lockwood weather. The people were forgetting Awad.

Through thousands of miles of travel and hundreds of speeches and tens of thousands of hands pressed in his own so that he needed salves and injections to control the pain in his horny fingers, Lockwood had almost drawn even with Franklin Mallory. The polls showed that the momentum of opinion was running in the President's favor. On the plane between stops he collapsed, exhausted; but when his feet touched the soil and his voice moved the crowd, he was rejuvenated. Taxiing to the apron of some airport in Illinois or Florida, he would be pale and trembling while Julian told him where he was, described the local issues, and repeated the names of the local politicians. But once outside, the color would rush back to Lockwood's skin, his shoulders would straighten and his stride lengthen; his huge voice needed no microphone.

That is how he appeared, hearty and American, each night on the news. Sometimes, flying back to Washington on a weekend, he would invite one important reporter or another to sit with him. The two men would sip bourbon in their shirtsleeves, and Lockwood would give the journalist a story for the Sunday papers.

"Where on earth is Patrick Graham?" Lockwood asked Julian. "Haven't seen him for weeks."

"Patrick will turn up, he always does," Julian replied.

But he, too, wondered where Patrick was. In bed one Sunday morning he asked Emily if she had seen him.

"Once, for a few moments," she said. "He seemed worn out. Like you."

Julian didn't pursue the issue. The children were back from their cruise. Julian had his Sundays with them again. Now Emily came on their outings, too. Elliott and Jenny spoke little of their trip to Antarctica now that it was over. Elliott showed Julian and Emily hundreds of slides of the things he had photographed; he'd made a tape-recorded commentary on the pictures. Jenny was finishing her book of birds, putting color in her sketches and a musical staff for each specimen's song below the bird, as if it were perching on its own music. This was to be Julian's Christmas present. She showed it to Emily, and Emily kept that secret from Julian as faithfully as she kept the larger one she shared with Horace.

Julian had extra security put on the children. The campaign made him nervous. A man had been arrested in a crowd in Phoenix with a loaded revolver in his possession; a shot had been fired in Indiana. A string of firecrackers had been let off in Cleveland and a Secret Service man had pursued the prankish boy responsible, wrestled him to the ground, and before his colleagues could intervene, smashed the bones in his nose and cheeks. The suspect, hardly older than young Elliott, had been taken away with his face a mask of blood, sobbing in a piercing voice, while the Secret Service man stood by, chest heaving in panic.

Life could end in an instant.

Emily still refused to be protected. She went about the city alone, riding the Metro and the buses, shopping, lunching with friends. Always, at the President's personal orders, two Secret Service operatives shadowed her. Julian wondered if she knew.

Emily read him her children's book. It was a story about Elliott and Jenny and their father and the veery in the garden and its eggs; while Julian was traveling with Lockwood, the eggs had hatched, and now the family of veeries had flown away. Emily made a sweet story of it.

Julian made love to Emily the night she read him the story. It was their first time since the loss of the baby, and Emily trembled and wept. In the early days of their love affair and marriage, she had often shed tears after the act; Julian remembered the taste and shine of them on her opened face. This was a different sort of weeping. He held her afterwards very close to him in the dark. The memory of the baby's death welled up in him, and glimpses of Jenny when she was very small, and a certain gesture of Emily's.

Julian himself began to cry. Tears came without warning and he was helpless to stop them. He thought Emily was asleep, but then he felt her hand on his face. She said nothing to him. They didn't stir, either of them, apart from the small movement of Emily's hand, brushing the tears away from his cheek. Julian knew Emily had begun to cry again as well. This was the last thing he remembered; he wondered for days afterwards if they had gone to sleep while weeping.

Julian was tired; in his job he could never show any loss of control, any flash of temper, any sign of fear. After the firecrackers had gone off in Cleveland, Polly Lockwood had put her arms around a young secretary who collapsed, sobbing, in the airplane. Polly's own face was expressionless and so was Julian's as he brushed past the two women, carrying some paper that Lockwood needed into the presidential cabin.

The children, on shipboard in the Antarctic when the story broke, had heard nothing about Awad, or so Leo reported. "Why tell them?" said Leo. "I thought, better not." By the time Elliott and Jenny returned to Washington, people had stopped talking about it.

"Do you think the children know?" Julian asked Emily.

"I don't know. It's as if Awad never existed. He's gone back to being a suicide in people's minds. One of the fools."

But not, Julian saw, in Emily's mind. She turned her back to him when she spoke these words. There was a new quality of withdrawal in Emily, there were things she didn't mention. Julian saw something of his mother in her sometimes: the day he'd almost drowned in the Seine and the older Emily had gone away and changed from her bikini into clothes that concealed her body. Neither woman knew the whole of what had happened to him; nor understood why the signs they saw in him meant something different from what they thought.

2

Patrick Graham saw no sign of worry in Franklin Mallory. The two men, one on either side of Susan Grant, were walking leisurely from picture to picture in a long gallery that took up one whole side of Mallory's house in New York. Cameras followed them. There were Picassos here and Braques and the works of American experimenters who had gone out of style.

"It was my wife who got me started collecting," Mallory said. "When we were still in college she saved money from the budget and bought reproductions at Brentano's—once a month, so we'd have a new picture. Finally we could afford the originals. On weekends I like to look in art catalogs and send away for things. Marilyn's taste still guides me—ah, I think, how she'd like this Juan Gris! Strange."

Patrick thought so. He stole a look at Susan Grant, but her face was serene. It was evening and Patrick was invited to dinner. Susan was transformed from her daytime self, Mallory's brain and sinew, into Mallory's handfast wife—hair loose, glasses gone, a long dress, her nervous corded hands softened by jewels and bracelets. In heels Susan was a trifle taller than Mallory. As they walked along the gallery she held his hand. Neither Mallory nor Susan had ever made any pretense about their relationship; she had been his hostess even in the White House.

Mallory paused before a Van Gogh landscape; it looked as if it had been painted by a man miraculously cured of color blindness and able for the first time in his life to perceive that wheat was golden and trees green.

"You know, this sort of art is over," Mallory said. "Beautiful as it always will be, it isn't enough."

"Isn't enough? What *is* enough?"

233

"*Humanity* orbiting Jupiter. That was the greatest work of art in the history of man."

"That was technology."

"So is this Van Gogh. It was done with tools—brushes, a palette knife. If ten thousand men create a form as beautiful as that ship, and send it hundreds of millions of miles into space with the human intelligence aboard, why is it less a work of art than anything Vincent ever did and sent into the future to us? Surely *Humanity* is as lovely as any cathedral ever made, and it has the power of infinite flight besides. It could sail forever if we chose to let it do so. That isn't art?"

Patrick could think of no reply. Mallory's idea was too strange to him. A machine beautiful? How could engineers and scientists—and slouching men like his brothers who put the rivets into the ship's metal—be called artists? How could thousands of uncaring hands make one work of art? It was an absurdity.

Mallory was watching him, his silver eyebrows raised just slightly. The expression on Susan Grant's face matched Mallory's almost exactly. Everyone around Mallory sooner or later came to resemble him; his people took on his gestures, his tones of voice, his healthy pinkness. *Mallory's clones.* The phrase pleased Patrick and he smiled. He would never be able to use it on the air; it required too much explanation.

Susan seemed to receive some signal. Patrick knew that this house was webbed with invisible electronic devices. Inwardly, he giggled—perhaps the eye in a painting had winked. Patrick had broken his strictest rule; he had had two drinks before coming here and two since arriving. He was beginning to see humor in everything. Drink made him admire recklessness.

"Dinner seems to be ready," Susan said.

She and Mallory turned, still hand in hand, and walked with Patrick along the rows of fabulous oils. The pictures were worth millions but there was no visible security system. It was all computerized; Mallory loved computers. Patrick knew that an alarm was hidden somewhere. Perhaps the heat of a burglar's body would activate a lightning bolt, striking him dead. Patrick laughed aloud. He knew the microphones were dead now. Neither Mallory nor Susan asked him to explain his outburst.

Throughout dinner, Mallory spoke of everything but politics. Susan asked after Charlotte; as a girl, she had spent summers off the coast of Maine on Chipmunk Island; like Charlotte, she was an expert sailor.

Mallory was a trencherman; when the platters were brought around again by the Filipino servants he took more of everything.

Susan said no. Patrick's plate, of course, still held most of what he had taken as a first serving.

"You eat a great deal," Patrick said to Mallory.

Mallory's mouth was full.

"Only once a day," said Susan. "Coffee in the morning, an apple at noon, and then this Henry the Eighth dinner."

"No eggs in the morning?"

"Really, Patrick," said Susan, "there *are* no new egg jokes. Franklin has heard them all."

Patrick was not here because he wanted to be. Whatever the world might think, he was not entirely his own man, and the president of news at his network had ordered him, in a curt memorandum, to interview Mallory. Patrick had not mentioned Mallory's name on the Graham Show since the interview during the convention in San Francisco. Patrick suspected the president of news of being a secret Mallory supporter. There were little signs: at staff parties, when the jokes about Mallory started, the president's maximum response was a grim smile. He complained that only unflattering still photographs of Mallory were shown on news programs. He had never congratulated Patrick on his Awad scoop, though it was a piece of reporting that was bound to win awards for the reporter and the network. Patrick felt a chill gathering around him: at a party, the president of news had made a point of rushing across a crowded room to shake hands with a young and unimportant correspondent who was covering Mallory's vice-presidential candidate; he told the youngster what a great job he was doing; he mentioned a stand-up he had done in a driving rain in Milwaukee. "Great work, Harry!" the president of news had said; and then he had fixed Patrick with a cold stare and, without uttering a single word to him, had taken one step backwards, and turned on his heel and walked away. Everyone in the room saw what happened. Later, Charlotte said, "Darling, don't you see? He thinks Mallory is going to win."

It was Charlotte who had given Patrick the idea for a different kind of interview. Mallory had said virtually nothing spontaneous throughout his campaign; he hadn't left his mansion. "Why not do that thing Ed Murrow used to do—at home with Franklin Mallory and his concubine?" asked Charlotte. "Stroll through the house, set up the cameras in the drawing room, be ever so civilized—and then go for him! Of course he'll go for you, too, if you're lucky. It ought to be thrilling, Patrick—two great white stallions bashing and biting on prime time."

Susan Grant had resisted the idea at first. Then, unaccountably, she agreed. But, as always, Mallory insisted that the program be broadcast live. He trusted no one to edit him. The cameras had followed them down the gallery of paintings, taping, but that footage, being edited now while dinner was served, would be used behind the credits as the show opened.

Susan and Patrick waited while Mallory finished his second helping. Talk died. The clock was moving. There was no dessert. The dining room was dark: candles on the table, sconces with weak bulbs on the fumed-oak paneling of the walls. Susan looked at her watch.

"We're on in two minutes," she said.

Both men were already wearing makeup.

"Remember," Patrick said, "they'll start shooting as soon as we come out of the dining room; the cameras will follow us into the living room. The mikes will be live."

Mallory nodded. They walked through the double doors into the glare of the television lights. Mallory, coming out of the dining room, which was as dark as a cave, didn't even blink.

Patrick paused by a window. "Miss Grant," he said, "there's something very unusual about this house. These windows aren't real, are they?"

"Not everyone notices that," Susan said. "You see glass. But there are sheets of some sort of everything-proof steel armor between two sets of panes."

"Let me show you," said Mallory. He went to a switch and suddenly the room was bathed in artificial sunlight that seemed to fall through real window glass. Mallory picked up a fireplace poker and rapped the glass with it; it gave off a ring like that of a tank struck by a rifle bullet.

"It's computerized, so that the light coming from the windows changes to simulate the angle of the sun," said Mallory. "Ridiculous, but security people fear the world."

Mallory put the poker back in its rack. "We should have had a fire," he said, "it's beginning to be the season."

"Coffee in the big room," Susan said. "There *is* a fire there."

One set of cameras followed them, another awaited them. Susan gave them espresso from a silver pot. Patrick realized how giddy he was. Mallory had drunk one weak cocktail; Susan had had a little wine with dinner. Patrick saw that they were watching him—four shrewd eyes glinting with amusement.

"Do *you* fear the world, Mr. Mallory?" Patrick asked. "Is that why you've spent this whole campaign locked up in this fortress while President Lockwood goes out among the people?"

"Why is it, Patrick," Mallory asked, "that you always bring

236

up this contrast between Frosty Lockwood's campaign style and mine? Do you suspect me of cowardice?"

Mallory's voice, as always, was light, even playful. Nothing offended this man or surprised him. Patrick wondered if Mallory had ever said or done anything that gave him remorse the following day.

"Cowardice is the last thing I'd suspect you of, Mr. Mallory. But you don't really seem to like the smell of the crowd. Everyone knows there's great danger in the world today, especially to public men."

"I don't think the people are dangerous, Patrick. They're an intelligence. I can speak to them as well from this house as from a platform in their home community; the nation is one community, thanks to your medium of television."

Patrick let a pause occur; he counted six heartbeats and then said, "But the fact remains that President Lockwood exposes himself every day to the people. It seems to have helped him and hurt you."

"Oh? How is that?"

"He's virtually even with you in the polls. It's remarkable, when you think of it; when the Awad story broke he dropped way down. A lot of people thought that would finish him."

"Did you?"

"The possibility entered my mind, yes."

Patrick still felt less than sober; it cost him an effort to keep his speech from slurring. This was a folly he hadn't committed for many years. He missed the first part of something Mallory was telling him.

Then Mallory's voice penetrated Patrick's reverie. ". . . Lockwood has done an amazing job of making people forget what he did."

His voice slipping from drink and emotion, Patrick said, "You say 'what Lockwood did.' Do you say to the people that the death of Ibn Awad was caused by President Lockwood and by him alone?"

In the days since he had heard the tape Emily had brought to his house, Patrick had been split into two parts. One part, the youthful believer in the morality of revolution, told him to suppress the story; the other, the implacable journalist, shook the bars of his conscience and demanded that the truth be let out. Suddenly Patrick, freed by alcohol, hoped that Mallory could be made to bring out the truth: that he could be manipulated just enough on camera, now, to make him say what Patrick couldn't bring himself to say.

Mallory had guessed the truth, or more likely knew it for a

237

fact. He had been the President; he knew what Presidents did. He had men in the FIS who must be loyal to him. O. N. Laster knew; it followed that Mallory *must* know.

"Of course it was Lockwood," Mallory said. "Only a king may kill a king. It's the oldest of rules."

"Would you have done the same?"

Mallory did not respond. Susan Grant was sitting next to him on a sofa, her long legs crossed under her skirt, sipping coffee. She seemed to take no interest in the conversation, but Patrick knew that nothing ever escaped her ear or her memory. She quivered under her load of secrets, under her burden of contempt for those who, like Patrick, had done Mallory an injury.

"Would he?" Patrick insisted, addressing himself to Susan.

"No," she replied. "If a President knows how to be a President, as Franklin does, he so controls events that he is never forced to do anything desperate."

"You think Lockwood is a desperate man?"

"I think that all you humanitarians, as you call yourselves, are desperate men, because you refuse to see the world as it is. I think Lockwood could as easily destroy Russia as he destroyed Ibn Awad, and that you, Patrick, would be on the air when the first Soviet missile hit Washington in retaliation, explaining that death and desolation were going to turn out to be excellent things for people. You don't *think*, any of you. You feel. You're proud of that. Honest emotion, whatever that's supposed to be, excuses anything."

Patrick felt the heat in his reddening face. Susan offered him more coffee. Her words to Patrick were only what Mallory said all the time in speeches; neither of them cared what stinging insults they delivered. An audience of millions or Patrick Graham alone, three feet away with his back to a snapping fire of apple logs, was the same thing to them. They said what they thought.

"And you," said Patrick, "if you win next week—"

"Franklin will win next week," Susan said flatly, interrupting.

"Will he?"

"Yes."

"Has he some bombshell that will change the trend? Lockwood's curve is up, Mallory's is down."

"A lot can happen in a week," Susan Grant said.

Patrick had never heard her talk so much. Patrick's head had cleared. He had not felt so alert for days. Once again, there was bait in the water. But some stubborn imp prevented Patrick from taking it. He was sure that Susan or Mallory would tell him almost anything. He would not ask. Let her, let Mallory come out with it.

They wanted something from him. Patrick had had enough of being used.

Mallory and Susan waited through Patrick's silence. He found himself smiling at Franklin Mallory, who smiled back.

"What did Miss Grant mean, 'A lot can happen in a week'?" Patrick asked at last.

Mallory's smile broadened. "Nothing sinister, Patrick. A lot *can* happen in a week in presidential politics. Four years ago you yourself made a great deal happen in a week; I was defeated when you told the world about the secret plan to join Canada to the United States."

"The people, as you say, are an intelligence, sir. They understood you'd deceived them. There was a rumor of an attempted assassination of the Canadian prime minister at that time."

"It wasn't a rumor. Terrorists actually tried to assassinate him."

"Terrorists?"

"Yes, terrorists—not the President of the United States, not any arm of the United States government."

Patrick let these words hang; a tight close-up of his worried, puzzled face went out over the network.

He said, "You really do think you'll be inaugurated as President again in January, don't you?"

"Oh, yes."

"That the Lockwood Administration, with all its concern for ordinary people, all its efforts to preserve what remains of the earth's natural environment, all its programs to restore eroded freedoms, was a mere interruption?"

"That it was an interruption, yes. As for the rest of your language, your viewers can judge its accuracy. Certainly the voters will do so in a few days."

"And they will choose another Mallory presidency—more huge expenditures on space; more development of biological weapons; more special quickie courts for felons; more imprisonment for life of men and women who are classified as criminal personalities in camps in Alaska; more sterilization of the poor on a mass scale?"

Patrick, as he spoke, shifted his glance to Susan Grant. Why did he keep on thinking he would catch her, when he could not catch Mallory, in an unguarded reaction? Her face showed nothing.

"The people know what I stand for, Patrick, and my policies are not quite as you describe them. It's pointless to contradict you. I have stated my intentions to the people very clearly. So, in his more roundabout way, has President Lockwood."

"And they'll choose you?"

"I hope so. I believe so. It's a choice between facing facts with me and chasing myths with Lockwood."

"On one matter you haven't been entirely candid. May I say what I think it is?"

"Say whatever you like, Patrick."

"You've refused, until tonight, to discuss the Ibn Awad assassination. Why?"

"Because it is not a political issue. It is a legal issue. Now is not the time to deal with it."

"When *will* you deal with it?"

Mallory paused. This time it was his face, perfectly composed, stern, unruffled by emotion, that went out over the network.

"When I am President again. That will be the proper time. I'll make it the first order of business of my second presidency, and I hope that I will be able to persuade the appropriate committees of the new Congress to make it their first order of business."

"You mean you'll stage an investigation?"

"Yes," Mallory said.

"You'd put the country through that? It would be a witch hunt."

"No. A search for the truth. Murder has been done by the President. By that act, he made the people his accomplices without their consent. They deserve to know the facts—surely they are owed that much."

"It would be an impeachment trial of a defeated President," Patrick said. "It would destroy him. It would destroy Lockwood's party. It would destroy everything."

"Everything? Not justice, sir; not truth. Not the principle that no man is so high in America or so pure in his political beliefs that he need not answer for a crime."

The hour had run out. It was Mallory, not Patrick, who saw the frantic signals of the floor man, and it was Mallory who had the last word. Mallory and Susan rose to their feet. Patrick, automatically, got up as well. He felt himself being walked towards the door. The cameras were following. Patrick straightened his back; the microphones were dead again; the three people smiled at one another. They paused, as they had rehearsed, to look for a moment at a Hellenic head of a youth; the nose was broken, but one could see what beauty the boy had had, two thousand years before. It might be a head of Alexander. It looked like Talil.

In the hallway, one of the Filipinos appeared with Patrick's coat; another stood by the front door, ready to open it. He could not open it in the normal sense—there was no handle; one of Mallory's invisible beams worked the latch. All was wizardry here.

Mallory, offering his hand, wished Patrick good-night and gave the journalists in the street his customary smile. He never waved. Too many photographers were waiting for just the right pose: Mallory with a stiffened right arm upraised before a cheering crowd.

Patrick went down the steps. One or two newsmen, acquaintances, spoke to him, but he wouldn't be interviewed.

In his car, overheated after its long wait, Patrick felt a wave of nausea rising. He fought it down, but it rose again. He hadn't vomited since childhood. Was that true? Patrick didn't know. His cameraman had vomited when they turned over that slain girl in Vietnam and he saw the blood. But not Patrick. He'd been too tough for that.

This was a different matter; something truly important, something invisible, was dying now.

3

The first of Hassan Abdallah's men exploded two days later in the crowd at the Alamo.

It had been Lockwood's own idea to spend the final week of the campaign visiting, at noon each day, one of the great historic sites of the United States. He would speak at the Alamo, at Gettysburg, at Valley Forge, at Plymouth Rock, at Williamsburg where Patrick Henry spoke, and finally on the steps of the Lincoln Memorial, with the brooding figure of the Great Emancipator behind him and the ghost of Martin Luther King beside him. Lockwood had the eye of a theatrical producer for the right background.

The terrorist at the Alamo was dressed in a white jibba and he was an Arab. He carried a hand-lettered placard that said, in English and Arabic, "Remember Ibn Awad!" The Secret Service watched him. There had been others like him all along the campaign trail: the jibba, the sign. They had been passive, but the Secret Service was never lulled into believing that anyone within gunshot of a President was harmless.

Therefore a young Secret Service man was close to the Arab when he exploded. It was the old Eye of Gaza method: plastic charges had been implanted in the man's thighs. He set them off with a battery connected to wires which were in turn connected to detonators inside his body.

Blood, bone, and flesh burst inside the crowd, twenty-five feet from Lockwood, who stood on a platform before the scarred gates of the Alamo. Hassan's human bomb created a geyser of fire and blood. The noise was deafening.

The young Secret Service man, standing between the terrorist and the President, was killed by a shaft of bone that pierced him front to back like an assegai. Five others standing near the terrorist died and many more were wounded. The President, before he was thrown to the floor of the platform and covered by the bodies of his guards, was spattered with droplets of blood. The television camera-men recorded this in the frozen instant before the Secret Service men could spring: Lockwood, tall and smiling as he spoke, being struck by a storm of gore. This, and the footage of the exploding fanatic that two networks had been lucky enough to get, were played and replayed in slow motion all that day.

Emily, watching in Washington, kept seeing Julian, standing in the crowd, facing it, just below Lockwood at the base of the platform. The force of the blast ballooned his unbuttoned seersucker jacket like a gust of wind before a rain. One moment, he was clean and neat, the next he was smeared with blood. She thought, Julian is dead.

Emily saw Julian turn and scramble onto the platform, his first and only thought for Lockwood. A Secret Service man, blinded by the rain of blood so that he couldn't recognize Julian, or merely acting on instinct, kicked him in the chest. Julian grasped the man's leg and threw him into the scattering crowd. His struggling body flew, clawing the air, as if it had been dropped from a helicopter. Emily had never know how much strength Julian had. She thought, It's adrenaline; he's mad with fear for Lockwood.

Lockwood, under a pile of bodies, struggled and heaved, trying to get free.

"Polly!" he cried. "Polly!"

The microphones picked up Lockwood's muffled voice. Amplified, his cry of anguish was replayed. There was a blurred shot of Julian rushing to the President's wife, who still stood erect and by some miracle unstained. Julian's great body shielded Polly Lockwood's; he carried her to the ground and covered her. She was wearing a pink suit; the bouquet of roses she had been handed was caught between Julian's upper body and her own. Polly's face was badly scratched by the thorns.

The crowd broke apart and ran. The last panning shots by the television cameras showed the plaza before the Alamo deserted except for the dead and wounded and the stain, bright red but really quite small, that the terrorist had left in the dust where he had been standing.

4

Lockwood insisted on remaining in San Antonio for the evening. Only that morning he and Polly had walked along the river followed by a mariachi band. Lockwood had eaten a burrito. A whole nursery school of Mexican children had skipped along behind him as if he were the Pied Piper. Here, as everywhere, the poor people loved him.

In the hotel, after the bomb went off, Lockwood and the others who had been soiled took off their clothes and washed themselves—all except Julian, who was too busy finding out what had happened; the facts. The White House physician had been deafened by the blast, but he insisted on examining Lockwood. He could hear nothing that was said to him, but he listened attentively to the President's chest with his stethoscope. Lockwood, lying naked on a hotel bed, let the doctor do as he wished. Julian, still in his stained clothes, watching, realized that the President himself was in shock.

Finally Julian went away to change and shower. Before he did anything else, he tried to call Emily, but the phone on O Street was hooked up to the automatic recording device. "I'm not hurt," Julian said to the tape. "The President is all right." He hung up the phone. He saw himself in the mirror. He said aloud, as if he were still speaking to Emily, "Have mercy on us." The words of the General Confession, unspoken by Julian since boyhood, ran through his mind. He saw himself again in the mirror. There was blood all over him.

That evening, inside a phalanx of Secret Service men and police, Lockwood visited each bereaved family. All but one of the dead, a girl who had been photographing the terrorist for a local newspaper at the moment of the blast, were blacks or Mexicans.

The President insisted on walking through the wretched streets. He went into the matchwood houses, filled with wailing, in which the victims had lived. As he walked, from one house to another, people came out and surrounded him, angry faces turned outwards to the world.

"An army of the poor, protecting President Lockwood," said Patrick Graham, following with the cameras; he had arrived that morning, to cover Lockwood in the last days of his campaign.

Later, airborne in the presidential jet, Lockwood said, "All those folks are dead. . . . But wasn't it something, the way they came out and walked with us this evening?"

Julian had had no chance to talk to Lockwood. The President had refused to listen to him, or to anyone. All his concern was for the dead and wounded. Now he began to talk about them again: the houses, the widows and orphans and bereaved mothers.

"In every single one of those houses there was the smell of *cooking*," Lockwood said. "There's something strong about people like that. That they should cook on the day of a death, a horrible death in the family. And the way the Mexicans all made me have a drink. . . ."

Both Julian and Polly had been with Lockwood in those houses, but he was turning the visit to the barrio into an anecdote for them. Julian looked very closely at him, and then at Polly. Did Lockwood not remember what had happened at the Alamo? Julian wasn't sure that the President knew what had occurred, that he saw its significance; that he made the connection. Julian himself had been blind to it until he talked on the telephone to Philindros.

"Frosty," Polly said. The President stopped talking, swiveled in his chair, and sipped his bourbon; his hand trembled, but only slightly. "Frosty," Polly repeated, "you ought to hear what Julian has to say."

Lockwood put down his drink and turned his attention to Julian.

"You're all right, aren't you, Jolly?" Lockwood asked. No one but Lockwood had ever called Julian "Jolly."

"Yes, sir," said Julian. "But we haven't talked. I wonder if you understand exactly what happened today."

"Somebody threw a bomb."

"No. A man exploded his own body."

"Did *what?*"

"He was dressed in one of those white Bedouin robes like the one Ibn Awad always wore. He carried a sign that said, in English and Arabic, 'Remember Ibn Awad.'"

"*Exploded* himself?"

"Explosives had been surgically implanted in his body. He set them off himself." Julian paused. "Like the terrorists in the airplanes over Palestine. It was the Eye of Gaza."

Lockwood looked hard at Julian. Taking Polly's hand, he gazed for a long moment at the windowless bulkhead as though he could see the endless Great Plains, brown with the stubble of the harvest, that flowed beneath the aircraft.

"Do you think they wanted to kill me?" he asked.

"No," said Julian. "Not yet."

At Andrews, the crowd beyond the fences was strangely quiet. A ripple of cheers, but not the usual bellow of welcome and affection, ran through the waiting people as Lockwood emerged from the airplane door into the glaring television lights. Though his image was broadcast in all its natural color, Lockwood's person at this moment was, to the naked eye, bleached by the klieg lights as white as a ghost. His landing in Washington was, as Patrick Graham told the audience, like a return from the dead.

Julian went down the rear steps of the plane. A car was waiting for him in the shadows there. It was not his usual White House vehicle, and he had to be led to it. Inside the black car, Philindros waited. He drove expertly, making a long, smooth turn, and then going straight across the aprons between parked warplanes and through a gate that Julian had never used before. There was no music in the car, and of course Philindros didn't speak, so that the only sound came from the grip of the tires on the concrete and the monotonous scream of the diesel engine.

Julian said, "We've already agreed on the phone that this episode is a Foreign Intelligence matter. I want to know what you know, in detail."

Philindros reported in his usual unhesitating way. "There's no question that the bomb carrier was a member of the Eye of Gaza," he said. "We've matched his photograph with a file picture of a known member of Hassan's organization."

"They've issued no statement claiming responsibility."

"I don't think they will. They want mystery, speculation. If they *kill* the President, then they'd have something to gain from confessing the murder. They would have avenged Awad."

"Then what is the point of what happened today?"

"The same as it always is. Horror show. We estimate they'll do it again, probably several times."

"On what basis?"

"We knew that seven members of the Eye of Gaza have entered the United States in the past two weeks. Now we know why."

"You *knew* they were in the country?"

Philindros said, "All that was reported."

"To whom?"

"To the Secret Service."

"I was never told. Didn't they take you seriously?"

Philindros, defending a sister service, spoke sharply. "They take everything seriously. But how can they take one potential threat to the President more seriously than another? Some psychopath with a cheap rifle is as dangerous as Hassan. More so—we *know* Hassan when we see him."

Julian told Philindros to stop the car. They were moving down a narrow street lined with ginkgo trees. Philindros braked and then backed smoothly into a short parking space. He left the motor running and kept an eye on the mirrors. Julian wondered if he was armed. No doubt he was.

"There's more to this than just a horror show," Julian said. "If it's the Eye of Gaza, they have a purpose."

"Obviously they didn't want to kill the President today."

"What, then?"

Philindros turned his body and slid towards the door. Julian's bulk in this confined space made him uncomfortable.

"To humiliate Lockwood publicly, literally cover him with blood. That picture will be on every television set in the world tonight, and in all the newspapers tomorrow, everywhere."

"We have to know more. Catch them. Question them."

"Everyone is trying to do the first. Nobody has ever succeeded in the second. They kill themselves."

"For the love of Christ, Jack! What good are you guys?"

Philindros took this rebuke in silence. It was remarkable that Julian was as collected as he was. Another presidential assistant might have been shrieking.

"We'd like to be better, but nobody—not Mallory, not you people—ever gave us the resources," Philindros said, "so these people have just been beyond us as a target. Only Horace touched them. Years ago he had an agent inside the Eye, but only for a short while. I don't know how to stop people who make a religion of dying a horrible death. No one does."

"Do they want the President to die a horrible death?"

"Not yet."

Julian had spoken these same words to Lockwood. Now, with Philindros, he searched for their meaning. He hardly knew himself; the feeling he had about what was happening was strong but he didn't yet see the details.

Julian said, "They're trying to influence the election."

"Possibly. Yes."

Julian's eyes burned with the obvious question. He said, "O. N. Laster?"

"Hassan Abdallah doesn't care who's President of the United States. Mallory's as much an enemy to him as Lockwood."

"But it was Lockwood who killed Awad. Therefore they want to punish him—humiliate him, as you say. Publicly."

"Yes. That's part of the profile. From now on, whether he wins or loses, he's under a threat. What happened at the Alamo can happen again—anywhere, anytime."

"And if he loses the election, he loses most of his protection. Retired Presidents, unless they're rich like Mallory, are only lightly guarded."

Philindros saw in Julian something rare in his experience: a man truly frightened for another man, and frightened by the things his intelligence revealed to him. Julian was beginning to know that there would never be any escape for Lockwood. Philindros let Julian see that he did not much want to say what he said next.

"To be realistic, the situation is this," said Philindros. "If President Lockwood is elected again and has the full protection of the American security apparatus, he'll be reasonably safe for four years. It's even possible we could penetrate and break the Eye of Gaza in that period. We've never put our mind or our money into that job."

"And if he loses?"

"Then he'll be a much easier target. Hassan might strike on Inauguration Day or he might wait years. But he's decided to kill Lockwood, Julian."

"Hassan himself could die."

Philindros nodded. "He knows that. That's why a baby is being born to replace him somewhere today, and another will be born tomorrow. And they'll beget sons like that fellow at the Alamo before *they* die."

"Is there anything we can do?"

Philindros put the car in gear.

"Stay inside," he said. "Pray."

6

Naturally Lockwood would not stay inside. As soon as he woke the next morning Julian told him what Philindros had reported. Lockwood received the information impassively. His mind was already leaping into the future as it always did.

"What happened in San Antonio is in the past," he said to Julian. "We'll go on to something else."

"No, sir. We'll go on to more of the same. Cancel the tour."

Lockwood shook his head emphatically. He wouldn't be driven into hiding.

"If I let them scare me, Julian, we'll lose. There's not the width

247

of a door crack between Mallory and me now. I've got the momentum. We've got to keep driving."

In New York, Susan Grant, returning a telephone call from Patrick Graham, heard his voice asking if the explosion of human bombs was what she meant when she had said that a lot could happen in a week.

Susan hung up the phone without responding to the question.

Polly Lockwood flew to Live Oaks. She took Elliott and Jenny Hubbard with her; Emily refused to go. The farm, protected by its ring of electronic devices, was, even more than the White House, the safest place in America. Two companies of Marines were flown in to reinforce the Secret Service; they camped in a woods beneath camouflage netting and patrolled the farm's perimeter.

Emily asked Julian to take her with him for Lockwood's last appearances of the campaign.

"It's mad to ask that," Julian said. "Don't you know what people are capable of?"

"Yes," she replied.

He refused her. But if Julian was going to die, Emily wanted to be with him. That night she phoned the editor of a woman's magazine in New York and got an assignment to cover the last week of the campaign from the point of view of the wife of a man in danger.

"Twenty-five hundred words," said the editor. "Just tell the reader how you feel, all of it, moment to moment."

The next day, at noon on the field at Gettysburg, Julian looked into the knot of journalists and saw Emily among them. She wore her glasses and a Burberry coat, stained from much use and travel. Her hair was hidden beneath a scarf. She wore that intensely interested look which she always wore when on assignment. She was scribbling on her pad.

Lockwood spoke on Little Round Top, with the thin crowd below him. It wasn't a crowd at all in the sense that it was packed together; groups of people who knew each other stood separated from other groups by yards of open space. Five or six outlandish young people carried placards with the message "Remember Ibn Awad"; they were herded together and moved to the far edge of the crowd and there surrounded by a ring of Secret Service men. Lockwood had forbidden arrests or even body searches. Two cameras stayed on this group. Another nosed the crowd, resting for a moment on one lone man, then trotting nervously to another.

A chill wind blew; the warm weather was over. That morning the battlefield had been white with frost, and the grass was cold and brittle still under the feet of the onlookers.

Julian's eyes kept straying to the journalists. Emily was watching, making notes. Once she smiled at a colleague who said something to her. She was as safe among the reporters as it was possible to be. Terrorists lived by the press; they would do its members no deliberate harm.

Lockwood quoted Lincoln's first inaugural address: " 'The mystic chords of memory, stretching from every battlefield, and patriot grave, to every living heart and hearthstone, all over this broad land, will yet swell the chorus of the Union, when again touched, as surely they will be, by the better angels of our nature.' "

At the end of the speech, the crowd went quietly away in the wintry sunlight among the monuments and the graves. The cameras watched them go and the microphones recorded, for somber moments, the deep hush that lay over the battlefield.

"Lincoln must have heard this same deep silence when he spoke here," said Patrick Graham to the audience. "There is always this stillness on old battlefields. Even the terrorists must fear to break it. Perhaps if they did, the brave men who died here, all so very young, would wake and ask them why."

In Times Square, noontime crowds watched Lockwood's speech on television sets in store windows. The same scene was repeated across the nation, and television crews photographed the crowds in New York and elsewhere. The watchers saw themselves on the tube and waved. When they dispersed in Times Square at the end of the speech, a young woman on crutches detached herself from the crowd and swung her body through the honking stream of taxis to the central island between the two parts of Broadway.

In a voice that afterwards seemed enormous to those who heard it issue from her small body, she shrieked, *"Remember Ibn Awad!"* The crowd, which had been walking away from the television sets in the store windows, shivering in a mixture of relief and disappointment that nothing had happened in Gettysburg, broke and ran. Some threw themselves to the pavement like people who had heard the whistle of an incoming shell.

The girl waited for the television cameras to find her. Then she repeated her cry and blew herself to bits.

No one else was killed or wounded, though a taxi driver, blinded by the blast, ran over the curb and struck a newsstand, scattering papers and magazines in a sort of sympathetic explosion.

249

Neither the FIS nor any other agency in the world was able to identify the girl. She had had long blond hair. The autopsy established that it wasn't dyed.

Almost certainly, thought Philindros, she had been got on an American mother.

It snowed at Valley Forge on the day Lockwood spoke there. The crowd was very small but the television audience was enormous.

Here the President quoted Washington. He spoke of the terrible winter, the loss of hope, the eventual triumph. His voice had never been stronger, but he spoke briefly: exactly twenty-two minutes.

In the twenty-second minute, in Union Square in San Francisco, a young man in a white jibba stepped out of a car and ran, limping painfully, to the middle of the park. A crowd of early shoppers and commuters had gathered round some street musicians: a boy in a curly wig, dressed like Shirley Temple as a child, was tap-dancing. The youth in the jibba ran straight into this group. The dancer and two policemen in plain clothes who had been pursuing the terrorist were killed in the ensuing explosion. The scene was recorded by a television camera with a long lens, shooting from the window of a room on a high floor of the Saint Francis Hotel, and within moments the crowd was able to see a replay of the explosion on television receivers flickering in the windows of the shops surrounding Union Square, and everywhere else in America.

7

"Sir, you have to stop," said Julian.

"They won't, even if I do," Lockwood replied.

They were aloft, flying from Valley Forge to the farm in Kentucky. Lockwood and Julian never saw the television pictures of the suicides instantaneously, as almost everyone else in the country did. They were always far from a television receiver, on a battlefield or in a speeding car, or airborne. In the evening, though, they watched the tapes.

"What the hell is this going to accomplish for them?" Lockwood asked after the girl killed herself in Times Square.

"This," replied Julian, pointing at the screen.

The whole of the evening news was devoted to the event. Lockwood's face and his eloquent words at Gettysburg; then the girl on Times Square, her cry and her death. One image replaced the other, over and over.

At the farm, Lockwood asked Julian to leave him alone with Polly. Julian, uttering no reproach, had had Emily brought aboard the presidential plane at Valley Forge; the press wasn't permitted even now to follow Lockwood to Kentucky.

Emily had never been to the farm before. Julian took her and the children to the paddocks. Elliott and Jenny hadn't been allowed by Polly to watch television. They asked no questions. They knew that something awful was happening in the world outside. Emily, silent, turned her back on the colts clustered at the fence in hopes of sugar, and looked long at the white columned house where Awad's death warrant had been signed.

That evening the four of them played hearts. Julian had forgotten the game and had to learn again.

The windows in this house, many-paned, ran almost from floor to ceiling. At three in the morning, Julian woke and found Emily standing before their bedroom window, with her slim shadow running behind her on the bare wood floor. He got up and put an arm around her. She didn't move towards him but remained as she had been, with her arms folded on her breast. The horses were galloping in their pastures, and their hoofbeats were transmitted through the earth and into the boards of the house so that Emily in her bare feet could feel the rhythmic tremor. Floodlights burned all around the perimeter of the farm. From the air it would appear that the President was inside a ring of light.

Emily thought, These are last days.

She didn't know what the thought meant. It had wakened her. She couldn't go back to sleep.

The next morning, the Saturday before the election on Tuesday, Lockwood came into Julian's room shortly after dawn. He hadn't yet shaved or brushed his hair.

He told Julian to cancel the next two speeches.

"We'll see what happens," he said.

8

Rose MacKenzie had once predicted the precise date on which a war would begin in the Near East by making a computer model of a phenomenon she called "semantic stress." Rose assigned an emotional value, expressed by a number, to each of a long list of words

251

and phrases in Arabic. Then she had her computers listen to the propaganda broadcasts of the two hostile countries, and count the frequency with which each of these words and phrases was used. When the ones with the highest emotive value were used with greatest frequency, war was imminent. Finally the pattern of hostile words on both sides reached a point where the computer stated that the chances for war on Tuesday were in the ninety-ninth percentile. On Tuesday, tanks rolled across the frontiers.

Now, in New York, Rose revived this old program. It was a lark, she told Horace. They were in the kitchen of her apartment. Rose was making baba ghanouj as the first course of the Persian dinner they had planned for that evening.

"What I did," said Rose, "was to work out the value of words and phrases used by people interviewed about the explosions, and about Lockwood and Awad, and also—this is *your* refinement—the tonal stress in their voices and in the voices of the TV reporters and commentators. There's a discernible pattern there, very much like the lie detector test that's based on voice tones."

Pushing eggplant through a sieve, Rose chattered happily about her techniques. These had always been a mystery to Horace, and he listened with only half an ear. He was lifting lamb chops from a marinade and putting them on a skewer. He waited for Rose to state the results of her work. Horace believed absolutely in Rose's results.

"Well," said Rose, licking her finger, "the word is this: Lockwood is going to lose the election."

"How do you know that?"

"I tapped the computers at Princeton. All the polls had him even with Mallory or a percentage point ahead before the Alamo. He went up a point in one poll, two points in another, right after that. But the trend ever since has been down. People's voices—the tone and the word choices—reveal what they really think and feel. And after all these kids blowing themselves up, what they think and feel is that Lockwood is putting them in danger. They're afraid. They're losing trust."

"Can't that change?"

"In three days, with more human bombs going off? Horace, you know Hassan. He's likely to have a fireworks display with parachutists exploding over the White House on Election Day."

"How much will Lockwood lose by?"

Rose added sesame and lemon to her eggplant and whipped it vigorously with a whisk. She tasted it, held out a gob of it on her finger for Horace to try.

"More lemon?" Rose asked. She added a few drops from a cut fruit.

"He won't lose by much," she said. "It'll be like last time—a few thousand votes in two or three states will make the difference."

"Is that you or the computer talking?"

Rose grinned. "The two of us," she said; "one flesh."

9

Patrick Graham had gone home from the interview at Mallory's to talk to Charlotte: "You see his intention. He'll wreck the party, discredit Lockwood, label the whole humanistic movement a lie. He wants to destroy his opposition totally in order to seize total power."

Mallory would destroy Patrick as well; they both knew it— Charlotte who had lost one glittering world, Patrick who had never quite got inside another.

"Do you really care so much for Lockwood? For Julian?"

Patrick could not return her smile. Charlotte had never really managed to teach him how to be debonair.

"They *are* the better angels," he said.

They were alone, of course. Charlotte, in their drawing room with its Hogarth and its Daumiers, put a languid wrist on Patrick's shoulder and lifted his left hand in hers as if they were beginning a waltz.

"After all this, Alaska," she said. "Imagine."

Barbed wire and snow. That was what Patrick had told his dark-haired girl to fear. He himself didn't fear those things, or the loss of what he owned, or the destruction of his place in the world. In a way he would welcome spending his last years in a concentration camp: his life had been a long process of reconfirming the truths he had perceived when he was twenty. American society, if he and his generation had been right about it in their youth, should have destroyed him long ago. Now he saw the irony: society had given him everything, but it had only been waiting for the arrival of Mallory in order to collapse and crush Patrick and everyone like him in its debris. He said all this to Charlotte.

"Well, perhaps it won't fall on you quite yet," she said. "I have something concealed in the bosom of my frock." She reached inside (Patrick had seen her make this gesture a thousand times as she dressed, settling her bare breasts in her décolletage) and produced a square blue envelope. "Poor Clive Wilmot has died," Charlotte said, "and left me everything. He had a house in Provence; I'd been there. And he had some new money, it seems."

"Clive? Why you?" Patrick took the envelope from his wife's hand.

"There was sympathy between us. We were cousins of a sort, you know, and when he came back from Ireland with that awful wound, I didn't mind."

"You were lovers?"

"You'd best read the letter."

Patrick did so. Evidently Clive had made some arrangement, only spies and characters in films knew how to do such things, to have the letter delivered to Charlotte in case of his violent death. It had come, without explanation, in the morning mail.

"I expected to read that he needed a loan," Charlotte said, "but he speaks of leaving me a great deal of money, buried in a cave. It's too Clivish."

Clive wrote of a great many other things—all he knew, in fact, about the Awad affair. Patrick put the letter in his pocket and went out the door without saying good-bye to Charlotte. He took the first available shuttle to New York; he took the dark-haired girl, too, when he found her still in the office when he stopped by to pick up some money.

Patrick Graham, having the run of the network's apartment, had no need for a club in New York (his Washington clubs were enough), so he had never joined one. The Millennium Club, like the house of a man who has grown old with inherited possessions, was less splendid than it had been. Its members liked it as it was. A whale-oil lamp burned on the cigar counter. The library contained, bound in red morocco, a copy of every book ever written by a member, and these were filed not in alphabetical order but in order of accession to membership: the volumes of Washington Irving, the club's founder, stood at the top center, and as the eye moved downwards and to either side the spines of the books grew redder according to their newness, scarlet near the floor and rose higher up; the effect, when the light was strong in evening, was like a sunset as painted by an amateur watercolorist.

Inside the door, Patrick found Horace waiting for him. Patrick had called him from the dark-haired girl's bed to make this appointment. Horace, with his unshakable good manners, took Patrick's coat. He peered into his guest's face, as if to detect signs of discomfort. "Are you all right?" he asked, pointing to the door of the lavatory that opened off the vestibule. Patrick shook his head in impatient refusal.

They went upstairs, and Patrick saw that they were quite isolated at their table. A group of younger men was drawn up in a circle at the other end of the long room, but nearby only one old member sat alone, wearing gray tweeds with the trousers hitched high to reveal argyle socks and chalky new tennis shoes.

"You don't still work for D. & D. Laux & Co., do you?" he asked.

"I'm on leave of absence."

"What exactly *are* you doing these days, Horace?"

"Nothing, really." The smile. "I'm out to pasture."

"You're not going back to Beirut?"

"Eventually, I suppose. I thought I'd hang around to vote next Tuesday, comfort Julian if that's necessary."

"You're really out of the FIS?"

Horace said, after the briefest of pauses, "What's *your* prognostication on the election? The bets in this place are pretty evenly split, I'm told. Funny thing—Frew, the barman, has been holding bets—people bet drinks on the outcome—on presidential elections for years. He says a majority have always bet for the winner."

The old member in tweeds and tennis shoes awakened; he stared in puzzlement at Patrick—this man with Horace was someone he recognized but didn't know. Patrick spoke cordially to the old man and the dim eyes turned away.

"Horace," said Patrick, "I suppose you have some way of communicating with Julian."

"Yes. Of course, I try not to bother him just now. Surely *you* can reach him."

Patrick didn't want to reach Julian. What he was about to do was an act of conscience. How could Julian understand that? All the wreckage of their two colliding lives lay between them. Horace was the only possible messenger: he would reveal his source to the right people and guard it with his life from the wrong ones.

"There's a bit of information I want to give you," Patrick said. "I expect you to keep the source to yourself."

"You want me to pass this on to Julian?"

"You can do anything you like with it."

Patrick laid stress on these words and Horace's eyes widened. Another politeness: amazed pleasure that a journalist should trust a man he knew to be an officer of the FIS. These expressions of Horace's flashed on his face like transparencies on a screen. He had spent his life paying silent compliments to men he must despise. No wonder Prince Talil and all the rest had fallen into his net.

Patrick handed Horace Charlotte's letter from Clive Wilmot. Horace got out his reading glasses and went through it. He was a rapid reader. Wilmot's handwriting was as flamboyant as the rest of his manners—large, with strokes of the pen running from one word to the next; the British public school hand was like the British public school accent, Horace reflected: plumage. Still, Clive had known a great deal; more than Horace imagined he could have known. Why, after his death, would he wish to have somebody like Patrick smash the secrecy he had always lived by?

Horace looked over the top of his glasses. "You're under some obligation not to use this information on the air?"

"No. If I could confirm it before the election, I *would* use it. But the network would never permit it. Mallory might win. They think he *is* going to win. I see the signs."

"And they fear his revenge?"

"Is there someone who doesn't? Mallory *wants* the presidency for purposes of vengeance—that's the real meaning of his whole political movement, to revenge itself on those who've stood in its way."

Horace was silent.

"What this does, of course," Patrick said, "is to lay out, naked, the connection between O. N. Laster and Mallory and the Eye of Gaza."

"Surely you don't think what's going on now, those terrorists blowing themselves up, is Mallory's work?"

"Don't you?"

Horace was sitting back comfortably in the old cracked-leather chair, one leg crossed over the other. "Let's say I'm glad I'm not in your position, Patrick; I wouldn't want to have to make such an accusation on television."

"Mallory would like nothing better. He could dismiss it as another last-minute attempt by television—by me, Mallory's known enemy—to swing the election to Lockwood."

"That's awfully subtle."

Patrick sat forward. His flesh quivered—all of it: manicured hands, knees beneath the perfectly creased trousers, facial muscles. "If Mallory gets in, Horace, you must understand what he's going to do. He's going to destroy Lockwood. He's going to put your brother in jail. He's going to turn the FIS into a personal secret police force. . . ."

Patrick stopped himself. Horace said, "I wonder if you'd mind if I just made a copy of this letter? There's a machine downstairs they'll let me use."

Patrick nodded. Before he left his guest alone, Horace called over the waiter. "More ginger ale?" he asked Patrick. When it came, Patrick drank it at a gulp, as though it were something a great deal stronger that he needed very badly.

Horace was gone only a short time; but by the time he came back he had phoned Philindros as well as making a photocopy of

Clive Wilmot's last letter. He handed the original, in its shoddy square envelope, the sort that can be bought in tobacco shops in France, back to Patrick.

"You will get this to Julian?" Patrick said.

"Of course. It's an interesting document, but then Clive was an interesting man. So, Patrick, are you."

Patrick shook off the compliment impatiently. "I wouldn't blame you if you thought I was a raving paranoid. But you don't know Mallory. If he wins this election, Horace, you *will* know him."

Horace said, with no smile, "Yes, it sounds that way."

10

In the talks room, Philindros came up from the depths of one of his silences. He held the photocopy of Clive Wilmot's letter in his hand.

"Why do you suppose Graham came to *you* with this?" he said.

Horace shrugged. "He said he wanted me to pass it on to Julian, but of course he could have done that himself. He wanted you to see it."

Philindros went silent again. There was no worry or anger in his face. There never was, once he had all the facts he needed.

"Really," Philindros said, "the man is very peculiar. What does he expect us to do? Strangle Mallory and throw him over a cliff?"

"Something like that."

"I hope no one else does. We'll get the credit. Idiots like Graham will see to that."

The day before, Clive Wilmot's body had been found, well preserved in the snow that had fallen on the night of his murder. Actually, one of Philindros's men had found it a week earlier, but he had left it undisturbed. A shepherd had stumbled onto the corpse finally, and called the police. Identity had been established, though the French had said publicly that the name of the dead man might never be learned as his face had been obliterated by the heavy slugs that had shattered his skull.

"Our surveillance team saw the exchange of money, saw Wilmot drive away in the Mercedes; the fellow in the white suit was Laster's man Hugo Fugger-Weisskopf; he's one of those Germans Laster has trained up to be mirror images of nineteenth-century Harvard boys. He *sends* them to Harvard."

Philindros's men had tailed Clive until they were sure he was on the old road where, a little later, he died. The idea was that another FIS team would pick him up and protect him at the Italian border, but Clive never reached the frontier.

"Hassan's people must have known he'd take that road," Philindros said. "*How?* Not that it matters; they have the money, and we have Hassan's people exploding all over the President of the United States."

"You think that's what Laster intended to happen?"

"I don't suppose he thought Hassan Abdallah was going to make a contribution to charity. Half a million Swiss francs; that's a million dollars. This could go on for a long time—longer than Laster may like."

Philindros's manner, still, was passionless. He took a drink of water. In the shadowless room with its utter absence of noise, Philindros and Horace were as isolated as the crew of a two-man submarine. They saw what was happening: the onslaught of terrorists against Lockwood was taking the election away from him. Hassan had his own purposes; these happened, for the moment, to be Laster's and Mallory's purposes as well. Like all conspirators, each partner believed he could overwhelm the other when his usefulness had ended. Laster and Mallory did not know Hassan Abdallah.

If Hassan made a victory for Mallory possible, Mallory's prosecutors would drag Lockwood and Julian and Philindros and Horace into the dock and convict them of murder. The best Lockwood's party could hope for would be a long, slow death like that suffered by the Republicans in years past. The FIS would perish. In its place, Mallory would put an intelligence service loyal to him, responsive as a whore to his wishes. When Philindros fell, all the men he had trained to love facts and despise politics would fall with him. It would be a coup d'état disguised as a defense of the Constitution.

Philindros gave Clive's letter back to Horace. "I suppose you'll go down to see Julian?"

"Yes."

Philindros nodded. He looked at the television monitors, showing their usual static images: the computers, the security system, the communications apparatus—the most advanced equipment in the world. Like Horace, Philindros had no feeling for the way fleshless things worked, but he knew what machines could do if the right humans controlled them. He cleared his throat. "You're still cleared to wander in and out of here, Horace?"

"No one has ever stopped me."

"You haven't talked to old Laux about this?"

"About the general situation, as you know. Otherwise Clive

258

wouldn't have had that million dollars to hide in his cave, and we wouldn't have had the bombs. I don't know what use they are to us now. Hassan's blowing up all these people makes the connection between him and Ibn Awad pretty obvious."

"Not everything works out. What's Sebastian's feeling?"

"Indifference to the election, to the FIS, even to the bank. He's going to die soon, after all. But he doesn't like the idea of Julian, his best friend's son, being paraded in chains. These old fellows are funny. If you're born with one of the names they know, they think you ought to be untouchable."

Philindros sighed—for him as loud a signal as the first gun fired in a war. "Your brother fears for Lockwood's life, and I think he has good reason," he said. "Hassan has no interest in keeping anyone alive for a show trial."

"What's *your* interest, Jack?"

Philindros drank some water. "You know what it is. I want to save the FIS. If I have to save Lockwood to do that—a strange thought—well and good."

"You think Lockwood is savable?"

"You've saved people who were in a worse state than Lockwood."

"Foreigners."

Philindros cleared his throat. He extended a forefinger and pressed it, hard, against Horace's heart through the cloth of his tie and shirt. "They're *all* foreigners to you and me, Horace," he said. "Do you think that you live—I mean *live*—in the same country as Julian, even?"

Horace looked at his friend for a long moment. He knew they were remembering the same broken men, the same lies about the things they loved. They had never spoken openly of the horrible death of the CIA; they couldn't do it now.

Horace said, "Are you licensing me?"

"No. You have no official position. That *is* your license." A cough. "You have this place, you have Rose. Do as you like. Nobody will interfere."

Horace let a moment go by, his merry eyes and Philindros's sad ones locked. "Maybe we can have lunch after the election, or something," he said.

"Maybe."

Philindros rose. There was nothing more to say. "Do you," he asked, "have a ride uptown?"

"Rose is waiting for me."

Philindros nodded. He unlocked the door, but instead of vanishing through it without ceremony as he usually did, he turned around. He had one more thought after all. "I've studied Julian," he said; "he's a man who likes to think that everything is his idea. He likes to feel his own weight."

"So did Talil."

"All the good ones do. But back to Julian: he won't *do* anything unless he thinks it's his own idea. Can you manage that, him being your brother?"

Philindros's feet moved, a whisper of leather soles against concrete.

Horace smiled, touched by his friend's embarrassment. "Maybe I can suspend sentiment this one last time," he said.

Philindros held out his hand. The gesture surprised Horace. Philindros nodded again, two or three times, as though recognizing all that was between them, the absolute trust, the years of facing the truth.

"Good-bye," Philindros said. "Do what you can. Julian will be thinking of the future. You and I, Horace, ought to remember the past."

Turning on his heel, he walked rapidly away down the long corridor of the inner vault, past the whispering machinery of his trade. If he saw Rose MacKenzie waiting for Horace, he gave no sign. Rose sent a look after him: amusement, the soft smile that women give to a harmless man.

11

Outside, Rose MacKenzie said, "The moon is full!"

She walked into the center of Hanover Square and looked up. Long streamers of cirrus crossed the white face of the moon. Rose's footprints were the only marks in the dusting of snow on the pavement. The streets of the financial district on Saturday night were as empty as a city of the dead, and as silent. The sky, threatening most of the day while Rose worked, unconscious of the weather, inside the vaults, was clearing before a wind blowing far above them. "Come out here and see this," Rose called. Horace crossed to her and she pointed behind him. There stood a tall curved building with hundreds of windows of black glass, and in each window hung a reflection of the moon.

"I wonder if the architect intended that," Rose said. "Some archaeologist, centuries from now, will discover the basis of our religion in the ruins of that building: moon worship."

Rose giggled and took Horace's arm. They decided to walk across the tip of Manhattan; Rose thought it was a good night for it, and she wanted to have a drink at the bar on top of the World Trade Center. The view of Manhattan was wonderful on a moonlit night.

Rose let go of his arm as they sauntered through the darkened streets. It wasn't difficult to see their way—the glass buildings reflected the moonlight, and so did the snow; they even threw shadows as they walked.

An idea had formed in Horace's mind when Rose, asking him to taste her baba ghanouj, had given him her election predictions. Now Horace presented this idea to Rose, as he had always presented everything to do with her work and his—as a scenario, a theoretical situation. Rose, as always, listened intently, then smiled as she saw the solution to the problem. Hundreds of times in the past, Horace had had some purpose to fulfill, something he'd brought into the computer room from the world outside. He was good outside, Rose was good inside. Often Horace's humans failed, but Rose's machines always performed as instructed.

Horace gave her an inquiring look. They had stopped to talk in the middle of the street, and behind them in the snow ran the long double line of their shoeprints like the tracks of a pair of night animals in a northern forest.

"Of course it's possible," said Rose. "It all goes over the telephone system on wires or microwaves. I can make the computers gossip. But it *is* wicked."

Her face shone with the fun of Horace's idea. She took his arm again and they walked on, weaving a bit—almost dancing. Rose's coat was open, she didn't mind the cold. Horace's voice was calm as he stated the problems one after the other. Rose sometimes burst into laughter as she saw the solutions. She was a mathematician, and finding solutions to new equations was mind-boggling joy to her. She did her work as she made love: for the pleasure of it. The idea of guilt, of morality, had never entered her mind; she cared only for skill and results. In all her life she had loved only science and Horace. Mathematicians and idealists, with their juggler's minds, had always loved Horace. He had never understood why; he himself, a nest of regrets, had never done any of the things he had done without knowing, to the last fraction, how much pain the act was going to leave behind it.

"It's possible, then?" he said. "I mean, possible with no conceivable trace being left?"

"I've already said so."

"You don't mind using the machines for this?"

Rose laughed. "It'll do them good. They'll have to stretch a little."

Horace and Rose had their drink by the window high above the city.

"'Come back, O glittering and white!'" said Horace.

Rose, looking uptown over the spires bathed in moonlight, didn't need to ask what he meant. Horace had already quoted Sebastian Laux's line to her. Among her books they had found the Fitzgerald short story and Rose had read it aloud. They had been together such a long time, anyway, that they communicated best in cryptic phrases. It was a sort of lovers' shorthand: a single name, a line of verse, could bring back a whole region of their lives.

"If we do it, you'll have to bring sandwiches," Rose said. "We'll be locked in the vault all night. Pastrami; hold the mustard."

12

Julian and Horace were alone in the house on O Street. The asthmatic walkie-talkies of the Secret Service detail, outside in the sleeping street, were muffled by drawn drapes. They listened to Beethoven— the *Emperor* Concerto again, but played this time by someone with a more timid touch than Horowitz's.

The brothers sat in silence in the half-light of Julian's study. Horace had just told Julian that Rose's computers were predicting certain defeat for Lockwood in the election. Julian closed his eyes. In the days since Horace had seen him, in New Orleans, he had been dehydrated by apprehension and fatigue. His collar was too large for his neck. He had heard the news Horace was giving him a hundred times in the last week; he had seen it in Lockwood's eyes.

"There are interesting times ahead," Julian said. "Mallory does plan a witch hunt if he's elected. A public burning."

Horace said, "Can Mallory really destroy Lockwood, destroy your whole political movement?"

"Of course. Lockwood's guilty and the movement is dying anyway."

"A lot of people will never believe that. Patrick Graham sees you as the last best hope of man—'the better angels,' he called you."

Julian laughed. "Patrick is not the American people. They're frightened of life as it is. A lot of them want what Mallory wants— want it enough to elect him tomorrow. If they do, it will be the last vote they ever cast for a President. I wouldn't be surprised if they wanted that, too."

Horace raised his big hands, pressed the fingertips together, and then flung them apart. It was an ancient gesture out of the

Near East, signifying gain and loss and the power of fate. The music had stopped. Horace rewound the tape and started it again. Julian watched him with a smile playing on his lips.

"You're taking all this pretty well, Julian," Horace said. "You know better than anyone what losing will mean."

"No, not better than anyone. Lockwood knows. But he believes in what he stands for—it's extraordinary. He doesn't *know* that power corrupts; there's nothing dark in him, he never has to struggle against himself. If the people elect Mallory tomorrow, Lockwood will believe in their wisdom."

"You won't?"

"No. Let me tell you what I've never said aloud before. I believe in their folly. Caroline spent years telling me I should realize that the people is a great beast. I always knew it. 'The two of you will fall,' she said of Lockwood and me, 'because you lack the guts to do unforgivable things.'"

"And do you?" Horace looked closely at his brother; in his weariness, Julian had become almost jovial. Horace had seen this in spies after a big failure: what they had, what they could never lose, was the knowledge that they had, for most of their lives, fooled the world into thinking that they were something they were not.

"Lockwood is Lockwood," Julian said. "That's what counts."

Horace returned his brother's smile. As if he were joking, he said, "There is a way to save the situation, Julian."

Calmly, he explained how Rose MacKenzie and her computers could steal the election for Lockwood. The smile left Julian's face; his eyes hardened.

He said, "Explain the technical details to me."

"Julian, it's just a game. Rose only worked out the details as a joke. She does that all the time. It's a what-if situation. Such things amuse her."

"But she could actually do it?"

"Yes, sure. According to Rose, it's just a very sophisticated telephone tap. She has the best computers on the planet. She can invade any other data processing system in existence, read its mind, change its results. I've told you, she's a genius."

Julian was not pausing for thought. "I can't believe this can be done without leaving traces. Those election computers were designed—designed by Franklin Mallory—to be absolutely secure."

"Only a fool," said Horace, "believes in the foolproof."

"*Would* she do it?"

Horace avoided his brother's eyes for an instant. It was the gesture of an embarrassed man. He was setting the hook in his own brother.

"Yes, if I asked her to. But Julian, you can't be serious."

"We're dealing with a serious matter. The control of the American government, the life of a great man." He gave a wry smile. "The murder of a great idea. You realize that personal freedom will simply vanish into history if Lockwood loses?"

"But if he wins by stealing the election, doesn't Mallory win anyway?"

"Mallory can have the moral victory." Julian straightened his spine. He was decisive. "Horace, I want this done. I want you and Rose to do this."

"Rose is an employee of the FIS; her equipment is FIS equipment."

Julian issued an exasperated sound, almost a bark. "You think there'll *be* an FIS, as you've known it, under Mallory?"

"If I do as you ask, and bring Rose into it, there won't be an FIS as I've known it, as Philindros has made it. Julian, this conversation has gone far enough. What you ask can be done. The technical means exist, I'd even say the risk of detection is negligible. But you can't do it."

"No? Why?"

"You say yourself the President wouldn't agree to it."

"He won't have the opportunity."

"You won't *tell* him?"

"Philindros told him about Ibn Awad. Was that a good idea?"

Horace started to reply, but Julian's head turned sharply and he held up a warning hand; this was his house, he knew its noises. In a moment, Horace himself heard footsteps, the rapid jabbing of a woman's heels, in the corridor. The door was flung open, striking the wall behind it like a slap, and Caroline burst into the room. A young Secret Service man was right behind her.

"She let herself in with a key, Mr. Hubbard," he said. "She was up the stairs before I saw who she was." His pistol was in his hand and his face was ashen.

Julian waved him his forgiveness. "Caro, you're lucky he didn't shoot you in the spine," he said.

The guard remained as he was. Caroline ignored the drawn weapon.

"Where are the children?" she demanded.

Julian told her. She knew that Live Oaks was the safest place in America. In her relief, she began to tremble. Horace touched her and she drew away; his hand might have been groping under her clothes. Without a word, Horace left the room. The guard went with him. In a moment Caroline and Julian heard the rattle of glasses and bottles from the bar downstairs. Horace came back with three glasses brimming with neat bourbon; a bottle of Maker's Mark was tucked under his arm.

Caroline drank her whiskey at two swallows and held out the glass to be refilled. "I want to be with the children," she said; her voice was thin, burned by the liquor.

"All right. I'm flying down tonight. You should be with them."

Julian hadn't touched his drink. There was no chair for Caroline in the tiny study and she refused the one Horace offered her. Instead she sat on the floor, cross-legged in tweed trousers.

"I only heard about the terrorists yesterday when we docked in Southampton; Leo won't listen to the news while we're at sea. I took the first plane."

Julian made no reply to this. Caroline drank more whiskey and coughed on it; she wasn't used to it any longer.

"Horace, what are you two doing? Discussing where to hide after next Tuesday?"

Horace gave her his twinkling smile. "Something like that."

"Frosty *is* going to lose? You *are* going to be kicked to death by jackboots? Julian's children *are* going to grow up in a stink of lies about their father?"

Julian said, "You've lost none of your wonderful subtlety, Caro."

"As a matter of fact," Horace said, "Julian and I were just discussing the possibility of stealing the election for Lockwood. Would you approve of that?"

To Caroline, Julian said, "Go downstairs. Watch television."

Caroline looked from one brother to the other; her eyes burned. "Like hell I will," she said. "What *is* this?"

"Caro, go. I'll have you taken out bodily otherwise."

Caroline stood up. She picked up the bottle by its neck. "*Do it*," she hissed, and went out the door. Soon the men heard the television, tuned very loud. Julian stared for a moment at the empty space where Caroline had been. Then he rubbed his eyelids with his fingertips.

Julian shook his head in annoyance and turned off the tape machine. Horace didn't know whether his brother was remembering the jagged years of his first marriage, or was merely vexed by the blaring television that drowned out the music they'd been listening to.

"I want to ask you something," Julian said. "Could you, if you put unlimited resources into it, stamp out this Eye of Gaza—kill Hassan Abdallah?"

"Possibly. They'd have to be hunted like animals. You'd have to pass new laws to make that possible, or place the hunters above the law."

"Don't misunderstand what I'm going to say next. In the context of what we've been talking about it may sound like a bribe to you, but the matter was settled long ago. When Philindros's term ends next year, would you like to be Director of Foreign Intelligence?"

"Under Lockwood?"

"I don't think Mallory would appoint you."

"But you would, if I steal the election for you."

"Yes. Lockwood wants you in any case. I want you because I think you'd protect him better than anyone else could."

Horace, playing his role to the end, spoke in a cold voice. "Do you really think you can justify what you're proposing to do?" he said to Julian. "Do you think Lockwood can go on being what he is—or what you think he is—if he robs the people in this way?"

"He'll stay as he is if he doesn't know, if he isn't told. If means are going to justify ends, let them be *our* means and *our* ends. That's what your work has been for your whole life. You and Philindros and the FIS *exist* to do illegal things, to give Presidents and the people the illusion that they live in virtue."

"Everywhere else in the world. Not in the United States. What would Pa have said?"

Julian laughed. "He would have said, 'Steal it!' It wouldn't be the first time. What do you think happened in Cook County in 1960?"

Horace let a moment pass. "There's never been any proof of that," he said.

"No. And there won't be any proof of this. Your friend Rose, she has all this 'gamed,' as you say? She could do it?"

"By Tuesday all could be ready."

"Then only this remains—the question. Will you do it?"

Horace looked steadily at his brother. "I don't know."

"I want to know."

"All right. Call me Tuesday at four o'clock, in the bar at the Millennium Club. Give me a code phrase that means yes. If I don't speak the phrase, you'll know my answer is no. If I do, you'll win the election."

Julian thought for a moment. The room, his most private one, was hung with photographs of Lockwood, and the many sheets of framed glass picked up what little light Julian's old lamp threw out. There was in Julian's face, and in his voice when next he spoke, a real anxiety. Horace had never conducted a more successful seduction.

"The code phrase will be 'the sunlit upland,' " Julian said.

13

That seemed a clumsy code phrase to Horace, but he went back to New York without mentioning his feeling to Julian. What did it matter? Julian had become his agent. On Monday morning, he saw where the words came from. Rising early, he switched on the morning news and watched the President mount the steps of the Lincoln Memorial. There must have been a camera in the Washington Monument, because Lockwood's lonely figure was shown from a height and a distance before the lens brought him closer. Another camera, sighted towards the southeast, showed a feeble sun rising beyond the Capitol and the Anacostia River. The Mall, indeed the whole city with its lawns and marble, was deserted wherever the cameras glanced. A voice explained that the President had decided to speak at this unexpected hour in order to eliminate any danger to others.

Lockwood paused a moment before the alabaster Lincoln, then moved toward the front of the Memorial. He wore a black suit. His expression was solemn. The awkward grace in the way he stood was as familiar as his face. There was no sign of a microphone. Lockwood seemed to be speaking out of the echoing depths of the white temple. Before he began, the cameras moved like reading eyes over the familiar words carved in the walls.

Lockwood did not speak long. A little breeze moved his clothing and his hair, and a camera with a long lens picked up the sympathetic ripples in the flag on the Capitol. Lockwood ended thus:

"There have been other times of blood and other times of fear. We have come through. Decency has lived. Brotherhood has been restored. The American dream has survived in its majesty and the heart has made room for fallen enemies. If we go on as we must, insisting that America has to be herself despite all danger and all sacrifice and all loss, then we will come out all right in the end. If we do not, if we falter, then we will have said to the invisible powers, 'We wish the end to come.' I do not wish that. No American, no man or woman or child waiting for freedom and food anywhere on earth wishes that. Nothing in the unconquerable human spirit has ever wished that. Let us therefore have the courage to make the new beginning we must make. Let us summon the strength to take step after climbing step until we shall emerge, all of us everywhere on this planet which is our only given home, onto that sunlit upland where at last the races and the nations shall join hands, knowing that their long dream of peace and goodness has come true."

Lockwood had been determined to speak at the Lincoln Memorial, and to do so at noon, the hour on which the Eye of Gaza always struck. He had a leader's vision: in any situation, he stood at one end of a long tunnel and saw the distant spot of light that was his goal. He ignored the darkness between.

Julian had said, "You simply can't do it. Campaign headquarters says they'll bus volunteers in if necessary to fill the Mall. It's all for the cameras. Everyone will see that—especially the terrorists. It will be the Alamo all over again, but worse. People will die in front of our eyes while you speak, and it will be our fault."

The Secret Service, the Bureau, the police were in despair. A regiment of airborne troops had been flown in secretly. It was all useless; if the Eye of Gaza wanted to commit murder and suicide, it would do so. The terrorists could not be stopped by uniforms and bayonets. At the cost of a handful of lives, Hassan Abdallah had defeated the United States, which could not protect its President or its people from him.

Finally Lockwood saw the reality. A detail of Secret Service men who had stayed up all night with the camera crews in a room where there were no telephones escorted the television technicians to the Lincoln Memorial. They barely had time to get their equipment working before Lockwood arrived by helicopter. As soon as he finished speaking and the video switched back to the studios, the President was surrounded by his guards, the tallest men in the Service, and rushed into his helicopter. It was during those panting moments, crossing the open ground from the Memorial to the aircraft, that Lockwood's face showed the intensity of the disgust he felt over this fear for his safety.

"If they keep this up," he roared at Julian as soon as they were alone, "they'll have the whole country rooting for my assassins. It's wrong, Julian, to show that kind of panic. It's better to let whatever happens happen."

Lockwood meant it. He was infuriated when others thought that he was something he was not. His whole life had been lived in the open; he looked as he looked, said what he meant.

"Where I come from," he told Julian, calmer now, "they've always liked a dead man a whole lot better than a coward."

On the morning of the election, Lockwood had a huge Kentucky breakfast cooked and served to the whole White House staff in the East Room. He made no speeches, but spent two hours moving from table to table, speaking to his people. For most of them he had a nickname, as "Jolly" was his name for Julian, and a memory of something that had happened between them. Lockwood had roamed the White House and the Executive Office Building for four years, perching on secretaries' desks, chatting with minor assistants. He and Polly always had them all for a Thanksgiving party. He loved the feel and the looks and the small talk of human beings; he withered without these things. From the plate of one secretary he took a piece of ham, and he munched a biscuit stolen from another.

They all knew that they might never see him again like this. They sang "My Old Kentucky Home" and "The Battle Hymn of the Republic." Lockwood's powerful off-key baritone boomed above all the rest and made them smile as they sang. But when he left they all fell silent, and their faces were those of people lost in a tender memory.

After breakfast, Lockwood and Julian and a handful of others flew to Live Oaks. At noon—he chose the hour himself—Lockwood had one of the farm workers bring his battered small sedan, unused in almost four years, around to the front of the house. He held open the door for Polly and then folded himself into the driver's seat and rattled down the drive through the green tunnel of old trees. With cars full of jumpy Secret Service men before and behind him and a helicopter overhead, Lockwood meandered along country roads to the schoolhouse where he and Polly voted. They marked old-fashioned paper ballots after identifying themselves to the election clerks seated in the front row of desks. Then they drove safely back to the farm.

While waiting for Lockwood to return, Julian took Emily and the children for a walk. Near a limestone wall, a grouse burst like a booby trap from a clump of grass, and Julian swept Jenny and Emily into his arms and spun with them as if to take shrapnel in his own back. Elliott stood a little apart, watching. Long ago, Julian had seen the look that his son wore now on Horace's face; he couldn't remember when.

14

As the explosions occurred during the day, Julian was informed. Every symbolic public building was flooded with police, but at the stroke of noon members of the Eye of Gaza—showing that nothing could prevent them from choosing their own hour as well as their own place—committed fiery suicide. They did so in the rotunda of the Capitol, inside the Lincoln Memorial, in the National Gallery of Art. Statues and paintings were pelted with blood as Lockwood had been at the Alamo. Everyone entering a public building had been searched by police but nothing had been found. All the terrorists on election day were females.

Julian, watching television screens and a computer display in one of the old slave cabins behind the big house that had been converted to offices, could not see that the day's bombings had altered anything. The early trend ran as expected. Mallory was ahead of his totals of four years before, Lockwood behind. The difference was not much. But what had been enough for Lockwood in the last election would probably be enough for Mallory in this one.

At about three o'clock Lockwood joined Julian, bringing with him the smell of the sharp November wind and the scent of the horses he'd been handling. A filly in heat had jumped a fence and scampered all over the farm. Lockwood had caught her himself. He sucked a rope burn on his hand. He drank from a bottle of beer.

"Has Franklin had anything to say today?" he asked. The runaway filly had erased every trace of bad humor.

"No. Just the closing speech last night. The media consensus is that you're ahead on points in terms of the final speeches."

Lockwood, with a shrewd look, let Julian pay himself this little compliment. He had been right about the timing of the speech at the Lincoln Memorial.

"It was the sunlit upland that did it. I stole that from Winston Churchill and saved it for the right moment. The whole speech was a bell-ringer—Lincoln, Stevenson, Kennedy, Holy Writ. Did you notice?"

Julian nodded; he had planted most of the phrases in Lockwood's tired mind.

Lockwood propped his wrinkled leather boots on Julian's desk and took another swallow of beer. Julian gave him the information he had. No one but the terrorists had died in the explosions; people were staying away from public places. Lockwood received this report in silence, but his eyes, peering over the tilted beer bottle, were alive with interest as Julian recited the voting figures.

"New York," Lockwood said. "Franklin's got to come down to the Bronx County line with a majority of a million to beat me there. Is he doing it?"

"It's too early for humans to know. The computer projections are beginning to suggest he might."

Lockwood's hopes for re-election would live or die in New York and Michigan and California. Because of the time differences, only New York had begun to report returns in any substantial way. Lockwood took his eyes off the silent television screen, where new

270

numbers had just been posted for scattered upstate small towns, and swiveled in his chair. He looked out the window. There wasn't much to be seen—the back of the big house with its wide veranda, a patch of lawn, the old brick cookhouse, a fragment of the horizon with stripped trees, shivering in the wind, against the sky. He spoke while his back was still turned to Julian.

"You know, Jolly," the President said, "if I have to come back to this place in January to stay I won't be sorry. Living in the White House hasn't been all that much—growing up the way I did, I always knew a boy could get there. But *here?* I never dreamed it."

He spun around in the squeaking chair and lifted the beer bottle to his lips.

"For years," he said, "all I had was a football suit and Polly, up on the hill in this white house."

Lockwood pushed his Stetson back on his forehead with a stiff forefinger. There was a look of mockery on his homely face.

"You missed a lot," Lockwood said, "never being poor." He grinned. "The suspense is terrific—you never know whether or not you'll stay that way."

"I've got the rest of my life before me."

"Everybody does, Jolly. That's a good thing to bear in mind."

"Are you saying," Julian asked, "that you wouldn't mind losing?"

"No. Just that I could live with it, I could go on to something else. So could you."

"I wonder."

Lockwood shrugged, dismissing the storm of lies and shame and ruin that lay ahead of him if he lost. "If you're going to die of bellyache," said Lockwood, "you'll never be kicked to death by a mule. We ought to believe in fate a little more, and accept it, like our granddaddies did."

Julian said, "I hate the idea."

"Hate what? My losing, or Mallory winning?"

"Both. You do, too."

"Yes, I do. We *are* the better people, Jolly. I'm not sure we're the smartest. Franklin is a genius, and it's always death to a people that chooses a genius to lead them. But it's out of our hands."

The television screen flickered. New numbers went up—pitifully small totals compared to the millions that would be posted by midnight, but as clear in their meaning to Lockwood as the green spots in a sheep's entrails would have been to Caesar Augustus, and he accepted them with as much fatalism.

Lockwood got to his feet and stretched. The empty beer bottle dangled from his hand. Lockwood winked at Julian. He balled his fist and swung it softly against Julian's chest.

The two men were close together. Just before leaving Julian, Lockwood always wore a look of expectancy in case Julian should have one more thing to tell him. He wore the look now. Julian said nothing.

Lockwood tossed his beer bottle into the air, end over end, and caught it with a little noise as the glass slapped into his palm. He turned and walked out the door. His boots scuffed on the rough boards of the tiny porch outside, and then Julian heard them on the gravel walk that led to the big house.

Julian went to the window. On the path, Lockwood had just met Caroline and Julian's children. The President's face lighted with pleasure; it was his first glimpse of Jenny and Elliott that day. He ruffled the boy's hair and swung Jenny into the air; the child was wearing long white stockings and a blue jumper, and she had never looked more like her mother. Caroline saw Julian's face in the window and stood, hands in the pockets of a sheepskin jacket that belonged to Emily, staring calmly into his eyes. Lockwood said something to Jenny and she gave him her slow smile; Lockwood hungrily kissed her cheek and Julian remembered how silken that skin was. Caroline went on looking at him, steadily, without expression. She was wearing one of Emily's scarves over her hair as well as Emily's coat; perhaps it was that—the clothes of his new wife on the body of his old wife—that caused such a shock of love and desire to run through Julian. Lockwood went on towards the house, and Caroline and the children, with their guards surrounding them, continued their walk; they were headed in the direction of the stables.

Julian turned away from the window. He watched the rolling images on the television screen for a moment. The phone rang but he didn't answer it. He looked at his watch, though he had no need to do so. It was four o'clock exactly. He took a slip of paper from his shirt pocket and, pulling the telephone to him, punched out the number of the Millennium Club bar.

Frew the barman answered on the third ring. His toothy New York voice sounded all the consonants in "Millennium Club." Horace came on the line. For a moment he and Julian chatted about nothing. Horace checked with Frew to see how the betting stood.

"Frew says Mallory is ahead by a hundred drinks with two thousand in the book," Horace said. "The betting is closed."

Horace must be alone in the bar or nearly so, thought Julian. He could hear no hubbub through the receiver, but of course it was early in the day for that.

"All the same," Horace said, "I'm telling Frew to put his money on the sunlit upland."

Frew hummed aloud as he polished glasses at the far end of the bar while Horace phoned Rose MacKenzie in the vault at D. & D. Laux & Co.

"If you're working late," said Horace, "I'll be glad to bring down some sandwiches."

"Marvelous. Pastrami?"

"And hold the mustard."

That was the agreed exchange, telling Rose to go ahead with the operation. Horace heard a note of laughter deep in her voice. Someone who knew Rose less well would mistake it for pleasure that Horace was bringing a picnic into the bank, where she was trapped by work. Horace knew better. He wore a fond smile as he rang off.

Horace walked down the stairs. In the strangers' room a television set was running. Returns from the five boroughs of New York City, and from Buffalo and Rochester and Albany, were beginning to be recorded. There was the hint of a change in the trend. As the big-city vote began to come in, Lockwood was gaining on Mallory in New York, though he was still far behind. In the anchor man's voice could be heard the vibrato of excitement.

Horace had his taxi stop at a delicatessen. He had phoned ahead and his bag of sandwiches was ready. A drizzle was falling—Mallory weather, the media kept saying; it was raining from the Rockies to Boston—and Horace ordered the cab to descend into the garage below D. & D. Laux & Co. He emerged from the elevator minutes before the door of the vault went on the time lock; he would be inside with Rose until seven the following morning.

15

It was Rose who had caused the anchor man's voice to tremble. When Horace found her, she was wearing her long white dustcoat and peering at a display of green symbols on a screen in a part of the vault that was called the branches room. Here the most sensitive of the FIS's business was done, and the senior technician on duty did it alone. The others, tending to the routine of the night, would not come in here, and if they did they would not notice what Rose was doing.

Horace put the sack of sandwiches on top of a file cabinet. The room was frigid. All surfaces were bare metal, light was at a minimum, there was no talk that did not serve a purpose. These devices lowered the psychological temperature, the real temperature having already been regulated to the chilly level at which Rose believed her computers functioned best.

"New York ought to be all right," Rose said. "I'm trying to find the best circuit for California. Michigan is all wired. The telephone system in this country is not to be believed. I hope to live to see wires vanish from the earth. . . . Ah!"

Rose had found the telephone circuit she wanted. She didn't bother to explain it to Horace; he couldn't possibly understand. She tapped out a message to the computer on a keyboard.

"God bless Franklin Mallory," she said.

Mallory, in his first term, had made federal money available to the states to install centralized computer voting. Not all states had installed it; Mallory's fervor for electronic gadgetry rubbed a nerve in some people. No state had completed the construction of a computerized voting system, but among those that had installed networks linking the largest cities into a central computer were New York and Michigan and California.

In those states, big-city voters, after identifying themselves at the polls, were given a plastic card that activated a computer terminal. The terminal in polling places worked something like an old-fashioned voting machine. The voter pressed a lever to vote for individual candidates, or he could vote the straight party ticket, as in the older method, by pressing a single lever.

The difference was this: instead of the votes being recorded in the machine in the polling booth and counted there, they were transmitted over telephone lines to a central computer, which tabulated them instantaneously and kept a running total. This computer had been designed to be absolutely tamper-proof. But it had been designed ten years before, and Rose's computers belonged to a new generation. Her computers could, in a way that was clear enough to Rose but very murky to Horace, create new artificial intelligences. They had been designed specifically to invade other computers. They could read other electronic minds with ease. With the application of Rose's ingenuity, they could, in effect, alter states of consciousness in other computers.

The weakness in the election computer system was the method of transmission. Telephone lines were vulnerable. All data went in and out of the election computers on telephone lines. If you knew the right combination of numbers, you could simply call up one computer with another. Rose called the result "gossip." The machines, under the right stimulus, talked freely to one another. They were *designed* to talk to other computers, to share data, Rose explained. That was their prime function. A sequence of electronic signals was, to a computer, the equivalent of a trusted face. On encountering a friend, they spoke freely.

Rose had induced the election computers in New York and Michigan and California to tell her computers how they received and counted votes. Then she arranged to have the votes pass through the FIS computers in the vaults at D. & D. Laux & Co. before they reached the central computer in each state. The votes traveled over the ordinary telephone system with something like the speed of light.

As they passed through Rose's computers, a certain number of Mallory votes were converted to Lockwood votes and transmitted to the central computers for counting. There were no false voters: the final tally of votes would agree with the final count of registered voters who had appeared at the polls. But several thousand votes in each state, just enough to swing the majority to Lockwood, would be changed. At the instant the polls closed, Rose would erase from the memory of the election computers all traces of her invasion. "A lobotomy," Rose said, smiling.

"In New York," Rose said, "Mallory has a much larger majority upstate than expected. It can't be made up from New York City alone. I've programmed Buffalo and Rochester and Albany to increase the Lockwood share by percentages expressed in fractions. That, and the very heavy Lockwood vote in the five boroughs, will give him the state by about twenty-five thousand votes. That's less than he managed last time, but he's not supposed to win and you've got a credibility factor to reckon with. We'll have to make adjustments in the other two states as the clock moves."

Her work done for the moment, Rose sat down in one of the cold metal chairs, smoothing her long skirts as she did so. Horace handed her the bag of sandwiches and she bit into a bagel with her strong teeth.

"The worst problem," she said, "has been reducing the probability that the Langley computer will monitor us. They've no reason to do so and I've covered it by representing what I'm doing as a gaming program. They may believe that and think I'm setting up a model to steal the Russian elections. And then again they may not. But they'll only see if they look, and that's an acceptable risk."

Rose drank celery soda and lifted her sandwich towards her mouth. The pastrami was very nearly the same hue as her tongue.

"Anyway," she said, "who would Langley tell? Jack?"

Not until four in the morning was the election finally decided. Lockwood's victory was achieved with a majority of fewer than one hundred electoral votes. Had he lost any of the three key states, he would have lost the election, but in New York and then in Michigan and California, he had been saved at the last minute by a rush of support from the big cities.

"These votes come from the poorest wards, from the forgotten precincts," said Patrick Graham in his commentary. "Lockwood's people, huddled in the threadbare cities, have shown that they are the ones who count after all. It reminds this reporter of that extraordinary scene in San Antonio when the poor teemed into the streets to protect their President. There was a look about them then —I don't know what you'd call it. Perhaps in some way they thought they were defending their only hope."

Lockwood's party won a majority in both houses of Congress. But Mallory's men took most of the state and local offices for which they ran. These results, Patrick and his colleagues agreed, defied easy analysis.

"Everything in moderation," said Rose of Mallory's smaller victories. She and Horace, released from the vault, lay together in Rose's bed, kept awake by the clatter of the morning traffic. One of Rose's plump Siamese cats leaped nimbly from the floor to the top of a tall stack of books, and the books came down with a crash. The cat snarled, twitched its tail, and walked away with dignity. Rose bit Horace gently and he touched her hair.

Mallory made no concession statement. Outside his mansion on Fifth Avenue the cameras waited in vain. From time to time during the night, as the inescapable pattern of Lockwood's hair-breadth victory formed on the great tote boards of the networks, one or another of the anchor men would call on a correspondent, shivering on the sidewalk in front of the tall house with its blinded windows, but all was silence. Silence fell, too, on the crowds of Mallory supporters who had gathered in cities across the nation to celebrate a victory. They were young people, mostly, neatly dressed men and pretty women.

"What you see in these faces," said Patrick, "is anger and bitterness. If you believe in a cause, you cannot believe in its defeat. This isn't the last we'll see of these people. They won't surrender, even to the will of the majority."

Julian did not wake Lockwood. The President had made an optimistic statement before retiring the night before, with the issue still in doubt. He knew then that if he carried California he would be elected.

At six, he found Julian before the television set in the little sitting room where the two of them, all those years before, had met

Philindros. Lockwood, wearing his bathrobe, hair rumpled, sat down on the sofa beside Julian.

"You carried California," Julian said.

The two men exchanged no congratulations. Lockwood was peeling an orange. He slit the skin with his thumbnail, spraying bitter juice, and tore off the pulpy skin with his blunt capable fingers. He divided the peeled fruit in half and gave one section to Julian while he ate the other.

When he said what he said next, he didn't look at Julian, but he put his hand on him, patting his thigh after giving it a hard squeeze. It was a gesture of forgiveness.

"Polly thinks they'll kill me for this—for winning," he said.

Julian didn't answer. Lockwood turned off the television set, and when he turned around his ruined gentle face broke into a smile.

"Don't take it so hard, son," he said. He retied the cord of his bathrobe. "I'd better go up and tell Polly," he said. "She's always hated California."

Julian climbed the creaking stairs and went softly into the room where Emily lay sleeping. She was, as usual at the end of her dreamful nights, uncovered, and Julian drew the blanket over her.

He felt nauseated and thought it must be lack of sleep. With hands that trembled slightly, he removed his clothes and put on his pajamas. He brushed his teeth; the aftertaste of Lockwood's orange was sour. He left his beard till later. He ached in all his long bones.

Julian, before he lay down to try to sleep, looked out the window over the broad lawns of Lockwood's farm. Just below him were two rows of lilacs. In spring—as when he and Lockwood and Philindros had walked through them—they formed a long bower, white and lavender, fragrant and shady. Now they were bare; brown and gnarled like arthritic limbs.

Two cardinals flying in opposite directions crossed midway between the rows of lilacs. One turned to join the other. For an instant they seemed suspended like impossible hummingbirds, wings beating, one beside the other. Julian watched until he could see them no more: they were so vivid, so simple, so easy to recognize. It was good to know shyer and rarer birds, but he had always loved the cardinal, scarlet sign of life stitched on the dull colors of the dying season.

MIDWINTER

THE GRAHAMS always gave their Midwinter party on the Saturday before Christmas. "That's near enough to the winter solstice to get away with, not that anyone knows when Midwinter Day falls," Charlotte had said, when she named the party, years before. "One can't call it a Christmas party—all the nicest people are Jews or atheists or pagans or Hindus . . . well, perhaps not Hindus."

She repeated these words now to Emily Hubbard and Emily smiled. This girl seemed sadder somehow. Charlotte wondered if something *had* taken place between Patrick and Emily in San Francisco. It didn't seem possible; Emily's eyes never stopped searching for Julian. But if it had, what luck for Patrick. Emily in her white dress, with a large green jewel touching the tawny skin where her breasts divided, was certainly the prettiest woman in the room.

She was, by fifteen years, the youngest. The Midwinter party was not at all like the Grahams' Midsummer party. Charlotte loved giving this one. The guest list was limited to forty people. Tonight there would be forty-two if the President and his wife came. Already here, besides Julian, were the Chief Justice, the majority and minority leaders of both houses of Congress, the president of Patrick's network; that range of people. In black tie and evening gowns, they filled the long drawing room, sending up a civilized murmur instead of the babble of the people who came on Midsummer Day and spilled out into Patrick's garden, leaving half-drunk glasses of Scotch whisky wrapped in damp paper napkins on the statuary. Tonight the Old Etonians served Taittinger's champagne and Beluga caviar and nothing else.

Emily said, "Is that an actual Tissot Patrick is showing that man?"

"Yes, isn't it a nice big one?" replied Charlotte. "You know Jack Philindros, don't you? Go rescue him from Patrick and the Tissot—I hate that girl in the painting, all his models were such heifers. Ask Jack if he thinks Horace can root out that dreadful Eye of Gaza. We all worry so about Frosty—and Julian, too."

The explosions had ceased after Lockwood's election. But tension still quivered under the skin of the government. The Grahams' house was ringed by private guards hired by the network and by the Secret Service men who had come with guests like Julian and other officials. One member of the Eye of Gaza, throwing himself through the french doors, could do a great deal of damage here tonight. The Grahams and all their guests knew it.

Charlotte led Emily across the room. Patrick, seeing them approach, turned to another guest, drawing the man nearer his new painting. He traced the line of the model's throat with his finger. It was the finest bit of painting in the picture, clean as living flesh.

"Jack, do you know Emily Hubbard? Jack Philindros. You two ought to be friends."

Philindros transferred his champagne glass, still full to the brim, from one hand to the other and shook hands with Emily. Charlotte went away.

"Charlotte was just suggesting to me that Horace can conquer the terrorists," Emily said. "Do you think he can?"

Philindros's head did not move, but his eyes followed Charlotte as she crossed the room. Emily had never seen eyes quite like Philindros's: no more expression showed in them than in two disks of smoked glass.

"The President thinks so," Philindros said.

"Do you?"

"Your brother-in-law is a talented man."

Philindros changed the subject; no one was supposed to know that Horace had been given the job of hunting down Hassan and the Eye of Gaza. It was Horace, not Julian, who had told Emily; since the election she had grown closer to Julian's brother; Horace had had time on his hands and he had spent much of it with her. Emily thought about Horace, his tender self-mocking good-bye. She might have been his real sister from the way he looked at her.

She had felt protected by Horace. Emily's own emotions were confused. Now that he was gone, she was overwhelmed by foreboding—but foreboding bent back upon itself. She didn't fear that the unknown was going to happen, but that it had, somehow, already happened. Something had vanished. Something had gone out of the air. Since childhood she had seen a force—an aura, she might call it if ever she were asked for a description, a *light*—in the space between people. There had always been a very strong light between Julian and everyone else. That was why she loved him. But it was dimmer now; there was less brightness between Julian and Horace, Julian and Jenny and Elliott, Julian and Lockwood. Emily turned away from Philindros and went to be near Julian.

Charlotte was talking to him, and to a corpulent man who was the minority leader of the Senate—one of Mallory's men.

"I know how grim all Mallory's people are supposed to be, but I must say, Julian, that Sam here is rather a dear. So freckled and nice. He carves things—he made me a lovely walking stick with all the Texas cattle brands carved into it. He brought it tonight as a Christmas gift."

The senator watched Charlotte go away.

"These high-bred Englishwomen behave a lot like rich Texas girls, have you noticed that?" he said. He turned to Julian. "I may be rather a dear, but you and Frosty may not think so when Congress reconvenes."

Julian said, "I don't think the President has many illusions."

"He'd better not have. The twin words from Mallory are repeal and re-enact. Repeal what Lockwood's done; re-enact everything of Mallory's that he's undone. Some of your own people may want to help us. They know a smell when there's a smell in the air."

Color rose in the senator's face. Julian began to speak, but stopped when he sensed a movement among the guests.

Lockwood and Polly came in. Lockwood's face seemed, as he stood for a moment in the door, pinched by the cold night out of which he'd come. Then, as always, he flushed in his pleasure in people and began to move among the Grahams' guests. Everyone here knew the President; they waited where they were for him to come to them. Lockwood and Polly, shaking hands and kissing, moved down the length of the room.

Lockwood took the fat senator's hand with cordiality.

"How's Franklin?" he asked. "Have you seen him?"

"The same as always, Mr. President."

"That's good news. I tried to call him, but he was sick with flu, or so Susan said. Good woman. Marilyn was a marvel, too. Franklin's lucky at love."

"Yes, sir. Unlucky at cards, though."

The senator, his shrewd eyes switching from Lockwood to Julian

280

and back to Lockwood, held the President's hand for a long moment. The President was unable to move away and the genial smile faded from his lips.

"Franklin," he said, "didn't deal himself a dead man's hand, did he?" He grinned again, the famous crinkling of the ugly face, and slapped the senator on the shoulder.

Charlotte, in her magpie way, moved a step closer, to hear what was said. In Polly Lockwood's face she saw fear come and go; only a woman as quick as Charlotte would have caught the expression.

Patrick made a gesture and one of the waiters approached Lockwood and Polly with a tray on which there were two brimming glasses. Patrick took the tray and offered the glasses himself.

Recovering his own glass, Patrick proposed a toast. "To the President and his lady, health and long life!"

Emily looked for Philindros, to see if he was drinking. His glass was at his lips, but it was empty.

Charlotte and Patrick, chatting easily, took the Lockwoods over to see the new painting. The party murmur began again, and grew. The Lockwoods stayed for an hour, drifting from couple to couple like any other guests. Lockwood drank three glasses of champagne and his large scarred nose grew a little red. Smiles of endearment were smiled. Everyone there knew that this happened to him when he drank wine.

The Lockwoods left at eight and the rest followed them out the door within minutes. Julian and Emily were among the last to go. Charlotte saw Patrick's eyes on Emily as she was helped into her wrap, and she wondered again about San Francisco. Julian as always was oblivious to Patrick's ardor. He had been the same with Caroline, he was the same with Lockwood. President and assistant had barely spoken at the party.

Of course, thought Charlotte, Julian is *alone* with these people Patrick loves whenever he wants to be.

She kissed both Emily and Julian at the door; she had to tug at the lapels of Julian's topcoat to make him bend over and give her his rough cheek. "Delicious," said Charlotte after the kiss; "rather like a poodle just back from the hairdresser." Julian and Emily went down the steps laughing, and on the brick sidewalk were surrounded by their Secret Service detail for the walk home. Snow fell through the glow of the streetlights and sparkled in Emily's hair.

The Grahams turned away from the door. They were dining in tonight, the two of them alone.

A sofa had been drawn up before their Tissot, as before a

fireplace, and they sat down to look at the painting. ffoulkes offered them champagne. Charlotte took a glass, but Patrick waved his away.

The servants had cleared away the plates and glasses and napkins, and the air conditioning had sucked the last traces of tobacco smoke and perfume from the room. Nothing remained but the Grahams and their pictures and sculptures, and that vague disturbance which lingers after a party, as if some invisible thing were filling in the spaces where the chattering guests had stood. It reminded Charlotte of sand running back into a hole. That, in turn, reminded her of a beach near Cannes where she had lain as a girl with a laughing mutilated lover.

"It's so quiet," she said to Patrick. "No Clive—that's it!"

Charlotte straightened her back and shot a glance to the other end of the long room, as though expecting to see the rumpled figure of their uninvited guest sprawled on the *duchesse brisée*. Then, with a sigh, she subsided and looked again at their new Tissot.

"No more Clive at all, ever again," Charlotte said, giving Patrick's smooth hand a little squeeze. "But at least all his murderers were here tonight, weren't they? Frosty and Julian and you and me. How chic! Clive would have loved it!"

"Frosty and Julian? You and me?" Patrick said in a biting voice.

"You don't much like that, do you?" Charlotte squeezed his hand again. "Suppose I had named other murderers—Mallory and Susan, O. N. Laster. Would you have snarled at me then?"

Charlotte looked into Patrick's face. She could only see his profile: his eyes were fixed on the painting, he wouldn't look at her. His lower lip was caught between his teeth and the skin was white where he bit himself.

"If Mallory had won, he would have been our guest of honor tonight," Charlotte said. "You and I, darling, don't care, really, who dies, as long as the survivors come and drink our champagne on Midwinter Night. They're all the same."

She saw that Patrick knew this at last. By tomorrow he would forget what he had learned.

Charlotte threw back her head, she had a finer throat than the girl in the Tissot, and drank her wine at a single swallow.